No Urn
for the
Ashes

No Urn for the Ashes

A Novel by
Alison Sawyer Current

Bayfire Press
BOULDER, COLORADO

First printing 2008

ISBN 978-0-9815464-4-5
LCCN 2008922141

ATTENTION CORPORATIONS, UNIVERSITIES, COLLEGES, AND PROFESSIONAL ORGANIZATIONS: Quantity discounts are available on bulk purchases of this book for educational, gift purposes, or as premiums for increasing magazine subscriptions or renewals. Special books or book excerpts can also be created to fit specific needs. For information, please contact Bayfire Press, 1750 30th Street, #197, Boulder, CO 80301; (303) 718-6395; www.bayfirepress.com.

CONTENTS

CHAPTER 1

Nederland, 1982

I'll never get out of here, Tennyson thought. He stood by the window, mesmerized by a fresh assault of heavy snow. The flakes, reflecting the light from the window, surged earthward like a sky full of comets.

Turning away, Tennyson gazed at his daughter, finally asleep next to the fire. Rebecca—what a mixed bag of emotions she'd brought to his life. There was no part of his life—past, present, or future—that she had left undisturbed. Nonetheless, he was enjoying this time alone with her. It was different without his wife, Taylor. Rebecca's total dependence on him deepened the commitment he already felt toward her. As he moved closer to the crib, checking for the rise and fall of her chest, he heard the crunch. It had to have been a boot sinking into the three feet of snow already accumulated outside the cabin. Certainly, it was too loud to have been an animal; it had to be a visitor. When he heard the knock at the door, he begrudgingly left his daughter's side.

"My god, I can't believe it! How'd you ever get through the snow tonight?" Tennyson flipped on the outside light. "I thought the roads were closed."

"Do I get to come in?" asked his visitor.

"Oh, sorry—come on in; get warm," Tennyson said flatly as he opened the door wider to admit his old associate. Kevin stomped his boots on the doormat and stepped inside but was hesitant to remove his coat. It had been a long time, and the tone of his reception was not yet completely clear. "I thought you hated the mountains?" Tennyson asked as he stepped next to the crib. Kevin shivered and rubbed his hands together as he moved, uncertainly, closer to the fire. "Just don't wake the baby."

"I'd heard you two had a baby. How's Taylor?" asked Kevin.

"She isn't here. She's visiting friends." Kevin sensed a "don't ask" in Tennyson's voice, left it alone, and congratulated him on the baby. "Her name is Rebecca; she's a year old. I'm trying out the lone dad thing for a few days." Again, Kevin sensed something askew but let it slide. He didn't care. He'd come for one thing and knew it was going to be hard to get.

He stretched his arms toward the fire. Tennyson was right: He hated the mountains, the snow, the cold, all of it—but he would put up with it briefly to get what he was after. "Actually, I wanted to talk to you alone anyway. It's about our work."

Tennyson raised his hand. "Stop right there. No way. Nothing has changed." He shook his head. "I should've known not much else would bring you up here. We've been…"

Not wanting to hear "no" so soon, Kevin cut in, "I know, I know." He looked down and waved his hands. "But I thought with a few years to think about it you might change your mind. I thought maybe a family would help you think about the future."

"I am thinking about the future. I have always been thinking about the future, and I'll never change my mind. The world's just not ready. You were my first example of that." Tennyson looked at Kevin, trying not to shudder. This conversation brought it all back—Kevin's intractable pursuit, the disappointment, and the gnawing doubts. "The change would devastate too many lives. I think it's funny, actually. You were the one who showed me the disastrous possibilities, and you're the one who wants it the most." Tennyson knew it was wrong to taunt Kevin.

Totally exasperated, Kevin was easily sucked into their same old argument. "You're such an asshole. I'm not the only one who wants this. Other people know. You've got no right to keep this to yourself. You don't own it. I could work on…"

"Then what are you here for? This is my research, and you know it. Go ahead. Try to figure it out on your own." Tennyson was haunted by his discovery. He'd given it life, but it had possibly been an exchange: his sanity for the kind of malaria one is never free of. Indecision had haunted him like a recurring fever. His passion was the hunt, not the prey. "The results are mine. I've got all the discs. You'd have to start from…"

"Where are the discs?" Kevin asked too quickly.

"In my head," Tennyson lied to cover his mistake. "Forget it. We aren't doing this again. Why don't you go before you wake the baby? It wouldn't have worked anyway."

Kevin's face reddened. "It would've worked, and you know it. God, you piss me off! You always were a flake, but this self-righteous crap is bullshit. When did you ever give a shit about other people?" Kevin had convinced himself it would be different this time. Coming up against the same attitude was just too much. He'd never wanted anything so much in his life.

He reached for Tennyson, a taller man but much thinner than Kevin. He had no idea what he was going to do, but he couldn't contain himself. He grabbed Tennyson's sweater and, with all his might, shoved him.

The sudden jolt knocked the air out of Tennyson. He lost his footing, floundered, and hit the floor. Kevin lunged and grabbed his sweater again. He jerked him up and drove him hard against the kitchen counter. Tennyson was pinned there. His first thought was for the baby. He had to keep Kevin away from her, but how could he?—the cabin was one room. His empty lungs denied him speech. He had to catch Kevin's attention and bring him back, but he couldn't.

Kevin's head spun. Their struggle had gone on for too long, and Tennyson's vulnerability was stimulating. The sum of Kevin's life was energizing the assault. He gritted his teeth as the frustration of his stymied existence digested the final crumb of constraint. Grabbing Tennyson's hair, he dug his fingernails into Tennyson's skull and bashed his head against the kitchen cupboards, over and over again, using all of his strength. Hate was running in his veins. Instead of getting tired, he was getting stronger.

Tennyson felt the hinge digging into the back of his skull, and, as his head was forced against the cupboard over and over, he couldn't see, yet somehow he was watching. He was aware of a ringing in his ears that seemed to block out all other sounds, as if his head were underwater. Stunned and barely conscious, he could only think one thing: *Rebecca!* His thoughts were drifting, never landing long enough to formulate a course of action. Blackness threatened him, crowding his vision from both sides, then spinning over the top of him, from his forehead to his chin. There was no way to fight back.

He never had a chance. Kevin kept hammering, a thwarted heart pumping blood through his system at a high speed. He was desperate and trying to fill a gap, that space where he'd allowed the dream to grow once again.

Kevin had no sense of time. He kept pounding and pounding until something hit his eyes, startling him. As his movements slowed, his head began to clear, starting again to record events, still not registering what it all meant. Clarity and panic reached him at the same time. It was blood on his face. There was blood coming from Tennyson's mouth and ears and dripping from his nose. Kevin was so taut he was still holding Tennyson's weight against the counter, but as the surge of fury receded, his strength left him, and both bodies slumped to the floor.

He knew Tennyson was dead. He'd always wanted him dead, but sitting next to the gory reality was not how he had imagined it. How long had they sat there? He felt incredibly heavy, with Tennyson's weight added to his own. Time had no significance. It never did. This had probably been fated, from the first day they had worked together.

They had been a part of each other's lives for all the wrong reasons—loneliness, envy, but never friendship—their differences rendered that impossible. They'd met at the University of Colorado, both graduate students in chemistry, appreciating each other's intelligence and working together smoothly until Tennyson emerged as the leader. His aptitude for new ideas was hypnotic—and far beyond Kevin's abilities. Working with Tennyson had been exhilarating, almost mystical, yet also confusing and frustrating. They were studying energy—improvements and alternatives. As time had passed, they had focused on alternatives, and as they had progressed, their research had focused on a substitute for fossil fuels. Finding an alternative had become the core of Tennyson's work, and the dexterity of his wisdom had been singular. Kevin had had nothing further to contribute but had stayed in the lab, to keep Tennyson company more than anything else. He had become caretaker as Tennyson sank deeper into his research and let normalcy fall away. Just being there had been enough for Kevin and much better than selling cars for his father, which he loathed—the work, the people, and especially his father.

Unfortunately, things did not happen as he had planned. Tennyson had met Taylor. After that, he had become more secretive about the project and no longer needed company. Kevin had tried to adjust, changing his focus to the project—its enormity. Ultimately, he had clung to the power of knowing Tennyson's deception. Tennyson had wanted to be left alone and told the university his work was based on a scarce substance, his hope being that if his research had little practical application, he would avoid outside interference.

How long had they sat there? He had to do something. If he called the police, surely rage would make a poor defense. *What to do?* They were in the boonies, roads closed; he was confident he had time to work this out. He had to find those discs. Warily, he raised himself, sliding to one side, trying to avoid the mound next to him. Kevin scoured every bit of the cabin. It was small and simple and yielded no discs, but his search did remind him of the sleeping baby. He'd heard her crying, but all was quiet now. *What next?* If he wasn't going to confess, then he had to destroy the evidence. They were back in the trees, above the small town of Nederland, Colorado. All movement in the area had been suspended by the unending snowfall, and the storm was not supposed to let up for at least twenty-four hours.

It has to be a fire, he decided—everything destroyed, a heartbreaking accident, a log rolling out of the fireplace in the night. Kevin started from there. With a scientist's precision, he projected the consequences that would be read from back to front. While surveying the cabin, he went through his plan many times. He knew he was procrastinating; he knew he had to move the body. Finally, he forced himself to wrap a towel around Tennyson's head and dragged him to the bed. There wasn't much to do; keeping it simple was part of the plan. After positioning the body, he turned out the light, placed the spark screen in front of the fireplace, and then laid it flat on the floor. Everything looked right, so he rolled a smoldering log on top of the screen. The rug didn't catch fire immediately. He knew the screen would keep it from the carpet long enough for him to check the scene again and get out.

Sooner than expected, the carpet fibers began to smoke. *Think, think— what do they look for? What survives? The starting point is first, then the position of the victims. What did they die of? Fumes. Okay, but there would be smoke in Tennyson's lungs if he were still alive. Come up with an alternative. How did he die first? He must have been frantic to save Rebecca. He leaps out of bed. Trips.*

Okay, he trips—on what? Put it there. Scanning the room, Kevin saw the rock doorstop. He moved it a body's length from the bed and pulled Tennyson off the bed, face up on the floor, his head next to the rock. *Blood on the rock, okay.* He gingerly rubbed the rock on the back of Tennyson's mashed head. Back to the bed, Kevin wrapped a sheet around the lifeless foot. He loved it. *So inept—trips getting out of bed, and they all die. It's just too good. Something else. What? Yes, rock matching blow to the skull. I've got to do it.* He was void of rage; the gore was too real. *Do it, you wuss.* He'd heard those words before. *Okay.* He closed his eyes, rolled Tennyson over, and bashed his head for the last time.

Okay, it's a story. The flames were beginning to burn the carpet, and Rebecca had begun to wail. *Walk out, walk out.* The baby was quickly crying in frantic gasps. *Walk out. It's clean—walk out.* The flames had moved across the carpet to the sheets wrapped around Tennyson's foot. Soon, the whole bed would go. *Walk out.* Kevin grabbed his coat. He knew that opening the door would fan the flames; there wasn't much time left. He bundled himself against the cold. *Open the door; walk out.* The baby's cries were coming in short bursts. Fear was exuding from the wooden crib. *Open the door; walk out. Shit, shit, shit.* The baby wailed, and the voice in his head kept repeating, *Walk out. Shit.* It was getting too hot to stay in the cabin. The baby wailed, the smoke increased, and the heat pressed against his clothes.

Kevin lunged for the crib. The heat was oppressive; the smoke was getting thicker. He grabbed for Rebecca. She was writhing in fear, and he couldn't get an arm under her until he used both hands to clutch the middle of the bundle and yanked her up. He unzipped the top of his coat and slid her inside. When he looked around, nothing was clear. Heat, haze: *Go!*, he told himself.

Frantic to escape, he reached his hand forward, trying to touch something. Finally, he made contact with the wall. *Left, left, yes…a door.* Feeling for the handle and knowing it would be hot, he curled his shoulder back to extend the sleeve over his hand. It took great force to open. The air came rushing in and shoved him back into the nightmare he had created. While the flames feasted on fresh oxygen, Kevin ducked as low as he could and then fell on his side and desperately crawled toward the opening.

There was no noise coming from inside his jacket, but he tried to stay on his side as he crawled and dragged himself out of the cabin. Finally, it was the cold that let him know he'd made it outside. He must have faded in and out, but he'd made it. The heat and smoke seemed farther away, and the snow was remarkably comforting. Lying on his back, he pushed with his feet, needing yet more distance from the flames. Kicking and pushing, he felt the cold, but the noise was still huge. Finally, he felt safe enough to rest. Lying on his back, he remembered the baby, ominously quiet. He unzipped his jacket and pulled the bundle of blanket up. She was still breathing but either asleep or knocked out from his fall, so he lowered her back inside his jacket and zipped it up.

CHAPTER 2

Eight Years Later

Taylor sat in her bedroom, an ordinary room but with a magnificent view. It offered the panoramic spectacle of the Beaver Creek Resort with ski runs flowing down through the trees like banners in the wind. Her husband had the means to own extraordinary things but could never pass the bland barriers in his mind, so the view was the cabin's major attribute. They had been discussing the dry remains of their marriage, which she feared would continue forever, slowly withering them both. Jack, her husband, had been steadily dehydrating for years. This was not to say he alone was at fault. It was the two of them and the marriage, which had become something so barren it was not a struggle but simply a void.

She had said something needed to change, which she'd said before—nothing earthshaking, just some deeper communication or maybe a spontaneous touch. But it was the request for warmth that did it. Jack leveled her with the comment that would change both their lives.

"You can have an affair, if you think that's what you need." There it was. Taylor thought that warmth was Jack's biggest challenge but realized now it was change that scared him the most. He would rather look the other way while she filled her nasty little shopping list of needs, thus reinforcing the accepted idea that their marriage problems stemmed from her personal inadequacies—struggles that she could not put to rest. "I've always known you'd forgive me the occasional extramarital excursion. Doesn't seem very romantic, does it?"

Taylor had just returned from a ceramic convention in Florida, where she had been featured as an up-and-coming artist. Although she usually preferred the solitude of her own studio, she had enjoyed the company of other potters. One young artist had been particularly interested in her lecture—and Taylor, as well. She'd felt a reciprocal attraction but was not used to flowing with such urges. Sorrow had squelched so much of her. One night the two of them shared stories as they walked along the beach, and later Taylor realized that the encounter only reinforced what she already knew to be true.

Timing being everything, it was not on the side of her marriage. After this wonderful burst of freedom, Taylor had returned to their mountain cabin. Jack and some of his family were already there. She tried to enjoy their company, desperately pushing herself to feel part of it all, but it couldn't be done. She could no longer convince herself that she felt anything more than habitual affection for her husband. Jack had given her time to heal, and for that she would always be grateful.

No plans for change were made that weekend, but the future had been defined. Circumstances were going to help them take the next step. Six weeks later Taylor was at home in Boulder, preparing for another visit to the mountains. They were going to leave for the cabin at 6:00 P.M. At 5:30 Jack backed out. Slightly relieved, she decided to go alone.

The drive between Boulder and Vail takes approximately two and a half hours if the roads are clear, and they were. The route follows the Clear Creek River as it always has, connecting old mining towns quietly tucked into the smaller valleys. Some of these towns are shrinking and appear more dilapidated every year, but others have grown, all depending on their proximity to a ski resort. Their frontier flavor and gold-mining folklore offer travelers a peek into the history of the Rocky Mountain pioneers.

An hour and a half into the drive, Taylor approached the Eisenhower Tunnel with trepidation. It burrows straight through a mountain for more than a mile and a half and made her feel claustrophobic. As always, she made it through, gratefully exiting the poorly lit passageway onto a wide mesa of rolling hills that circle the small town of Frisco. *We should've bought a cabin here*, she thought, enjoying the easiest part of the drive and yet wary of the rapidly approaching Vail Pass. Holding the steering wheel tighter, Taylor paid more attention to the highway as it sloped sharply upward and narrowed to two lanes. Although she was pleased to see that the pavement was dry, she remained anxiously aware of the sharp drop-off on the left. With relief, she finally drove down into the Vail valley, from where it was just a short distance to the cabin.

The cabin was cold and dark, so she lit the fire first and then busied herself settling in. She decided to unfold the hide-a-bed couch in front of the fire and sleep there rather than go upstairs to the master bedroom.

The fire had spread warmth and color through the room like sunglasses with softly tinted lenses. Taylor snuggled deep into the blankets, feeling cozy, but her respite was brief as her mind became agitated over her uncertain future. She knew that the troubles she was facing now were based on the unsolved mystery of her first mountain home. Her marriage to Jack had offered her a reprieve, but it had been an offering of time, not growth.

When she had married Jack, she had been numb from the loss of her family. For three years grief had squeezed the life out of her. Sometimes the intensity forced the air out of her lungs and then wouldn't allow it back in. Mornings had been the worst. She dreaded waking up and realizing she had to live through another day. In the night there were no expectations, but in the day she was expected to get up and do something, and this was too much to ask. Jack had been a comfort. He didn't require much from her, just a wife, in the leanest sense of the word. Taylor had appreciated him; he was good company; but as the fog lifted, it became clear that it ended there. Things had to change. It couldn't be right to be lonely and married at the same time.

Just a brief recollection of those times, even the slightest brush with the crushing pain she'd experienced after the fire, was too much. She turned out the light and was determined to sleep.

Saturday was beautiful. It was warm for November and perfect for skiing. Taylor loved getting up alone and shaking herself loose of the night at a comfortable pace. It was still early when she left the cabin. She parked her car at the bottom of the mountain and rode the bus to the ski hills. This was a hectic trek for her, burdened as she was with all of her equipment and wearing heavy ski boots—but all that was quickly forgotten when she reached the top of the lift.

Preferring to ski the bumps and knowing she had to stay loose, she reminded herself to bend her knees and not be afraid to fall. *Loosen up*, she told herself. *Second run's usually better.* The mountains were as majestic as always. The view from the top offered an expansive portrait of at least a dozen other snowy peaks. *Take it in*, she thought, gliding off the lift toward her favorite bowl. On these back areas of the mountain there were always fewer people, more snow, and more room.

In an exaggerated effort to relax, she hit a huge lump of snow head-on, and rather than bending her knees as high as she could to compensate, she bounced straight ahead over one bump after another until she landed facedown in the cold. The safety bindings on her skis released, and she rolled down the hill without them. Her slide was slowed by a section of flat relief, which offered her enough level space to stand up. After shaking the snow out of her hair, she scanned the hill for her equipment and other skiers. She wanted to see whether anyone had witnessed her fall and also wanted to ask for assistance as most of her things were uphill from where she stood. Luckily, a skier appeared before she had to commence the arduous hike up the hill.

"Stop! My skis!" she yelled, trying to catch the skier's attention before he or she glided past her skis. The distraction was probably what caused the fall. Feeling stupid, Taylor yelled, "Sorry." No reply. Again, she yelled, "Didn't mean to distract you." Still, no reply. Soon, the skier was standing up and checking for damage. Apparently none was evident because he or she was now staring in Taylor's direction and preparing to ski forward. Completely oblivious of her pleas for help, the other skier came toward her, smiling. *You idiot*, she thought unkindly. He stopped on her oasis in the steep grade and removed his hat and goggles. Instantly, Taylor had the strangest feeling—something or someone was askew. Before her stood an old schoolmate she'd completely lost touch with. "God, Michael, where'd you come from?"

Recognition was not immediate.

"Taylor! That's right. I'd heard you lived in Colorado."

"For a long time now. Where've you been?" Taylor asked. "God, it's been years." Michael was so handsome. They'd known each other for a long time.

"I've been all over the place," he answered as he scanned the hill above them. "Took a fall, eh?" Taylor nodded. "Let's get you put back together and then talk about it." They collected Taylor's equipment, put everything back where it belonged, and skied to the bottom of the run. "Are you here alone?" Michael asked.

"For this weekend, yes. We have a cabin nearby, but Jack couldn't make it."

"Lucky me." Michael's smile was so friendly and familiar. "I'm here with my kids, but they don't want to ski with me. They say it's like an all-day ski lesson."

"Aren't you with your wife?" *What a tart,* Taylor thought as she asked, fishing for information.

"Nope, separated."

Wow, was that ever casual. Is that what it'll be like? They skied a few runs together and then took a break halfway down the mountain.

"I like to ski hard, have a late lunch, and then quit early; how about you?"

"Works for me," replied Taylor. "I'm not really good for a whole day."

Lunch was exciting. Taylor had a glass of wine—it helped her relax and talk like a normal person. Her life was so askew that she didn't know where she was or where she was going, but she was having fun. They ate at Michael's very elegant hotel. Then the kids showed up, not seeming the least bit surprised to find their father with some woman. *Funny,* Taylor thought, *me, in the "some woman" category.* Afterward, they didn't bother with any more skiing. They said goodbye, maybe tomorrow, and Taylor headed back to her car feeling very lonely.

In twenty minutes she was home, putting away her ski gear and lighting a fire. Warm and tired, she fell asleep on the foldout couch. Then the phone was ringing, slowly erasing the strange places and characters that, as was often the case, crowded her dreams.

Taylor realized where she was and swung her feet over the side of the couch. She hated sleeping during the day—it took so long to clear her head—but she made it to the kitchen and picked up the phone. "Hello."

"Hi. I was just about to give up. It's Michael."

"Sorry, fell asleep. I'm not used to wine at lunch."

"What a lightweight you are." Taylor loved his casual manner. He seemed to exude self-confidence and ease.

"I thought you might like to come out for dinner. The kids are going to Pizza Hut with some ski buddies, and I wasn't invited, and you're the only other person I know around here."

"You sure know how to make a person feel wanted. Good thing I've already seen your nice side." *Flirting was entertaining.*

"Well, do you want to come out, or do you want to ask me over? I'll bring the dinner."

"Oh, come on over. Everything is so crowded this time of year." She gave him directions, and he promised to be there in an hour. This was incredible. After so many deadening years, numb days and nights, and then growing confusion, all her focus landed on the next few hours. The anticipation was stimulating. Taylor felt ten years younger. She found a bottle of white wine above the refrigerator and poured a glass. Better to be calmer, she told herself, feeling like a jittery schoolgirl.

Michael arrived with a pizza, a bottle of red wine, and a smile that intensified her enthusiasm. *Did he always smile like that, or am I just super-susceptible to any offering of gracious attention?* Dinner was uneventful, their appetites extinguished by potential romance. They caught up on old news, and Taylor tried to project the best of herself. She was so relieved that he didn't know about or chose not to mention the fire. *Would it always be a danger zone? Would it always ground anything light or fanciful?* she asked herself.

Michael seemed to notice a change and suggested they move to the couch. *Was this smooth or sensitive?* she wondered. Soon it became apparent that he was getting touchier as they got more comfortable, but so subtle were the movements, so in sync with the conversation, Taylor thought maybe she was imagining the whole thing.

"Can I use your bathroom?" Michael asked as he rose.

"It's over there," Taylor pointed and settled back into her seat, glad for a little time alone. *What's really going on here?* Was she constructing the scene, or did she detect some real romantic possibilities? And if so, she needed to make a choice, now, before her resistance became negotiable. She would never have an affair. It would make going home unbearable. For now her life was sluggish, but she had a comfortable routine. If she slept with Michael, the deciding would be over.

When he returned to the room, he definitely settled into the couch closer to Taylor. The conversation remained casual, and the situation felt controlled. Then, during a lull in the conversation, he leaned over and kissed her—a long, soft, sumptuous kiss. *Pretty nervy,* she thought as she kissed him back. *I'm married. I must be giving off a scent, like a dog in heat. No one else has kissed me like that in eight years.* It was a passionate, long, consuming kiss. Her entire existence was behind her skin wherever he touched her—where he had his mouth, where he put his hands. Then Michael did something that completely dumfounded Taylor—he stood her up and guided them both up the stairs and into her bedroom. *Things sure move faster at thirty,* she thought. She was still enjoying the kisses but wasn't sure she could make that final leap. It would change everything.

Later, she tried to recall some resistance. All the touches and smells were so unfamiliar, but what Taylor remembered most was relief. She was getting what she wanted, choices removed. She tried to assure Michael that she'd never cheated on her husband, concentrating on looking as sincere as possible. Everybody probably says that. He shrugged it off, and they lay in bed, feeling satisfied for a long time. He left around midnight, departing without an awkward moment.

The next morning Michael called early before she left for Boulder. He told her he was returning to Colorado in a few weeks and asked if she'd like to see him again.

"Love to," Taylor answered, trying to sound casual. She left the cabin early that day. The drive home was rough. Michael was a step she'd taken to change her future—beyond that, she wasn't sure of much of anything.

CHAPTER 3

The University

George Landell begrudgingly drove through the snow on his balding tires. He was slipping at every stop, go, and turn and had to start everything thirty seconds before normal to compensate. As the maintenance man for the science building at the University of Colorado, it was his job to clear out storage rooms in the basement. The university was remodeling the lab facilities. This would be counted as overtime, and he wanted the extra money but not the work. Ultimately, he wished they would leave his building alone.

George didn't like scientists. He thought they were a bunch of airheads with bad tempers and no sense of humor. When any small thing interrupted their mission, they took it out on him. *But,* he thought, *do they ever say a thing when things are running right? Never. Bastards. So full of themselves.* He made his usual face when thinking about scientists.

As George entered the back gate to the university grounds, his parking space came into view. It was taken—some junk heap. *Probably some student slumming it,* he thought. How he would love to slide, "accidentally," into the car—except that it was in worse shape than his. The only people who bothered him more than scientists were their students.

"They leave the labs a mess, and every year, without fail, they try to blow something up. Guess who has to clean up the mess?" he'd told his drinking buddies a hundred times. "They're a bunch of peons."

George found a parking spot a little farther away from the backdoor and placed his standard nasty note under the culprit's windshield wiper. It was 5:00 P.M. He'd already worked an eight-hour day, but Boulder was getting more expensive by the minute. *New young upities thinking it's the place to be, driving the price of everything through the roof.*

George knew this building better than his own apartment; he'd descended these stairs every day for fifteen years. Carrying everything up each step was what he dreaded the most. He was tired, and his short, stocky body was already carrying extra weight. His wife had never minded his widening frame, but now his daughter was caught up in some new fitness craze and brought it up constantly. If George hadn't wanted to see his granddaughter so often, he'd have kept his distance.

There were two rooms to be cleared. Usually, students took their research with them when they left, but there was always something left behind. *Heaven forbid they throw out any evidence of their brilliance.* George's job was to figure out what to do with it all. Things were smaller now, all on discs. "But you put enough discs in one box, and they're heavy, too," George had said a million times.

Just start, he told himself, standing in front of the huge piles. He started top front, ruthlessly discarding anything he didn't recognize. *If it's so important, they should be down here helping out.* Some boxes had the names of students he remembered and some did not. Generally, if he remembered the student fondly, he saved the box. Part way through the first room, George came across something that saddened him. It was the work of Tennyson Garland and Kevin Levine. Kevin he had no time for, but Tennyson had been a good guy. He'd always been friendly and down to earth. At lunch or dinner, if they came across each other (with similar looking paper bags), they'd sit and eat together. He never said much, but neither did George. When Kevin was around, it was a different story. *That little prick wouldn't stop for anything that didn't get him something.* George had always wondered why Tennyson had hung around with such a jerk.

There were two boxes, one with Kevin's name and a second smaller box with Tennyson's name. Since George knew that Tennyson's widow still lived in town, he felt obligated to send on the material. Then he thought that Kevin would probably hear about it so decided to send his carton off as well. He didn't want to mess with that jerk.

He'd put in enough time for one night. There was lots of time to get both rooms cleared. After carting most of the cartons to the dumpster, George carried the boxes for Kevin and for Tennyson's widow to the car.

He hoped the stuff he was going to send Taylor wouldn't upset her. He'd always liked her as well. *Not like all those other stuck-up girlfriends who thought they'd landed a gonna-be-rich hubby. Those two were a nice couple. They didn't deserve that awful fire.*

CHAPTER 4

Kevin

Kevin woke up in a fog. When he rolled over to get out of bed, he noticed he wasn't alone. *Oh, fuck, who the hell is this? Think, okay— party, group went to the bar. Who was in the group?* Unceremoniously, he pulled down the sheet to find the answer. Yes, he knew her; no, he didn't want to have breakfast with her. He jumped out of bed quickly and headed to the shower.

"What's up?" his night companion murmured sleepily.

"Damn, it's late; sorry, got an early meeting. How 'bout I call you later?" Then thinking she might hang around after he was gone, he added, "Maid's day today; I like to keep out of her way."

Perhaps she was used to waking up in other people's beds, or maybe she just got the hint. She dressed and called, "Later," as she walked toward the door.

Hardly a love match, Kevin thought cynically. At least he'd been saved the trouble of pretending to leave. Feeling clever, he continued his morning routine: shower, dress, paper, orange juice, and plans for the day.

He was coming to the end of the sports section when the door buzzed. The apartment was on the top floor of a four-story building in Boulder, near the University of Colorado. It was a nice place, out of the price range of most students, so no parties, but not big enough for young families, so no kids, and they didn't allow pets. Perfect.

Kevin pressed the intercom button. "Yeah," he said in an unfriendly tone, worried it might be the return of his night bunkmate.

"I've a package for Kevin Levine."

"I'm on the fourth floor; I'll ring you in." Kevin was hoping it was policy that the man should deliver the package up to the fourth floor.

"I need someone to sign for this, sir."

"Just a minute; I'll be down." Kevin left his apartment and walked down the hall, purposely avoiding the elevator. He hated elevators and always used the stairs. "Free fitness," he would say to guests, as if he had a choice. When he was a student, he'd been in an elevator that had malfunctioned and dropped a floor. That was the end of his elevator days.

As he walked back up the stairs, he noticed the return address: "University of Colorado, Science Dept." He ripped off the brown paper. The box underneath was marked "Kevin Levine, March 1977." Tearing into the box, Kevin's heart skipped a beat, until he saw it was only the research he had done with Tennyson. He'd hoped for more, some silly mistake that would drop what he'd always wanted right in his lap. He flopped onto the couch, suddenly worn out by the shock, the possibilities, and then letdown. *What's this all about? Why would they send this stuff now? Who sent it?*

It was Saturday, no work, so he had time to figure this out. Kevin went downstairs and out to his car, a Ford from his father's dealership. *There had to be at least one advantage, right?* He didn't even get that big a break on the price. "You've got to pay for things in this world, son, or you just don't appreciate them." *What a pompous ass,* Kevin thought. He was so out of touch with his father. Even when he wanted to please him, Kevin wasn't sure what would do it.

Shaking his head, he hopped into his Explorer and drove to the university. On Saturday the offices would be closed, but it was only a few miles from his apartment, and he'd hoped somebody might be there. It was strange to pull onto the grounds and then, without forethought, into his old parking spot. First, he checked the front of the building, but the door was locked, so he went around to the backdoor. Although the area seemed totally deserted, the door was open. He walked in slowly, not feeling like he owned the place anymore.

"Anyone here?" No reply. There were stairs that went up and stairs that went down. He moved toward the stairs leading up and called again. No reply. Giving it one last try, he called down the other stairs, "Is there anyone here?"

"Who's that?" came from below. Unprepared for the question, Kevin hesitated.

"A…an old student."

"How old?" The voice came back, sounding amused. "I'm old," the voice was getting closer, and Kevin waited for the source of it to come into view. It was George. Who could forget him? He'd been the plague of the labs, constantly harassing anyone trying to concentrate. Was he really still here? "Oh, I remember you. You and Tennyson…got my package, did ya? Wanted to visit the scene of the crime, eh?"

For a moment Kevin was speechless, but George's casual stare brought him back to reality. "Yeah, yeah, we did a lot of work here. Actually, that's why I'm here. There were more notes…or was that all of it?"

"Yeah, there were tons more," George rubbed his back, "just not with your name on it."

"How," Kevin took a deep breath, "how about Tennyson's notes, from later years?"

"Yup, found some. Just one box, full of discs, but you put enough of them discs in one box and it's just as heavy as the rest. Sent that one out to his widow. I know she's got a new husband here in Boulder."

"When did you do that?"

"Do what?"

"Send the box to Taylor?" Kevin was trying not to let his impatience show.

"Same time as I sent yours, but it came back. I'd put the wrong address on it. I had to send it again. You ever see her? Nice lady." Kevin's mind was racing; he'd see her now.

"Yeah, yeah," Kevin replied, walking out the door. He was already developing a plan, and George had served his purpose.

Jerk, George thought as he reluctantly started back down the stairs to finish his work. *Stupid little punk! Gee thanks, George, for sending me that stuff. I really do appreciate the time you took—that was so thoughtful. Ha, not a word—same crappy kid I remembered.* Entering the storage room, George moved most of the boxes he'd put aside to be mailed over into the dumpster pile.

That was close, he thought. He didn't want Kevin to know he still had the box for Taylor. It had just been returned that morning. George made a mental note to send it soon.

Kevin sat in his car, trying to arrest the commotion that was raising his blood pressure. He wanted to make a plan but couldn't keep his thoughts straight. Over the years he'd let the dream fade. Occasionally, when there was something in the news about unrest in the Middle East or general concern over the cost of living, he'd allow himself to fantasize. Or when his father was interrogating him for the hundredth time about his future, he'd try to visualize a different scene, one in which he was respected for his part in the discovery. The possibilities were endless: a new fuel, something the whole world could afford. No more dependence on oil-rich countries. The entire balance of the world would change, and he would be the center of it.

Then there was the added prospect that their discovery would be the downfall of his father. What good would those old cars be? Kevin fantasized about his father asking him for a loan, remembering all the rhetoric he'd been forced to listen to. He had to find Taylor. She'd listen this time, and if she didn't, he still knew something that she would give anything to know.

CHAPTER 5

Taylor

Taylor arrived home from Vail feeling totally adrift. She had wanted so badly to love Jack. It would've been so much easier—and she knew he was a good man. There had even been times with Jack that were so comfortable she could almost believe their life together was possible. After years without intimacy, Taylor thought she'd tidied away the need, but that weekend had woken the beast.

She had a trick. Whenever she had trouble making a big decision, she would imagine herself at eighty or ninety years old, rocking on a porch, looking back over her life. From that vantage point she could view her choices without fear. Today, as she projected herself onto the old porch, there was no choice. Either she stayed where she was and said, "That was easy," or she made a change and said, "Good going—go for it—wow, did we live or what?" Where's the choice there? There wasn't one; there was only one course possible, or she was going to be a very disappointed old lady.

Taylor had no idea what she was going to do or say when she saw Jack—and luckily it didn't come up right away. He left town over the weekend to visit his sister, so she had a slight reprieve, some time to think—not that it was going to do her any good. She was suspended between her decision and acting on it. So she did what she'd always done when things were baffling—she cleaned. That meant everything. It was great. With loud music and a vacuum, there's no chance for thought. Confusion was held at bay, and that night she finally slept well, her muscles winning the battle for rest. Awake and alone in the dark had become the norm, and it was such a dangerous place, ripe for pessimism's best work.

The next day Jack was supposed to return. Taylor wondered how it was going to feel when he looked at her for the first time, as a wife who had slept with another man. She wondered whether it would show, like an old "A" flashing on her chest. Then, too, there was the fear that in her volatile state she would handle things poorly, as she sometimes did.

Amazingly, when she first saw him, he was the same man, and she, apparently, must have looked like the same woman. So much had happened, and she felt so different. How could it not show? In order to give herself some time to adjust to the mere sight of the man whom she had betrayed, she put her feelings in her back pocket and made him dinner. The respite was short. She had changed, and this no longer calmed the waters.

Days passed, and she desperately tried to stay calm, waiting for the right moment. It was never there. She couldn't push herself to start the conversation that was now mandatory. Instead, her feelings kept oozing into her attempts at seeming normal, and biting comments would leap out of her mouth with a life of their own. Obviously, it was a manifestation of her incredible need for change. Mainly, it was her inability either to patch things up or to bail out, but there was nothing really left to patch.

They rarely fought, maintaining a mutual respect, so as she flung nasty and mostly unjust abuse in his direction, he looked at her with amazement and eventually anger. At these moments she resented him the most, hating the way she was acting and wanting to scream, "See, I told you we needed change, you idiot. Look what's happening now. And by the way, I've slept with another man, and it's too late." Just a few words of truth, and their turmoil would be over forever.

Lazily, she wanted Jack to know it all without having the heart attack of telling him. So, in a self-proclaimed chicken-shit manner, she was able to send enough confusing garbage his way to give even him, uninformed as he was, the idea that something had irretrievably changed. She felt pathetic and knew it was manipulative, but it worked, and she managed to encourage Jack into questioning their future rather than having to bring it up herself.

They lay in bed when he posed the question, "What's going on?"

With relief and nervous anticipation she replied, "We need to talk." *Here we go. This is the discussion I've wanted and dreaded for years.* She was standing at the edge of an enormous river. Should she jump in or stay dry on the shore? If she wanted to be a happy old porch-rocker, she knew she had to get wet.

"Things are not working," she said. "We've discussed the need for change, and nothing has changed, and now I'm afraid it's too late." What she really wanted to do was scream her guilt at him, somehow making it entirely his fault that she was an unsatisfied—and now unfaithful—wife.

Taylor had always thought she would have to talk him into any split-up, yet he didn't put up a fight; he merely complied with her motion for a separation. They both decided they wouldn't tell anyone for a while until some details were worked out. Taylor went to sleep feeling odd but honest and closer to Jack than she'd felt in a long time.

Soon, it was apparent she was stepping off dry land, not to float on a river but to sink in a marsh. Any weight she had accumulated in her life, any unresolved issues forced her deep into the muck.

She and Jack had lived with friendship rather than romance, and she had hoped this would protect them from the usual pitfalls of divorce. They stayed in the house together for the next few months, even slept in the same bed without romance or sex. Mockingly, Taylor felt like they had been practicing for this all of their married life.

Leaving Jack was much harder than she'd anticipated. She wished he would hit her or tie her up and leave her in a closet for a few days— anything that would give her a clearer mission than passion over comfort. When he finally did move out, she wasn't as sad as she was empty and lonely.

Ruby saved her. They had known each other since they were eight years old. They had started their long friendship by butting heads, figuratively speaking, and trying to determine who would be the Big Chief and who the Little Indian. They had met at a private school, all girls, and the drama was intense—at least they thought so. The two of them fought and made up. They backstabbed and made up. They manipulated and made up. After six months of making each other miserable and needing to put some of their energies elsewhere, like into school work, they gave up and joined forced and had been close companions ever since. Sometimes they were together and sometimes they took different directions, but they always remained committed to one another and available in emergencies.

This wonderful friendship has been swaying comfortably back and forth all of their adult lives, between need and strength, one path or another. Taylor needed Ruby now, and she was there one hundred percent.

At thirty years old Ruby looked like a hippie, long hair parted in the middle, dressing according to what was clean that day, anything to erase the scent of upper-class New York. She'd taken to writing with the same devotion Taylor had for pottery, and they both appreciated their good fortune at having discovered an unshakeable passion early in life.

Jack had never understood how close they were. Taylor had tried to explain: "Our relationship feels as if we took the same train but somewhere mine headed into town and hers headed into the wilderness. I was always sharper, she was odder; I was better read, she was less bound; I worked harder, things always seemed easier for her; I was part of a community, and she was a community all by herself. I have never wanted to be her, and she doesn't want to be me, but we love each other and try not to judge. It's been too long, too many circumstances. We know we're good people, and when we mess up it's just stupidity. Who can avoid that all their lives? I'm not saying we couldn't piss each other off. It happens all the time, but with a wonderful security—a few bumps in the road, so what?" He never could understood, or he didn't want to, because the truth was that Taylor loved Ruby much more than she would ever love Jack.

She needed Ruby now. She had attempted two marriages: one had been taken from her, and the other was over. "I should marry you," she laughed, sitting at lunch with Ruby.

"Why do you have to marry anybody?" Ruby replied. Taylor was joking. Ruby was serious. "I mean, really, Taylor, you don't need the money, and you could use some practice at independence." Ruby lowered her voice, "You haven't spent all that insurance money. Have you?"

"Of course not; I've never even touched it. It just didn't feel right, getting money like that."

"He did that for you; you should take advantage of it. Tennyson wouldn't have set up the policy if he had thought you were going to let it sit in the bank."

"It wasn't really like that. Tennyson had bought the homeowners and life insurance from a friend, someone who had dropped out of the science department and started selling insurance. Tennyson wanted the homeowners for the cabin but bought the life insurance as a favor. He was so young at the time, it hardly cost anything. Actually, my father stuck it all in a mutual fund. I didn't want to think about it at the time."

"So what did you live on after the fire?"

"I had a little money, and after that was gone I used the homeowners insurance. Then I married Jack, and he insisted on paying all the bills."

"Good, then you've got tons of dough. You don't need to do anything for a while except figure out what you want. Right?"

"Right." The conversations had been one-sided. They were spending so much time discussing Taylor's situation, but she knew that so much of what Ruby was saying could be turned around and plopped in her own lap. Ruby is married, but she doesn't love her husband—or doesn't think she does. You would think this would naturally enter into their discussions about marriage, but it never did. There was a certain comfort for Taylor to see that Ruby didn't have a clue either. Their lunches sometimes stayed light, and they would laugh at everything, mainly themselves. At other times they would cry, which felt safe, but they never ended on the grave side. General mirth was their gift to each other.

This day Taylor was having a rough time, finding it hard to stay out of the muck. "Whenever things feel this empty, I think of Rebecca," she told Ruby. "She would be nine now. Imagine that. Would she be happy, smart, artistic, tall, short, what?" Ruby had always been a place where Taylor could embrace her daughter.

"She would be beautiful, smart, artistic, and amazing—just like her mother."

"She still feels like such a part of me. Even after all this time, I can feel her—not just when I need her to ground me, but when I have things to share, when I talk to myself, when I need you. Maybe you were actually her mother, a spoof perpetuated by some alien plan." They both chuckled and then broke into laughter. The thought of the three of them together was such a happy one. It felt good to let go of the pain for a while and enjoy the memory.

"Who cares who her mother was—we're one person anyway, and she definitely would've had to deal with the two of us. What a wonderful thought."

For now, Ruby and Rebecca were going to be Taylor's family, and Taylor's work was going to be her relief. It had always been that way. The clay always dragged her back—since the first time she had touched it, she was in love. She needed time, and even as dispirited as she was she knew the answer—go back to the things you know. For her, that meant pottery.

When Taylor hadn't worked for a while, it often became difficult to take that first step into the studio; but this time she charged in. On the first day she threw different shapes on her wheel. She loved the feel of the clay running through her fingers like a warm hug. Smooth and liquid, it glided over her skin, responding easily to the gentle pressures she used to form the contours she was after. The next day, when everything was leather hard (still wet but firm enough to handle and assemble), she would put things together. It's the part she loved the most, watching the rough, odd-shaped pieces meld into one, each part meaning nothing without the others. Then she worked with the assembled piece back on the wheel until it was smooth and made sense. If successful, the project should look like it was born as one piece. If the sections stand out and don't flow into one vessel, then it's not finished.

She loved to work in groups, sometimes only making large pieces, then at others making smaller pieces that she enjoyed for their grace and simplicity. She believed it was a better learning experience if she stuck to one theme or type of pot for as long as she could, but she never forced herself to the point of boredom. Starting at seven in the morning and working until night was her idea of a wonderful day.

The weeks flew by as she filled up the limited amount of shelf space in her small cubicle at the local potter's guild. Then the pieces needed time to dry, and she preferred to dry the pots slowly, just to pamper them.

The clay, as usual, had been a reprieve, but the solitude was not always her friend. Taylor had heard of an organization that sends potters to third-world countries to volunteer. The program was designed to help the local clay workers and to share ideas and information. After looking through some pottery magazines, Taylor found Nicaragua intriguing. It had been in the news a great deal, and though she was not well acquainted with the politics, she could appreciate a struggle.

She needed to tread through someone else's altercation and felt that the problem would have to be of national proportions to do the job.

CHAPTER 6

Nicaragua, January 1991

Taylor was on her way to Nicaragua with less preparation than a trip to the store. It was a raw decision. As soon as the plane took off, she felt alone and unnerved and was sure she'd made a huge mistake. She kept asking herself, *What was I thinking?*

Arriving in Florida, she met up with Richard and his traveling companion, Mary. They were all part of the same group. Richard was a well-known potter and, therefore, a face Taylor had seen in magazines. Just this brief brush with something familiar gave her some comfort. Everyone introduced themselves and then sat down at the airport bar for a drink. Richard, who was also a teacher and couldn't help himself, asked each person to share why he or she was on this trip. The other members of their troupe had magnificent and scholastic responses for their motivation. When Taylor's intentions were requested, she could only reply in confusion, "I needed to get out of town." Not exactly what they were looking for, but definitely original.

The last flight was destined for Managua and put Taylor into a state of utter emotional chaos. She wondered, once again, *Why have I put myself into this situation?* No one spoke English, and the other members of the group were nowhere to be seen. She had been seated in the middle of a team of men who were part of a singing octet and were practicing their harmony techniques all around her. It made her feel like she didn't exist or maybe they couldn't see her. Was this a sign? She wasn't supposed to be here. She was on her way to an unstable and war-ridden little country she knew very little about.

Her anxiety increased as they approached the airport, which looked more like an army base. There was camouflage netting over all the ground equipment, and tanks were at the end of the runway. As the passengers deplaned, their route to the airport terminal was lined with armed guards. Being five foot nine, Taylor was a head above everyone, and her height along with her blond hair made her incredibly conspicuous. Inside, the building was bulging with people and confusion. As her eyes adjusted to the murky interior, she was totally lost. She was powerless. *This is it,* she thought. *I haven't done well with my life. At thirty I don't know how to manage it, and now I've stranded myself in a third-world country with no resources and woefully inadequate language skills. I certainly found a way to think about something other than "those old, easy problems." Talk about from the pan to the fire.*

An angry-looking man was yelling at her while smacking some papers. The man next to him was yelling at someone else. None of her meager Spanish was coming to mind. Then, just in time, although a little earlier would've been nice, her deliverance came on a dirty piece of cardboard with the word "potters" on it. She cautiously lowered her feet back to earth and, without much more fuss, was outside, in front of the airport, meeting with the other potters that were part of the group. They had been preauthorized; they had a mission. The organization was under the label of a delegation because no tourists were being allowed into the country. Taylor surveyed the odd collection around her; it was not what she had expected.

What a gang, she thought. There was an old, withered couple who looked like the president and secretary of some obscure bird-watching society. Then there was a very prim, nervous-looking woman in her mid-fifties, and next to her was a short, heavy woman with a highly determined and righteous look about her; lastly, there were Mary and Richard. They still had to wait for over an hour for one more member of the group to arrive on a different flight. It was hot, they were all tired, and they hardly spoke to one another. Finally, Cathy landed. She was a young graduate student from Iowa who looked very confident and passed over the introductions coldly. As soon as her luggage came through, they piled into a car and a truck and headed off through Managua.

There wasn't enough room for everyone inside the truck, so Taylor volunteered to sit in the back. She was desperate for some open air. It was warm and wonderful, but the view was disturbing. Looking around, she felt like she was in a newsreel. This city, in the dark, was a remnant. This wreckage couldn't have been caused by anything except an enemy bent on destruction. There was a feeling of past splendor in the larger buildings, but for now, in the dark, they were big piles of rubble.

When they arrived at their new home, it was not what they expected. It was a small house, not very clean, and the five women were to share one bedroom. Each was given a cot, one sheet, one thin blanket, and the use of the space under their beds. A nice surprise, however, was that an attractive woman, about Taylor's age, had already moved into this humble abode; Taylor felt an instant connection with her.

She watched them try to adjust to their new home with amusement and informed the group that the house was immaculate compared to what it had looked like that afternoon, before being prepared. Diane had come in around noon from Guatemala, where she was living with her husband, who worked for some large American company

"What do each of you have in mind for the Nicaraguan potters?" This question was being put to each member by their local leader, once again reminding Taylor of her selfish quest for an obstacle larger than her own existence. It was morning, and the delegation was looking tired. During the night they had been constantly woken by wails and sobs and strange moans coming from inside the house. In the morning, when they shared their experience with the host, he told them about his son, who'd been shot in the head in the early days of the war. He was now bound to a wheelchair, without speech, and could only move one hand. Apparently, the nights were the hardest for him, wracked by memories and disability. After this, the moans continued, but sympathy overshadowed their discomfort.

Eventually, the question rested with Taylor, and she was determined to sound more generous. "I want to help in any way I can." Next in line were the birdwatchers, who were bursting with suggestions on how to enlighten the native potters.

Later that day the group was given an itinerary; for the first ten days they were going to travel the entire length and width of the country, at times staying out "in the field" for a day or two in places that would make their current situation something to wish for.

The weather was warm during the day, but in the morning and at night it was chilly. Painfully, they started each day with a cold shower. There was a shortage of clean water throughout the country, so adding to the shock of the cold shower on a chilly morning, it was suggested that they turn the water off while soaping up. Everyone was always wide awake for breakfast.

The next obstacle was food and drinking water. "Try this," Mr. Birdwatcher said as he plopped a small pill into Taylor's water glass. She waited the required sixty seconds, gave the glass a swirl, and took a big gulp. It was revolting. From then on it would be boiled coffee in the mornings and beer the rest of the day, sometimes up to six or eight when it was hot. The Nicaraguan potters must have thought they were a bunch of lushes, starting to drink at 10:00 A.M. every day. There was also Coke available, but it was bottled in Nicaragua, and they had the mix all wrong, or at least everyone in the group thought so.

After that, there was the food to deal with. Taylor's normal diet was fruit and vegetables, some meat, and a little bit of everything else, generally pretty healthy. All one needs to have a complete functioning kitchen in Nicaragua are a bucket of water, a hot plate, and a large iron frying pan, full of oil, never changed, just topped off occasionally. They fry everything—rice, plantains, any vegetables available, and meats until they're unrecognizable. Taylor thought she would starve and started rationing the bag of trail mix she'd brought with her—two peanuts, two pieces of dried fruit, and four wheat Chex at each meal. As the trail mix dwindled, beer became her food and water.

CHAPTER 7

Patricia

Patricia hated this moment every day, watching the last parts of Emma disappear into the school bus. After that, her day was just filler until the bus returned in the afternoon, with her world. *Grade three—how did that happen?* Patricia had been so overjoyed these past eight years that the time had flown by. Turning, she walked across the porch to the front door and was grateful for the warmth as she stepped inside. Her days were anything but exciting—pick up the house, dishes, beds—all the normal chores she'd been doing for most of her forty-three years.

She'd been forced to start household chores at the age of five when her mother died. Sadly, her childhood passed away the same day. Her father was hopeless around the house and had way too much to do on the farm to even think about it. At first, neighbors had come around, bringing food, tidying up, taking laundry home, but the visits became less frequent. In the fall, when she started kindergarten, the neighborhood women must've thought that would be all the care she needed. The bus took her there and brought her home, plus the school provided lunch, so she was cared for from 8:30 A.M. to 4:00 in the afternoon.

Some diehards still brought food occasionally but never cleaned or did laundry anymore, so it was left to Patricia. Harry, her dad, didn't seem to care much. He worked, and he slept and hardly noticed anything else. He'd been such fun while Celia, her mother, was alive. The family had done things together on Sundays and, occasionally, Patricia and Celia had gone out to the fields and ridden on the tractor, enjoying the sun and just being near Harry.

Near the end they hadn't done any of that. Her mother had been too uncomfortable and had spent most of her time reading and trying to keep up with the house. If Celia did do anything strenuous, she would get a sincere but loving lecture from Harry. They all wanted a boy; it sounded like such fun. Then the "bad day" came, and Celia left forever. No son, no little brother, no more mother. *And for that matter, no more dad either*, thought Patricia as she put the last dishes on the rack.

Now it was time for the books, the only part of the day she did find interesting. She had invested in a computer—there was no one to tell her not to, and it sounded intriguing. Something new was going to fill her days, or she would go mad. When she bought the computer, it came with a flyer about classes offered in the nearby town of Newmarket. Since the classes were during the day, she could attend. After learning the basics, she'd started by putting all the ledgers from the farm on a business program. Now, she was venturing into other areas, and it was getting easier. The more she learned, the more fun it became.

It had been twelve years since her father had died, and the farmers on each side of her property had approached her about working the land and sharing the profits. This whole region, north of Toronto, in Ontario, was famous for its corn, so every field was planted to its maximum capacity. The money was good enough to cover all the bills and put some away, as well.

Patricia had been so lonely back then. The farm was hers, hers alone. She wanted to leave but couldn't think of anywhere to go. Gradually, the years passed by, and she was still there. She'd had a few lovers but no one she wanted to share her life with. As time passed, the idea of a family started to fade. She was already into her thirties, and everyone she'd known in school had two or three kids. It was children she wanted, not a husband. She could only remember her father as a shadow who had shared their house; any happier memories had dwindled to a vague recollection. She was open to alternatives. What if she did just have a child without the husband? She didn't care what people would say. Hippies, free love, and unwed mothers were common…just not in her part of Canada.

Not knowing where any of this was going, Patricia decided to have a checkup and touch base with a doctor, just in case. The only doctor she knew was Dr. Spencer. He'd taken care of her mother. He didn't practice anymore but had gone into partnership with some younger doctors and still hung around his clinic. He was there the day she went in and was pleased to see her. He introduced her to one of his young partners and told him to take good care of her. Her checkup was extensive. She had to confess, "It'd been a long, long time." Patricia also mentioned her desire to have a baby, and not knowing anything about boyfriends or possible husbands, the young doctor never questioned her timing and simply added an internal examination to his list of probes.

A week later, Patricia's world changed. She was summoned back to the clinic and escorted into an office occasionally used by Dr. Spencer. Later, she could hardly remember what he'd said—something about a severely tipped uterus and then a whole slew of medical terms that meant nothing to her until she heard "same as your mother" and then the blow: "possible death, like your mother."

The year that followed was long and empty. Patricia didn't want to see people. It was too much just getting dressed, and she was having trouble completing the same work she had done easily for years. Then she got a call from her cousin, Kevin. His father and her mother were brother and sister. Both Kevin and Patricia were only children and had experienced many of the same struggles. When they were younger, they'd shared secrets and often pretended they were brother and sister, truly wishing it were so. They were best friends until Kevin's father moved his wife and son to Colorado. Still, for a while the families came together on holidays, and she and Kevin continued to enjoy each other's company, but when he called, Patricia hadn't seen or heard from him for years. Then, when he asked if he could visit, she thought it might be good for her and maybe even fun. She desperately needed some family.

Just the anticipation was already an improvement. Prepping the house was giving her a boost, and caring about something was bringing her back to life.

Kevin arrived at 11:00 A.M. on February 4, 1982—the date of Emma's birthday. He came to the door looking tired and nervous, immediately asking who was at the farm. He looked overly relieved when Patricia informed him that she lived alone. This was hardly the hello she'd been looking forward to, and Kevin didn't seem in the mood for a pleasant visit.

It was cold that day, but when she asked him to come inside, he nervously kept glancing at the car and finally ordered her to wait there. He astounded her by returning with a sleeping baby and shoving past her, into the house. Looking around the car before she shut the door, Patricia wondered what was going on.

Once inside, Kevin's entire focus was on the baby and trying to find a suitable place to lay her down. After lowering her onto the couch, he pulled out the back pillows and put them in front for security. Finally, he turned and looked at Patricia. She was speechless, this being so far from what she'd expected. She didn't know what to say, so she waited for Kevin to start.

"Just give me a little time. I'll explain everything," he said quietly as he removed his coat and slowly sat down in the chair next to the couch.

"Would you like something to eat or drink?" she asked, not knowing whether she was to get an explanation sooner or later.

"Yeah, sorry about this; I'm just so tired, and I knew you would help. How about coffee; is that okay?"

"Just relax; I'll make some." It'd been a long time since Patricia had taken care of anyone, and she craved an assignment. When she returned to the living room, Kevin was fast asleep, so she covered him up and turned her attention to the baby. At first she just stared but then couldn't resist the temptation to open the bundle and find out whether she was looking at a little girl or a boy. She unwrapped three layers of blanket and discovered the baby was wet. Looking around, she remembered no supplies coming through the door with Kevin. Anything was better than soaked clothes, so Patricia unwrapped more to discover a beautiful baby girl. The baby's eyes had opened during the fuss, and she was smiling up at Patricia as though they were old buddies. She undressed her completely and bundled the treasure back up in the warm blanket from the back of the couch. The baby seemed quite content to lie warm and secure in her arms.

The afternoon passed dreamily. Having a baby and a sleeping man (even though it was her cousin) relaxing in her living room was a kind of soothing experience Patricia had not had in a long time.

Kevin woke up as the light started to fade. For a while he laid his head back with his eyes open and took deep breaths, so she didn't press him. This had to be something monumental. Finally, he said, "I'm so hungry; do you mind?"

"Let's go into the kitchen," she suggested. They both got up and headed in. Kevin sat down at the kitchen table and Patricia handed him the baby.

She was impressed by the tenderness he displayed. As she started to make them something to eat, he started his story. In the previous days he had decided to give an "as-close-to-the-truth" story as he could, so it would be easier to remember. Besides, he needed to share some of the burden.

Kevin went through all the events just as they happened, with two major changes: Tennyson's death was an accident, and Taylor had deserted both Tennyson and the baby and didn't want anything to do with them. He ended with, "What do I do now?"

Halfway through the story, Patricia had started her dream, realizing the possibilities, realizing what Kevin was really thinking. It was so much. Everything she had lost started flooding into the emptiness that had ground her world down to a whisper. They sat down to eat, making small talk and feeding the baby little bits of their dinner, marveling at her appetite and little fingers.

"What's her name?" Patricia asked.

"It was Rebecca, but I've been calling her Emma."

"Then Emma it is," said Patricia, making the first of a thousand decisions that involved Emma. Neither of them really noticed the passage, but it was significant.

The three of them spent a week together, and it was a wonderful time for all. They relaxed around the fire, shared their struggles, told secrets like they used to, feeling very much like family.

They also spent time pasting together a story that would introduce Emma into Patricia's life without suspicion. The tale they came up with was that an American, second cousin to Patricia, was the daughter of Kevin's mother's sister; therefore, Kevin's first cousin was married with one baby—the idea was to make it family but too complicated to be of interest. Both parents were killed in a car crash coming home from a party. There was no other family that was young enough, so Emma came to live with Patricia. Family farms were notorious for taking in stray relatives, and the story worked very well. There was no one to dispute it—Kevin's parents appeared to have forgotten that Patricia existed.

Soon it was time for Kevin to leave. He said he couldn't be gone for too long without raising questions. Patricia was sad but excited, because as soon as he departed, Emma would be truly hers.

CHAPTER 8

Dusty Truck Rides

Nicaragua was just what Taylor needed. It had nothing to do with her. There was so much destruction in every part of the country; it easily downsized her troubles at home. The delegation traveled everywhere in two trucks, sometimes returning to Managua for a day or two and sometimes staying out for two or three days. Taylor's friendship with Diane added so much richness to the experience. They were together twenty-four hours a day.

One night near the Honduran border they were put up in a hotel called The Frontier. The war and a lack of tourists had shut it down. It was a dry, hot, inhospitable area, and the atmosphere was definitely not vacation-friendly. The hotel had a vacant disco, mirrored ceiling ball included, an empty swimming pool, and out of the six rooms they had rented only one had running water. The days were hotter in this region, and the nights were cool, bordering on cold. Diane and Taylor shared one room. There were two beds with mattresses but no sheets or blankets, and they were the lucky ones—some of the rooms only had box springs. As darkness fell, they discovered there were no lights either, so everyone put on every piece of clothing they'd brought along and hoped to fall asleep before the cold became impossible to ignore. Many of the locals had not seen newcomers in the area since the war had started and presumed there was opportunity for all in this situation. As Diane and Taylor lay on their bare beds, vendors actually came to the open windows and tried to sell them things. They were shocked at first and then couldn't control their laughter at the predicament they were in, by choice.

All of their most basic needs became paramount. The food continued to be inedible, the beer flowed as needed, and the surroundings were awesome. The population's attitude toward Americans was surprising. It seemed to the group that most people inside the USA had only heard what they were supposed to hear.

The United States had portrayed the Sandinistas as bloodthirsty rebels who wanted to set up a communist government. They were described as uneducated and cruel, and it was said that they offered nothing positive or constructive to their country. Manuel, their delegation leader, told them that the Sandinista National Liberation Front took over the government in 1979, ousting President Anatasio Somoza Debayle. He pointed out that this ended a forty-two year rule by the Somoza family, whose lifestyle and that of anyone remotely related to them was a sharp contrast to the rest of the population. As poor as the poorest Nicaraguans were, these people lived over the top on a decadent scale.

Initially, the Sandinistas tried a series of changes. The top needed to be lowered, and the bottom needed to be raised. They started by offering a broader range of liberties and did what they could to encourage economic development, but there was such a long way to go.

The delegation heard these things while visiting different communities. In some towns they were welcomed with open hearts. A man named Marcelino offered his garden for them to lunch in. He was proud to be part of a slowly emerging middle class. "See," he said in his broken English, "wall strong." He pounded his fist on the wooden side of his house. "Good for hammock." This was a sign of good living. If you had a wall strong enough to support your hammock, you could sleep inside.

"The Sandinistas have been part of that lifestyle change," Manuel continued to explain. "They knew how much was needed. Daniel Ortega became president in 1984, and according to some people he tried very hard to improve healthcare, built new schools to reduce illiteracy, and promoted business. However, these improvements were so slow.

"The US government opposed Ortega. They crippled his leadership by severing trade between the two countries. This, and constant attacks by the United States-backed Contras, was devastating. He couldn't fight them both. The progress of his improvements was slowed to such a pace that the people began to lose faith. By the tenth anniversary of the government takeover in 1989, the standard of living had dropped sixty per-cent. They'd promised a better life, and our people who had waited so long had little patience left."

Someone asked Manuel what had happened to the Sandinistas, so he continued. "In 1990 Violeta Barrios de Chamorro took office as the leader of the coalition that opposed Sandinista rule. She promised the country democracy, but the problems she faced were huge. The work that needed to be done was overwhelming. So we continue to struggle."

On the way back to Managua, Manuel pointed out a piece of land covered with shacks. In fact, shack was probably generous for the sea of hovels they saw. The shelters were built out of anything obtainable, mostly cardboard nailed to wooden posts with bottle caps. They were constructed so close together that from a distance they gave the impression of one decrepit roof covering the entire area.

Manuel explained, as they watched from their trucks, that the prob-lem with these makeshift neighborhoods is the people do little to improve their living conditions. They considered them temporary. They'd had homes before the war and presumed they would be returning to them soon. Aside from the obviously disgusting environment, there was also a health risk for any adjacent city. Due to the lack of any formal sewage system and the abundance of garbage and human waste, the settlements were polluting the groundwater around Managua.

It was a horribly sad sight but also odd, because many of the women and children were wearing uniforms from American fast food chains. Baskin Robbins, McDonalds, Dairy Queen, and others had been donating their used clothing through relief groups. The uniforms were mostly striped and colorful, designed to offer a cheery atmosphere for the business they came from—which made an odd joining of the two worlds.

It seemed that the people living in the hills were the best off. They, at least, still had their homes and a place to grow food or keep livestock. These groups of families were used to being self-sufficient. They suffered only if their men went off to fight or if there had been fighting near their communities. It was obvious, however, that there wasn't one Nicaraguan untouched by the civil war. There was no one whose life had avoided new hardships in a country where survival was already difficult.

After many days in the hills and hours in their old dusty trucks, the group needed a break. It was time to think about something else for just a few hours.

Outside Managua is a volcanic freshwater lake called Xiloa. Formerly, a few wealthy families had owned it, but the Sandinistas had made it public, available for recreation and watering local livestock. The area was lush and hilly and sheltered from the sights and sounds that had been assaulting them daily. The lake water was a murky brown, and they would have to pass over a muddy shore to get to it. Still, they couldn't wait.

"Boy, do I need this," Taylor said to anyone within hearing distance.

"I think the roads are rougher than the land around them. I gotta get a cushion for the back of this truck," Diane said as she jumped down. She was wearing shorts that were too big for her small frame, a shirt she had cut up to cover as little of her body as possible for tanning purposes, and her long black hair tucked up under a ridiculous hat. Aside from her ill-fitting clothes, any exposed skin was covered with dust and then crisscrossed with streaks of sweat.

"You should see yourself," offered Taylor. "It's bordering on scary."

"Thanks a lot; if I look anything like you, it must be." This said, Diana ripped off her hat, shook out her hair, and charged for the water. Everyone followed. The water was brown and gritty, and they'd been warned ahead of time that cows took precedence over people, so to stay out of their way—as if, someone pointed out.

Manuel had taken a truck to find some food and beer, so the group of nine crawled up on shore to wait, wondering whether it would be edible. For once they were pleasantly surprised—somehow, Manuel had found something different. He presented them with a warm treat wrapped up in banana leaves. It was a spicy and delicious kind of corn mush called polenta, sort of like wet cornmeal. They were also thrilled to find oranges and bananas in the bag. It got very quiet as the group attacked the first decent food they'd had in days.

Generally, they had all warmed up to one another, finding something special in each member of the group. When faced with one difficult situation after another, everyone had something special to offer when it was needed the most. The delegation had been trucking around the country for ten days by now, encountering situations that would press the most tolerant of people.

"Are you ready for the brick factory?" asked Manuel. He was young, energetic, and wanted to change the world. Once you got past his rhetoric, he handled all with a touch of humor, which was forever a relief. A few days earlier, when they had hiked up a mountain to visit a remote family of potters, they discovered there was no drinkable water for someone not raised in the area. Manuel entertained them all by demonstrating with great exaggeration what the new governmental sculpture was for. Worried about sanitation in remote communities, the local officials had issued a large hollow cement block with a hole in the top. This was actually supposed to be a toilet, which should have arrived with instructions to dig a hole and place the block over it, then plans to build a small house around it—presto, outhouse. Well, the block was delivered with no explanation, and the people had put it in their tiny town square as a sort of sculpture. Manuel proceeded to sit on it and go through all the mimicking gestures of someone defecating. He had everyone, including the entire community (who had come out to greet them), in great fits of laughter. They were easily entertained and did forget their thirst, albeit momentarily.

"Do we have to leave?" Diane had finally found a soft spot outside of the truck to get a tan.

"We can stay, but today is the only day I could arrange to have someone show us around." Reluctantly, the members of the group rose to their feet and started to gather their limited possessions. Once they were under way, the breeze in the back of the truck felt good.

Everything to do with clay or firing was on the agenda. The factory they were visiting had a unique and efficient system for firing bricks. They had already visited a more primitive setup, where they removed their shoes and stomped in a pit to mix clay, cow dung, and straw. This mixture was then packed into brick-shaped wooden containers and dumped out onto the ground to dry in the sun. All those who participated were left with straw and manure between their toes for the rest of that day.

This brickwork was to be more of a hands-off experience. "This is different," Taylor said as they approached a fenced-in compound with an entry gate, gatehouse, and all. The place looked totally deserted.

"This was one of the Sandinistas' prides and joys. It was originally built by the government to supply bricks for special projects," Manuel explained. "When the Sandinistas took over, they gave it to the workers to run as a profit-sharing company. They were making bricks for new housing in Managua, and it was running around the clock. You won't believe the kiln."

"Why isn't it running now?" one of the group asked as they got out of the truck.

"When Violeta Chamorro took over the government for the US, she tried to privatize the factory again, but the workers refused to give it up. Chamorro let them keep it but canceled all the orders from the government, and the whole operation fell apart."

"Could they start it up again if demand was increased?" Diane asked.

"There's a lot of equipment here. It's never good for it to sit around unused; plus, I'm sure some things have gone missing. There really isn't much security." They had already seen evidence of the kind of scroungers the whole population had become. There was just so much need and so little supply. The war and changing governments had brought the whole country to a halt.

"Come on—let's go inside and see if we can find José. He's going to give us a tour." They all crowded behind Manuel and made their way into a huge brick building. It had at least twenty chimneys on top and high windows all the way around, just under the roofline. The inside was like nothing any of them had ever seen before.

"Wow," everyone said. "This is unbelievable," said Cathy, the young student from Iowa. In front of them was an enormous brick donut. It was at least sixty yards long and thirty yards wide. They could only see the outside but were told it was just one big hollow bagel with the inside tunnel three yards wide.

"How does it work?" asked Richard, our most experienced potter, who had fired just about every kind of kiln there is.

Now it was José's turn. He was one of the few employees left. He was only thirty-five but already had years of experience around clay and kilns. "This thing is fired with coffee husks," he explained in Spanish, and Manuel translated. "Twelve hundred bags to go all the way around the kiln once. You can start anywhere in the circle, stacking a three-square yard area with raw bricks. In the first area that is being fired, you pack the coffee husks loosely around the bricks. There are holes in the roof of the tunnel every three yards, so they can feed the fire from the top, once it's going. But before you start to fire the first section you put up a thick paper wall and stack at least five more spaces of three yards. Now you're ready to start the fire. There are air holes all along the walls with plugs in them, so you can light the husks there and then control the airflow and therefore the strength of the fire.

"The first area is fired over a twelve-hour period; meanwhile, more 'three-yard areas' are packed with paper separating them, one after the other. Actually, I think they stack about six areas before they light the kiln."

José moved down the length of the kiln. Everyone followed, still amazed by its size. "The idea," José continued, "is that this is fired continuously. It should never go out. As one area is firing, the next area is completely dried and preheated. After the first area reaches the right temperature, the next area is fed with coffee husks to raise the heat level there. And so on—no heat is wasted. Some workers are always unloading bricks, and some workers are always stacking the three-yard areas."

"This must take lots of people to run it?" Mr. Birdwatcher asked.

"It takes less than you would think, but it's round-the-clock work. This is the only one like it in Nicaragua and an amazing thing to see up and running. The men who worked here did so with a great deal of pride."

"Where are they all now?" Taylor asked.

"Hanging around," Manuel stepped in.

"How many bricks does one circle of firing provide?" Cathy asked.

José was the detail man. "One complete go-around fires a hundred and twenty thousand bricks, more or less, depending on the stacking. I hate that it's just sitting here unused." José's frustration was apparent. This was his country.

"*Hola, señor.*" Another worker was approaching José.

"*Ah, buenas tardes. Como estás?*" José replied, stretching out his hand. As the two men talked, Taylor turned to see Diane's reaction to everything, but she wasn't there. Taylor scanned the crowd, but she wasn't with the group. She walked outside, and after her eyes adjusted to the light, she spotted Diane at a payphone by the gate. The outlying areas had very few

payphones, but some could be found in more populated spots, often looking incongruous, attached to some dilapidated building or fence. Diane
seemed to take advantage of every phone they encountered and never
looked like she was having a good conversation. Whenever Taylor asked
about it, Diane was vague, so she stopped asking and reminded herself of
the short time they'd actually known each other. Diane smiled at Taylor
as she came closer. "I'm sick of kilns," she said, rolling her eyes. "We
should've stayed at the lake."

Diane was a beginner potter and often seemed uninterested in anything technical. "Let's walk around a bit," Diane suggested, seeming a
little depressed.

"I'm just having trouble with my husband, and it's bugging me more
than it should. You ever think about yours?"

"Not Jack," replied Taylor. She had never mentioned Tennyson. She
wasn't in the habit of talking about him to anyone. "But my first husband—I've thought about him a lot." Diane stopped walking and turned
to look at Taylor.

"What, you sneaky little devil, how many have you had?"

"Just two," Taylor replied, feeling silly. She never meant to keep
Tennyson a secret; she just never wanted to talk about Rebecca. "It was a
long time ago. He died." This brought a quick change to Diane's face.
Taylor thought that maybe she'd been too blunt.

"What did he do?" *Odd,* Taylor thought, for the first question, after
such shocking news.

"He was a scientist, really brilliant actually. We were young and in
love, but it's never easy—you know those egghead types are hard to get
along with." Taylor was trying to lighten things up. She already regretted
the discussion.

"The strong, silent type, eh?" Diane was obviously taking her cue to
keep things from getting too morose.

"Definitely silent. It seems so long ago now."

"How did he die?"

Taylor wanted to stop this. It was a bad idea, but they were new friends,
and she'd brought it up. "He died in a fire. It was an accident. We lived
way up in the mountains of Colorado." Her hands were balled up into
tight fists. "There was so much snow at the time that no one could get

near the place for days." This was the most that Taylor had talked about the fire in years.

"How'd you know it was an accident?" Again, this seemed like an odd question, or maybe she was just feeling odd because of the subject matter.

"That's what I was told. I was out of town at the time, and there was no reason to think anything else. I mean we're talking boonies here. The nearest town was only a little more than a gas station, and the sheriff was about one hundred and ten." Taylor hesitated and then, before this went any further, she said, "It was a long time ago. I really don't know why I brought it up. Let's go see what the others are doing." Diane didn't push, and Taylor was definitely done with the conversation.

"I'm sure they'd love to leave our troublesome butts behind; we'd better make ourselves unavoidable." They entered the building and joined the tour.

CHAPTER 9

Ruby

R uby was never good at getting up in the morning. As long as she could remember, she'd been plagued by her dreams and needed time to shake them off. This morning the struggle had been light, and she was prepared for the day quickly.

She loved her automatic coffee machine. It helped her pretend that her husband didn't depart early every morning, leaving her to wake up in an empty bed. She was the one who set up the coffee and the timer, but it still had the feel of a breakfast companion.

Her days were full. She was part of every activity involving art in the growing town of Boulder. In fact, she had to be careful; there was always a cause. This day she had two meetings, one before lunch and one after. Committees were the plague of her existence, but at least these didn't start too early.

Ruby had gone through all the "don't-know-what-to-do-with-but-can't-throw-them-out papers" cluttering her counter. That was always a huge accomplishment. The phone hadn't rung yet, and that was a blessing. Sometimes she didn't answer it, but she always suffered afterward, inevitably wondering who it was.

She was on her third cup of coffee, which never tasted as good as the first two, when the doorbell rang—not a usual intrusion. Ruby opened the door. "Yes?"

"I've got a package for Taylor Barrett."

"Okay."

"Are you Taylor Barrett?"

"No, but she's had all of her mail forwarded here."

"Okay. Wait." The deliveryman checked his clipboard. "Are you Ruby Starkey?"

"That's me."

"Well, we've had a hard time tracking down the right place to send this, so we sent it back to the university. I guess they called the post office, who said to send it to a Ruby Starkey."

"Where do I sign?"

Ruby returned to the kitchen with the package. She placed it on the table and sat down next to it. There was no way to get hold of Taylor in Nicaragua. She had to wait to be called.

What's this? It was from the University of Colorado. *This can only be trouble.* Based on her long-term relationship with Taylor and Taylor's vulnerability at the moment, Ruby had designated herself as protector of Taylor. With that in mind, she opened the package. It was all of Tennyson's work, numbered on discs.

They were also catalogued by date, and Ruby knew when Tennyson had left the university. The dates ran right up to the day he'd left. She remembered it so well because it was the same day that Taylor had moved to Nederland with him. Ruby had had reservations about the whole arrangement. She'd liked Tennyson. He was a good man but moody and hard to get to know. Taylor had never talked about him much, and Ruby had felt left out. Men had usually been great material for hours of conversation.

What am I supposed to do with this? she asked herself. *One, I stow it for now and present it to Taylor after she gets back. Two, I put it in my safety deposit box and forget all about it. Three, I try to get hold of her through the organization she's with, and four, I go to Nicaragua and talk to her about it before she comes back to the real world.* More than bored with her own life and in need of her old friend, Ruby decided on number four. She was instantly excited at the prospect. The committees could easily exist without her, and that in itself was the real problem.

Ruby had been in a strange mood ever since Taylor had left her husband. She knew that all of the discussions they'd had applied to her as well. She'd been grateful to Taylor for not bringing it up. But that was

Taylor, letting her figure things out for herself, supporting rather than criticizing. Sometimes there was a nudge but never a shove. Ruby knew Taylor felt that people learned things when they were ready to. Ruby, on the other hand, would say what she thought anyway.

CHAPTER 10

A Visitor

The trucks finally rolled up in front of their dingy little house in Managua. Taylor was up and out first. There was a taxi on the road where they usually parked the trucks and loud voices coming from inside the house. After Taylor went in, the commotion got louder. Diane wasn't in the mood for any brouhaha, so she took her time. They had purchased a huge variety of pottery in an effort to put together a good example of work from each region they visited. She helped unload, carrying the boxes and some loose pieces to the side of the house, where they were secure. The pottery ran from lusciously naïve to beautiful examples of the nation's best works in clay. The group generally preferred the more primitive pieces, which never left the country because of their unsophisticated style. Trade with the US, however, was still suspended, making any work they collected even more precious.

After everything was safely stowed, Diane finally went inside. There was Taylor, hugging and talking quickly to a woman she'd never seen before. She was about five foot four, not fat but not skinny, with long brown hair falling halfway down her back.

"Oh, my god, Diane, you're not going to believe this," Taylor said excitedly. "This is the Ruby I've told you so much about. Can you believe it?"

"Hi, Ruby; I'm Diane," she said flatly, stretching out her hand, "and, yes, she does talk about you all the time."

"Ruby's been handling all my stuff while I've been here. I don't know what the hell she's doing here." Taylor turned back to Ruby. "I'm not complaining. I'm just in a state of shock. I want to hear about everything."

57

Taylor's face was red with anticipation as she hugged Ruby again. Diane left them to catch up and walked into their crowded dormitory. Taylor and Ruby went outside, talking the entire time.

It was only four o'clock in the afternoon, and the rest of the delegation seemed to be occupied, so Diane plopped onto her cot and tried to figure things out. Kevin had told her that he'd arrived at the cabin and found it entirely engulfed in flames, yet Taylor said no one could get there because of the snow. *If Kevin was there, wouldn't he have mentioned it to Taylor? And if not, why?*

Diane had always known that Kevin was no saint—in fact, far from it—but, somehow, nothing he did put a dent in the feelings she had for him. She couldn't believe the position he'd put her in. She'd never considered that she might like Taylor. Kevin only had bad things to say about her.

A free trip for a little info—Diane never thought this would be complicated, just a simple, "Did you get a package from the university?" or "Where's your mail going while you're gone?" or "Where's your husband's research now?" She could've started working toward that last question today, but she didn't want to. Taylor seemed so uncomfortable discussing it at all, and now it all seemed so slimy. *Kevin, you jerk.*

Taylor just couldn't get over the arrival of Ruby. She was so delighted to see her. After the discussion she'd had with Diane about Tennyson, she was feeling edgy and couldn't shake it off, and here was her friend just when she needed her. She didn't find the actual fact that Ruby was there that unusual; it was so like her. Unexpected arrivals were one of her specialties.

Ruby had arranged to stay a few days. She'd had to work with the organization to make her travel plans; there were still no tourists allowed. The owner of their little house had already been informed of her arrival, and he was planning to add another cot to their overcrowded room. When she saw them bring the flimsy cot around the corner, Taylor knew she was thinking this was something else they were moving before setting up her bed. Ruby thought rustic was more than two people sleeping in one room. True, she was an aging hippie, but her rebellion was now solely in her mind—comfort had wooed her and won. Taylor held her laughter until it was time to tell her about the cold showers and bad coffee, then lost it completely. She could hardly finish the explanation she was laughing so hard.

The delegation was to spend the next week in Managua, helping to build a high-fire kiln. The problem was twofold: lack of fuel and lack of experience. The delegation was only allowed to teach the Nicaraguan potters completely new techniques. They were in the country to rebuild and repair existing workshops and were not allowed to give any one group of potters information that would improve their current production over their competition—this they had to obtain on their own. The establishment in Managua, however, had already built a high-fire kiln, and this was not a threat to anyone because it was the only kiln of its kind operating at the level of "small business." They also suspected that the government was somehow involved in the enterprise and, as usual, most rules were flexible for the right people at the right price.

Almost all the families of indigenous potters they'd visited fired their work in dirt pits with straw for fuel. They'd position these makeshift kilns in front of a wall to help the air flow. The highest temperatures reached were in the area of twelve hundred degrees Fahrenheit, less than what's required for the most basic unglazed earthenware flowerpot. Even still, a firing would only get that hot if there was just the right kind of wind and the straw was dry enough and positioned properly.

They were isolated and starved for information, but, sadly, the delegation was limited by protocol, which was frustrating and seemed counterproductive. The Nicaraguan's thirst for inspiration was comically illustrated by an old newspaper the group had seen stuck on the wall of a work room. In it there was a picture of a lion. The date on the paper was years earlier, but half of their ceramic figurative pieces still resembled that lion in some obscure way.

Ruby had arrived at the end of their travels. They would now be staying in Managua and working on the kiln. She emerged the next morning, looking more like the rest of them after a night on the cot and a cold shower. Leaving her bad coffee on the breakfast table and nearing the end of her tolerance, she insisted on sitting in the cab of the truck on the way to the project. They had been told that the buildings in Managua were modernized, and they were, by the country's standards. Lucky for Ruby, working there was going to be plush, comparatively speaking.

"What's for lunch?" asked Ruby. "I'm starved." Taylor had been dreading this moment all morning.

"Have a beer," she suggested, trying to keep a straight face. Diane had joined them and was enjoying the situation. No one could face the food lightly.

"What do you mean, 'have a beer'? It's only eleven o'clock in the morning." Ruby was eyeing Taylor with distrust.

"The problem is," Taylor started, "that lunch isn't served until one. Until then—and believe me, we've sampled all of our choices for fluids—beer is the best one." Taylor gave Diane a look that said "don't say a word" and thought, *One step at a time.*

"Okay, you lushes, bring on the beer." Ruby seemed quite content to watch everything and occasionally sat outside and admired the green hills around the city. As one o'clock neared, Diane and Taylor kept making eye contact. They knew exactly what they were going to be fed: the usual unidentifiable meat, fried rice floating in oil, and fried plantains. Even the plantains were inedible.

Ruby was not amused, but everyone had a good laugh at her expense. They told her that dinner at the house was usually edible and handed her another beer. As they worked on through the afternoon, Taylor felt rested, almost content. The work was all-consuming, and the respite was worth all the hunger and the heat, even the cot and cold showers.

That night Ruby couldn't get to sleep, so they sat outside in front of the house, leaning against each other for support.

"I've another reason for coming down here," Ruby started.

"What—you didn't just come to try out the local beer?" Taylor could sense a seriousness but wasn't ready to go there. Ruby gave her a look. "Okay, what?"

"I got some strange mail for you and thought I'd better talk to you about it in person." Taylor turned to face her friend. This didn't sound good. It'd been such a gift not to think about her situation, and she wasn't ready to give it up.

"It was a box, actually, from the university, all of Tennyson's work while he was there—or I assume so. It's full of discs, dated right up until the time you two left for Nederland." It was odd: two unrelated discussions about Tennyson in two days, when usually Taylor never talked about him. "I knew he was working on some pretty important stuff, and I didn't know if you thought it might've burned in the fire, so I thought you should know right away."

"I guess I'd always assumed his research had burned. He must've thought it was safer locked up at the university." Taylor felt relieved. *This is history. If I separate Tennyson from Rebecca, I can handle this*, she thought.

"What fire?" Diane had come outside unnoticed and was standing behind them.

"It's nothing," said Ruby, quickly.

"Is it okay if I join you two?" asked Diane, obviously sensing Ruby's hesitation.

"It's okay." Taylor motioned to Diane to join them and turned back to Ruby. "Ruby, I've told Diane about the fire." Ruby was visibly shocked; she knew Taylor never discussed it. Taylor looked at her, wanting to say, "I don't know why; it just came out."

"It's just some old stuff I thought had been destroyed by the fire I told you about. Stuff I never wanted to deal with." Taylor explained to Diane.

"Something to do with your husband?" she asked. Ruby shifted uncomfortably.

"Some old stuff of his, that's all." Taylor stretched her arms and yawned. "Time for bed," she said as she got up. "My cot awaits me." As she left, she thought the two of them would follow, but neither moved, so she continued inside.

The next day there seemed to be tension between Ruby and Diane, so Taylor avoided them both and worked hard on the kiln. She needed time to think. She wasn't sure how she felt about this; clearly, she was going to have to make a decision. Tennyson had suffered over what to do with his discovery. He didn't think the world could handle the change. If his formula could be used in place of fossil fuels, it would affect the entire economic structure of the world. He'd made it work, but then he didn't know what to do with it. *Things haven't changed so much since then*, she thought. *The troubles in the Middle East are even worse now, but just imagine if we didn't need oil from there anymore.*

They'd talked about it endlessly. There was a lazy side of him that wanted someone else to make the same discovery—then, it wouldn't be up to him. But that wasn't all that caused him to struggle. He'd read about other discoveries that had been used for things not intended by the person who developed them. Some of the things Kevin had said illustrated the disasters that were possible. *Poor Kevin*, thought Taylor, *he just wanted to be important. His father had pounded him down for years. God, how can I inherit Tennyson's struggle. Okay*, she told herself, *I don't have to decide right now. I'm going to let this settle a bit, deal with it when I get home. I wonder what Ruby did with the box?*

Taylor was relieved the day Ruby left and wanted to go with her at the same time. The idea of a salad and a hot shower—oh, please. But there were a few more weeks of work that she'd committed to, and she wanted to go back to thinking only about the project. She hadn't enjoyed the invasion of her respite; it was going to be over soon enough.

She asked Ruby to put the box somewhere safe and not tell her where. It was a "kind of" decision—enough, at least, to give her a break until she got home.

Diane was back to her cheery self after Ruby was gone, so Taylor assumed she'd been jealous. They attacked the kiln reconstruction with renewed energy, and every day by five they were feeling tired and tipsy and looking forward to the good food at the house. A few nights after Ruby left was lasagna night. It sounded so normal; they couldn't wait. "I think we should dress for dinner," Diane announced when they got back to the house. She was talking to Taylor, but others overheard, and pretty soon the whole delegation was in on it, including Manuel.

"A toast," said Diane, rising out of her chair, "to the weirdest group of people I've ever grown to love." Everyone hesitated for a moment, trying to figure out the meaning of this strange statement. Then they all jumped to their feet and toasted, smiling and laughing in the comfortable manner that comes from going through so much together. Manuel had scrounged up a jug of repulsive red wine for the occasion, and everyone enjoyed the party. Dressing up only meant clean clothes and a little makeup, but it brought everyone into the mood.

Diane's wonderful, thought Taylor. *She has been helping the other women get past their discomforts, and she was a lovely companion to me. She's always eager to please.* Taylor thought about the hardships that had overpowered them at different times and how one of them always had enough resources to keep both of them out of the muck. They seemed to know each other without getting to know each other. They were the kind of quick and easy comrades that one needs on an adventure. Taylor, though, found it odd that Diane never talked about her husband or Guatemala. She decided it must be really bad, especially after all the phone calls. They had become good friends, and Taylor hoped they could spend more time together.

Finally, after two more weeks, they finished the kiln and fired it. It wasn't perfect. They couldn't get it up to the temperature they wanted, but they wrote out some ideas on how to work the bugs out. Kilns are complicated things; like sound acoustics, the heat has to be directed in the right way to achieve the really high temperatures.

Then, everyone went home except for Diane and Taylor. They spent the afternoon in central Managua. It was an appalling site. Obviously, there had once been beautiful buildings with big paved squares in front of them. Now there was just destruction. Since they had not seen the city before the war, they had no idea whether the buildings had been ravaged by war or age or earthquakes. It didn't really matter.

Back at the house, Diane seemed ill at ease, as if she needed to talk but didn't want to. "What's up?" Taylor asked.

"Oh, I'm just sad about the end of the trip. I've really enjoyed getting to know you."

"I feel the same way; in fact, I feel as though I've known you for years."

"I've had that same feeling," Diane agreed.

"I hope we can see each other again," Taylor said sadly.

"Well, I may be coming to the States soon, so I'll give you a call if I do."

"Really, that would be great. Promise you'll call me."

Diane had never mentioned a trip to the States before, but the possibility made saying goodbye more palatable for Taylor.

CHAPTER 11

Fresh Water

"Sometimes you are so paranoid," Taylor told Ruby. They were at their favorite restaurant for lunch. Taylor had been back from Nicaragua for two weeks and wanted to hold onto the way she felt forever. She appreciated everything, literally everything. It pleased her to have gone, and it pleased her to be back. The trip had been the best thing she could have done for herself. The wealth and possibilities of her life had been laid out in bold print on every square foot of Nicaragua. When she woke up in the morning in her soft bed and looked forward to a warm shower, she already felt lucky. Every bite of fresh food was a delicacy; just a glass of cool water pleased her and reminded her to appreciate all she had.

Ruby and Taylor had been spending a lot of time together, working hard to build up Taylor's emotional immune system. Taylor had put all of her possessions in storage and was house-sitting for a friend. Not finding a place right away made her feel unencumbered, but at times it could make her feel lost as well. This was a short-term solution until she knew where she wanted to live. Ruby, as usual, was the presence that grounded her.

"Really? Well, I think it's odd she has contacted you so soon. Plus, I told you I know I've seen her before."

"You're not my only friend, you know. Maybe you're jealous. She was jealous of you."

"Did she tell you that?" asked Ruby.

"No, she just seemed weird around you and happier after you left." It already seemed like a long time ago.

"That's because I gave her shit. She was asking too many questions about you, and I told her to mind her own business."

"Very nice—no wonder she didn't like you." Diane had called and wanted to see Taylor. They were going to meet in Vail. "You can come if you want."

Ruby gave a shiver. "I hate the cold. Why would I go to a higher altitude where there's snow, too?"

"Then I'm going to have to go off with this strange woman, alone."

"Just be careful."

CHAPTER 12

Vail

As Taylor drove up the mountain, she went over the events since the last time she'd visited the cabin. She hoped this time would be less eventful.

She arrived at the cabin around 7:00 P.M. on Thursday. Jack had suggested they share the property for the time being, and Taylor was grateful to have a place to get away. It felt good to be there, and the snow was refreshing after all the heat of Nicaragua. It was a good place for her to relax. When Diane had called about a visit, Taylor had thought a weekend in the mountains would be perfect, so they had made arrangements, and Diane was due to arrive the next day.

After lighting the fire, she made herself a salad, still savoring every bite. She was in bed early, book in hand, once again on the foldout couch in front of the fire.

There was no hurry to get out of bed in the morning. Taylor had promised to wait at the cabin until Diane called or arrived. She read, cleaned, watched the ski hills, and kept the fire going. Finally at 4:00 P.M. her cell phone rang. Sure that it was going to be Diane, she answered, "Where are you?"

"Oh, sorry, I must have the wrong number," came a male voice.

"Wait; I was expecting a friend—who is this?"

"Is this a friend of Diane Hastings?"

"Who's this?" Taylor asked again, not about to give any info until she got some.

"Sorry, sorry; this is embarrassing. Diane was supposed to get there first and tell you about me—that is, if you're Taylor?"

"Yes I'm Taylor, but Diane isn't here yet."

"Okay, sorry for the confusion. I'm Shane. I'm Scott's brother. You know, Scott from Nicaragua?"

"You're kidding." Scott had arrived the last day they were working on the kiln in Managua. He'd taken their instructions and promised to get the kiln up to temperature before he left the project. He'd talked about his brothers nonstop, telling everyone how much they could've helped if they'd been there. "Scott was great; we were very grateful to him for sticking with the kiln since we had to leave before it was running properly. Where are you?"

"Well, that's a long story. At the moment I'm in my car, driving from Steamboat Springs. Diane told me she was staying with you and wanted us all to get together."

"How do you know Diane?" Taylor asked.

"After your group left Managua, I came down to see Scott and Diane was still there. She had four days before leaving, and we spent that time together. The three of us went all over the place."

This wasn't making sense to Taylor. "Where are you staying?" *Better not be here.*

"I've got a room at the Hyatt in Beaver Creek. I rep sunglasses and ski clothes, so I come here often."

"Well, Diane should be here by now. I'm sure she'll call any minute, and then we can give you a call." Taylor scribbled down the number and hung up, feeling a little betrayed. If Diane wanted to have an affair, Taylor didn't want any part of it.

Diane never called. Finally, Shane called back, and they decided to meet for dinner. Taylor left a note in case Diane arrived. They met at his hotel. The restaurant was very nice, and the staff was familiar with Shane. First, they sat in the lobby in front of a huge warm fireplace, hoping Diane would get there before they started to eat; then, after a while, they went into the dining room.

Conversation centered on Scott. Apparently, there were four brothers, all with names starting with "S." Shane had heard thirty different explanations from relatives, but the reason was never clear. Their parents had died when the boys were young: their mother of cancer and then, shortly afterward, their father of liver disease. Shane was the oldest and had taken over the role of mother and father. He told her all about it: how they had worked together and how close it made them. He explained how proud of Scott he was and complimented Taylor for participating in such a great project. Taylor felt guilty immediately.

Diane never arrived. They went over the possibilities together—a missed connection, air sickness, a traffic jam, and then blazing amnesia as the final, light contender. Taylor had her own car, so said a stiff and worried good night and drove home.

The next morning she was about to call Shane when the phone rang. It was Diane. She sounded out of breath. "I've been worried about you," said Taylor, slightly annoyed.

"I know. I'm so sorry. I just couldn't come last night. Things just got out of hand."

"Something about your husband?"

"No, something you don't know about. I wasn't going to come, but I'm on my way now." Diane sounded stressed.

"You mean you're just getting on the plane. Where are you?" Taylor was completely confused.

"No, I'm in Boulder. I'll tell you all about it."

"Does this have anything to do with Shane? He's here, you know." Taylor was getting tired of the mystery. None of this was what she'd expected—they hadn't known each other long enough for all of this.

"Oh, yeah, I forgot about that; sorry. That must've been weird. No, this is different. I should be there in a couple of hours. I'll explain everything."

Taylor hated waiting for things like this. *What are you going to do, forget about it until they get there? Hardly! You're going to spend the next hours wondering what the hell is going on.* By the time Diane finally drove up the driveway, Taylor was angry and nervous from the anticipation.

The first sight of Diane was nothing she was prepared for. Her hair was stacked on top of her head but coming loose everywhere. She was pale, her eyes were red, and she had a bruise on her cheek next to a swollen lip. "Oh, my god," was all that Taylor could manage. Diane moved past her into the cabin and stood nervously next to the fire. Taylor immediately forgot all her anger and gave her a big hug, then helped her off with her coat in an attempt to make her comfortable before asking for an explanation.

"This is such a long story," Diane said nervously. "I just need a moment near the fire before I start because I really want to tell it right." Taylor made tea, and the two of them sat next to each other on the couch. "I've thought so much about how to do this, and I want to tell you all the bad parts first, but you have to promise to let me finish my story before you hate me."

Taylor couldn't imagine anything that would make her hate Diane. "Okay," she said quietly.

"First of all, I live in Denver. I've never lived in Guatemala, and I'm not married." Diane had stopped looking at Taylor, so Taylor stared straight ahead, trying to hide her surprise.

"I was on the Potters for Peace trip to meet you. I was sent by my boyfriend to get some information." Diane spoke quickly, wanting to get it all out before she ran out of courage. "I guess he'd worked with your first husband and wanted to find their research."

Taylor got up quickly. She needed some distance. *Kevin*, she thought. She'd done everything she could to avoid seeing him over the last eight years, yet somehow she knew they weren't finished with each other. How he'd tormented Tennyson, hounding him, saying the research was half his, threatening to expose Tennyson to the university about his true project—but then, of course, never doing it because it would have belonged to everyone, not just Kevin and Tennyson. He'd wanted the research for all the reasons Tennyson had kept the project a secret. Kevin wanted power, money, and fame—and most of all to impress his father. His concerns had nothing to do with the project, only what good it would do him. He'd become obsessed. The two of them had actually moved to Nederland to get away from him and to decide what to do. The pressure had been a huge strain on their marriage.

Diane went silent after Taylor stood up. She wanted to give her time. It was a lot to take in all at once. After a few minutes, Taylor turned and looked at her again, so Diane continued. "I've known Kevin for a long time. I know he can be a shit, but for some reason that's never stopped me from loving him—if that's what it is. I went to Boulder to tell him I didn't know anything and that I felt awful sneaking around and that I wasn't going to spy for him anymore. That's when I got this." Diane pointed to her bruised face. "He's never hit me before. He just went crazy."

"What started all this up again?" Taylor had an idea before she asked. She wasn't angry with Diane; she was more surprised by the connection. Mostly, her emotions were focused on Kevin.

"I guess Kevin got some stuff from the university and figured that you had, too. I've never seen him like this. We've been together off and on for years, and he's done some rotten things, but never like this." Again, Diane pointed to her face. "I don't know what to tell you. I didn't know you. It seemed so harmless, and I wanted to help him. He told me that your husband had stolen the research and wasn't going to give him credit for his half of the work. He knew I wanted to do some volunteer work and offered to pay for my trip and only wanted me to ask a few questions. He was the one who found the Potters for Peace Organization. When we first talked about it, I guess I didn't think of you as a real person, and Kevin said you were a stuck-up bitch." Diane looked up at Taylor sheepishly. "I should've known he would say anything to get what he wanted." Diane stared at the fire for a moment. "I believed him because you were married to someone who had run off with Kevin's idea." Taylor rolled her eyes and started to say something but changed her mind and let Diane finish. "It never even occurred to me that I'd like you. After that, the whole thing became a nightmare. I kept calling Kevin and saying I didn't want to do it anymore. I told him he must have the wrong person. He'd get furious and yell at me like he never has before. It was awful. It had just started as a free trip. Then everything seemed like a horrible nightmare."

"You should've told me." Taylor sounded colder then she felt.

"That is what this weekend was for. I was going to tell you everything. Here we were, living so close to one another, and I wouldn't be able to see you. I went to tell Kevin that I was going to talk to you and that I didn't want any more secrets about any of this. I even invited Shane so that if you really hated me, I'd have a friend nearby."

Diane took a deep breath and looked at Taylor. She had a sad, "I'm-ready-for-my-punishment" look on her face. The two of them faced each other. *So much stuff,* Taylor thought. First, she smiled, and then, unbelievably, she started to laugh. This had happened to her before. When she was really nervous and everything just seemed too unbelievable, she'd start to laugh. Then, as she tried not to, it would get worse, like trying not to laugh in church or at a funeral—not that anything was funny, just that you're not supposed to.

The shock of it was too much for Diane, and she burst into tears. Now it was Taylor's turn to feel bad. She hugged Diane close to her and apologized profusely, trying to explain the laughter.

They went back over the whole thing again, filling in more details. Finally, Taylor assured Diane that she believed there was really only one bad guy in all of this; the rest was stupid mistakes.

Worn out, they called Shane. He came over with wine and beer. Both women went straight for the wine. They scrounged up some food and managed to relax. Taylor could see how comfortable Diane and Shane were together. He was warm and understanding, and this evening was a deep contrast to the one she'd spent with him the night before. Shane went home late. Taylor and Diane fell asleep in their clothes, completely spent.

The next day Taylor thought about what Ruby had said. She'd known something was askew; she was amazing.

CHAPTER 13

Boulder

"You never cease to amaze me," Taylor said for the third time. She and Ruby were sitting on Ruby's back porch. Winter had turned into spring in Boulder.

It had been a month since the weekend in Vail. Ruby had been in New York and then swamped with her usual stuff. They'd spent very little time together, and Taylor needed a good dose of Ruby. She'd told her the whole story a few times now, and Ruby wasn't surprised that she'd been right about Diane. Now the question was Kevin and the research.

Diane had kept in touch with Taylor and had stayed away from Kevin. The resurrection of Tennyson's struggle with Kevin had caused Taylor many sleepless nights. She'd thought this was all behind her. Since that weekend she'd become hyper-watchful, avoiding her usual places. Her biggest relief was that he didn't know where she was staying. The homeowners were going to be gone for another three months. House sitting had turned into a perfect hideout.

The doorbell rang, and Taylor gave Ruby a look. "Be nice," it said. Diane was coming over to see them both, and it would be the first time she'd seen Ruby since Nicaragua. Ruby was a very forgiving person when things were done to her, but she was not as kind to those who betrayed her friends.

Taylor brought Diane back to the porch, and she and Ruby sparred for a while until it got old. Then the two of them settled down. They were all going to be friends, and they knew it. Ruby, however, had to get a few answers first.

"Can I ask you a few things about Kevin?" she started.

"Go ahead. You both deserve any clarification you want. I want everything clear, and then I want to forget the whole thing."

"Okay—did you know Kevin when he was working with Tennyson?"

"I didn't actually know him then. I knew of him and thought he was cute." Diane looked embarrassed. "He was a friend of a friend who was at CU. We started dating after Tennyson had left school; I remember him mentioning it. Kevin was already working for his father at the dealership by then."

"Had Kevin ever talked about getting this research stuff before?" Taylor was eyeing Ruby, wondering where all these questions were going.

"No, he hadn't talked about it in years. One time he said he was going to Nederland to talk to Tennyson, but I never heard anything about that."

"When was that?"

"I remember perfectly. It was Christmas, 1981; Kevin had come to meet my parents. It was one of the best times we ever had." You could see the pictures forming behind Diane's eyes. "But by spring we were off again—that's the way it's always been."

Ruby gave Taylor a look. These dates were a little too close to leave the subject alone. "Did Kevin ever talk about Tennyson's death?"

"I was actually surprised that he didn't talk much about it. I'd thought they were good friends, but he was out of town for a while after it happened."

"Did he say anything about it?" Ruby pushed.

"You know, there is one thing that's a little weird. He told me he was at the cabin when it burned, but it was already engulfed in flames." Taylor sat up and looked at Diane. "But when we were in Nicaragua, you said…"—Diane noticed Taylor's added intensity—"that nobody could get near the cabin, that there was a snowstorm, and it was some days before anyone could get there." Diane looked down at her hands. "But I wondered how both things could've happened or why, if Kevin was there, he didn't tell anyone."

Taylor had gone pale. Nobody said anything. This could mean a lot or very little. Ruby looked at Taylor. "They never investigated the fire, did they?"

Taylor told herself, *Keep talking; don't go anywhere with this; keep talking. You're with friends.* "You have to remember we're talking about Nederland in 1982." She tried to sound casual. "There was one cowboy-type sheriff. There was no reason to think it was anything but an accident, and then…there was the other stuff." Both women were waiting for Taylor to fill in "the other stuff," but nothing came.

Finally, Ruby leaned forward and asked quietly, "What other stuff?"

"Oh, god," Taylor slumped in her chair. "I try not to think about it. It'd been a hard winter. They couldn't get to the cabin for days. I guess some kind of animals had scrounged through the fire site. They told me there wasn't much to see." Taylor was deflating as she spoke, as though the memory of it all was sucking the life out of her. She was allowing herself to go there. "They asked me if I wanted an investigation. I was a mess. Why bother? So they could tell me a light switch overheated or something?" Tears were pooling in her eyes. "What difference did it make? They were both dead; nothing was going to change that." She leaned forward and dropped her face in her hands. Her friends could see her shoulders moving with her sobs, but there was no sound. Ruby knelt beside her and put her arms around her. They stayed like that for a while, and then Taylor looked up and with difficulty said, "It was my father who actually made the decision. He was there, too, you know."

Diane watched, respecting the ties of an old friendship, but her mind was racing. *Didn't Taylor say they? Who was "they"? I'll ask Ruby later,* she decided.

Ruby's husband was out of town, and the three women had planned to spend the weekend together. After Taylor composed herself, they explained to Diane that she'd had a daughter, just over a year old, and that she'd died in the fire as well.

Taylor went to bed first. For eight years she'd avoided discussing the fire. She'd never learn to live with the details. Now she needed to be alone. Ruby and Diane stayed up.

"I think we should check out some old records. They have to have some reports on the fire somewhere," said Ruby.

"Sure, they're all on chips or something." Before they went to bed they decided to check it out. They were going to run it by Taylor, and if she wasn't too keen, they'd do it anyway, without telling her.

CHAPTER 14

Nederland

Ruby and Diane never did run the idea by Taylor. After their weekend was over, they met in Boulder and drove up to the mountain together. It was a beautiful ride. Everything was green and bursting to get greener. It had been a rainy spring, and the vegetation was flourishing. The drive took forty-five minutes. They listened to music and enjoyed the new comfortable relationship they were developing. As they followed the road into Nederland, the reservoir came into view. The water was brilliant and alive as the wind passed over it. Behind the lake, the hillside rose sharply, dotted with rooftops. Somewhere near the top were the remains of the cabin.

The land still belonged to Taylor. She paid the taxes and tried to forget she'd ever lived there. She assumed that what was left of the cabin must be slowly settling back into the landscape. Ruby didn't know where the cabin was but had called ahead and talked to the sheriff. He'd been the sheriff for sixteen years, and, yes, he remembered the fire.

Ruby turned left into town. Nederland was still very small. They'd been told to go past the gas station and then to the right. The sheriff's office would be the third building on the left. When the car was parked, the two women were slow to get out. Now that they'd arrived, they weren't sure what to expect, Ruby especially. She was usually a woman of expectations; she always had a plan and a projection of events. If it didn't go according to her design, it was still a comfortable way to approach new experiences. Diane, being younger and less secure, never anticipated her own impact on an event and, therefore, entered every new situation with trepidation.

The door to the office was ajar, so they walked right in. Henry Small was sitting behind a high counter that cut the room in half. There was a low swinging door at the right of the desk, and chairs were under the windows to their left.

Henry Small was exactly what Ruby had expected. It seemed almost comical, making it hard for her to suppress a chuckle. He was tall, with beautiful gray hair. When he stepped through the swinging door to greet them, he was wearing jeans, cowboy boots, and a khaki shirt over his solid torso. An enormous silver belt buckle completed the look. Ruby was sure there must be a cowboy hat somewhere.

"You two lost?" he asked.

"Hi, I'm Ruby. I called you from Boulder about my friend, Taylor Garland. You know, the fire?"

"Oh, yeah, have a seat." Henry motioned toward the chairs under the window.

"This is my friend, Diane," Ruby said as they settled themselves into three of the four chairs.

"Pleased to meet you, ma'am. Oh, I remember that fire. It was a terrible thing, with that baby and all. Watching the smoke and not being able to get there was frustrating as all get out."

"Can you tell me why there wasn't any investigation?" Ruby asked, getting right to the point.

"Mrs. Garland didn't want one. She came back as soon as we contacted her. She'd been out of town, visiting friends or something. Her father arrived soon after and took over. Mr. Mendel said he didn't want to put his daughter through anything more."

"What did you think?" asked Ruby.

"Well, I sure didn't think that little lady could've survived an investigation. You see, when we were talking about it, it'd already been three days since. It took so much time to clear the road that far up the mountain. My deputy finally got up there and said the animals had been digging through what was left. It'd been a hard winter, and there were lots of coyotes and wolves coming down closer to town, looking for food."

"You mean they would have messed things up too much for an investigation?" Diane asked.

"Not so much that, though it would have made things tough. It was more that we didn't think Mrs. Garland could handle hearing the details. It was bad enough that the little baby was dead, but then to hear it was possible that any remains had been dragged off and eaten by animals…" Henry was slowly shaking his head. "I talked about it with Mr. Mendel, and we agreed. There was no reason to think that anything suspicious had happened."

"What about the funeral?" asked Ruby, beginning to sense some missing pieces.

"Well, we collected all the human bones left on the site and handed them over to the coroner. He dealt with the funeral home. They used one in Boulder."

"Neither of them was ever positively identified?" asked Ruby.

"Nope, there were two people in that cabin, and it burned down. That's what happened. There was no reason to look for anything else." Ruby sensed that Henry was getting defensive, so she backed off on that part of it.

"Was there anyone else around the cabin when it burned?" she asked. Henry got up and started to wander around the small space they were in.

"We were having the biggest snowstorm in ten years. We couldn't get our fire truck anywhere near the place. Maybe something smaller with four-wheel drive and chains could've made it halfway up the hill, but the problem was that the cabin was all the way at the top. You would've had to hike in. It was a hell of a storm. The place burned fast but didn't spread—there was just too much snow."

An older man had come into the office some time during their conversation. He looked just like Henry, except smaller and older.

"That was the worst. You could see the smoke from town after the snow let up a bit," the older man said. "That fire went up and out before we could even think about plowin' the road to get there."

"Oh, this is my father, Joe Small. Dad, these are some friends of Mrs. Garland."

"That poor little gal. I never seen anybody look so sad in all my life." He was looking down and shaking his head, as if he was seeing her all over again. Ruby was amazed at how they seemed to remember it all so well.

"Sheriff, do you remember the name of the funeral home?" asked Ruby.

"Yeah, Johnston's Funeral home. I was just in Boulder short time back at a funeral there, old pal of Pop's. Same place, wasn't it, Dad?"

"I don't really recall, but it's been there a long time; that's for sure."

Ruby asked whether they could see the cabin. Henry was only too happy to take them up to the site. He said there wasn't much left, but they were welcome to have a look. They all got in Henry's mud-covered jeep, including old Dad, and headed through town, which took about thirty seconds, and then up the hill. The road wound back and forth all the way to the top. After the first few switchbacks, they couldn't see the reservoir for the trees. There were huge boulders and huge pine trees. Everything was huge.

It felt like they had gone back and forth fifty times when they finally slowed down, nearing the top. "I think this is it," said Henry, getting out of the jeep. Ruby and Diane climbed out of the backseat. *I love this women-in-the-backseat thing,* thought Ruby. She turned to say something to Diane about it, but she was already following Henry across the ditch and up an embankment.

This is country living. Dirt roads, no driveway, and a hike to what used to be the house, thought Ruby. After a short walk, the four of them found the site. The only evidence of the house was the crumbling fireplace. The chimney was half gone, but there was still a stone floor in front of it. There were weeds coming up between the stones and signs of small, va-cated dwellings in the firebox. The whole sight gave Ruby the shivers. *Taylor shouldn't ever come here.*

Standing back, she could picture the cabin, with Rebecca in her crib to the left of the fireplace, where Taylor had described it. Ruby had never been here before. Taylor would always bring Rebecca to Boulder, and they'd stay the night. What a magical time that had been! They were such good friends, more like family, really, and Rebecca had been cherished by both of them.

Ruby had seen enough. Her knees were getting weak, and, if she didn't sit down, she was going to fall. "You look like a ghost." The voice seemed far away. Someone was holding her around the waist as she sank to the ground. She heard someone say, "Hey there," but didn't know where it was coming from. Then there was something caustic in her face. Someone was lifting her, and she felt as though she was there but really didn't want to take part in the whole thing.

Ruby's mind rejoined her body on a bed somewhere. They'd taken her to the small health center in Nederland. Slowly, she remembered the whole thing. "I'm fine," were the first words she produced. Not used to being the "faint-of-heart damsel in distress," Ruby was annoyed by all the attention and perplexed by her reaction.

Diane drove the car back to Boulder as Ruby rested in the passenger seat. When they arrived home, she asked Diane to spend the night and went straight to bed. Diane stayed up for a while, trying to dispel the eerie feeling she had.

The next morning both women slept in. Finally, they had to get up and discuss what was on their minds. "She's not dead," said Ruby, watching Diane closely for a reaction. "I just know it." She was answering Diane's first question before she could ask it. Diane said nothing. She didn't know what to say, so she opened the refrigerator, supposedly looking for something to eat.

"I know it; I feel it. I swear it's the truth. Don't even ask me why. I loved that baby, and I would've felt it if she'd died there." Ruby sat down at the counter; she didn't seem to know what to do with herself.

"I don't know what to say. This is all new to me. I saw you faint, and the place was so eerie, but I've no insight one way or the other."

"Well, you wouldn't; you weren't emotionally involved. Why would you feel anything, other than a reaction to a sad remnant?" This was not meant in any kind of exclusive way, nor was it taken as such. This was too monumental to let any petty feelings cloud the issue. "I'm still overwhelmed. I don't know how to stress how completely I believe this to be true. I'm sure it sounds silly, but then, I know it's not. I know what I know, and there isn't one speck of doubt in my mind." Ruby still looked like she couldn't get comfortable. "Not only am I amazed by the realization, but I'm amazed by how sure I am that I'm right."

Diane was feeling strange. This was a strange moment. Ruby was sure. Diane was sure that Ruby was sure, but what now? Diane knew that she was the one who was going to have to start speaking in concrete terms. She owed Taylor, and she was going to do everything in her power to pay that debt so she could live with herself.

"Okay, the one thing we know is that Kevin said he was there, and no one else seems to know that, so let's start there," said Diane.

Ruby appreciated the guidance, and she agreed. Part of her conviction came from the revelation that Kevin was there yet failed to mention it to anyone. Maybe if there hadn't been any discrepancies she wouldn't have been open to different possibilities. Or maybe some things are just too close to the heart to miss.

She spent the day going over all the details. Finally, she focused on one last question: What did they bury at Rebecca's funeral? Ruby called the funeral home and asked to speak to Mr. Johnston, assuming that would be the name of the owner. Surprisingly, he came to the phone. She made an appointment to meet with him that afternoon.

"Nice to meet you, Mr. Johnston; I was given your name by Sheriff Small."

"Yes, Sheriff Small; he was just in Boulder. Mr. Henderson's funeral, I think." They were sitting in Mr. Johnston's office. The funeral home was a beautiful, old Victorian house. His office was just what you'd expect: antiques, wooden paneling, and soft lighting. Collectively, it offered a soothing atmosphere. It had been designed well for its purpose.

"Mr. Johnston, I'm here about something rather sensitive." Ruby had decided she needed to be charming yet needy—ultimately, vulnerable. He was an older man and from all that surrounded her at the moment, she assumed, old-fashioned.

"What can I do to help you, my dear?" He definitely had the mannerisms of someone who was used to dealing with people in pain.

"Well, I have this friend, and she lost a child eight years ago, Taylor Garland."

Without hesitation he said, "I remember her, a terrible tragedy." Ruby was surprised. It seemed that everyone who had anything to do with the fire remembered it well. It must be that the death of a baby is a scar to the entire community.

"Yes, it was a terrible tragedy. Actually, I'm here because Taylor Garland is my dearest friend. She's still having so much trouble dealing with the loss of her child. She's in therapy still."

"These things are so difficult to get over," Mr. Johnston replied sympathetically.

"Well, I hate to say this, but she's having trouble with reality." Ruby had a plan. It was horrible, and it was wonderful. The author in her had written the script. She'd convinced herself that the situation required some "really itfy behavior." If this didn't work and it ever got back to Taylor, she couldn't even imagine what would happen. "The problem is, I'm assuming that you remember the circumstances, that Taylor could never stand the idea that animals had disturbed the body of her beautiful daughter. She's having a tough time coming to terms with that."

"I completely understand."

"Yes, and I want to do everything I can to help her. It was such an awful thing."

"I can see that you're very concerned. How can I help?"

"Well, the sheriff told us," she was hoping he would assume that "us" included Taylor, "that all the remains were handed over to you."

"That's correct."

"Well, how should I put this? Um…were the remains just Tennyson Garland or was it both of them?"

"This is a delicate matter. What did the sheriff say?"

"He said that the baby's body was gone." The sheriff had never actually given her that exact detail, but she wanted Mr. Johnston to have the impression that he wouldn't be telling her something she didn't already know. "We're trying to get as many clear details about the entire tragedy to help Taylor get well." *Almost true.*

"What the sheriff said is true; he gave us no remains of the child. Her coffin was empty."

There it was: the last piece. She had accepted the fact that Tennyson and Rebecca were dead for eight years; now she was surer than sure. Rebecca was alive. There were enough missing pieces; it was "an accumulation of doubt."

CHAPTER 15

A Different Life

Diane didn't have a job, and she hated her apartment in Denver, so for the time being she became Ruby's temporary, permanent houseguest. They were already spending so much time together it just seemed to make sense. She was hardly noticed by Ruby's husband because he was never there. His absence was never discussed, so Diane didn't ask about it; she simply settled in and enjoyed Ruby's company and generosity.

The two were sitting on the back porch. Boulder was beautiful, with lilac and fruit trees all in bloom and a coolness that was wonderfully comfortable.

"Do you really want to do this?" Ruby was asking.

"I did it for him. Why shouldn't I do it for Taylor?" They had decided that they needed some confirmation on where Kevin had been at the time of the fire. Diane was going to feign renewed interest in him and had arranged a meeting at the Fishbone Café that evening. Her biggest fear was not getting "found out"—her fear was of getting sucked back in. He had sounded so glad to hear from her, and they had reconciled many times before. Meanwhile, Ruby was going to research his life, looking for any personal or family facts that might help them.

Diane was nervous, and she wanted to call Shane. He was such a good guy, and maybe he could help her out. She reached for the phone and then sat back. *This was it, wasn't it?* she thought, taking a deep breath. *There always has to be a guy. From one to the next, focus on them and they will run your life for you.* This was her life-long pattern.

She had been the middle of three sisters. She didn't consider herself beautiful but knew that she could "dress up pretty."

In retrospect she saw everything in her history as completely average. She'd done what she was told. All of her efforts were passable and consistently unnoticeable. She often felt as though she were walking alongside of her life, just flowing with it, not participating. The fact was that she even bored herself. The only thing that seemed to add any depth to her existence had been boys and then men. They made her feel, and they ran her life. Or she ran her life according to them. Her self-respect depended on the man she was with, good man—good girl, bad man—bad girl.

Diane knew all this, but so far it had not inspired her to live differently. But this thing with Taylor had been unique. She hadn't had many female friends, for obvious reasons, and for the first time, she cared more about what she was doing to Taylor than about her relationship with Kevin. Leaving him the way she did had been huge, not to mention topping it off with the full confession. She was making a break by telling Taylor everything. Laying herself wide open, ready to take the consequences, had been a new experience. It had rendered so many fears unnecessary. She had admitted her guilt, divulged her worst behavior, and after the fear of disclosure had passed, she was still alive and well. She survived and was offered relief in return for honesty. Exposure had been such a deterrent. Maybe her inner self didn't need to be a secret. How bad did she really think she was? She'd expended so much energy hiding. What didn't she want people to know?

Diane *did* feel different, but she knew meeting with Kevin could be a setback.

I need a cue, a key move, a prompter, she thought as she considered the possibilities. She wanted some solid thinking, total participation, and the belief that she could change things. As she tried to find a cue, she brushed her hair away from her face, and there it was—a perfect prompter. Every time she made this move she would check herself—was she paying attention? Was she in control? Was she accomplishing something? This was going to be a good test. Perfect practice for the kind of awareness she was trying to achieve.

Brushing her hair back, Diane was finally reminded of her plan. She had most likely made the motion several times but hadn't thought of it as the cue. The sight of Kevin had overwhelmed her, as she had loved him for many years. This was actually the first time she'd remembered her strategy. Their dinner had not been served yet; luckily, there was still time.

They had a quiet table against the wall. Kevin had ordered a bottle of red wine and had already drunk half of it. Diane had insisted that he get a table for them if she was late. She knew he would start drinking—and that could be helpful. They had finished ordering when he reached for her arm. "I'm really sorry about that night. I've been under a lot of stress lately. I don't know what came over me. I didn't mean to hurt you. I was just so frustrated, I…"

This is different already, thought Diane. Instead of letting him off the hook at the first "I'm sorry," she was letting him go on. She'd decided to say very little—better that than the wrong thing, yet this was a result she hadn't anticipated. When she looked up, he was staring at her with a "hurt dog look" and some obvious expectations.

"Well, I've never been hit before," which was a lie. "It was very upsetting." She let that hang. Now his "hurt dog look" flashed a hint of irritation. *You thought this would be easier, didn't you?* Diane was thinking, only feeling a portion of her habitual discomfort.

"Well, you did really piss me off. I held up my part of this thing, and after you got your trip, you were backing out of your half," Kevin said defensively. Again, Diane waited a while before speaking.

"I was down there with all those people, trying to do good things, and I just felt guilty that my mission was so sneaky. I must've called you five times to tell you I didn't want to do it." *Guilt isn't going to work on him,* thought Diane. *He doesn't have a conscience.*

"We made a deal. You got your trip, and I got no information." Kevin was getting angry, and that wasn't going to help. Diane wanted to direct this conversation. She was enjoying the challenge. If she kept her distance and her composure, she could hopefully manipulate things properly.

Miss Fentner is taking her time. Diane was enjoying the person inside her head more than the one in front of her. She was feeling a control she didn't know was available, at least to her. Even her long pauses seemed to give her an advantage.

"Did I ever meet Tennyson? Did we ever see him after he left school?" The leap didn't seem too great. After all, they were discussing information about Tennyson.

"No," he replied abruptly.

"I just wondered…" *Casual, sound casual.* They were interrupted by the waiter arriving with their dinner: a steak for Kevin, fish for Diane.

"Can I get you anything else?" asked the waiter.

"No," said Kevin, abruptly waving his hand across the tablecloth, possibly a dismissal, possibly a crumb.

They were quiet for a while. Kevin appeared to be regrouping. Whatever power Diane was exercising was definitely depleting his supply. "What was his work about?" she asked.

"Fuel," he said without looking up from his plate. He was forming his words around the food he was chewing. "He was always fascinated by an alternative. He hated the way our government behaved, all for the acquisition of oil."

"Do you think he found something? Is that why you want those papers?" she pushed.

Kevin put down his fork and looked away, as if he needed time to go there. "We started everything together, and it was my research, too. He always thought he was so much smarter than me." As he spoke, Diane could sense his anger. Aware of his mistake, he tried to lighten things up. "Actually, he was; we all knew that, but we can't all be geniuses."

Diane tried to look sympathetic. *Time for the plunge.* "It must've been hard for you when he died. I remember you told me you actually saw the cabin burn."

Kevin looked up from his plate again. He was looking at her, not angry, more like he was making a decision. "I told you that?"

"Yup, a few years ago. I remember because I've never seen a fire and wondered what it would be like."

"I did; I saw it burn. I went up to talk to Tennyson, but the cabin was already burning when I got there." Diane looked down, trying to hide her surprise. She never thought he would actually validate what he'd told her so long ago. She had come to doubt that he'd said it at all.

"That must've been awful for you" was all she could think to say. She had to be careful; she knew more than she was supposed to. *Calm down,* she warned herself.

"My poor uncle had a fire once, lost everything. It was in Utah. My poor aunt lost all her baby pictures." *Shit, did I actually say "baby"? Cover it; talk on.* "It was really neat. All our family got together and made them new albums with all the pictures they had. I just thought that was so sweet, don't you?" Diane looked up to see what damage she'd done. Kevin seemed uninterested, the way he usually looked during their conversations. *Have I ever noticed that before?* she wondered.

He had finished the bottle of wine and then ordered another glass. He was getting drunk and sleepy. *I've got to get out of here. I know he thinks I'm going to go home with him.*

The waiter cleared their plates. Diane had been concentrating so hard she had eaten very little. "No, no dessert," she said, and then, before Kevin could order, "I have to be home early tonight: job interview tomorrow. I really should have left by now."

They ordered coffee. When enough time had passed, Diane stood up to leave. "Why don't you sleep at my place tonight?" Kevin asked.

There had been so many times she would've been thrilled by this request. He had always called the shots, but not now. On the way home in the car Diane felt better than she had in a long time.

CHAPTER 16

Mexico

Patricia was at the bus stop when Emma was dropped off after school. After all the years of stepping off the bus to nobody, followed by a lonely walk home, it was essential to Patricia that she be there every day. There were so many things she did for Emma, not just because she wanted to, which was also true, but because she'd missed so much in her own childhood.

Emma was glad to see her, and the two walked home, chatting about their day as if it was all that had happened in the world. After positioning Emma's new art project on the mantle, the two started to prepare dinner together. Everything was done together; loneliness was never going to be a part of Emma's childhood.

Patricia had something very specific to discuss tonight, but she held back until they had eaten most of their dinner.

"What do you think about taking a trip? Somewhere really different?" she asked.

"Do you mean like, travel, like Marco Polo? We're learning about him; he found spaghetti, you know."

"Really? Yes, I mean travel like Marco Polo, but it will be easier for us. I thought we might fly somewhere—somewhere warm."

"But it's getting warm here now."

"Pretty muddy, though," Patricia said. She wanted Emma to want to go. She wanted her to take part in the planning, even though everything had already been decided. She always wanted Emma to listen and to feel a part of things. She wanted her to learn how to make decisions for herself.

The fact that she was guiding those decisions had no impact on the lessons Emma would be taught.

"You should see the side playground at school," Emma said. "It's so muddy, we aren't allowed to go over there, but Becky did; she got mud all over her shoes. We tried to clean them off before recess was over, but the bell rang. We didn't want to go in because our hands were muddy, too. The teacher came over and saw us. She told the whole class what we did and said that's why the area is blocked off. Then she helped Becky clean her shoes and put them in the sun to dry."

"It's really muddy around the barn, too." Patricia got up and cleared the dishes away. "Would you like to look at the map?" The two of them huddled over the map and picked Mexico. Then they decided they should work on the rest of the plans at breakfast.

After Patricia tucked Emma into bed, she sat in the kitchen. Her day had started poorly. Christine from the county records office had phoned her to say that someone had called and was asking questions about Patricia's family. Christine had gone to school with Patricia and still lived with her parents. She didn't like strangers, and she guarded the records as if they were her children. Patricia had always thought she was silly, but this time she was grateful. Her first reaction had been to call Kevin, but he wasn't at home, so she left a message. She spent the rest of the day trying to get things done, only to have her fears immobilize her. She had always harbored a veiled fear concerning Kevin's story about Emma, but once the possibility of keeping her had taken root, Patricia had become afraid to ask. She knew there was a mother out there, but Kevin said she didn't want anything to do with a baby.

Since there was no way to do or think about anything else, Patricia had called Christine back. She wanted to get more information on the caller and was upset to find out it was a woman. The stranger had asked about her father, Harry, and did he have a brother in Colorado. Christine had said he did, but Harry was dead. Then the woman asked whether he had any children and was told yes again. "I gave her your name and address, and that is all I told her. Nothing else is anybody's business," said Christine, faithfully standing guard.

No one in the community had ever asked much about Emma. They had accepted the story as told by Patricia. She had depended on the kind of people who lived around her. This group of families had lived side by side for a long time and protected their own: "None of our business," they would have said. "That Patricia's a good woman—had a rough time of it."

Hanging up the phone, Patricia felt vulnerable and exposed. Then, when another attempt to reach Kevin failed, she knew they had to leave. She needed to do something, and she wasn't going to wait for someone to knock on her door. She had feared this for years. It had faded slightly with time but had never been totally excised. She'd lived in constant dread of a woman arriving at the door, looking like Emma and asking whether she knew Kevin.

How fast could Patricia remove all the pictures, the toys, the signs of a young life in her home?

There had been nightmares, too, and times when Patricia would watch people for signs of Emma in their faces, but over the years there had been a reassuring accumulation of papers, health certificates, school ID cards, even a fun fake birth certificate with a footprint, part of a promotion at a local shoe store. This had included one large, two medium, four small pictures, and the certificate. Of course, the footprint was too large—still, it had been a comfort. But the fear had remained.

Now they had to go. Anywhere in Canada was too close to home, and the US was definitely out—so why not Mexico? But ID: How could she handle that? She decided to take everything she had and bombard them with paperwork. Patricia had called a travel agency in Newmarket. There was a woman in Burntwood who booked trips for people, but that would be too easy to trace. Newmarket was bigger than Burntwood and had two agencies. She asked for somewhere remote, by the water, and was recommended the small island of Isla Mujeres. Two weeks were reserved for now; it was low season, so there was no trouble finding a place to stay. Yes, they could change their tickets later, for a fee. They were set to leave in three days, on June 10th. If things got too scary before then, they could go to Toronto ahead of time—anywhere but the farm, waiting for that knock on the door.

In the next days things were fast and efficient. Schoolbooks and assignments were acquired. The farmers on either side would keep an eye on the house and continue to work the fields. Her banker, whom she'd known all her life, was going to pay her bills for her. This was amazing and depressingly easy. She had performed certain tasks all her life and then had managed to replace herself in twenty-four hours. *Except for Emma,* she thought; *no one is going to replace me there.*

CHAPTER 17

Throwing

Ruby and Diane were sitting in Taylor's cramped studio. Actually, it was more like a cubicle. She rented some studio space from the local potter's guild and was working on the wheel. Taylor had been a potter for so long her movements were slow and direct, with a calmness based on experience. She loved what she did; she'd said it a million times.

She was throwing a bowl, starting with a ball of clay the size of a cantaloupe. The wheel was spinning quickly as she leaned her weight into the clay, changing it from a glob that wobbled from side to side into an even lump, perfectly centered. The two friends watched as she pressed one finger into the middle of the mound and turned it into a donut. Then, with one hand over the other for strength, Taylor pulled the hole open, creating a bowl with three-inch thick walls. At this point she sat back. "Don't you two have anything better to do?" She was rinsing her hands in a muddy bucket as she spoke.

"You're always late, so we decided to escort you to my house. We can see that you have some cleaning up to do—that is, before we do anything with you."

"I'm not supposed to be there for forty-five minutes. Give me a break."

"Then we came to help you get ready." Ruby gave Diane a look as if to say, "Right?"

"You guys are too much. What would I do without you?" Taylor said sarcastically. Then with seriousness, "Actually, it's been lonely in that big house. I've been here all day, just to avoid the empty spaces."

Ruby could tell that Taylor hadn't been sleeping well. It was obvious from the droop of her shoulders and the dark circles under her eyes. Plus, she hadn't heard from her, and Taylor usually called when she was happy and hid when she was sad.

Leaning forward again, Taylor returned to the bowl she was making. She tucked the knuckle of the first finger of her right hand at the bottom of the clay and another knuckle from her left hand in the same position on the inside and lifted. Slowly, the walls rose, magically thinning and changing the form. After repeating this several times, the shape was more open and the sides curved smoothly from foot to rim. She leaned over after each lift to check the profile. When she was satisfied with the height, she used a wooden rib shaped with a curved edge to pressure the walls from the inside and round the belly of the piece. After this, she smoothed the upper rim, making it thick and strong. Then she sat back for the final inspection. Pleased, she pulled a wire under the bowl to separate it from the bat it had been formed on. The bat and bowl were then lifted off the wheel head and set on a shelf. She was done. A little clean up and a change of clothes and she was good to go.

They were all making dinner together at Ruby's house. Shane was in town on business and planned on joining them. Ruby's husband was out of town on business; evidently, a new project was keeping him out of the state. No one even asked where he was anymore. He was never there, and Ruby never talked about it. It simply was not up for discussion.

When the girls parked in front of Ruby's house, they spotted Shane sitting in his car. "I was starting to wonder if this was the right place."

"You must be Shane," said Ruby. "You should've gone in; everyone else does."

"Next time I will," he replied. They all entered the unlocked house and walked through to the kitchen in the back. It was a big room, with a fireplace and a wooden table in the front of it. There was an island in the middle, a couch against the wall, and plenty of room for everyone to be comfortable.

"If we all pitch in, we'll have this dinner whipped up in no time." That was the way things went in Ruby's house. It was comfortable and felt like everyone's second home.

There was a purpose to this dinner—they had all discussed it and decided they should tell Taylor that they were looking into a few things. Ruby was not going to mention her certainty about Rebecca. There was no point until she had some facts. She wanted to discuss the basics, like the lack of investigation and other decisions made after the fire.

Ruby had also been trying to get hold of Taylor's father, Mr. Robert Mendel. He had not been much of a participant in his daughter's life. Apparently, he'd only shown up after the fire because Taylor had asked him to. The situation had been too grave for him to ignore, and he was the last of her family.

They cooked and ate in high spirits, and it all felt easy. Then it was time to talk to Taylor. Ruby explained everything, even going to the cabin but leaving out her fainting and her thoughts about Rebecca.

"How did the place look?" Taylor asked, appearing remarkably unconcerned.

"It's beautiful up there," Diane replied. "All that's left is a fireplace, and it's starting to crumble." Diane looked around, afraid she'd said too much.

"Tennyson always loved that fireplace. He had it built with rocks from the property. It's so appropriate that it should sink back into the ground." Taylor had completely detached herself from the land. To her it was a memory; in fact, it was strange for her to think it still existed.

"Maybe you should sell it," said the practical Shane.

"No, it's better left alone, a memorial to Tennyson. He loved it up there. It can just sit there forever. No one has to own it." The conversation had not bothered or surprised her; she'd known something was up. She could read Ruby. They'd found nothing new and wouldn't.

The next day Ruby continued with her research, feeling better about it now that Taylor knew. She was very organized and had mapped out all possible connections to Kevin. His father and mother were still alive and living in Boulder; he was an only child. On his father's side there was a brother and two sisters, all living in Denver. Ruby had called them all. She'd pretended she was with the census office and easily acquired all the information she needed. Then she had taken that information and checked it with the County Record's Office. Everything checked out—no extra children anywhere. Then there was Kevin's mother's side—one brother in Ontario, Canada. A call to the small town's record office revealed there was a family farm there. The brother and wife were dead, but there was one unmarried daughter living on the farm. That was all she could get.

The woman on the other end of the phone had been very officious and unfriendly.

Ruby had a few scenarios she was working with. The first was that Kevin was there, saved the baby, but didn't want any suspicion roused, so gave the baby to someone in his family or left the baby at a hospital or adoption agency. If Tennyson had left the baby with anyone, that person would have come forward. The only reason for not hearing anything would be that there was something to hide.

When all the research was done, the only family member Ruby wasn't sure of was a Patricia Weston.

Next, she would start matching the dates of the fire with adoptions. While she was working on her notes, the phone rang. It was Robert Mendel returning her call. He wanted to know whether Taylor was all right. "Yes, Taylor is fine, Mr. Mendel. I just wanted to ask you a few questions about the fire."

There was a pause.

"What for?"

"Well, Taylor and I are really good friends, and I found out some new information about the night the cabin burned." Ruby paused, but the phone was silent, so she went on. "I thought maybe you could tell me what you know, since there was no investigation."

Again a pause. "Are you there, Mr. Mendel?"

"Yes, I am here. This was all a very long time ago. I cannot imagine why you are going into it now."

"Well, I was just wondering why you didn't request an investigation." Ruby wasn't about to give Robert Mendel a bit of information. She didn't like him before she called him, and she didn't like him now. He had been a non-participating father. He was some big hotshot New York attorney. "Selfish" and "cold" were the words Taylor had used. He'd left her mother for some young trophy wife and then dumped her, too. Taylor's mother had died the year before Rebecca was born, and he hadn't even gone to the funeral.

"There was no need for an investigation. There was a fire, two people died, and that was that. No mystery, no questions."

"But isn't it true that they never found Rebecca's body?" Ruby replaced the word "identified" with "found." She wanted a specific answer.

"Whatever was left of the body was dragged away and eaten. That information would have been more than Taylor could have handled. It was better left unsaid. She heard there had been some animals but not the full extent of the carnage."

"But there was nothing left—no sign of Rebecca at all, right?"

"Young lady, how many ways do I need to say the same thing? The body was gone. The truth was too painful; we left it alone." Pause. "Does Taylor know you are looking into all of this?"

"Yes, she does." Ruby was relieved it wasn't yesterday.

CHAPTER 18

Galashiels, Scotland

Darby Wallace was born in 1896 in Galashiels, a small town forty-five miles south of Edinburgh. Galashiels was on the down side of a textile boom that had started in 1849, when the railroad was completed. The new connection with Edinburgh supplied a huge market for the fine textiles the area produced. The population had swelled to eighteen thousand by 1891, until cheaper cloth manufactured with new machinery folded the market. Soon, jobs were hard to find, and life became increasingly difficult.

Darby's family was poor, but they always ate, and they had a home. It was small: The roof was low, and the inside was dark with a dirt floor. Darby was the second oldest of nine children, so it was crowded and uncomfortable, and by 1909 he was on his own.

He had jumped the train as it left the loading dock and ridden it to Edinburgh. There were more jobs there. He had heard other boys bragging about making money, more than their fathers made in the mills. It was a hard way of life. He was just one of the hordes of young boys forced to leave their families too soon because of a lack of food or space.

He managed to stay alive, but life was cruel. He learned to do anything to survive. Any conscience he had he deemed useless after three days without food, or trying to recover from a brawl, or a night in the cold. Yet Darby was different; he enjoyed the cruelty he used to survive. As he grew and developed a life for himself, his need for cruelty remained, even though the use of it was no longer needed to survive.

Sarah worked in the bar he frequented the most. She had been born in Edinburgh and was familiar with the kind of lives her customers led.

She was a good girl—that is, if the women she knew were to be divided into good or bad. Sarah could hold up her end in tough situations and kept a distance from anyone making persistent advances. She did, however, like Darby, and Darby liked the idea of his tough virgin.

They were married in 1914, and from the beginning he supported them both, but he would never discuss how he made his money. At first their life together was rough, but so was everything in their neighborhood. Sarah was pregnant within months and then every year after that until 1919. She produced three girls, pretty like their mum. At this time and in their neighborhood it seemed to be the norm that as more children were born, fathers were home less and less. Sarah and Darby were no different except that when Darby did come home, he would be agitated and aggressive. Other families accepted the alcohol that made life for their men bearable, but Darby didn't like to drink; he wanted control. He had discovered at a young age that as everyone else drank, his power increased, just by staying sober. As the years passed, he became even more mysterious, and some of his crueler habits started to find a place in their home.

Sarah would defend herself with trepidation, trying not to aggravate the situation or let Darby's attention fall on the girls. She found just the right place between submission and preservation to survive his harassment. She was strong and healthy and believed in doing what was necessary. That was what was expected of her; her life was not unusual.

One night, while Sarah and the girls were alone in the house, the police came pounding at the door. "No, Darby was not there. Yes, you may come in and look, and, yes, there are only two rooms." Days passed and still no Darby. More pounding on the door and searching the house. Finally, Darby showed up in the middle of the night, and Sarah knew better than to ask where he'd been.

Within hours of his return they had left everything they couldn't carry and boarded the train for London. Darby had money, and they were going to America, and that was all Sarah needed to know. She'd heard that life there was full of opportunities and easier for women with families. She loved her girls. She didn't care much about Darby anymore, but if he had money and took them to America, he was okay.

The family had not been prepared for the magnitude of the ocean or the vile conditions aboard the ship. Sarah's gift was Darby's illness. He was incapacitated for the entire crossing. She didn't have to tolerate his shameful treatment as well as fend for the girls. Her middle daughter, Elizabeth, could not hold anything down. It started as soon as they set sail, and Sarah prayed they would reach America before Elizabeth became too ill.

They arrived in Boston on a Sunday, and Elizabeth was still alive but vulnerably frail. Sarah was surprised when three men met them at the dock. Darby was looking thin but alert and greeted them without affection. The men were instructed to carry the family's few belongings and deliver them to an address she'd never heard before. Apparently, these men worked for her husband, and when they arrived at the small house where they were to live, there were more men inside waiting for Darby. He sent one of them to find a doctor and left without a word, taking the rest of the men with him.

For five years they lived in Boston. Sarah had three more children, two girls and a boy, and the family was okay if Darby didn't come home. He had become untamable, unmanageable, and a stranger to the woman who had married him. His visits were increasingly disruptive, and Sarah dreaded his homecomings. Life was difficult enough with six children, and he devised new and crueler ways to remind her that he was master of their small world.

Then it started over again: the police pounding on the door, the searches, and the questions. But this time Darby's name was in the newspaper.

"Looking for suspect, gruesome murders, history of cruelty in Scotland."

Sarah had spent all of her married life paying Darby like a loan. She had her children, and his money helped her care for them well, so when a payment was due, she was ready. But this felt different. It wasn't just her problem; everybody wanted to know what she had never asked. What had he done?

This time they *did* capture him, and they *did* find out that he had killed four people in a cruel and perverse manner. This time they *did* send him to jail. Sarah *didn't* care; he couldn't collect on his loan anymore.

It was time to find a new life, so she moved from Boston to Cambridge and changed the family name to Mendel—she'd seen it in the newspaper. Anything but Wallace.

She never visited her husband in prison. She preferred to say he was dead and lived for a while on the small amount of money he had left behind. But life was still hard in Cambridge, and Sarah was just another immigrant with too many children and no money. There were so many women in her position and no jobs that allowed a mother to care for her children and make enough to support the whole family.

People were not kind to those who recently had landed; there was a hierarchy set up to keep them in their place. Soon, she was doing for strangers what she used to do for her husband. She had six children and no skills, but she was tough, and she knew how to do what needed to be done. This didn't destroy her; in many ways, the men she knew were kinder than her husband had been. She set a standard for herself and never walked the streets and learned to live with her new profession.

Robert Mendel was the last child born into the family of Sarah and Darby. He couldn't remember his father but had heard everything about him from his sisters. Darby came to represent the devil to Robert, and his mother was an embarrassment, as he reluctantly witnessed her vocation.

Robert's goal in life was to leave, which he did at thirteen. He found a job cleaning the butcher's stall at the market and eventually just stopped going home. He worked hard and was rewarded with a small cot in the back room of the shop. The owner was glad to have him there for security; there were so many hungry people in their part of town. But when the windows and doors were closed for the night, the smell was hard to sleep with at first. He got used to it, though—anything to keep him from going home.

Robert had learned to read from his oldest sister and was determined to learn more. He was convinced that there was some part of himself that he could use to go beyond the obvious barriers. After work he studied for as many hours as he could squeeze out of his young body. He had a mission, and nothing was going to keep him from getting far from his family and their way of life.

Robert had never thought of himself as part of the family he deserted, but family life had taught him how to work hard. He was used to feeling alone and didn't have or want any friends. His ambition was to have money and live well, and the thought of it kept him company. As he got older, he told people he'd lost his family, and in his heart it was true.

Darby had been evil. When Robert had learned enough to understand, he read the transcripts of his father's trial and found no evidence to change his perception. There was nothing redeeming to be found. Everything he read and everything his sisters and mother had told him confirmed that. Ultimately, the question that plagued him the most was: "When had his father not been evil?" Robert had never heard one thing that led him to believe such a time had ever existed.

After many years and help from people who appreciated a young man dedicated to hard work and study, Robert became a lawyer. He started as a prosecutor—every bad guy was his father, and every time he won; he put him in jail again. Yet people didn't seem to like him; he was too intense. A sense of humor was a waste of time.

Carol Hurley worked with Robert as a legal aide. She was serious and seemed to have an understanding of how alone Robert felt. Before they married, Robert told Carol he did not want children, and she had agreed. He never said why, but there was no doubt he was sure. He didn't want a family; he had never witnessed anything good about being in one. He truly believed that his father had been evil—not just mean but inherently evil. When he added this to the fact that it was a family that had forced his mother to sell herself to pay the bills, he couldn't come to terms with starting one of his own.

When Carol became pregnant, there was only one thing to do; they had agreed on it. But Carol wasn't sure, and then she was: She wanted the baby. Robert was not going to hand down his genetic code of evil to terrorize the world again and implored Carol to do what they had agreed on. She would not. He left. He would have no part in bringing another member of his family into the world.

He stayed in New York and watched, detached but concerned. His concern was not for his daughter but for what she might become. As she grew, he became relieved—no unusual behavior, but there was no way to determine at what age his father had started to enjoy the awful things he did or when his mother had abandoned the need for morality. What generation would these defects show up in and expose his origin?

When Taylor had called about the fire in 1982, Robert had wanted to help her. He knew he was all she had. Then, when asked whether they should have an investigation and told that the baby's body wasn't there, his mother's face was all he could see. He hadn't wanted a daughter, and he didn't want to have to watch a granddaughter the way he had Taylor. He believed or wanted to believe that animals had dragged off the baby's body. Yet, if for some reason the child had survived and nobody knew where she was, it could no longer be connected to him. Either way, he wanted no investigation. Even a daughter's grief could not overpower a lifetime of fears.

Robert was annoyed by Ruby's call. *Why now?* He had put all of this behind them, including Taylor. Taylor was better off without a baby—she could be on her own. Look what his mother had to do, without a husband, with children to feed.

When Robert returned to New York after the fire, he hired an investigator to compose and go through a list of people connected with Tennyson, looking for anyone who might want him dead. Kevin became the prime suspect. After searching through family records, much like Ruby was doing now, they found Patricia. It was easier back then; the trail was fresher. The baby had arrived on the farm and was being talked about by neighbors.

Robert paid the investigator and started watching Emma the way he had Taylor, from afar. He hired someone he'd not used before. He didn't want any connection to his work. Some new man in town had put flyers in the office boxes, looking for work. The timing was perfect, and Robert knew that someone looking for work was not going to be too picky or ask too many questions.

He never allowed the label of evil to adhere to his behavior; he had a goal and never wavered.

CHAPTER 19

Ontario

R uby and Shane flew into Toronto and rented a car. They were on their way to Burntwood to find Patricia. Ruby had to rule her out before she went to the next stage of her investigation. Diane had stayed home. She couldn't afford a ticket and refused to take advantage of Ruby's generosity—that is, any more than she already was.

Ruby wanted to go. She recognized her denial as she embraced any chance to get out of town. It was taking on a familiar ring. How can you call a place home if no one wants to be there? She'd been moving from one day to the next without considering her situation. But it was easy to see—her marriage was over. It had been for some time, yet finally admitting defeat and then splitting, dividing, and settling was a hard chapter to begin. The more she was out of town, the longer she could delay the inevitable.

Shane's reason for the trip was different. He'd started his company alone, and things had gone well. He always said he "was in the right place at the right time." The truth was he was hard-working and imaginative. The pragmatic behavior he'd learned while raising his brothers had served him well in the business world.

After his brother Shawn had finished school, Shane hired him to run the company. Now it was time to leave Shawn fully in charge. Shane wanted to start something new but needed a break first. He'd raised the boys and built a company, and now he wanted more—something unusual, an adventure, something unplanned. He went to Nicaragua to let Shawn try to run things for a short while, and he'd done very well. Shane was confident that the business would be okay. There were no more excuses for not stepping out. He used to tell the boys, "Discovery is all about timing."

Shane wasn't clear on Ruby's status, but he enjoyed her company, so here he was, helping her with the investigation. They had planned a very short trip, two nights.

After finding their way out of the Toronto airport, they headed north on Highway 400. Ruby had been driving only in Boulder and Denver for so long that the ten-lane highway heading north was intimidating at first. Once the road narrowed to only six lanes she could relax enough to discuss their plan.

Shane had the first suggestion. "How about we just get a look at the farm today and then find a place to stay?" It was two in the afternoon, and there was still enough daylight left to locate Patricia's house.

"That's a good idea. Maybe we can find a nice dinner somewhere?"

Ruby agreed that just looking at the place would be okay; however, after traveling all day, she was tired. The chance of knocking on a door and having a little girl with Taylor's face answer it had to be prepared for. She wanted to see the area, the people, the town, and get a feel for the community. If this woman had Rebecca, she would not be happy to see them. Ruby had considered this side of the story for the first time as she sat on the plane. She'd been so focused on finding Rebecca, she hadn't considered whoever had her. Was she a loving mother? If so, what to do then? This was a whole new dilemma; if she found Rebecca happy, wouldn't it be better to leave everything alone?

It was the bond that changed her mind, even before she got to other issues like right and wrong. There was that bond Taylor had with Rebecca. And then there were the three of them on those wonderful weekends in Boulder. It was the closest thing to motherhood Ruby had felt. *Blood isn't everything*, she thought, *but whose case am I arguing now?*

"If the child is happy and loved, what difference does blood make? What havoc would her true history cause?" Without meaning to, Ruby had spoken out loud.

"I've been wondering the same thing," replied Shane. "When my parents died, there was talk of foster homes and adoption. I'd just turned twenty-one and, therefore, was barely into legal adulthood. My two youngest brothers were only ten and twelve, and Scott was sixteen, so we were a marginal case, and it came down to blood or care. Was it more important to keep us together as a family or to find us homes, most likely separately? It was our strong collective voice that won. We never wavered. We wanted to be together and knew we could do it. It was two years before there were formal papers. I was named guardian. It was a legal stretch but the right thing to do." There was a pause as the two looked out the window and privately contemplated the problem.

"This is one of those circular things," Ruby broke the silence, "so how do you know if you've done the right thing? You can't go back and try the other way for comparison's sake."

"I knew it was the right thing for us to stay together. Nothing else could have compared with the life my brothers and I had together. In some ways we were lucky. We all understood each other perfectly. There may have been times we lacked guidance or pissed each other off, but we shared, and we worked together, and I wouldn't have wanted it any other way."

"Okay, well, let's forget the obvious pros and cons of this situation. There's a whole other part that's weird. I'm not a religious person, but I try to do the right thing and be kind. You really want to get into this?"

"Have at it," Shane encouraged.

"Okay, I don't believe in the organized God thing, but I believe in energy, just generally in a vague way. I believe in good. Like, for example, you're at the grocery store—you're going through the checkout counter, and you smile and chat with the checker. You don't even have to chat, just smile and be nice. Okay, now the checker has a good day and goes home with a good attitude or good energy to share with his family." Ruby held up her hand. "I know, this is simplistic, but consider the other side: You've had a bad time because some asshole honked at you in the parking lot; you get your groceries and either act grouchy or ignore your checker. Not that this alone could do it, but it could add to other crappy things and send the checker home to his family in a way that isn't going to do anyone any good." Ruby was making big circles with her right hand as she watched the road and drove with the left. "I mean, bad adds to bad, and good adds to good.

"The point is kindness, in every way, in every little thing—like you don't always have to prove someone wrong. Do they need that, or do you just want to be right? Do they need to learn, or do you just need to feel better? I'm rambling, I know, but my point is that it has to be the right thing to reunite a heartbroken mother with her child if you can. Then, if everyone continues dealing with the situation with kindness in mind, it'll work. A good attitude will create the right energy. I mean, once I felt what I did at the cabin, I had to act on it, right? Oh, I hate this. I confuse even myself. Sorry for going on and on, but this thing has just brought up so many issues. Someone needs to organize my brain."

Shane laughed. He admired her willingness to drift aloud. "The more I get to know your brain, the more I enjoy it. I'm always way too practical, too cautious. Too much responsibility at a young age, I think. When I was twenty-one, my friends were running around making asses of themselves and having a blast, and I was playing Susie Homemaker."

"So now it's time for you to have some fun."

"You're right about that. They are all old enough to take care of themselves now. The boys, I mean." Shane moved his shoulders up and down and moved his head from side to side. "I just need to loosen up." Ruby laughed at his exaggerated gestures.

They were getting closer to the area where the farm was. The scenery was hills rolling into hills and waves of green trees. This was a huge contrast to the barren plains of Colorado. Shane started checking the map. "The first turn off will be the easiest, then the roads will probably be harder to identify," he said. "Okay, we need to look for Highway 88, then turn right, that is east. Then we need to look for 48, where we head north, then we…"

"Wait! Can we do this one road at a time, please? Just tell me where to turn when it's time. I'm terrible with directions." They made the first turn and then the next, each thoroughfare getting rougher and smaller as they neared Burntwood. The last turn was away from town on Route 83. This was definitely farm country. Lines of corn marched away from the road in an orderly fashion. Every few miles there would be a clearing with a farmhouse. Next to each red brick house stood a large wooden barn that had turned gray from years of rain and snow. These buildings would be surrounded by enough open space to include a yard and driveway before the tall stalks of corn would line up again. The collective effect was charming.

Five miles after their last turn they found the farm. The mailbox had "Harry T. Weston, Rural Route 83" on the side. Ruby pulled off the road but didn't enter the driveway. Her heart had started pounding, and she needed to sit quietly for a moment. "Are you all right?" Shane asked.

"I will be; just give me a minute." She laid her head back on the seat, closed her eyes, and tried to envision a river flowing over and around smooth rocks. If she could really go there, it would actually calm her down, but not today. She opened her eyes and walked around the car to get a better view of the farmhouse. Maybe she would feel something like she had at the cabin.

The house was old but appeared well kept. It was two stories, with a large wooden porch on the front. It looked very much like the other farms. Ruby was hoping someone would come out of the front door, and she was terrified they might. She studied the windows, the steps, the yard, searching for a clue.

"It looks like a real nice place," Shane said as he stepped out of the car. He'd waited to join her, recognizing that she was struggling.

"I don't feel anything, and I don't see anything that gives me any information either way." She rested her back against the side of their rented car. "I was sure I'd feel something."

"It's been a long day," Shane said. "Why don't you let me drive?" Her disappointment was magnified by the long day's travel. He opened the passenger door, and Ruby lowered herself into the seat, never taking her eyes off the farm. They drove to town in silence until Ruby said, "I was so sure I'd feel something, either way. But it's just a farmhouse; they all look the same."

"Let's find a place to stay and then get something to eat." The town was much smaller than they'd expected. Shane pulled into the first gas station and rolled down his window as an older man in greasy overalls came out to the pump.

"What'll it be?"

"Could you fill it up, and can you tell me if there is a hotel in town?"

"Nope. Used to be a small motel, but no one ever stayed there."

"Is there some place to stay for the night?"

"Well, Ramona Jennings' got a place, sort of a bed and breakfast, she calls it. But no one ever stays there, either."

"Could you tell us how to get there?"

"Yup, go through town; it's the last house on the right, biggest too."

Shane paid in cash, glad that he'd changed money at the airport. They were in and out of town in a minute. It had one wide main street with cars parked on both sides, diagonally to the sidewalk. The stores seemed to be one extended building on each side of the road. The first open space was between the hardware store and Ramona Jennings's house. It had a small sign hanging under the mailbox: "Bed and Breakfast, Welcome." Across the street was what looked like a courthouse and then the post office.

"I hope the workers there are happy," Shane said, but his sad attempt at humor was totally lost on Ruby. She was studying the house.

"Let's try it," she said. "Looks quaint." They climbed up the front steps and rang the doorbell next to a "Home Sweet Home" sign. The door opened, exposing a short, gray-haired woman in a flowered smock.

"Yes?"

"We were told we might find some rooms for the night here."

"Yes," she said again, offering no other information.

"Do you have rooms…for rent?"

"Yes."

"Do you think we could look at them?" Shane gave Ruby a look, rolling his eyes.

"Yes."

"Mother," came from behind the old woman. "I've been looking everywhere for you. I thought you were in the garden."

"Yes," the door lady replied again as she turned slowly back into the house and wandered past a younger woman who was approaching the open door.

"Sorry. I was in the garden looking for my mother and didn't hear the bell. She's driving me crazy. She just wanders around, so I have to keep a close eye on her. I think she's completely senile, or maybe I am." Ramona smoothed out her dress. "Well, what can I do for you?"

"We're looking for a couple of rooms."

"Oh, wonderful, I just love having people stay. It's so nice to have someone to talk to with a larger vocabulary. My mother has honed her speaking down to, I'd say, around ten words. Come on in." Then, extending her hand, "I'm Ramona Jennings, and that was my mother, Ruth."

"Pleased to meet you. I'm Shane Smith, and this is my friend Ruby Starkey."

"How many rooms did you say you wanted?" Ramona was eying Ruby suspiciously after hearing the different last names.

"We need two rooms," replied Ruby, amused by the "back-home morality."

"Well, come with me. I actually have five rooms. Mother sleeps downstairs. Can't take the stairs anymore, and I'm in one of the five upstairs. I could stay downstairs with mom if I ever actually had five guests, which has never happened, so you have four rooms to choose from. I keep them all clean just in case. There are two bathrooms. I use one, and then there is another one for guests. If I rented out all four rooms, I'd give up my bathroom, too. Here we are." They had reached the top of the stairs, and Ramona opened the first door to the right. They were standing on a large landing with a door every few feet going all around the walls.

The room was charming in a Victorian sort of way. There was too much furniture and doilies everywhere. The light switch on the wall was two small knobs. When you pushed one in, the other popped out and the lights went on, which is just what Ramona did. They picked two rooms and got a tour of the bathroom and then moved their things in from the car.

Ruby unpacked and went downstairs. She found Ramona in the large kitchen at the back of the house.

"Ramona, I was wondering if you knew a place in town where we could get dinner?"

"Oh, here, of course—there's a diner, but it isn't that clean, and the food…" She shook her head. "I haven't had anyone to cook for in a while. Mother's food all has to be soft, and it's no fun cooking something special just for myself. I've already started planning something. I know the sign says 'Bed and Breakfast,' but I always cook all the meals for whoever stays here. I can't call it a 'Bed and Breakfast and Lunch and Dinner'—the sign would be too big to hang on my mailbox. You will be wanting dinner, won't you?"

Ruby was amazed at how this woman talked. There never seemed to be a pause where someone could comfortably break in. "We'd love to stay, thank you. What time do you usually eat?"

"Let's see…it's five o'clock now, and I need to pick up a few things; don't worry, it's only a few doors away. Then I need time for the potatoes…" She closed her eyes as if she could not take any visual input while she was calculating. "Is seven o'clock too late? I would like to make something special and just need a little time to prepare. Just you wait and see. It'll be worth it. I learned to cook on the farm for the family, and the hands and I never had any complaints…"

"Seven is perfect." Ruby had to time her answer carefully; she waited till she knew that Ramona had to breathe and spoke fast. "I'll go tell Shane." She left the kitchen as she was saying this so Ramona couldn't stretch the conversation any further. Ruby was going to need a nap to get through this meal. She told Shane the plan and lay down on her four-poster bed.

Waking up after an hour, she wondered where she was. It took a few seconds to reacquaint herself with her surroundings, and then she lay there for another half hour, questioning what they were doing there. After freshening up, she went to Shane's room. He was reading and looked absolutely ridiculous sprawled out on his four-poster bed surrounded by pillows decorated with lace and frills. "I don't know if I've enough energy to sit through a whole dinner with Ramona; she never shuts up."

"I've been thinking about that," said Shane, sitting up against the headboard. "I think we're really lucky to be here."

"What are you talking about? She'll probably describe every meal she's cooked since she was ten." Ruby crossed the room and sat on the edge of the bed.

"It's perfect; someone who talks that much is probably a busybody and knows lots of things about lots of people." Shane was raising his eyebrows in a playful way as he spoke.

"God, you're right; I bet she knows everybody's business around here. We have to get her to talk about Patricia."

They all sat in the formal dining room, Ramona at the end by the kitchen door and Shane, temporary man of the house, at the other end. Ruby now knew what farm cooking meant: mashed potatoes, corn, pork chops, rolls, and a pitcher of milk. Ramona spent the whole time she was serving dinner talking about how she'd "put up" the corn, how she never wastes any of it, how if she cans too much she gives it away, and on and on and on.

The "give away" part was Ruby's cue; she waited for Ramona to take a breath and plunged in. "I bet there are tons of people who would love this corn. You must know everyone in the area."

"Pretty much. Sometimes people leave and new ones come in, but not very often. We all know each other's families from way back. Most of these farms have been in the same family for generations. We're not that big a community, and all the farmers come into town for anything they can't grow. We have these…"

"We saw people's names on their mailboxes as we drove into town. You know, I'm from Boulder, Colorado, and one of my neighbors there had a brother around here. Her name is Anne Levine, but she used to be Anne Weston. Do you know her family?"

"Oh, sure, the Weston family's been here forever. They've had a rough time of it, though: poor Celia dying so young. I used to go to school with her. She was older than me but in the same school. I thought Harry was going to go crazy, and then that poor little girl, just sad, sad. We all took over food and helped with the house for a while when it happened, but that poor little girl just plain had to look after herself. Harry wasn't ever good for much more than farming after Celia was gone."

There was a slight pause, so Ruby asked, "How did Celia die?"

"Oh, she was told not to have another baby. She was lucky to have Patricia and live through it. She knew she shouldn't do it, but there she was pregnant again, and she died trying to give birth to a little boy. I know because we had a funeral for both of them. Harry couldn't even talk, and that poor Patricia, she was such a little thing and no mother and Harry just being kind a queer after that. Poor little thing, she…"

"Is Patricia still here?" Ruby was hoping that this wasn't too obvious, but Ramona didn't seem to notice; she was so caught up in the history of the Weston's. "I mean, is she still on the same farm?"

"Oh, yes, she doesn't farm, though; her neighbors use the fields now. She never married. I think she just got so used to living alone in that house; that was how it was when she was growing up. Harry wasn't much of a talker, and he just worked and slept. Poor little thing always seemed so alone."

"So she still lives alone?" Ruby pushed.

"Oh, no, she's got that little Emma. What a godsend she was! The two of them are just two peas in a pod. They're always together except when Emma's in school. I've never seen anyone change so much as Patricia when she got Emma. All of a sudden she was chatty and happy and coming to town more and talking to people more, just like her mom. Her mom used to talk to everyone, and she had the best laugh. She was really popular in school. I used to watch her with her friends and wish I were older so I could hang around with that bunch. She and Harry were so in love. High school sweethearts, you know. He never was much of a talker, but he lit up like a candle when that Celia was around. Everyone knew they would get married. They were just…"

"What do you mean Patricia got Emma?" Shane asked. He wanted this question to come from him. He thought it might distract Ramona from thinking Ruby was being too nosy. There was no need to worry, though—Ramona was having a grand time, talking away with someone to listen.

"Oh, well, Emma came from some relatives. Both parents were killed in a car accident or something like that. It was so sad. Everything seems to happen in that family. Not that the rest of us don't have our pains, but it just seems they got more than the rest of us—too bad about the parents, but it made Patricia so happy. I think everyone was happy for her. The two of them are inseparable. She brings her to all…"

"How old is Emma?" Shane asked. Ruby was very quiet and listening to Ramona with glazed eyes and nodding a lot, like she wasn't all there.

"Oh, well, you know, I'm not quite sure. She's just a little thing and still in grade school, so she has to be under eleven or twelve, doesn't she? Let me think."

Taking the final plunge, draining poor unsuspecting Ramona of all he could, Shane asked the big question, the one that made this trip worth it: "Do you remember what year she came here—Emma, I mean?"

Ramona was still deep in calculation, trying to determine how old Emma was. *Maybe Ruth wanders around just to get away from her daughter's chattering*, thought Shane as he fought frustration, waiting for her to answer the question.

"You know, I'll have to think about that. It's hard to separate the years. After a while they all string together. Usually, I can figure it out by some other big event."

They had all finished dinner, and Ramona was starting to clear the table. "I've made you a pie. I haven't made one since the autumn festival, and it was such a pleasure. I had to use canned fruit, though, but I canned it fresh, and I'm sure you'll like it. Peaches can be really nice if you use the best ones. Apples, you really need to cook, applesauce or apple chutney, something like that. Now pears…" She was chatting away as she went through the swinging door, in and out of the kitchen. They would hear some of it, and then the next bit would be muffled as the doors swung shut, then out she would pop, still chatting.

Ruby was discouraged by the change of subject, just as they were posing the big question. She hoped Ramona would think about it and get back to them. They were there for two nights, so there was still time.

The next morning they ate breakfast in the same dining room. Fruit and rolls had been laid out on the table with a cloth over them, and next to them was a note. Ramona was so sorry, but she couldn't join them for breakfast. Could they please leave a note telling her whether they would be there for lunch and dinner or just dinner? Signed, "Your Hostess, Ramona Jennings."

"What a relief. I'm not sure I could take our dear Ramona first thing in the morning." They happily served themselves. "By the way, thanks for stepping in at dinner last night. It just felt so strange to think we could actually be right and that this could really be where Rebecca grew up."

"I could see you were in a zone somewhere, and I also didn't want it to look like all the questions were coming from you. Not that I think it made one bit of difference."

"What do you think we should do today?" Ruby was enjoying this; it'd been a long time since she had said that to a man. She'd never shared any kind of leisure time with Mark. They might have gone to a party together or to a business dinner, but they never had a "what-should-we-do-today" kind of day. That kind of question was reserved for her women friends. Shane was good company, and Ruby liked his tall athletic appearance, his blond hair and brown eyes—*an unusual combo*, she thought.

"I think we should relax. We should look around town a bit and then go back out to the farm. Or maybe the opposite order would be better, so you don't have all that time to get worked up about it." As Shane spoke, Ruth wandered into the dining room.

"Nice morning, don't you think, Ruth?" Shane asked with a huge grin on his face.

"Yes," Ruth replied as she wandered into the kitchen.

"I thought I should ask her a question we know she could answer."

"You're such a brat." Ruby was slicing the last of the strawberries onto her plate. "I think you're right; we should go to the farm first. Let's just head out there after breakfast. The rest of the day will depend on what happens there."

They finished eating, cleared the table, and prepared to leave. The trip to the farm felt longer than the previous afternoon. Finally, they pulled up in the same spot, and then without a word Ruby backed up and drove down the driveway. They left the car in front of the steps and knocked on the door. No answer. Shane knocked a few more times—still no answer. Ruby cupped her hands around her eyes and leaned her forehead on the window. Peering in, there wasn't much to see. It was very tidy, almost generic. They went around to the back of the house and knocked on the kitchen door. No answer.

"They're not there," came a voice from the barn. Turning, Ruby saw an older woman, maybe in her seventies, walking toward them and eyeing them distrustfully. "They're out of town."

"We just wanted to talk to Patricia Weston. We know some of her relatives in the US," Ruby said defensively, walking toward the woman with her hand out. "Hi, I'm Ruby; will they be back soon?"

"Pleased to meet you. I'm Martha Nelson, Patricia's neighbor. I'm just watchin' over the place while she's gone."

"Did they both go?" Ruby prodded. Martha ignored this question and answered the first one.

"Don't know when they'll be back, but she deserves a nice holiday. You're welcome to look around. I remember now—Harry's sister lived in the US." Martha shaded her eyes and looked up and around. "Just like to check on the house every day. Sorry you missed her." Martha turned and walked back to the barn. "Should be a nice day," she said and was gone.

Ruby sat down on the back step. This was the kind of attitude she had experienced with the record's office lady. She was starting to feel very grateful for chatty Ramona.

The two of them looked around the farm a little longer, but nothing told them anything. It was like someone had wiped off all the fingerprints. Disappointed, they drove back to town and had some coffee at the diner. There were only booths or a counter to sit at, so they opted for a booth. The vinyl was ripped in places and had been repaired with duct tape. The table had a linoleum top that was peeling up around the edges, offering refuge to the remnants of messy eaters. Coffee was as far as they dared to go.

"You were right about Ramona. We are lucky to have her. We're going to have to get her to give us the year Patricia's little girl got here tonight at dinner."

"Didn't you think it was weird at the farm? It looked like no one had ever lived there or a place that was being sold furnished and the family had already moved out."

"I can't believe you said that," said Ruby. "I thought the exact same thing. I mean, it could be that one woman living alone could be a neat freak, but she lives there with a kid. There were absolutely no signs of life. You know, when I called here to check the records, the lady was like our friend Martha, very stingy with any info. Ramona said everyone knows everyone. What if the records lady called Patricia and told her someone was asking about her?"

"Yeah, and if the little girl really is Rebecca," Shane took over the scenario, "then Patricia would be terrified of anyone asking anything about her. I would leave town, too, if I thought someone was going to take my kid away."

"It makes perfect sense. Where do you think she went?" They both sat back. The vinyl was cool and took a while to deflate under pressure. "If she took off to hide," continued Ruby, "she wouldn't tell anyone where she was going, at least no one around here."

"I've got an idea. Let's go back to the farm and see if there's a car there. She would have to have a car, living in the boonies. If it's not there, then she's traveling by car, but if it's there, then she probably took a plane."

"She could've taken a bus," suggested Ruby.

"Nah. Why would she take a bus if she has a car? If she's going some-where where she can drive, she would have more freedom with a car, and she wouldn't leave an easy trail like a bus schedule."

"I didn't see a car. Did you?"

"No," replied Shane, "but it could be behind the barn or in the barn; let's go see." The two of them happily abandoned their coffees and drove back to the farm. There was no car anywhere. Shane finally climbed a tree beside the barn and looked inside. The interior was dark, but he could make out a medium-size car just inside the door.

"She must've flown," said Shane, climbing down out of the tree, "but I can't imagine this town having a travel agency."

"Let's tell Ramona we're thinking of spending more time in the area. We'll ask her where to go for travel information."

"Another stimulating meal with Ramona-the-Mouth and her mother—yes—you better take another nap."

CHAPTER 20

Newmarket

"So, who would you call if you needed travel information?" Ruby's tolerance was being challenged as Ramona rattled on. Dinner was as heavy and wholesome as the night before, and Ruth was sitting across from Ruby, staring at her like she couldn't figure out who she was.

"Oh, well you know there's Irene. She went to travel school, and you can go to her house, and she'll make some calls for you. But then there was that thing last year when she messed up for Tony Presley and his family. Oh, the whole thing was such a mess, and everyone was so mad. Tony wanted Irene to pay him back the money, and Irene said that she'd done everything right and that he just hadn't listened, and then it…"

"Does she still help people with travel plans?" Shane cut in.

After a lifetime of chatter, Ramona didn't seem to mind or notice the interruptions. The only one who probably didn't interrupt her was Ruth: She'd run out of words. "Well, I think she does it for some of her friends now, but she can be awfully grumpy. Most people go over to Newmarket. There are a couple of shops there, and that's all they do."

The topic of Patricia didn't come up until after dinner. They were having coffee when Ramona surprised them. "You know, I was thinking about that little girl—you know, Patricia's little thing. I started going back through things, and I think I remember. The Christmas of 1981 was the year mother fell. She slipped on some ice on the front steps. You know, you just have to put that salt on, but then it isn't very good for your shoes— stains them wherever they get wet." Ruby would be grateful for any information, and if she had to sit there all night, she would. "Oh, yes, mother slipped on the ice and hurt her hip. She didn't break it, thank god, but she was awfully sore. Well, Patricia was a doll; she brought over soup and watched mother if I had to go out somewhere. She's just like that, you know. Well, she didn't have little Emma then—I would remember that."

Shane was having trouble staying awake. He was sitting next to Ruby on a Victorian loveseat with red velvet covering, and Ruby had her hand wedged between them and kept pinching him every time his head started to roll forward. He was more alert after he heard Emma's name. This was what they had been waiting for.

"Well, the next Christmas we had so much snow, we had to get Johnny, who works at the grocery store, to shovel the walk, and he started salting it, too—made a huge difference. I remember Patricia coming to town with that darling baby bundled up in a red snowsuit. She would pull her around town on a sled. I remember she came over the day before Christmas, and we had tea. We were warning mother not to go out alone and reminding her that it had only been a year since her fall. Oh, and that baby, all decked out in a frilly Christmas dress. It was charming, and Patricia—I thought she would just burst, she seemed so happy. That was a wonderful Christmas."

It was the silence that caught their attention. Ramona had come to the end of the story, and she actually stopped talking. For Ruby the timing was close enough. The fire had been in January of '82, so it didn't matter how old Ramona thought the baby was; the timing was too close. They had to find Patricia.

They rose early the next morning, had breakfast, and paid their bill. The travel agencies were in Newmarket, so they had some time before their flight out of Toronto at 6:00 P.M.

Newmarket was not hard to find; it was bigger than Burntwood and closer to Toronto. They stopped at the first phone booth in town and looked up the agencies. There were two: Adventure Travel and Jones's Travel. Ruby wrote down the numbers and addresses, and they found a café to talk strategy. This town seemed more up-to-date than Burntwood, and they were able to find a clean, cozy little shop in which to have coffee.

"So how are we going to do this? I'm not even sure it's legal to give out other people's travel plans," said Shane.

"Anybody will tell you anything if you ask them the right way." Their coffee arrived, with a little foam on it. *Ah, the modern world,* thought Ruby. "Do you think people from here know people from Burntwood?"

"Well, if this is the nearest bigger town, it's possible." Shane sipped his coffee. "But I don't think, from the look of the farm, that Patricia is much of a shopper."

"Okay, then this is what I've been thinking," said Ruby.

The door opened at Jones's Travel, disturbing the bell above it. There were two desks, but only one was occupied. Mr. and Mrs. Cramer approached the woman behind the desk. She rose and said, "How can I help you?"

"Good morning, I'm Mrs. Cramer, and this is my husband, Paul. Oh, that's the first time I've ever said that," giggle, giggle. "We just got married yesterday, and I'm just so excited."

"Well, congratulations. Then you're probably here for honeymoon plans; am I right? Please sit."

"Well, sort of—we kind of eloped," Ruby looked up at Shane adoringly. "We didn't tell anyone, and now we want to go on a honeymoon. My best friend just took a vacation and told me she booked it through you. We thought we'd surprise her. She's traveling with her little girl, my goddaughter."

"Let's look; what's her name?" The agent turned to her computer and started punching some keys.

"Patricia Weston—do you know her?" Ruby asked, better to know up front what they were dealing with.

"No, the name's not familiar; let's see. What day did she leave?"

"I'm not quite sure." Ruby tried to look star-struck. "I've just been in such a state over all this. My head just hasn't been on straight, has it, sweetheart?"

"No, honey, you sure have been a scatterbrain lately," answered Shane flatly, not quite as good with the charade.

"Well, can we narrow it down? Was it this last week? Today is the fifteenth." The agent must have felt it was necessary to point this out to her love-struck potential customer.

"Oh, yes, definitely in the last week."

"I don't show anyone that I don't know making travel plans here in the last week. There was just the grower's convention that I've been working on, then a couple of people from town. That's it; I'm sorry."

Ruby let her disappointment show. They thanked the agent and went back out on the street.

"It's okay," said Shane. "We have one more to try." Ruby tried to reenergize herself for the second act as they headed for Adventure Travel. They went through the whole performance again, but this time it ended differently.

"Yes, I see here a Patricia Weston, flying out on the tenth of June, two tickets."

"Oh, isn't this exciting sweetheart? I told you we'd be able to surprise her." Ruby's excitement was real.

"Well, you know, I'm not supposed to give out this information."

"Oh, please, just this once? We won't tell a soul, will we sweetie-dove? It would just be the best surprise ever. We're *such* good friends."

The agent continued to look at the screen as if her struggle could be solved by something there, and then she looked over her glasses and smiled. "All right, but you can't tell anyone. I could get into big trouble."

"Oh, thank you, thank you." Ruby jumped up and down, making short claps with her hands.

"She left on the tenth of June from Toronto and flew to Houston and then from Houston to Cancún, arriving at 3:00 P.M."

"Do you know where she's staying?" asked Ruby, trying not to sound as anxious as she felt.

"Says here she's staying at The North Shore Condominiums on the island of Isla Mujeres, and she has reservations for two weeks. Can I book you into the same place?"

"Oh, yes. Isn't this wonderful, darling? But we need to get our credit cards out of the car. We parked at the other end of town and walked. We'll be right back. Thank you, so much,"

"Take your time. I'll be here all day."

CHAPTER 21

Boulder

"This is great." Diane was astonished. She kept shaking her head as Shane and Ruby shared their trip with her. They were all sitting on the back porch of Ruby's house. It was five o'clock, and the sun had already dropped below the foothills. Everything was spring green, and the air was warm. It was the kind of temperature that's so perfect you can't feel it.

"The big question is what to do now? When do we tell Taylor about this?" asked Ruby.

Diane sat forward in her chair. "I don't think we should tell her anything until we've actually seen Rebecca—until there is no doubt at all." She had seen the look on Taylor's face the last time they had brought it up.

"I think she's right," agreed Shane.

"Then we have to go to Mexico—at least I do. I would love for you two to come, but I'm going no matter what." Ruby had been anxious since she found out where Patricia was; knowing it and not going there immediately was making her crazy. The possibilities were hard to fathom. What expertise did any of them have as a guide through this? What event could they possibly draw experience from to help commandeer their actions from here forward? "I really want to go soon. This is driving me nuts. Do either of you want to join me?"

Ruby knew that Diane couldn't afford it and knew she wasn't going to take any money, so she had an idea. "Listen, Diane, I know you don't want to take any money, but I need you there. How about if I pay for the trip and then you pay me back later, with money or work? I've so many things that I need to get organized—you could help me. I would be eternally grateful."

"I would love to go. I thought this might come up, and anything we can work out suits me. I know that I'll be able to pay you back someday. It's just that right now things are really tight."

Ruby was relieved. She threw her arms around Diane and hugged her close. Then the two of them turned to look at Shane. "Well?" they said in unison.

"Of course, I'll come, but I can't come right away. You go ahead, and I'll come down in a few days. I just need to spend some time with Shawn."

Ruby turned to Diane. "I'll make all the arrangements. You and I will leave as soon as we can. How many days do you need, Shane?"

"You had better give me four days."

CHAPTER 22

Isla Mujeres

The airport in Cancún was bigger and more modern than they had expected. As they stepped out of the plane, the air landed on them heavily. The difference in humidity from Colorado was as far from dry as one could feel without actually being wet.

They had to go upstairs to enter the terminal and then downstairs into a large room with lines of travelers. There was one line for Mexican nationals, in which three people waited, and separate lines for "Other." This was their line, and there must have been two hundred people ahead of them. They dropped their carry-ons and proceeded to shuffle through the maze, back and forth across the room six times. Immigration was easy when they finally got there: a few questions and then many loud stamps on their passports.

The final stop was customs inspection. After retrieving their luggage, there was yet one more line to endure before they were permitted to leave the airport building. There were actually two lines, arbitrarily set up; either one would do. Each line ended at a traffic light on a four-foot pole with only two colors, green and red, and a large silver button. One was instructed to press the button; if the green light came on, you sailed through, bags undisturbed, but if the red light came on, you were escorted to a table where all your belongings would be scrutinized. What had Ruby so amused was that every time someone got a red light all the people waiting in the other line would move into that line, figuring the odds were better for a while. As a result, the whole situation became very confusing. People kept switching sides, moving two or three suitcases with them, and then, of course, the lines would be getting longer and shorter. They were at sea, rocking forward and back in their row and then side-to-side from one red light to the next. Luckily, they got a green light and left the airport without any more delays.

They'd been instructed to get a cab to Puerto Juárez, where they could catch a boat for Isla Mujeres. The ferry was large and air conditioned, and they arrived at the island in twenty-five minutes. When they stepped on the dock, they spotted a man with Ruby's name on a sign. He put their luggage in a three-wheeler bicycle with a big carrying basket in the front and instructed them to follow on foot.

Walking along the road next to the ocean was a pleasure. There were fishing boats pulled up on the sand and nets strung between the palm trees. The other side of the street was lined with shops, occasionally separated by a restaurant or bar. It was nice to stretch their legs for the quarter mile it took to reach the condos. Halfway there, a four-legged friend joined them. It was brown with large, oddly-shaped white spots, almost like a beagle but bigger. This new companion accompanied them to the end of the road and then disappeared into the brush. Since Ruby had not picked the accommodations, she was pleasantly surprised as they rounded the corner. The gardens around the buildings were beautifully groomed, with flowers and tall palms neatly bordering well-swept walkways. Their room was on the third floor. It was clean and warmly decorated with a view of the ocean, which was five different colors.

Ruby had been so involved in her surroundings that she didn't think about Rebecca until they were settling in. *Was she really somewhere in this building? Could I actually see Taylor's dead child today, alive and nine years old?* She sat on their balcony, looking over the grounds. *Is she there?* Diane came out and sat next to her.

"I'm terrified," Ruby confided.

"I hope so," was Diane's surprising reply. "If you weren't, I'd be worried. There isn't anything this monumental that has ever happened in my life. Up until now we've been dealing with potential. Even at the farmhouse, you were not as sure as you are now." Diane turned to face Ruby. "This is the dividing moment. You're the center, the only connection, and here and now is the link. If you weren't scared, it would be weird." Diane had meant this last part as a joke, but Ruby wasn't laughing. She was crying.

Diane gave her a hug and suggested the two go down for a drink. An attempt at relaxation was all they could hope for. Alcohol might add enough to the mix of sand, ocean, and sea air to make it happen. "I think we should hang out here tonight and go to bed early. In the morning we can ask the lady in the office if there's a Patricia Weston here." Diane was taking the leading role for the night, and Ruby was grateful.

They sat in the restaurant and enjoyed the salty breeze. "You know, there's one thing we have never talked about." It wasn't going to be possible for Ruby to discuss anything else.

"What?"

"If Patricia has Rebecca, then Kevin was at the fire before the whole cabin was in flames. He had to have been inside at some point. I can't imagine why he wouldn't come forward with the baby unless he had something to hide."

Diane had wondered when this was going to come up. She didn't mind deceiving Kevin to get some information; in fact, she'd enjoyed the duplicity, but she'd avoided thinking about his culpability. "I've been trying not to think about it," Diane confessed. "I mean, in addition to being a bad judge of character, I wasted a lot of romantic energy on that man."

"Well, really, Diane, no matter what he did, the guy's a schmuck." Ruby knew this was unsympathetic, but she had often wondered why Diane had ever been with him in the first place.

"I know, but, come on, schmuck or boring or aloof, none of us is really doing well on the soul mate scale."

"Touché. If I get cantankerous on this trip, can I make all my apologies in advance?"

"Absolutely. Be as surly as you want. You'll need to conserve all your social skills for other circumstances."

"We should talk about this. I need your help. Okay, we're walking down the street and coming toward us is a child with Taylor's face and a woman between forty and fifty. What then? 'Excuse me, ma'am, is that really your child?' Or, 'You know, your little girl looks just like a friend of mine.' Or, 'Show me your papers.' I mean, what? I've got to prepare myself, but every time I try to come up with a plan, my mind goes blank." Ruby sat back as the waiter set two more margaritas on the table.

"Some more chips and salsa, *por favor, señor?*"

"I want to help you come up with something brilliant; I want you to be amazed by my genius, but I don't think any plan will endure the shock of it. I think rather than design what you're going to say we should decide what we're going to do, and since we don't know if she's here yet, why don't you tell me about Shane?"

"What do you mean tell you about Shane?" asked Ruby

"Oh, please, you're about to go on your second trip with him. He's cute, he's intelligent, he's responsible, etc., etc."

"He was great company. It's been so long since I've shared anything with a man. It felt…let's see…easy, comfortable, supportive—I don't know—friendly."

"Well, I would just like to point out that he's not hanging around because of me. The truth is we tried to get romantic one night in Nicaragua. We'd been drinking the usual amount of beers and were feeling loose." Diane sat back for a bratty pause. Ruby was giving her a "fork-it-over" look. "Well…nothing happened; it just wasn't there. That was part of what woke me up down there. It really was an epiphany. Normally, I would've pretended it was great just to please the guy, but I didn't. We ended up laughing and decided that this meant we could be really good friends. Sex would never get in the way. We would never have to wonder." Diane sipped her margarita. "I've never had a male friend. I've never had a brother. I barely had a father—he just didn't seem that interested in me; that's why all this is so amazing." Diane had spent many hours thinking about her life lately and had looked forward to talking to Ruby about it. "I mean, what if my dad did care about me? What if I was just so bored with myself that I never noticed anyone noticing me? What if I go through the rest of my life missing so much because I'm too wrapped up in my own performance? Trying to please people so they'll like me? Trying to pretend I'm not boring but not living, just monitoring my exhibition, not knowing there is any other way to live—actually *being* alive. Performing takes a lot of energy." Diane sipped her margarita. "I've never thought it was much fun to be me. So why would anyone want to hang out with me if they had the choice? I mean, I have to." Diane finally stopped. Ruby was so impressed with her objective analogy. These are the things that usually go around in your head; it was great to hear them come out of Diane's mouth, and she couldn't take them back.

"If that was the first time you weren't performing, I mean with Shane, and you guys became friends, and we became friends, imagine the number of things you must've missed. If you two had finished having sex just because you'd started, you probably wouldn't have become friends. So thank you for being a boring lover."

"Wait a minute." Diane looked up and saw Ruby had an enormous grin on her face, and they both burst out laughing. They drank too much, had a wonderful fish dinner, and managed to talk about everything but their quest for the rest of the evening.

The next morning Ruby was up early and agitated. The respite had been short. The office opened at nine. It was torture to wait, and she spent most of the time staring out over the balcony with anticipation and dread.

When she entered the office, the woman was just putting her purse under her desk. "Hi, we checked into 310 last night; you left the key for us. My name's Ruby Starkey."

"Oh, yes, is everything okay?" Nancy, the receptionist, was used to people coming in only when they had a complaint.

"Everything is great, no complaints." *How should I start this?* "Just one question: I have this friend who's staying here, and I've come down to surprise her. I wanted to find out what room she's in. Her name is Patricia Weston. She's here with her little girl."

"Oh, yeah, I know who you mean. She left."

Deflated, Ruby tried to stay calm. "She was supposed to be here two weeks."

"Oh, she's still on the island, just not here. She wanted to stay longer and needed to find cheaper accommodations."

"Do you know where she went?" Ruby was so relieved she could have hugged the receptionist, but then the poor lady wouldn't have had any idea why, so Ruby controlled herself.

"I knew she was looking, and I made a few suggestions, but I'm not sure where she ended up. I wasn't here when she checked out. You know the island is so small; I'm sure you'll find her."

"Do you remember what you suggested?"

"Let see, I usually suggest a woman downtown who has some apartments. She could also help with ideas if her places don't work out. Her name is Jeannie Tull. She has a little shop on the main street called Tull's. You can't miss it; this island just isn't that big."

Ruby went back upstairs to enlist Diane for the next set of inquiries.

CHAPTER 23

Pueblo de Dolores

Ruby and Diane went in search of Jeannie Tull. They were in no hurry. Ruby's fear had slowed her down; she had developed a reluctance to step over the edge, to be the link. She had started to question her motives. This was Taylor's life, and maybe she should be helping, not heading up the search.

As she lay in bed that morning, having woken up at 4:00 A.M., Ruby struggled with some debatable material and forced herself to embrace the most controversial of it. Why had she taken on Taylor's life with such fervor? Was she simply avoiding her own? As she let the wheels turn, she encountered a plethora of clutter.

Ruby started her life in New York. She came from a "good" family. Her mother, Denise, was a lawyer, an officious and intelligent woman. She could have some patches of warmth, but they were reserved for Ruby's two brothers. Denise had a problem with women, and, sadly, daughter status did not exempt Ruby from this category. Ruby had decided that her mother, quite plainly, resented being one—a woman, that is, and therefore resented a daughter as well.

She was a very good lawyer—criminal lawyer. People considered themselves lucky if she took their case. Nevertheless, she wanted a family but obviously resented being expected to give anything up for it. To Ruby, this made sense, but the confusion was why *did* she want to have a family at all?

Taylor always teased Ruby about being a hippie, yet she was only half a rebel, if that's possible. She embraced anything off-color, anything provocative. She wasn't going to be ignored. Yet she'd been well-trained for upper-class New York. She could turn into her mother at the drop of a hat and knew how to carry on in the most socially demanding situations.

She'd always admired the fact that no one messed with her mother if they knew her at all. Things seemed unquestionably clear to Denise; if something's not right—fix it, not acceptable—alter it, trivial—don't bother, uncivilized—invisible. Ruby could play her mother, but she would never be her mother. Ruby was going to use it, but she didn't buy it, and it was never going to matter.

Her father was a different story. He loved having a daughter. She was his warmth, his family. The boys were achievers. Coach Mom made sure they would be the best at whatever they did. Denise was trying to create the man she could never become. Daughters were different. If Ruby didn't demonstrate the kind of drive necessary, then she was just another woman, like the rest, buying into the norm, beyond redemption. Denise had sacrificed her humanity to get where she was; she had no currency left to spend on a daughter.

Ruby was a smart woman. She had gone over her own childhood many times, and she had some understanding of its manifestations. The problem she faced was that it was an intellectual evaluation and lacked emotional perception. *How do you make that leap? How do you come to terms with it and then leave it behind?*

She thought about her husband—they existed under the same roof and understood the same lifestyle. Her mother had liked him, but her father never had. Ruby had tried to love Mark. When they met, the timing had been right. She was experiencing a lull, that space when your formal education has come to an end and it's time to make some supposedly brilliant choices for your future. Nothing, however, was immediately clear to Ruby, but he was her chance to get out of town with approval. For some reason, when it came to that major life decision, she lacked the stamina to bulldoze forward as she had done with everything else.

There had not been children because Ruby realized almost immediately that she could not love her husband. Eventually, they'd discussed it, and he had confessed he didn't love her either; but they really liked each other and made great roommates. Until now there'd been no reason to change their status; it was perfect. He worked all the time but didn't suffer the usual dilemma of neglecting his family. Ruby had not missed romance so far and had enjoyed the distance from New York. It gave her the freedom to do as she pleased without explanation. She preferred the company of women—not sexually, but in her thirty-three years she had not found a man as compelling.

She wrote freelance articles for a few magazines and spent the rest of her time volunteering. Soon it was meeting after meeting: committees, sub-committees, and politics. Progress on programs was so sluggish, though, it was hard to maintain forward momentum.

Ruby and her two brothers had inherited a real estate development company from their grandparents. Her mother had bragged that her parents had built half of New York. It was a big company that neither Ruby nor her brothers were qualified to run. They were on the board of directors and left the rest of it to the people who had been running it for years. But this did afford Ruby a lifestyle. She could do whatever she wanted, and this was not necessarily a gift.

Writing had been her passion, but she always seemed to find something else to do. So there was the question: Why was she avoiding her life, married to a man she didn't love and doing things she didn't want to do?

As they headed into town, Ruby tried to shake off the remnants of her disturbing night. She noticed that the same brown-and-white dog was following them but keeping a distance. "Do you think that's the same dog that walked with us yesterday?"

Diane turned around to check. "It looks like it, but maybe all the dogs on this island look the same." They reached Jeannie's shop and forgot all about the dog. Jeannie Tull was inside. She was an enormous woman with a beautiful, happy face. She told them she'd been born in London but had come to Isla and taken to island life so completely that she never left. She talked about herself as though that was why people came to the store. Jeannie had a pleasant, contagious accent and easily made the most mundane things seem more interesting. Ruby was sure that most of what Jeannie said likely suffered some embellishment, but she was enjoying it all and liked Jeannie immediately.

"I showed Patricia and her daughter a couple of my places. She wasn't a taker. I think she wanted something a little more out of the way. All my flats are in town."

"Do you know where she went?" asked Diane

"I gave her some names. There're lots of bed-sits, and June is one of our slowest months."

"Do you remember what names you gave her?" Ruby asked.

"You guys want this bad, you do. What did she do, something smashingly awful?" Jeannie's eye's lit up with anticipation.

"We aren't sure she's done anything; we just have a few questions for her."

"I can ask around. There are no secrets on this island; it's just too bloody small."

"Oh, Jeannie, that would be great. We haven't been doing too well on our own," admitted Ruby.

"On one condition," Jeannie said loudly. Everything about her seemed bigger or louder.

"What?"

"Come to my house for dinner. I need some new faces, and I like both of yours."

"We'd love to," said Ruby, without even looking at Diane. The island felt good, and she loved the idea of enjoying some genuine, even if imported, local color. They exchanged information, set a time, and it was a plan.

"Aren't you worried she might tip Patricia off in some way?" asked Diane as they left the shop.

"I don't think we have much choice. I don't know; I just decided to chance it. I liked her."

There were many shops on this street, so they continued along, just looking.

"Cheaper than K-mart," one vendor said.

"You'll like it here, lady: best prices."

"What you need, lady, we got it; just have a look."

"Can you imagine employees hanging out in front of their shops in a mall and saying this stuff? It would be hilarious."

"Did you get that list of names that Jeannie had recommended to Patricia?" Diane asked.

"Nope, we'll have to get them tonight." Diane didn't mind this new pace; she hadn't been to Mexico before and wasn't in a hurry to dive right into the dilemmas that were sure to come up.

They arrived at Jeannie's apartment at around 7:00 P.M. Their new canine friend escorted them once again, so Ruby decided to nickname him Boo, because he appeared and disappeared like a ghost. Jeannie's apartment was like Jeannie, big and colorful. She'd painted murals on the walls with broad, bold, unencumbered strokes. There were a few pieces of carved wooden furniture, not too many, but each piece was huge. Her fabrics were like the vibrant colors you see in Mexican travel posters, and they were everywhere—draped on the furniture, over the table, and hung on the walls. The refrigerator was painted, the rugs were faded and threadbare, and the general feel of the place was warm and alive. Jeannie offered them wine, and they sat out on her veranda and spied on the neighbors—there was nowhere else to look.

"Have you been in this apartment long?" Ruby asked.

"Well, actually, I've had a few different ones, but I'd been waiting for this one to come up ever since I opened the store downstairs. I've been collecting these things," Jeannie made a wide sweep with her arm, "since I got here. They're so Mexico, don't you think? Anything un-London is the bee's knees to me. I've always felt that all the colors in London were muted and grayish. Not a warm, worn look, more a soiled rendition of the original. That's actually what I'm here to avoid, being a soiled rendition of my former self. I was on that path when I came here. Fat people are not popular in most places, least of all in crowded cities. I wasn't about to get skinny, so I had to get out."

"When did you come here?"

"I've been here ten years now. Things have changed a lot, but I've no complaints. This island has an interesting history, and change is always good. I didn't come here to stay the same."

"Can you tell us some of the history?" Diane asked.

"Sure, let's see…how far back do you want to go?"

"Start anywhere you want," suggested Diane.

"Okay, the Spanish discovered it in 1517, and because they found so many female statues here, they named it The Island of Women, or, in Spanish, Isla Mujeres. I've always loved that—when they say they "discovered" the island—like it didn't exist until they got there, and then they named it, like they invented the place. Anyway, apparently the island was uninhabited for three hundred years after that, except for a few fishermen, and then, of course, there are stories of pirates. I've been told that famous pirates like Jean Lafitte and Henry Morgan landed here. Islanders love to tell stories about the pirates burying treasure somewhere around the coastline, but I don't know anyone who has found any yet.

I guess the fishing was a bit of all right, so the fisherman started to stay here, and shortly after the independence of Mexico, some families started a small community where the downtown area is now. By 1850 the village was big enough to get a name, so Don Miguel Barbacona—don't you love that name?—anyway, he was the governor of the State of Yucatan, and he named the village Pueblo de Dolores. I have never been able to find out who Dolores was."

"Was it just fishermen and their families?" asked Ruby.

"So far, I guess." Jeannie poured them all some more wine. "Although there was one famous pirate who did actually settle here—there are some ruins of his house you can go see. It's called Mundaca. The old codger got rich capturing Mayans and selling them to Cuban plantation owners as slaves. Nice, eh? Well, he must have figured that wasn't such a romantic way to get rich, so he played up the idea that he was a pirate. Anyway, he came here around 1860 and started building a house or hacienda. He called it Vista Alegre, which means happy view. The place must have been huge. I've heard that at one point his lands took over forty percent of the island. Can you imagine?"

"What did he do with all that land?"

"He became quite the farmer, raising livestock and planting fruit trees and vegetable gardens. They say he had a sundial made from a rose garden; he called it 'The Rose of the Winds.' I read somewhere that he had exotic plants brought in from all over the world."

"Did he have a family? I mean, who'd he feed with all those gardens and livestock?" asked Diane.

"There's a whole legend around that. I've no idea if it's true."

"Tell us, anyway." Ruby was fascinated.

"Okay, let me check dinner first."

"This is so great of you to have us, Jeannie," Diane said.

"Are you kidding? It's my pleasure. It's so great to have someone new to talk to. I can tell all the same stories and not be boring," Jeannie chuckled.

"So tell us about the pirate," Ruby prodded.

"Okay, so this is it. In 1876 Fermin—that was his name—fell in love with a green-eyed island beauty. She was only fourteen, and he was fifty-one—what a randy old bastard, eh? Anyway, she wouldn't marry him, and the legend says he was so broken-hearted he slowly went insane. My guess is that he probably had syphilis," Jeannie added with delight. "He named the arches over his gate after her, 'The Entrance of the Triqueña' and 'The Pass of the Triune.' 'La Triqueña' means 'the brunette.' They also say he carved his own tombstone with a skull and crossbones and the words 'As you are, I was. As I am, you will be.' I love that part—he had to say she rejected him because of his age—it couldn't have been that she just didn't like the old guy. What an ego he must've had."

"What happened to him?"

"I don't know much after that. I know he wasn't buried here. He died in Merida. That's a city about a four-hour drive due west of Cancún."

"Even if it isn't true, it makes a wonderful story," concluded Ruby.

"There's more to tell about the early history and how the statues got here, but it's time for dinner, and I want to hear more about you two." They went inside and settled around the table. Jeannie had made them some sort of vegetable casserole and a salad. She had corn tortillas on the table and showed them how to put the stew on the tortilla over some shredded lettuce, add a little cheese, and roll it up. It was delicious.

The three of them drank two bottles of wine, shared stories, and had a terrific time. Ruby and Diane walked home around 12:30, Boo trotting along beside them.

The next morning they realized that, again, they'd forgotten to get the names of the other people Jeannie had recommended to Patricia.

CHAPTER 24

La Playa

R uby and Diane sat in the restaurant in front of the condos. It was another beautiful day: hot but no problem if you were at the beach. They'd decided they would spend some time on the sand in the morning and then find Jeannie and get those names. The ladies ate light, aware of their pending bathing suit plans.

Ruby kept noticing a good-looking man at the next table. She'd seen him in town the day before and didn't realize he was staying at the same place. He was reading the paper and glancing at them occasionally. *Why not?* Ruby thought. *We're not so bad.* After paying the bill and gathering all their beach items, they were on the way.

This was, without exception, the most stunning beach. The sand was white and soft. There were large clean stretches between the water and the palm trees, offering room to spread out, play volleyball, jog, whatever tourists considered recreation. Because this was the leeward side of the island, there was no surf, just a tender roll at the water's edge.

They picked their spot, rented two loungers and an umbrella, and tried to relax. As much as Ruby had been enjoying her time, it took a distraction to unwind and forget the task ahead of them. Diane was deep into her tanning-sun-goddess mode but Ruby was restless. She decided to take a walk. The beach wrapped around the north point of the island. Possibly she wanted to explore, or possibly there would be a woman and her daughter enjoying the sun—what did it matter?

She headed north, and as she neared the point of the island, the beach got wider. There was a series of congregations along the way but no groups of two. If Patricia was hiding, they would keep to themselves. At the end

135

of the island was a separate, smaller island with a large hotel on it. How funny it looked—most of the dry land was covered with buildings.

"Looks strange, don't you think?" Ruby heard from behind. She turned and found herself looking at the man from breakfast. "If they wanted a hotel that big, you'd think they'd have looked for a bigger space."

"It looks deserted," replied Ruby.

"It is. There are three or four stories going around as to why. Who knows which one is true?"

"How long has it been like that?"

"I don't know. Some say it was condemned after a hurricane. Some say that the owners didn't pay their taxes. Then there is the story that they started building more rooms without permission. Who knows? I am sure, though, that it was open for business for a while."

"Are you allowed to go across the bridge?" There was a long wooden bridge over the shallow water between the two islands.

"Yeah, I've been over there. It's a little spooky, but the ocean side has some magnificent tide pools. Want to see?"

"I suppose I should know who you are first." Ruby took a closer look and could see other people over there, so they weren't going to be alone.

"Sorry, that was rude. My mother taught me better. My name's Roger Bates, here on vacation and your travel guide to abandoned hotels."

"A pleasure to meet you. My name is Ruby Starkey, and I won't tell your mother." This was some sort of dating schlop that Ruby hadn't experienced for a while. It felt transparent and silly, but Roger was tall with brown hair and a friendly face, and she needed a diversion, so they crossed the bridge to the old building.

As they approached the entrance of the hotel, they were amazed at the decay obviously promoted by the heat and sea air. First, they came upon a collapsed palapa roof that was now a mound of wet, muddy palm branches covering the ground and probably a world of insects. They took a path in the sand to what must have been a terrace. There was a large cement pool with a shallow area on one side. Here there were cement lounge chairs positioned so that the water would be just the same height as the top of the chair. The thought of lying there with turquoise water lapping at your side was very appealing, but now the pool was empty. There was some brown water collected in the deep end that was evaporating fast in the June heat and leaving a moldy residue as it receded over the once-turquoise paint.

Another collapsed roof must have covered a pool bar, with stools in the water where tourists could swim up and order a drink. The end of the pool was a glass window looking into an enormous dining room. The view for diners would have been above and below the water. *Sort of like a large aquarium with human fish*, thought Ruby. The dining area was three stories high and filled with white wrought-iron tables stacked up in the middle.

"It must've been very elegant," commented Ruby. "It's spooky to see it like this and to imagine people once lounged in the pool or dressed for dinner. I wonder if there was a chandelier—maybe three or four."

"What a view, too! You have the ocean all around, not a bad sight from anywhere," Roger pointed out.

"This must've been a very upscale place," said Ruby.

"It was, and it was going to be even better, but all the construction was shut down. Come and see this." Roger led her past the large building to an area where someone had obviously been working. It was an interesting sight. There was a row of condos on both sides, each one on the ocean, with a wide garden path down the middle. It was like seeing a progress projection. The condos closest to the hotel were almost finished, and as they got farther away, they were in earlier stages of construction. It all had an eerie feel. Vegetation was reclaiming things fast, and iguanas had found multiple dwellings among the cinder blocks and old cement. Ruby thought she saw Boo next to one of the buildings, so she walked toward the spot, but whatever it was disappeared fast.

Together they walked over the construction debris toward the windward side of the island to see the tide pools. The shoreline was rough coral, yet among the jagged rock an exquisite turquoise pool had formed. The waves were broken by the outside strips of coral, but it didn't completely encircle the pool, allowing water to flow around and into the area, keeping things fresh and trapping the occasional fish.

"This water must be as turquoise as turquoise can possibly get," commented Ruby as she stepped into the pool after removing her sandals. In its deepest parts the water was up to Ruby's waist, and the bottom had filled with sand, making bare feet possible. As she leaned against some of the smoother coral, she could see small crabs racing to find new hiding places. Small black and yellow-striped fish came closer to investigate, and the sun wrapped up the whole scene, completing this package of paradise.

"Imagine, realizing a place like this exists on a cold, cloudy day in Chicago." This was unsurpassed in Ruby's catalogue of luxury. It was a quiet place, and the desertion brought up feelings too intimate to share with a stranger. After Roger joined her in the pool, the two sat in silence, absorbing the sensations.

As her body relaxed, her mind revved up, all questions and no answers. Ruby wondered if she put her head under the water—would her brain *shut up? Trying not to think about something is just about the most contrary project ever attempted*, Ruby thought. *What a drip torture this has become.* As wonderful as this pool felt, it left her mind to wander. It was time to go. "I'd better get back. Diane will be wondering where I am."

"Sounds good," said Roger, and he helped Ruby out of the water. They walked back down the beach, still quiet, holding onto the physical repose they'd been gifted with.

Diane was still on her lounge, cooking the flipside. She was awake, and Ruby made introductions. "Where are you from?" she asked Roger.

"New York…not exactly where I thought I'd end up, but that's home for now." Roger covered his eyes as he spoke; fine sand was being whipped up off the beach. As they continued to talk, heavier sand began gliding along the ground, arranging itself around obstacles. "Where did this come from?" asked Roger. He turned and scanned the bay. The water was being agitated as well. The tips of the waves were forming foamy peaks just before they rolled over to become the underside of the next rise. It was all happening very fast.

The boats that had been aimlessly tugging on their moorings were now pulling more insistently to the south. The sunbathers were packing up, more irritated by the sand than the wind.

Roger helped Ruby and Diane gather up their beach paraphernalia, and they ducked inside the restaurant. Ruby held back at the doorway and turned to watch the turbulence. Storms intrigued her; they demanded attention, and they determined the timing. She liked the excitement. She'd been trained to think fast, because in her family if you weren't smart enough or fast enough to get out of the way of a bulldozer of a mother, you paid an emotional price—your confidence was squeezed out of you as the rollers flattened you against the floor. Since Ruby had refused to ride along, she had become apt at dodging its destruction, anticipating its movements. She developed all the qualities that increased your chances of survival in storms.

The beach had cleared quickly—most of the boats had up-anchored and were motoring off for safer moorings. One large sailboat remained; it had shifted closer to shore and was listing oddly to one side. While Ruby watched, two men hurried through the water and climbed aboard. They disappeared below deck and emerged a few minutes later clad in wetsuits. It was hard for them to move around; the angle was already more askew than when they had arrived. Their growing concern was evident in the acceleration of their movements.

A crowd was accumulating on shore, and some of the early arrivals were hurrying off, looking important. Ruby decided she wanted a closer look. "Have you noticed this sailboat?" she asked. "I'm going over to see what's going on."

"I'll take our things upstairs and come and join you," replied Diane. Roger had already left. By the time Ruby reached the shore closest to the boat, the crowd was larger. Some people had brought their chairs over and were enjoying beers with the show. They looked concerned but detached. The men on the boat were now in the water, where the waves were making everything they did more strenuous. The boat had moved. The centerboard was obviously wedged in the sand and was being shifted downwind, but the grip was still tight.

After a while, a shrimp boat came into view, rolling from side to side like a waddling old woman. It was rusty, and the decks were covered with a mishmash of cables and pulleys. Several smaller boats were scurrying around behind it, coming close enough to yell at people onboard and then dashing off in different directions. These boats managed to connect a thick rope from the shrimp boat to the sailboat and then backed off. The rope lifted out of the water and created a perfect line as the strain increased. Ruby felt as though the entire crowd had taken a deep breath and was holding it in expectation. Motion was suspended; only the tension increased. The sailboat remained wedged and without any warning; the rope disappeared. There was a delay, and initially the crowd was unsure of what had just happened. Disappointment surfaced as people realized the rope had broken. It was unbelievable; the rope had been four inches in diameter.

After much ado, the whole thing was repeated. Perhaps the rope was old? Again, everyone held his or her breath, and again there was a collective exhale as the rope disappeared. Now, Ruby could see urgency turning into panic as the crew waved to the boats and screamed to one another over the wind, which was blowing harder. It was getting late, and this situation would not spend the night well. The boat was tilting so far over now that one side of the deck was submerged. It looked like it should go all the way over but was suspended by its centerboard still stuck in the sand.

In a last attempt before dark, a new rope joined the two boats, but this time a cable had been attached to the top of the mast. One of the crewmembers was fighting the rough water in an effort to deliver the cable to a small motorboat nearby. The crowd had now grown to some two hundred people. The cable was tied to the bow of the smaller boat, and everything was ready. The small boat started first, pulling the mast farther over, tilting the boat to an even more unnatural angle. Then the shrimp boat started to pull. Ruby found it hard not to yell at the small boat to stop. The mast was only a few feet from the water.

Then there was something—just a difference—no pop, just a difference. More people became aware of it, and a murmur could be heard along the shore. Now it was obvious. The sailboat was moving. Not much, then a little more. The small boat was easing up on the mast, but the angle was still odd. Soon, it all moved, upright and away from the beach. There was a loud cheer from the spectators, who clapped and hooted as though they were at a sports event.

Sometime, during all of this, Boo had found a spot under a tree nearby, but Ruby didn't notice as she hurried toward her room. She wanted to lie down. She knew why she hadn't asked Jeannie for those addresses. She could push and pull all she wanted, but there had to be another connection, another force. Rebecca was Taylor's daughter. This had to be approached from all angles to be done right. Ruby had done the heavy work, but now she needed something more. She needed Taylor.

CHAPTER 25

From Two Sides

It was Thursday, and Taylor was tired when she got home. She'd worked on the wheel all day. The clay had felt so good. She's thrown her favorite forms—tall vases and large bowls—and on a good day these bowls were the size of large sinks. Taylor almost felt as though she could've gone on forever, but there comes a time when you just get sick of being wet, of noticing the drips running down your arms and being irritated by them. At that point, she was done. Taylor never threw anything worthwhile when she was irritated.

The phone was ringing when she walked in the door. She wasn't going to answer it, but it rang forever, so she picked it up. "Hello."

"Hey, Taylor, it's Ruby."

"Oh, hi—you're the only call I want. Where've you been?"

"I'm in Mexico." Ruby's voice sounded strained.

Taylor was shocked. "What do you mean you're in Mexico? I just thought you were busy."

"No, I'm in Mexico, and I want you to come down and join me. I've already bought your ticket."

Sure that this was some kind of joke, Taylor said, "Sure, I'll come right away." Nothing came over the line for a moment, and then Ruby said, "Okay." Not the response Taylor had expected.

"I know this all sounds bizarre, but I'm serious," Ruby said. "I've some really important stuff to talk to you about, and I'll tell you what it's about over the phone; but if you want my advice, I think you should wait until you get here."

How do you know when your life is going to take another one of those huge flips? There's never time to prepare. How would you prepare? "Ruby, I'm going to trust you and come, and if you think I should wait to know…I will."

"That's great. Then we can go to plan B. I booked you a flight for tomorrow night, but they said I could change it to tonight if you could get there on time. What time is it there?"

"It's five."

"There's a flight at 8:00 P.M. I can come to Cancún and meet you, but we'll have to stay there for the night, because we won't make the last ferry to the island."

"What island?"

"We'll have the whole night to talk, and if you get that flight, you won't have to wonder too long. It's United Airlines to Cancún, eight o'clock. They'll have your ticket at the counter."

Taylor hung up the phone and just stood there, trying to organize what was going on; but she didn't have enough information to do so. Nonetheless, Ruby was correct: She was glad she was leaving right away. It wasn't until she started to pack that she realized how little she actually knew, and even if she wanted to call back, she didn't have a phone number.

It wasn't necessary for Taylor to call anyone to say she was going out of town. *How did that happen? So many of the friends I had with Jack were couples. All those dinner parties were geared toward a good seating plan. Actually, that's not true. I could've kept in touch with my old friends if I'd wanted to. Somehow, I've just been too busy, or maybe the days are shorter. Mostly, I don't have enough energy to function outside myself.*

Ruby and Taylor laughed about the stoplight customs check as they taxied to their hotel. They chatted lightly, avoiding explanations. The hotel was stunning: five floors of marble and plants with a beautiful beachfront. Their room was marbled, as well, and spacious with an ocean view. When Taylor emerged from her shower, Ruby had already started on the bottle of wine she had chilled for them. Poor Taylor didn't know that she was about to jump out a window, to lose all the ground she'd taken eight years to tamp down. She had often felt like land reclaimed from the ocean, filling the space with everything available, until finally you can stand on it without sinking. Then it all needs time to settle before you can safely build. She'd been thinking that maybe she was ready to do a little building, something small, but Ruby washed away the fill with one tidal wave of memory, grief, and fear.

After Ruby explained why they were in Mexico, Taylor was understandably agitated, walking back and forth. She couldn't stay still; each step required concentration, and her hands were a burden. "God, Ruby, what do I do with this? I can't afford to jump in. I can't lose her again."

"Oh, Taylor, I'm so sorry. I just couldn't go any further without you. I wish I could have just arrived with Rebecca, but I was stuck in the sand. It needs the two of us."

"I don't know what to do. I remember this feeling. Each second is a minute, each minute an hour. There's too much. The beginning doesn't matter, and the end is miles away. If you can stand the next second, there is another one after that. It pushes back on you when you think it's too much already. The thought of getting her back only brings back the pain of losing her: all the need, the emptiness."

Ruby was looking up at Taylor with so much pain in her eyes; Taylor wanted to help her. She tried to smile, but she was overcome with the need to touch something. She was crawling back into that space, a dangerous place. Finally, she reached out and touched Ruby's shoulder.

"We don't have enough wine," she said, not knowing why. It just flopped out of her mouth and landed between them as silly as a fish out of water. Ruby looked up at Taylor as if she'd just spoken in a foreign language, but Taylor kept smiling and then she started to laugh, like the time with Diane. There was a moment, a suspension, and Ruby looked like she was holding her breath, trying to decide what to do with the air in her lungs. Finally, she let go, haltingly at first, and soon she had no choice but to laugh as well; it was either that or cry. Then they fed off of each other, laughing at themselves laughing. It went on and on; they were witches cackling, rubbing their hands together, agreeing to try some magic.

CHAPTER 26

The Group

The group sat in the restaurant on the beach, enjoying each other. Shane had flown in the same day as Taylor. He was already settled into his own condo.

Jeannie Tull came in from the beach and spotted Ruby. "Hey, you—I thought I would've seen more of you by now." She approached the table in a swoosh of size and color, her face an open book.

"Oh, Jeannie, I'm so glad to see you. I've some friends I'd like you to meet." Ruby made introductions while Shane found an extra chair.

"Well, I've some info for you," she said as she sat down. "That lady you're looking for, she's staying down island, a rental by the lighthouse." Everyone looked at Taylor.

"How did you find her?" Ruby wanted to keep the attention on Jeannie Tull.

"It was the oddest thing. There's very little crime on this island. It's just too small to get away with anything." Jeannie signaled to the waiter. "Anyway, we islanders love to dish the dirt, and I heard there'd been a break-in. When I asked around, it turned out to be the lady you were looking for."

"Is she all right?" asked Taylor.

"As far as I know, she's just fine. They pinched her passport and some money."

"Is that normal?" asked Shane. "I mean do people usually steal passports?" The waiter arrived, and Jeannie ordered a *chaya* shake.

"No, theft isn't normal on this island, but I suppose there's a market for passports. Hers would've been tough, though. I assume her little girl was probably on it, too."

"But they're okay?" Taylor asked again.

"I don't think they were home, so I'm sure they're fine. The police are looking into it, but whoever did it is probably from the mainland and long gone."

There was a loud bang; Taylor had knocked her chair over as she bolted up. "I...I've got to go." She looked pale, and her eyes hurt anyone they landed on.

"I'll go, too." Ruby rose and gave the others a look that said "stay."

"I don't know where you're going, but you can use my golf cart. I'm gonna hang out here for a while. I've heard the food is a bit of all right. Just bring it back in one piece."

"It could be a while."

"Don't worry; I can walk to work from here. It's supposed to be good for me." Jeannie Tull made a face.

CHAPTER 27

The Point

She stepped into the sun, one hand on her hip, the other shading her eyes. Her skin was a luscious bronze, her long, lean legs set apart, bare feet in the sand. Patricia seemed to be trying the day on, comparing it to the day before. Were her legs still strong, and did this ground still feel steady? Mainly, though, she was wondering whether they needed to leave.

There was a small restaurant around the corner, more like someone had simply put chairs out in the front yard and made guests pay for their meals. Emma liked it there. The owner was teaching her Spanish. *She is so quick*, Patricia thought. But yesterday when José came with the bill for their lunch, he'd told her a man had been asking questions about them. "I no tell him *nada*," he said, but the encroachment had begun. After that, they went home and found that someone had broken into the house and taken some money and Patricia's passport.

That was the query. *Was it the same man? Was he just a thief researching his next job, or are we being targeted? Was this about Emma? Do we need to move on? What precedent would I set by leaving?* Patricia didn't want to run; she liked Isla Mujeres. She'd been thinking they could live off the small allowance from the farm or even rent the farmhouse, and she could home-school Emma. *When Emma's older, we'll return*, she thought. *By then she'd be too old to be relocated with some old family member. She'd have a mind of her own.*

After a sleepless night, Patricia decided to look up the woman she'd asked about apartments. She'd been so friendly and seemed to know a lot about everything.

As Patricia surfaced from her reverie, she noticed a golf cart parked next to the road. The house was across the street from the very southern tip of Isla Mujeres. This part of the island was narrow, and the road wrapped around the property she had rented. Her privacy was protected by thick foliage that only gave way at the entrance to her driveway.

There were often people milling around in golf carts or scooters. They came to see the lighthouse and a small Mayan ruin. Yet this seemed different. The people were still sitting in the cart instead of getting out and walking toward the sites. There wasn't much of a view to be had from their location, other than her driveway. *Maybe I'm just getting paranoid*, she thought and turned back toward the house.

Patricia joined Emma inside—she was looking at a Spanish picture book. Patricia felt a rush of love as she viewed her daughter lying on the tile floor. She was on her stomach, completely absorbed, absently swinging her bare feet from side to side. "It's not hot out yet. Do you want to sit outside and have some fruit?" she asked.

"What kind of fruit?" Emma asked without looking up. *What a comfortable rhythm we have*, thought Patricia. *We are our own world.*

"Let's take everything we've got out to the table and decide there. Whatever looks good, that's what we'll eat."

"Can I bring my book?"

"No, it's rude to read at the table if someone else is eating with you, but we can look at it later; how's that sound?"

"Yeah," Emma jumped up and joined her mother. Together, they took their breakfast outside and settled at the picnic table.

"Why don't we each pick one, and while I cut it up, you can bring out some napkins?" This was serious now; Emma wanted to make a good choice. She ran her eyes the length of the table. They had a papaya, half a pineapple, three mangos, small bananas, and two grapefruits. This was going to be tough. After picking up each item, trying to check it for ripeness, the way her mother did at the store, Emma picked two mangos. Patricia picked the pineapple and started to cut it up as Emma went inside. This was better than the farm—no school bus took Emma away for the day. This island had a pace that was perfect for a mother and daughter to enjoy each other.

"I'm going to learn everything in that book. Won't I be able to surprise José?" They were eating with their hands, and Emma had fruit juice running between her fingers. "He thinks I just know numbers." José was always delighted with Emma. His children were grown, and his son had recently gone to Mexico City to attend school. Unfortunately, he'd also taken José's two grandchildren with him. The loss was somewhat appeased as he and Emma sat for hours after other customers had left. They would trade languages while Patricia read. Sometimes, José would take Emma back to the kitchen, where they'd sort beans, looking for bad ones or stones. José's wife was shy but no match for Emma's friendly manner.

Some days, two girls would appear, and then all four heads would lower over the paper on the table. At these moments Patricia would lay her book down and watch, enjoying the blend.

"Would you like someone to come to the house and teach us Spanish?" They were almost finished with breakfast, still picking at remnants.

"I already have José, *es mi abuelo*." Emma replied proudly.

"He's a wonderful grandfather," Patricia, who had learned some things too, said, "but he has to run the restaurant, and I thought it would be fun if we took classes together." Emma eyed her mother suspiciously.

"You mean the teacher coming here? I wouldn't have to take a school bus, and you would be in class, like me?"

"You bet. We'll learn it together." Patricia so enjoyed this gift that was her daughter she had a hard time not smiling whenever they spoke.

"Would José be there?"

"No, José would be at his restaurant. We can go there and show him how much you have learned."

"Will he like it if I learn more than him? We like learning together."

"He'll love it. Then you'll be able to talk about more things," Patricia said, handing Emma a napkin to stop her from licking her fingers.

"Okay, but you're not supposed to show off."

"We won't show off; we'll share, and that's always a good thing, eh?"

"Okay."

"Why don't we clean up and go to town? We can get you that sun visor."

Patricia parked their rented golf cart on a back street, and the two of them strolled toward the shops. They were just approaching Jeannie Tull's store when they saw her hurrying toward them. "I'm just about to open; give me a minute." Jeannie Tull looked up, "Oh, I remember you." She fussed with her keys and raised the metal door that fronted her store.

"Don't let us get in your…"

"No, no, it takes me two minutes to get up and running; besides, I want to hear all about your time on Isla so far." Jeannie Tull was debating whether to mention Ruby or Diane; she still didn't know what all this was about. "Did you find a place?"

"Yes, something close to the south point, just perfect for us." They all went inside. "I'm looking for a visor for Emma."

"You said I could pick it out," complained Emma.

"Of course, you can; I was just…"

"I've got tons of visors. You can try on every single one if you want; they're over there. One size fits all." Emma marched over to the shelf and started her search.

"So, are you two enjoying yourselves?"

"It's been wonderful, just what we needed." Patricia was poking at some T-shirts as she spoke, doing a poor job of looking casual. "We did get robbed, though."

"I'm so sorry. I heard about it; news travels fast. Did they mess the place up?"

"Not really. There just isn't that much in the house to mess up. But they did take my passport, and I wanted to ask you about getting a new one; is it hard?"

"Nah, there's a US consulate in Cancún."

"Well, actually, I'm Canadian. Is there a Canadian one?"

"Absolutely."

"I wanted to ask you some other things if you have time. Just to get your opinion, if that's all right?"

"Ask away."

Emma was completely absorbed with her visor selection, so Patricia took the chair Jeannie Tull offered her. "Well, the whole thing has made me a bit jumpy. Before we were robbed, José, who has the little restaurant near us, said that someone was asking about us."

"Yeah, I know José; he's a peach."

"He and Emma have been trading language classes. He's been very friendly, and, anyway, I was just concerned. I wasn't sure if we were targeted or if the thief was just doing some research. I can't even be positive it was the same man. I just thought maybe you could tell me if this has happened before or generally what goes on."

"Are you sure it was a man asking questions?"

"That's what José said: *hombre*, right?"

"That would be it. You know, we just don't get many robberies around here. Probably the guy hasn't had that much practice and just wanted to find out who was there, but I'll for sure keep my ears open."

"That would be so nice of you. We've been keeping to ourselves, and we really haven't met too many people here."

"No problem. You just come to me for anything. I'm easy to find. I mean you can't miss me, right?"

CHAPTER 28

The Lighthouse

The ride to the south point is an ocean-lovers dream: tropical foliage to the right and the rolling waves stretching out to meet the sky on the left. Taylor and Ruby didn't notice. Taylor was furious with herself for worrying about a dead child that she didn't believe existed. She didn't have the strength for this, but the "what ifs" were too powerful to ignore. Plus, things were going to have to happen fast. Either it was or it wasn't, and doubt was too painful to entertain.

They reached the point, saw the lighthouse, and navigated from there. There was only one possibility, and they parked with a view of the house. Taylor felt light; her body didn't come into contact with anything that she was aware of. This was not the real world, and no hard objects could intrude. There was a woman standing outside a very small square house. She looked tanned and healthy and attractive in a natural way. She stood there for a long time and then turned and walked inside. No sign of any young girl. Then the door opened, and out walked mother and daughter, laden with fruit.

Taylor and Ruby stared. Frozen. Searching. "Shouldn't I know? Shouldn't I feel it…either way?"

"She's too far away; we have to get closer," said Ruby.

"Just let me sit here for a minute."

"Well, she's the right age, and she's definitely your coloring."

"I need to see her face, closer, but…Ruby…I can't move."

"It's okay; we have time." Taylor leaned back in her seat and continued to stare at the pair eating their breakfast. They seemed so relaxed, chatting and eating in the morning sun. If this was Rebecca, how many breakfasts had she missed? Taylor laid her head in her hands—her head was spinning.

Suddenly, she sat up and looked at Ruby. "I...I..." and then she was over the side, vomiting. She was retching every thought, throwing up all the pain and making room in her wounded heart for the loss. It was a massive eruption, anticipating the possibility of all the time irretrievably gone. She rolled slowly off the seat and crouched on the ground, avoiding the mess she'd made. At first she was on her hands and knees, and then she moved back on her heels, into a fetal position. Ruby left her there. What could she possibly offer?

Time passed. Occasionally, a tourist would ask Ruby whether things were okay. "Bad food," she'd say. Everyone understood. Eventually, Taylor climbed back in the cart, at first sitting very straight and then slowly slump-ing into her friend.

Ruby nudged Taylor when she spotted the golf cart coming toward them, down the driveway. They watched it get closer and turn onto the road. Then, as it passed by, the girl on the passenger side looked straight at them. She seemed curious about the two women huddled together by the side of the road. Taylor had seen that look before—those were Tennyson's eyes.

Ruby didn't see what Taylor saw but felt her friend stiffen. They re-mained, sitting in the golf cart, reluctant to join this future with their past. *How is this possible?* Taylor was searching. *Yes, they found Tennyson's body, but the animals had been there. No little bones—was that it? Was she dragged off and then survived?* Taylor's mind rested there for a while. Other possibilities were too hard to fathom.

They left the cart by the side of the road and walked toward the Mayan ruin. "I know my life should be opening up, but I can only feel it pressing in on me. I mean, I've found my daughter, but she has another mother. Did you see them together?"

"You're her mother; nothing can ever change that."

"Okay, I'm her mother, but what does that mean? What does it mean to her? What does it mean to the woman she's with?" Ruby remained silent. She had always thought Taylor was everything she couldn't be—strong and kind—but this beat everything. Not to rush in, not to disturb things on her own behalf. Was this the selfless side of motherhood that she hadn't experienced, or was this the selfless side of Taylor?

"You need time, but no matter what a person wants, everyone deserves to know where they came from."

"Can we go back to the condos? The sun's too bright."

CHAPTER 29

Those Eyes—Boulder

Taylor had spotted him eating lunch with the maintenance man from the science building, both with their brown paper bag lunches and neither one saying much. It was so like Tennyson to prefer George to his colleagues in the science department. Not that he really had any colleagues left there. He worked alone now, and even though Tennyson would never say it, Taylor knew he had surpassed everyone in the department.

It was the story of his life to be alone. As a boy his life had been very difficult. He'd been different; he stood apart, even from his family. Taylor often wondered what life was going to be like with this strange man. There was so much she adored about him. When she became the focus of his intense nature, she felt completely blanketed in his love. She had imagined that the love and security he offered in those moments would be enough to carry her through, but that was also what made it so hard. To go from the center of his universe to barely noticeable was by comparison more painful.

Would her child be brilliant like his father, intense, often unreachable? Could she live with such a family? There has to be a way to bring someone down to earth, if you understand them early, help them adjust, and make things safe. She knew he trusted her.

Tennyson had looked up and smiled that wonderful smile as she approached the table. His eyes were a soft blue, and strands of his sand-colored hair constantly fell across his forehead. He hated his hair longer; it got in his way, but Taylor had told him how much she had liked it, and so he'd let it grow. Taylor felt privileged to be loved by such a genius, like being in on some secret, some higher knowledge.

Tennyson had stood up and taken her arm, easing her onto the bench. "How far have you walked today?" He had read books on pregnancy and childbirth and had taken an overpowering interest in her progress.

"I've walked enough." Taylor shook her head. Once she caught his attention, it was usually more involvement than she wanted.

"I don't want any attitude from you in front of my daughter."

"Then you don't need to worry because this little boy is definitely in front of me." George rose and started gathering his things; this was definitely too much family chatter for him.

"See ya, George," said Tennyson.

"Yeah, yeah, try not to blow up the lab today." George hated scientists; he thought they were "stuck-up jerks," but Tennyson knew he was the exception.

"How was your appointment? Is everything on schedule?" He laid his hand gently on Taylor's tummy, rubbing it as if he were polishing something breakable.

"He said everything looks great, that it could be any time now. It's time to keep that bag by the door." Taylor was in no hurry; she loved being pregnant, feeling special, never feeling alone. She was nervous, too. She'd been an only child and didn't think she knew enough about caring for a baby.

They picked up his things and walked slowly across the grass to their small apartment off campus. At first she thought that her bladder control problem was getting worse, but soon she realized this was more fluid than normal. She pulled on Tennyson's arm to stop and stood for a short time to be sure. Then she looked at her husband. "I think my water just broke."

They arrived at the hospital by cab. Tennyson had printed out all the information the nurse needed. He had prepared it months ago. The doctor was not at the hospital yet, so they proceeded to the second floor. Within an hour Taylor was in a labor room in a wrap-around hospital gown covered with little brown bears. Her contractions had started and were seven minutes apart, which meant she had a long way to go.

Together, they'd done all the classes and were using the breathing techniques they'd learned. Tennyson, of course, had a few ideas of his own. He was instructing Taylor on his "heartbeat and exterior body theory," and she decided she would put up with this for a while. He usually had his own theories on things, and more times than not they were better. Childbirth, however, seemed a long way from his field of expertise.

Things proceeded very slowly. At first Taylor felt the pain was manageable; she *could* handle this. But after five hours three things happened: the contractions got very close together, the pain became extreme, and she started to tire. No distraction was enough, not her husband's ideas nor the breathing techniques. It was time for some relief, time to call the nurse and ask for something, anything. Tennyson didn't object; seeing her writhe in agony was more than he'd expected and painful for him to watch.

"What is it, honey?" asked the nurse.

"I can't stand this anymore. Please, please, give me something for the pain."

"Let's have a look." Taylor rolled on her back and spread her knees for yet another examination. "Oh, this is good." The nurse removed her rubber gloves with a snap. "You're so close; it's really too late for any pain medication. By the time we'd have you set up, you'd be heading for the delivery room." The nurse looked at Taylor sympathetically. "Do you think you can handle it just a wee bit longer?" Taylor couldn't answer; she was being assaulted by another contraction, starting off painful, peaking at unbearable, and easing off slowly. They were coming one after another now. "I'm going to call your doctor and have him take a look. I think we're almost ready for the delivery room now." Taylor nodded; she could already feel another contraction coming on. Tennyson held her hand and urged her to breathe, three short then one long. He felt helpless and was doing his best not to hyperventilate.

"Let's have a look. The nurse told me you're doing very well, Taylor," the doctor said as he entered the room. Taylor rolled over for the exam and prayed that the next contraction would not come before he was finished. The doctor smiled and said, "I think it's time, Taylor. We're going to move you into the delivery room and introduce this baby to the world. You're doing very well; everything's going along fine." The doctor disappeared, and then there were three new people in the room, two to move her bed and one to come along with the IV bag. Tennyson did his best to stay out of the way as they all moved down the hall.

Once in the delivery room, they slipped Taylor onto the delivery table and laid her gently back on her pillows. Tennyson was horrified to see them strap his wife's feet into the footrests. This position kept her knees high and far apart. He'd seen it in the books, but actually seeing Taylor in this position was an image he wasn't prepared for. He leaned on the bed to support his wobbly legs and talked to Taylor. "Not long now—you're so brave."

"I hate this. I'm so tired. You do it for a while. I hate this room; I want to go home; I...*ohhhhh.*" The next contraction hit her hard. Taylor scrunched up her face and gritted her teeth. "*I can't do this.*" Tennyson was shocked by the panic in his wife's voice. He looked at the doctor, who was busy getting things ready.

"Is this normal?" he asked. The nurse came to the side of the bed with a wet cloth for Taylor's head.

"You just keep talking to her and cooling her with this; everything's going along fine."

"Okay, Taylor." The doctor was slightly muffled behind his mask. "With the next contraction, I want you to push. Hold onto those handles by your knees and give it all you've got. That's right—good job." Taylor was pushing with all she had; it helped with the pain. After the first push, she lay back and looked for Tennyson. He was leaning on the table behind her and looking very pale.

"I love you," he said as he mopped her brow. "You're everything to me." Taylor pushed and pushed until the doctor told her to stop.

"I can see the head. Now what I need you to do is resist the urge to push."

"You can do it," said the nurse as she positioned herself next to Taylor's head. "I want you to breathe with me honey; we're almost there." Taylor made eye contact with the nurse and followed her breathing. She was frightened by the powerful urge to push. "That was perfect."

"All right," the doctor said, "this time you can push, and we're going to have this baby in your arms soon." Taylor began to push, watching the doctor for instructions. "Now ease up a bit; that's good...oh, look at this: We have a head." The nurse suctioned out the nose and mouth as Taylor took a rest. "Just a little push now...here we go now, yes...good, good. Oh, look at this: a beautiful baby girl." He handed the baby to the nurse, who was waiting with an open blanket.

"She's beautiful, honey. You hold her for a minute, and then we'll weigh her and all that, and you can have her right back." She laid the bundle on Taylor's tummy. *Oh, my god.* Taylor was mystified. Tennyson was leaning over her shoulder with his arms around her. They were speechless.

CHAPTER 30

The Condo

"How did this happen?" Taylor was sitting on the end of her bed. She had not left her condo for twenty-four hours. Shane had promised to keep an eye on Patricia so Taylor wouldn't have to worry about her leaving the island.

"You've got to come outside with me," Ruby said. She thought two days was enough of the "in-a-dark-room" kind of processing. The weather was beautiful, and she was determined to get her friend outside.

"I can't. I've got to figure out what to do. I'm lost: back and forth, back and forth, good for her, good for me."

"Just come outside. You, Diane, and I, we can talk, or not talk, whatever it takes, or…whatever you need." Ruby started going through Taylor's clothes. "Here, put on this suit and this T-shirt. Let's go; you've no choice." Taylor didn't move. "I'm going to bug you until you come with me, so you can give in now, or you can give in later, but I'm not leaving without you."

Taylor looked at her friend. They'd been through so much together. "Okay, okay, okay, but I can't talk to anyone, just you and Diane."

"No problem. We'll move down the beach and sit under the palms. It'll be beautiful." Ruby worried about exposing her pale friend to the sun. "Just for a while."

They were settled under the trees, and it seemed a long way across the beach to the water. Most people were playing in the ocean. Their spot was perfect, quiet with a slight breeze. The three sat in silence and enjoyed the view. They hadn't been alone together for days, and just the company was pacifying to them all.

"Talk to me. I've already heard everything my head has to say."

"Okay," said Ruby, "let's get clinical. There are three main characters: you, Rebecca, and, whether we like it or not, the woman with her. Her name is Patricia. For you, you want to have your daughter back; for Patricia, she isn't going to want to give Rebecca up; and for Rebecca, we all want what's best for her. Those are the starters. Okay, who's the most important to everyone? Rebecca, right? So let's start there. What's best for her?"

"That's just it. I don't know. She seemed so happy with…Patricia. Whatever I do will only complicate her life. I mean, what is blood anyway? It's only biology." They fell silent again.

"I have the answer to this," Diane offered.

"Okay, go."

"Okay," she swung her feet onto the sand and sat facing her two friends. "If this is all about Rebecca, let's think what she would want. Imagine you're Rebecca and you find out Patricia isn't your real mom, or maybe she already knows. What kid in the whole world wouldn't wonder, wouldn't want to know? Who wouldn't want to know her own mother and how they were separated? No matter how it stands now, she'll know some day that Patricia isn't her biological mother, and how will you explain that you didn't go to her when you found her? She would never understand." They all sat quietly for a while.

Diane astounded them both. She could make such a mess of her own life, and then, every once in a while, she would come up with something brilliant. She was right. Not that Ruby ever believed there had been a choice. If Taylor did nothing, she would have to ask herself the same questions over and over again for the rest of her life. Ignoring the truth was never going to be an option.

Taylor didn't seem ready to discuss it further, so they all closed their eyes and listened to the ocean. "This is a beautiful sight." Ruby looked up, and there was Roger.

"Hi, Roger, how are you?"

"Wonderful. How can you beat this?" Roger swept the air with his arm.

"I know. Do you think it ever rains here?"

"Hi, Diane. How are you doing today?"

"I'm in heaven, thank you."

"Oh, I'm sorry. This is Taylor Barrett; Taylor, this is Roger Bates from New York."

"Pleased to meet you." Taylor held out her hand, and they shook. There was something familiar about Roger, but she didn't have the energy to try to figure it out.

"Where are you from, Taylor?"

"Colorado."

"We're all from the same town," Ruby broke in, trying to save Taylor. She didn't want her going back to the room. "What are you up to today?"

"Not much, just trying to get a little exercise, walking up and down the beach. It's pretty quiet around here today."

"Well, that's what we're all here for, isn't it?" Ruby knew this was rude, but she had only one purpose at the moment, and he wasn't helping.

"Well, I guess I'd better keep going. My walk just got started. I'll see you around; nice to meet you, Taylor."

"That was pretty rude, Ruby," said Diane after Roger had left.

"Nah, he's from New York, and he's a big boy; he'll get over it. I just didn't want him to join us." As Ruby watched him walk down the beach, she noticed Boo in the trees. "Hey, Boo, come here, boy." The dog trotted over immediately and settled next to Ruby's chair. "I think I've got a friend."

Ruby hated to push, but since their quiet had already been interrupted, they had more to discuss. "We've one more thing to decide here, and I don't think we should wait too long."

"I know," said Taylor. "What do I do next?"

Ruby was a little hurt by the "I" but let it go. Instead, she reminded herself of how alone Taylor had been most of her life.

"Well, I think you need to talk to Patricia first, alone, without Rebecca there. Then, depending on what kind of a person she is, you two can decide together on how to approach Rebecca."

"Good idea," said Diane. "How do you think we should approach Patricia?"

"And how do we separate her from Rebecca? She isn't going to send her off with us; she doesn't even know us." Ruby lay back and closed her eyes.

"Let's talk to Jeannie Tull," Diane said after a long silence. "She knows Patricia and us; maybe we could meet at her house."

"Good, that's good. What do you think, Taylor?" Ruby turned toward Taylor, who had been silent this whole time. She'd been lying back with her eyes closed.

"What is Jeannie Tull like? Does she know what's going on?"

"She seems like a very nice person," Ruby answered, "and she doesn't know what's going on. I can talk to her myself, and we can go from there. What do you think?"

"That would work, Ruby. I just don't seem to have much energy. In fact, if you don't mind, I'd like to go back to my room now." Ruby escorted Taylor back to her room and then went to town.

She found Jeannie Tull in her shop and asked whether they could go upstairs for privacy. Without giving it a second thought, Jeannie Tull pulled the metal door down to close her store, and they went to her apartment. She sat quietly as Ruby explained the situation.

"This is incredible. I wondered what all this was about but never imagined anything so amazing." Jeannie raised herself up off her couch and headed for the refrigerator. "I have to have a drink; you want something?"

"Sure. Have you got a beer?"

"You bet." Jeannie settled herself across from Ruby and handed her one of the beers. They sat quietly for a while. Ruby wanted to let things settle.

"Okay, right—why are you telling me this now?"

"We need to figure a way to get Taylor and Patricia together without Rebecca there. I thought maybe…if you didn't…."

"Well, here, of course—it's perfect."

CHAPTER 31

Jeannie's

Patricia finally decided to leave Emma with José. She knew she could trust him, and Emma was thrilled. *Maybe it will be good for her,* she thought. *We probably shouldn't spend all of our time together.* Patricia had been invited to Jeannie's house for dinner. She was a little nervous, but if they were going to stay on the island for a while, she was going to have to socialize.

Jeannie answered the door in her usual bouquet of colors. "I'm so glad you're here; we should've done this sooner."

"Well, I've always been a bit of a hermit. Thank you for having me; I'm flattered."

"Flattered? I'm the one who needs entertainment. I'm just using you as a fresh audience for all my old stories." Jeannie shut the door and led Patricia to the couch. "Actually, I'm having some other women tonight, as well. Visitors like you, whom I've met around town."

"I wasn't sure who would be here. I brought a bottle of red wine. I've no idea if it will be any good, but I'd never heard of any of them at the store, so I just picked the one with the label I liked the best."

"Perfect, it'll be perfect. Wine's always good." As she led Patricia into her apartment, there was another knock on the door. Jeannie called over her shoulder, "Come on in; it's open. We're in the salon." She drew out the last word with a wave of her arm. Ruby, Diane, and Taylor came through the door, and hugs and introductions were offered all around. "That's it, then; we're all here. Who wants a drink?"

Patricia felt intimidated. All the other women obviously knew one another, but she was determined to enjoy herself and asked for a glass of wine. They settled around the room, grateful to be inside under a fan. Jeannie'd put a tub of ice with beer and white wine on the floor in the center of the room.

Ruby poured Patricia some of the red wine and then some white for herself. "So where are you from, Patricia?"

Patricia was glad that Ruby was the first to talk to her; she had a warm manner and a lovely full face. "Canada." Patricia knew that she should be more specific, but she'd not prepared herself for questions. She'd been so private and careful lately that she was set back by even a casual question. "Ontario, actually," she added, trying to sound relaxed. "I grew up on a farm."

"Oh, a farm. How wonderful. I grew up in New York and yearned for the country. We lived right in the middle of the city; it was intense. Some-times it's hard to remember that there's a world outside New York City." Ruby sat back. "Now there's a scary thought."

"No, no, no," interjected Diane. "You should try the Midwest. From there it seems like the whole world is somewhere else." Diane looked like a cheerleader to Patricia. She had that small, cute look that totally eluded anyone over five foot seven.

"None of you has any idea. Try being a fat person in London. I grew up with Twiggy." Jeannie scanned her guests. "You probably don't even know who that is, right?"

"I know who she is. She was all eyes on a stick body," Ruby said.

"Okay, well, just imagine growing up as me, and I swear to you I was born this way. Can you picture me in London next to a Twiggy poster? I was the Antichrist." Jeannie scanned her company once again. "None of you are religious, are you?"

"Not enough to be bothered by that comment," said Ruby, looking around for support. "Childhoods are always a bitch, eh?" A silence fell over the room, so Ruby hurried on. "You seem pretty happy here, Jeannie."

"Oh, I am, but I had to travel halfway around the world. I would've been balmy to stay in London."

"Ha," said Diane. "Try growing up looking like a cheerleader." Patricia had to suppress a smile. "You're stereotyped the minute you walk into a room. Everyone thinks they know all about you right off the bat."

Patricia joined in, "Maybe growing up on a farm is a relief? You just don't think about it that much—not that it doesn't matter what you look like, but I just tried to look clean and presentable."

"I love the thought of that," said Diane. Patricia looked at Taylor, who had said nothing during all of this. She looked pale. Ruby noticed the glance and said that Taylor was a little under the weather but not contagious.

"I'm sorry; is it something you ate?" asked Patricia.

"I talked her into coming," said Ruby. "It probably was something she ate, but she's much better and needed to get out."

"I'm...much better, thank you," said Taylor. "Just feeling sort of...quiet."

"Well, that's a bit of all right; just let us entertain you," said Jeannie. "I've made something different for dinner. They have a million different squashes down here, so I bought every one I could get my hands on and put them in a casserole. Who knows? We may be on the brink of a magnificent discovery." Jeannie looked at Taylor. She obviously needed help. "Taylor, will you help me toss the salad?"

"Sure," Taylor said as she stood up. The two of them went into the kitchen.

"We need some spices off the deck. I'll show you my herb garden."

"Is she going to be okay?" asked Patricia.

"Oh, sure. She's quiet anyway, and this really knocked her socks off." Patricia, Diane, and Ruby sat inside and talked until dinner was ready. Patricia found it all very enjoyable. She hadn't had enough friends in her life, and she liked these women. Dinner was delicious. They drank more and talked more—little bits of their lives, shared in a secure environment—all but Taylor, who never joined in.

After the party, Patricia picked up Emma. When she left the restaurant, José said, "Man back, *mismo hombre antes*...before."

"He was here?" José nodded. "Did he ask anything?"

"*Quiera hablar con* Emma. *No permitar, yo la tuvo en la cocina.*" José looked worried, so Patricia decided to come back the next day to find out more. When she got home, she thought a few things looked out of place but couldn't be sure.

CHAPTER 32

No More Time

When Patricia returned from the restaurant the next morning, there was a note on her door. Jeannie wanted her to come over at three o'clock. Patricia wanted to talk to her, anyway. It was time to go, and she needed to get a new passport.

"I'm glad you asked me over. I need some information about getting a passport," Patricia said as Jeannie led her into the apartment. To Patricia's surprise, Taylor was sitting on the couch. "Hi, Taylor—are you feeling better today?"

Taylor was finding it hard to talk—behind Patricia stood Emma. Tennyson was there, too, somehow, showing through the face of this pretty girl. "I...I'm still having some trouble," she said with difficulty.

"I have to check something in the store. Is it okay if Emma comes with me?" asked Jeannie.

"Sure. Emma, you do what Jeannie tells you, okay?"

"Sure, mom."

Patricia thought she heard Taylor gasp as Jeannie led Emma out the door. After they had left, she turned back to Taylor, who was pale and looking very ill.

"Oh, Taylor, you look terrible; can I help?"

"Patricia, I'm so sorry...I don't know where to start...I..." Taylor put her head in her hands. Her ears were ringing, and blackness was threatening her peripheral vision. "Just a minute, I..."

Patricia was getting nervous. This woman was such a mess she didn't know what she could do for her. Maybe she needed a doctor? "You don't have to be sorry. If you're that sick, maybe we should get you to a doctor."

Taylor sat up, determined to compose herself. "No, I'm okay…I…I think I'm Emma's mother." This wasn't how Taylor had planned it. But nothing was working the way she had planned. *I mean, how can I plan a thing like this, anyway?*

Patricia was backing toward the door. She looked like she'd been hit on the head and was trying to figure out what happened. "What…what are you talking about? I'm Emma's mother. Are you nuts?"

"Tell me, did you give birth to Emma?" The horror on Patricia's face was hard to look at.

"Of course, I gave birth to Emma. What are you talking about? I'm leaving now." Patricia turned and moved toward the door. She had to leave. *Where is Emma?*

"Please, Patricia, I know you didn't give birth to Emma. I know you told your friends she was the child of your relatives who died. Please, don't leave. I'm not going to go away. We have to talk about this." Taylor wanted to get up, to move toward the door, but she didn't think her legs would support her.

Patricia's mind was racing. All these years, this had been her biggest fear. "That's right. I just don't usually tell people that. It's none of their business, and certainly isn't any of yours."

"Please. I know you must be scared, but we have to do this. It's too late to go back. I can see my husband in your daughter's face. The timing, everything, I know it's the truth." Patricia reached for the door, so Taylor rushed on. "I don't want to take her from you. We need to talk; please, we can work something out." Taylor waited. Then she saw the top half of Patricia's body slump. Her head and her shoulders dropped like someone had pulled the plug. "I can't imagine how you're feeling. I must be your worst nightmare. Please stay. I want us to work this out together."

Patricia turned. She had her hand over her mouth, and she looked like her chest had caved in. She was not a liar. She couldn't make this go away, and she couldn't keep running. "I…I just can't do this. I've thought about this moment so often, prayed that it would never happen. Please, please don't take my daughter." Tears were sliding down Patricia's cheeks. She couldn't hide anymore.

Taylor found the strength to stand. This woman needed her help, and she needed this woman. She went to Patricia and led her back to the couch. "I won't take her. We'll work something out, something good for all of us.... I don't know what, but we can do this." The two women sat on the couch, looking ahead, trying to adjust. They were simply out of words for the moment.

After a very long while, Patricia said, "Don't tell Emma; she's not prepared for this."

"I swear, we'll work together; it's all about her," Taylor said, and then they were silent again. There were so many questions and so many decisions, but for the time being they simply sat.

The door opened slowly, and Ruby looked in and saw the two women sitting quietly on the couch. She closed the door behind Diane and approached Taylor. "Are you okay?"

Both women looked up. They had the same lost and tired look in their eyes. "We're okay," replied Taylor as she looked over at Patricia. She had an odd sense of having known her for a long time.

"Have you talked?" asked Diane. Taylor looked up again, as though she had already forgotten they were there.

"Yes, we've talked. We haven't answered any questions, but we know it's true." Taylor looked at Patricia, "I've so many questions. You must, too." Then Taylor looked up at her friends. "I've assured Patricia that I'm not here to run off with her daughter."

It is so like Taylor to refer to Rebecca as Patricia's daughter, even now that they both know the truth, thought Ruby. "Do you know how this happened?"

So far, Patricia had said nothing and had not made eye contact with anyone. Suddenly, she turned to Taylor and said, "You didn't want her!" Taylor was surprised by the accusation.

"That's not true." She tried to keep her voice calm. "I thought she was dead. I was told she died in the fire." Taylor could no longer control her own tears. How could anyone have thought she wouldn't want her daughter? Patricia looked confused.

"Where's Emma?" she asked.

"It's okay," said Ruby. "She's downstairs with Jeannie, and they're having a good time."

"No one is going to take her from you," said Taylor. "I promise you that. You're her mother. I don't want to hurt you or...Emma." Patricia appeared to relax a little.

"I don't understand how this happened," Patricia said.

"If you're up to it, can you tell us how this all started?" asked Taylor. Patricia looked up at Diane and Ruby. "It's okay; they know everything, but if you would rather talk to just me, that's…"

"It's okay," said Patricia, waving her hand in defeat. Here were all of her worst fears, and her time was up. "My cousin brought her to me."

"Do you mean Kevin?" Diane asked.

"How did you know?"

"We've been slowly putting the pieces of the story together, and Kevin was a friend of Taylor's husband."

"Well, he called me and wanted to come for a visit. I hadn't seen him for years. I was glad to have him, but when he arrived, he was a nervous wreck, and he had Emma with him."

"What was the date?" asked Ruby.

"It was February 4th, 1982." Patricia was silent for a moment.

"What did he tell you?" Taylor knew she should give Patricia time, but she had to know.

"He told me that you had abandoned them both, father and daughter. He told me that he was a good friend of the father and that they got into an argument and somehow a fire got started and that he only had time to save the baby. He was frantic and told me the baby had nowhere to go. I believed him, or…I wanted to believe him. He stayed with us for a week and then was gone. I haven't seen him since." Fresh tears rolled down her cheek as she finally gave up the truth.

Ruby and Diane sat facing the couch, keeping a protective eye on Taylor. "There was a fire," said Taylor. "But we never knew anyone else was there. We thought it was an accident and that both Tennyson and Rebecca died. There was a huge snowstorm, and no one could get there. When they finally did, animals had been digging in the wreckage, and so many things were out of place…" Taylor still couldn't bring herself to say animals had dragged the baby off, even though she now knew it wasn't true. The pictures of it had haunted her for years.

"Kevin and Tennyson had worked together at the university but hadn't seen each other for a long time. Tennyson didn't trust him…it's all so complicated. Tennyson had made an enormous discovery but wasn't sure the world was ready for it. Kevin had pestered him for the formula, and Tennyson thought he only wanted it for power and money and…"

"Do you think Kevin could have caused the fire?" asked Diane.

"I don't know. I remember he had a bad temper," said Taylor.

"He always had a rough time," said Patricia. "His father was a terrible man and was often mean and abusive with Kevin. When his family would come to visit, Kevin and I spent all our time as far away from him as we could get. He scared me to death."

"But if he didn't do anything wrong," said Diane, "why wouldn't he take Rebecca to Taylor?" Everyone turned to Patricia.

"I don't have the answers. He came to me for help, and I…" Patricia couldn't say it, not in front of Taylor. "What do we do now?"

"I have to think," said Taylor. She looked at Patricia. "Promise me you won't run with…Emma, please. You can't hide, and it would be no life for the two of you. We can work this out."

"I won't run. I thought about it when you sent the man to ask questions, but I can't do that to Emma." Patricia had started to put everything together.

"What man?" asked Ruby.

"Did you send someone to watch Patricia?" Taylor asked, looking at Ruby.

"Well, Shane was keeping an eye on them after you saw Rebecca, but I don't think he asked any questions." Ruby turned to Patricia. "Someone has been asking about you? Do you mean the robbery? Jeannie told us you were robbed."

"It started with the robbery. I didn't know if the two were related, but then the other day, a man was asking more questions. José told me. He runs the restaurant, where we eat all the time. It's right by our house."

"Wait," said Diane, "let me get this clear. You were robbed, and a man has been asking questions about you?"

"We were robbed, and then I found out a man had been asking questions about us beforehand. Then yesterday, the same man was asking more questions. At first I thought he was getting information for the robbery, but now I don't know what's going on. That's why we were going to leave."

Taylor looked surprised, "You were going to leave?"

"I was frightened. I thought it might have something to do with Emma. That's why we came here in the first place. Someone had been asking questions about us at home."

"If you mean at the records office, that was me," offered Ruby. "I actually went to your farm, but I've got nothing to do with this."

"Do you feel safe?" asked Taylor. "You're awfully isolated out there."

"I don't know what to think."

"Why don't you come and stay at the condos? I know they have lots of space available, and you would be closer to other people if you needed help."

"Let me think about it," responded Patricia, not willing to give up her time alone with Emma. "What about Emma? She knows she came to me from relatives but has never asked anything about it."

Taylor thought about it. She didn't want to intrude in any way that would scare Patricia off. "You and I should probably figure that out together. Whatever is best for Emma, right?"

Patricia found Emma downstairs, and they hurried home. She was spent. When they arrived at the cottage, she told Emma she wanted to lie down and went into the bedroom. Her body was heavy, and her thoughts were clogged, but she wasn't scared. Taylor didn't have horns, and she didn't appear to have any expectations either. Maybe this could work somehow, and Patricia would be free of the nagging apprehension that had tainted her otherwise perfect life with Emma. Just in the few hours since meeting Taylor, she had experienced a mixture of confusion and fear but also just a shadow of liberation.

CHAPTER 33

Beans

"Does he have an English menu?" Shane asked Patricia. They were all sitting at José's restaurant, near the south point of the island. The chairs were red plastic with Coca Cola written across the backs. The table was wooden and rustic and big enough for all of them. José's kitchen was part of his house, and the group was essentially sitting in his front yard.

"I can translate for you. I'm learning Spanish, and we eat here a lot," said Emma. She was thrilled to be eating with so many people, and they all seemed so friendly.

"Okay, what is '*tres tortillas de harina llena de ingredientes deliciosos y frito en aceite vegetal?*'" Shane was trying his best to pronounce everything correctly but realized it was a wasted effort.

Pointing to the menu and feeling very important, Emma explained each item. She had tried them all and felt like an expert. "That's a chimichanga. It has different things wrapped up in a flour tortilla and then is fried. See, here they list all the different things you can get inside it."

"And what's this?"

"Oh, that's a plate of chips covered with different things and then heated up. Those are really good; they make you full, though." Emma pointed to another place in the menu. "These are burritos, and then here are the fajitas. You get to pick what you want with any of them. José is really nice. He'll put anything in there; you don't even have to pick from the menu."

"Anything he has," corrected Patricia. She was so pleased at how comfortable Emma was with everyone. She felt oddly proud with Taylor there. *See what a good job I've done.*

Patricia had been up most of the night and had finally decided that maybe she was lucky. Her biggest fears had come to pass, and the sky hadn't fallen. If Taylor was as straightforward and reasonable as she seemed, maybe they could work this out. She liked Taylor. She felt like a distant relative who had shown up, unexpectedly—someone she'd never known existed.

Taylor was in awe of this incredible child. She was bright and friendly and interested in everything around her. *Is this really my Rebecca? How do I sit at a table with my dead child and put it all back together?* Rebecca had been dead for eight years and alive for two days, and this wonderful little stranger was the link.

Taylor's world was tangled. She supposed that she should be ecstatic, but that wasn't one of the many feelings she was experiencing, and there was guilt, even in that. Ruby had given her a Valium, and the two had laughed as Taylor nervously nibbled away at half of it. She wasn't used to drugs, but she wanted to be relaxed, and she didn't want Rebecca to see her as a nervous weirdo. She wanted Rebecca to like her.

During the night, Taylor had made thirty different decisions and changed her mind as many times. Maybe she should just go home, leave this mother and daughter alone, and get on with her own life. But this was her life. They could say she was an aunt, and she could be part of Rebecca's life yet not take away from Patricia…and then Taylor would reprimand herself for thinking that lying to her daughter was a way to go. Back and forth it went all night, until Taylor decided it was okay not to know what to do. She decided to spend time with Patricia and Rebecca and see how things unfolded. That, however, didn't stop her from being a nervous wreck at the thought of sitting down to lunch with Rebecca and Patricia. Ruby's Valium was a great idea. It was working well, and she was feeling more relaxed, a little detached, but she decided that was good because she didn't know where she fit in yet. She was happy to watch but had yet to say one thing to Rebecca. The thought of speaking to her was a whole new challenge. Maybe the menu was a good place to start.

"What's a burrito…Emma?" Other people were discussing the menu and stopped to look at Taylor. She could tell her timing was off. *What do you expect? I'm on a different planet here.* When Emma turned her Tennyson eyes on Taylor, Taylor tried to remain casual.

"Oh, those are yummy. They put anything you want in a giant flour tortilla and heat it up. That's my favorite, and they give you guacamole and salsa with it."

"What do you like in it?" asked Taylor, trying to act like she was talking to anyone.

"Well," Emma was feeling the excitement of having been asked her opinion, "I like it with rice and beans and chicken."

"Then that's what I'm going to have."

Patricia was watching the two of them closely. She thought she would feel jealous or threatened by anything they shared, but she didn't. She wanted it to go well. She wanted it all to go well.

Ruby was sitting at the head of the table with Boo next to her. Somehow, this dog covered the entire island, finding her wherever she went. Ruby was watching all of them. She was less confused than Taylor and less afraid than Patricia and would have been enjoying herself completely had she not also been worried about this man—this mysterious man asking questions. She wanted to talk about it but not in front of Emma. Ruby had mentioned it when they first had arrived, and Patricia had assured her that Emma always helped in the kitchen after they ate and that there would be time then.

So for now she watched. This was an incredible, incredible thing. There sat their Rebecca. Ruby had always thought she would be the lively one; she would have to be in order to engage her parents, who were quieter and more withdrawn than most. It had been clear in that first year that this was an energetic and charismatic child, and here she was, just that. *What a study this would be for genes versus environment.*

With Emma's help, everyone ordered. When the food arrived, everyone tried a bit of everything, and the meal had a warm feeling of friends enjoying the best of things. When they were done, Emma went into the kitchen as Patricia had predicted, and the group became more serious. "Let me get José out here. He can tell us what happened. Jeannie, maybe with you translating, it will be clearer."

"No problem. My grammar is dicey, but I get by." José returned to the table for more dishes, and Jeannie asked him to sit down for a moment. *"Puedes decirnos mas del hombre que pregunto de Patricia y Emma?"*

"Si, pero no se mucho."

"Cuantos tiempos vino aquí?" As Jeannie talked, the rest of the group was silent, waiting for the information to be given to them in English. After five minutes José went back to the kitchen with more dishes and Jeannie explained what he'd said.

"Okay, he said that he has seen the guy three times, the first was a week ago when he had lunch here. He thinks that Patricia and Emma were here at the same time. Then he came in the afternoon a few days later and asked José if he knew where the mother and child lived and how long had they been on the island. He said he didn't tell him anything except they'd been coming to the restaurant for a few weeks. Then, the next time the guy came, he asked if Patricia and Emma had been around and if they drove a golf cart. José told him you had a golf cart." Jeannie looked at Patricia. "But nothing more. He didn't think that was too private, but he didn't like the man."

"Did you ask him what he looked like?" asked Ruby.

"Yeah, he said he was tall, that he looked like an average gringo, was well-dressed, and he drove a rented *moto*."

"Anything else?" asked Shane.

"Only that his hair wasn't black or white and that he wasn't skinny but wasn't fat."

"Did he ask any other questions?" asked Diane.

"He asked where they lived, but José said he didn't know. Then the man asked him again, saying that it must be close, because they were on foot. When José heard that, he stopped telling him anything. He said it sounded like the man was following them. José told me he was sorry and that he hoped he hadn't told him too much."

"I hope you told him it was okay," said Patricia.

"Don't worry; I told him everything was fine and that he hadn't done anything wrong."

"The second time the guy came was definitely after the robbery?" asked Shane.

"Absolutely, he remembered that specifically."

"Can you think of anyone who would want to know about you and Emma?" Shane turned to Patricia as he spoke.

"I can't think of anyone. My biggest fear has always been Taylor." Patricia looked apologetically at Taylor. "I've no idea who this could be."

The group quieted down as they collectively pondered the situation. "I have a plan," said Shane. "At least, if José will agree to it. One of us spends some time with José every day. We situate ourselves in different places downtown: one day for lunch, then maybe for drinks, then maybe dinner, so we cover different places at different times. Since he's the only one who's seen this guy, he can point him out, and then we'll have him."

"How can José run his restaurant and hang out with us at the same time?" asked Patricia.

"We could offer to pay for help to take his place," said Ruby. "I think it's a great idea, if José doesn't mind hanging out with a bunch of gringos."

"He may not be comfortable with this," suggested Taylor.

"Well, let's get him out here and ask him," said Jeannie as she raised her arm.

They worked out that Patricia and Emma would help in the kitchen at the restaurant while everyone else in the group took turns around town with José. The first day it would be Jeannie and Ruby at lunchtime.

CHAPTER 34

Old Friends

The next day was Saturday, and Ruby decided to spend some time at the pool with Shane. Diane felt that three was a crowd and headed out along the beach. She had been worried about things, and when she wasn't thinking about Taylor's situation, her own life was crowding in on her. She had no job, no money, and didn't even know how long she would be in Mexico. All her choices seemed to depend on Ruby, and that was starting to feel familiar.

She walked north toward the old hotel. It had such an abandoned demeanor; she thought the two could get along. After crossing the wooden bridge, Diane turned left to inspect the half-built condominiums. *They could've been so beautiful.* She approached the round staircases. There was one in front of each condominium, and the effect of having six in a row on each side was very appealing. She climbed the stairs to one of the buildings on the right and went inside. The room was bright. The whole side by the ocean was open, obviously a spot for sliding glass doors leading out onto the balcony. There were white tiles on the floor with dried mud and debris settled in the corners. *What a waste.*

"What a waste." Had she heard that or thought that? Turning to check, Diane was faced with an old debt.

"What are you doing here?" But she knew. She knew she was going to see him again, but this was not where she'd expected it to happen.

"Hi, to you, too. I told you at the restaurant I missed you." Diane could not believe he actually thought he could still say things like this to her.

"Kevin, I know why you are here, and it isn't to see me. I just can't believe you would follow us here."

"I followed *you* here. I need to know what's going on. What's happening with Taylor, and where are the discs?"

"You mean what is happening with Taylor and your cousin, and I don't have a clue about any discs." *How guilty is he?* "What did you do?" Diane asked this before she thought about it. She really didn't want to know.

"You don't even know what you're talking about, but you're going to tell me some things."

"Why would I tell you anything? You and I are so over, and you've done some kind of thing I don't even want to think about. None of this has anything to do with me."

"Actually, it does. You picked an odd group of friends for someone who didn't want to be involved with this." Kevin shifted from one foot to the other. "Besides, this is no big deal. I just want to know what's going on. I haven't done anything."

"Why don't you just talk to all of us, then?"

"Taylor has never liked me, and she never knew what a big part of the research I actually conducted. I could never reason with her. You guys have become friends, right? So you can help me out here."

Diane didn't want to ask how. "What about your cousin?"

"I thought you said cousin. What are you talking about?"

"I'm talking about your cousin Patricia and Taylor's baby."

Kevin was partially prepared for this. He knew something was up when he got the messages from Patricia. "What about my cousin Patricia? She has always been a bit nuts. What's she got to do with anything?"

"You're sick. Do you actually think you can deny this? These are people, people you should care about. You can't..." Kevin took a step closer to Diane. "You...can't possibly think I'm going to keep your presence here a secret."

He took one more step and grabbed Diane's arm. "I'm not here, right? You're not going to say anything to anyone." Kevin's cheeks were red, and he was leaning toward her, face first. Diane had seen this posture before. "I'm not walking away from this; it's mine. Why would I walk away?" Then, abruptly, he dropped her arm and left.

She couldn't move. Past, present, and future were holding her in place. She had a sense of the now that doesn't exist; she wasn't anywhere. Kevin had brought so many things with him. He'd treated her like he always had. Didn't he know she'd changed? He couldn't depend on her fear anymore. He wasn't going to control her. Yet in ten minutes he'd resurrected her old self. She hadn't changed; how she felt about herself still depended on the people she was with.

Diane moved out onto the balcony and slid down the wall until she was sitting on the cement. She could feel how cool and rough it was. Kevin was her nemesis; he wanted from her everything she hated about herself. As Diane studied her toes, the waves filled the air with sound. *But there is no wave without the shore, so everything changes. Yeah but it's still caustic salt water. God, listen to me—what an idiot.*

CHAPTER 35

Ruins

K evin couldn't think of anything to do but leave. He was losing his temper, and that wasn't going to do him any good. He felt no regret over the things he'd done, only the fear of being caught. He wanted those discs. *Now that goddamn baby's going to get in the way.* How was he going to explain that? How could he have ended up with the baby without being at the fire, and why would he have taken it to his cousin?

Kevin sat down on the bed in the small room he'd rented. It was over one of the many convenience stores on the edge of the downtown area. He'd been pacing since he got back. This was getting more complicated.

Wasn't I Tennyson's only friend at school? Everybody knew that. So maybe Tennyson had asked me to take the baby so he could have some time alone to think. Kevin had sensed some sort of rift between Tennyson and Taylor the night of the fire. *This is good. Who's going to say he didn't ask me to baby-sit? Who's to say he didn't tell me that Taylor was abusing the baby, that he was afraid for Rebecca? Then…then he died in the fire, and I didn't want to take the baby back to a bad mother. This could even make me look good. So, I took the baby to my lonely cousin, who I knew would take care of it. Oh, yeah, this is good. Those guys lived in the boonies, and if Tennyson stayed true to form, they probably kept to themselves. Maybe I only have to tell Taylor my version of the story and she'll give me the discs just to shut me up.* What did he care as long as he got the discs? He wasn't going to wait much longer. They were his. He started the research. He could get Diane to help him; he knew how to manage her.

Diane was sitting at a table by the beach, having coffee with Ruby. She hadn't mentioned anything about Kevin. She wanted to take yesterday's events and insert them farther back in her history, where she felt they belonged. She wanted to keep moving forward. Things were feeling possible. He reminded her of the shame she'd suffered as she confessed her part in his stupid, conniving behavior.

"I think I need more sunscreen today. I'm just going to run upstairs; do you need anything?" asked Ruby.

"No, I might have a bite to eat."

"Okay, order me some fruit, would you? I'll be right back." Ruby went upstairs, and Diane started to look at the menu. Earlier, Diane had noticed a Mexican boy hanging out on the beach. He was walking aimlessly in a small area and then settled on the sand near a palm tree. He appeared to be waiting for someone. Diane had made a mental note to check on him later; he seemed so young. As soon as Ruby left, he started walking toward her table. *He must be selling something*, she assumed.

"No, *gracias*," she said. He was holding something toward her, an envelope. He dropped it on the table and was gone before she looked back up. Diane knew what this was; she knew that Kevin wasn't going to conveniently disappear. Looking around her, she opened the envelope. He was still going to single her out. She was weak, and he was going to use her.

When the waiter returned, she ordered "*dos frutas y dos cafés*" and waited for Ruby to come back. As they ate their breakfast, they made plans for the day.

Ruby put the bread from the table in her bag. She was sure she would encounter Boo on the beach. "Who was with José yesterday?" Diane asked.

"Shane took him out for pizza. I think José is enjoying all the meals out, and he says it's improving his English. Still no sign of this guy yet, though."

Diane had wondered whether the guy might've been Kevin but decided his surprise at hearing his cousin mentioned was genuine.

"I'm taking him for drinks tonight, and I think Taylor wants to come. I want to go into town this morning. Do you need me to get you anything?" Diane started to gather her things.

"Can you pick up some mangos? That little store by the cemetery has good fruit. I want to do some reading, so I think I'll hit the beach."

"Well, maybe I'll join you later." Diane picked up her beach bag and walked into town. Everything was within walking distance, and she wanted time to gather her strength before meeting Kevin. The note had told her to come to his apartment and given her directions.

"Welcome to my home away from home. Not as nice as your place but a little more private." Diane moved inside and sat on the only chair in the room. He would have to sit on the bed.

"Look," she had a whole speech planned, "I'm not interested in any more conspiracies; this has nothing to do with me."

"I just thought you might want to do your newfound friend a favor."

"Kevin," Diane put up her hand, "I'm not in on anything with you."

"You're right; this is more like a 'saving-face' kind of thing."

"Look, just tell me what you want, and then I've got to go."

"You used to like time with me."

"Come on, Kevin; let's not confuse things. You know we're over, and we both know you want something from me, and it isn't a relationship. I don't think it ever was." Diane regretted the last comment instantly. She didn't want to discuss anything about their times together.

"Okay, I'll tell you a story, and then you can tell your friend Taylor or not. I've even written it down for you. The bottom line is that I want those discs."

CHAPTER 36

New Lies

"This is so bad." Taylor had that fogged-over look again. Ruby had considered not telling her but knew better this time.

"It's the stupidest thing I've ever heard; no one will listen to him. Everyone knows what kind of person you are. People in Nederland will remember you."

Taylor walked over to the window. "You know we kept pretty much to ourselves. The only one I hung out with was you, and Tennyson hardly left the property. He was working on the cabin and trying to resolve his ambivalence about what to do with his research. He said he'd figured it out, but I knew he hadn't. That was one of the reasons we'd moved up there, to give Tennyson time. But the decision wasn't any easier with time. It plagued him night and day. It was affecting everything, even our marriage. That's why he was alone that weekend." Taylor closed her eyes. "I just had to get away from it all for a few days."

"Why don't you just give him the discs, and he'll go away?" Diane was feeling as though she had somehow caused all this.

"I just couldn't. It's exactly what Tennyson didn't want to happen. You have to realize this fuel could change the balance of things forever. If oil companies or oil countries even knew the possibility of it existed, it could be dangerous. I've thought about destroying it, but that doesn't work either; it's just too big."

"Do these discs have Kevin's name on them anywhere?" Ruby asked.

"I don't know. I know Tennyson started the research with Kevin but quickly left him behind. You've no idea. Tennyson was brilliant." The weight of those years was settling down onto Taylor's shoulders. Inheriting Tennyson's struggle was something she thought she'd avoided. It was the only good thing about the fire, or so she had presumed.

"Have you guys told Shane about this?"

Diane looked over at Ruby. "No, we wanted to talk to you first. Besides, he's in Cancún today. He went over to play golf with that guy I met at the old hotel. You know, the one from New York. We saw him after dinner last night."

"I think that guy has a crush on you, Ruby," said Diane.

"You think everyone has a crush on me. It's got to be some way of avoiding your own contact with men." Diane made a face but said nothing. "Diane, weren't you and Taylor going to take José for drinks tonight?" Diane nodded. "Well, why don't we all meet for dinner afterward? We can talk about all this then. I mean, really, if you think about it, we have lots of questions for Kevin, and since we know this is bullshit, we can't let him go anywhere with it."

Ruby waited for Shane in his condo. She wanted to explain things to him before they all went out. He came in around 5:00 P.M. He'd taken the four-thirty ferry with Roger, then came straight back to the condos. "Hey, Shane," she said the minute he entered the room. She didn't want to startle him.

"This is a nice surprise. What's up?" Shane removed his hat and sat in the chair across from Ruby.

"I wanted to tell you what's going on with Taylor. That scumbag Kevin is in town and is making up some stupid story about child abuse to cover his own ass."

"Wait a minute; I need to catch up. Patricia's cousin is here—the guy who brought Taylor's baby into Canada?"

"Right. And he cornered Diane and told her he took the baby away at Tennyson's request because Taylor was abusing her. Then, he added he's so big-hearted he will be glad to forget the whole thing if Taylor hands over all of Tennyson's scientific research. Remember those discs she got from the university? The whole thing is ridiculous. We need to turn it all back on him. He's the one with all the explaining to do."

"So what's happening now?" Shane had gone into the kitchen to wash his hands and get a beer. "Do you want some wine?"

"I'd love some. I can hardly stand to see Taylor go through one more thing."

"Everybody goes through what they go through. You can't protect Taylor from all of this. She's a strong woman, and you can't solve all her problems."

"Thanks, I feel so much better now. Really, Shane, I know all that. It's just that we're all here, and there has to be something we can do to keep this jackass from causing more trouble. He's got a lot to answer for." Ruby accepted a glass of wine from Shane. "I thought we'd all go out and talk about it after Diane and Taylor take José for drinks. José hasn't spotted this guy yet, and I wonder if he's left the island."

"Well, I played golf with your friend Roger today, and he wanted to join me or us for dinner. Should I tell him another time?"

"He's not my friend. I just met him one day on the beach, and tonight probably wouldn't be a good time."

"He sure had a lot of questions about you. I think it's a crush."

"Oh, my god, you sound like Diane. She thinks everyone has a crush on me, including you."

"Ha, crushes are for kids. I don't have a crush; I just adore you; you're unavoidable."

"That's an odd choice of words, and don't you even try to get cutesy with me. I'm way too focused."

"I know. I often wonder why."

"Quit it. Are we going to get together tonight or not? And can you un-invite your friend?"

"Okay, let's get together and, yes, I'll un-invite my friend if I see him. Other than that, I don't know how to get a hold of him." Ruby got up to leave. "Are you going to wear that great blue dress again?"

"You know, you're getting far too familiar." Ruby was not looking at Shane.

"Well, I hope so. We've known each other for a while now. That's what usually happens. You look great in that dress."

"Ha, then I'll wear something else." Ruby was smiling as she left the condo. It had been a long time since someone had asked her to wear something special or even noticed what she was wearing.

Diane and Taylor joined Ruby and Shane at the Sunset Grill, the restaurant in front of the condos. "Anything new?" asked Shane.

"Well, we're not sure," said Taylor. She was desperately trying to spend more time outside her head. She'd been letting too many conversations go on around her. "José thought he saw the guy, but it was very brief, and when he tried to show us, whoever it was had gone. It's the closest thing we've had."

"Was he sure?" asked Ruby.

"He actually seemed pretty sure. He was visibly frustrated when the guy disappeared so fast." Diane turned to Taylor. "Didn't he seem upset to you when he left?"

"I think he's been looking for so many days now that to get a little glimpse and then end up with nothing would drive me nuts, too. I really want to know who was watching Patricia and Reb…Emma."

"This island is so small. I'm sure if he's still here, we'll find him eventually." Shane looked at his companions and puffed up his chest. "So what do my girls want for dinner tonight?"

"Huh!" came from three different directions. They were all feeling very comfortable together despite the complications.

Families come in many forms, thought Diane as she looked at her friends.

"Hey, I've been looking for you." Roger was looking at Shane. "My new golf buddy," he said, addressing everyone else at the table.

Shane stood up, "How're you doing? I was hoping you'd find us here; otherwise, I didn't know how to get hold of you." Shane moved toward Roger. "Everyone here has met Roger, right?"

"How are you?" asked Diane with a "know-it-all" look toward Ruby.

"I'm great. We're in paradise, right?" Roger asked this as Shane guided him away from the table.

"Just a minute—we'll be right back." Shane led Roger toward the bar. "Listen, do you mind joining us a little later? We've got some stuff we have to talk about. I didn't know this was coming up…sorry."

"Hey, no problem; I'll just have some drinks here, if that isn't too close?" Shane wasn't sure how this was meant but nodded as he went back to the table.

"He's just going to have some drinks at the bar," Shane said as he sat down. "He really is a nice guy."

"I'm sure he's great. I just don't want to have dinner with him to-night," said Ruby. The waiter returned with their drinks and left menus. "Let's have a toast." Ruby raised her glass and waited for the rest to join her. "To really great friends." They all touched their glasses and drank. "I really wanted to toast Taylor and Rebecca but decided it's too monumen-tal for a dinner toast. Besides, we need to get something resolved about this phantom, and now we've got Kevin to deal with, too."

Taylor could feel herself sliding inward but fought it. She reminded herself that these were conversations she needed and wanted to be a part of. It was so alluring to fog over, go numb, and let Ruby run interference. "I've been thinking about Kevin," she said. "He's always been very clever. If we try to make him answer for his actions, he'll pull out all of this gar-bage. So, no matter what, this will end up in court somewhere. If not with charges against him, maybe charges against me, or some custody issues would come up, and the whole thing would roll over my life and Patricia's and Rebecca's. Something none of us wants." Taylor was interrupted by the waiter, so they all ordered dinner and then waited for her to go on.

"If I give him Tennyson's research and he goes away, it won't help either because the work is so monumental that it will bring attention to Tennyson and anyone around him. I can just see the fire and all kinds of details being dredged up. So we've got a problem. I don't know what this other phantom guy has to do with this, but he couldn't possibly be as dangerous as Kevin."

"I'm sure you're right about that," Shane said, "but I think we should keep looking, for at least a few more days. As far as Kevin is concerned, he's definitely a menace. Do you have the letter with you?"

"No, it's in my room. He wrote out all of his stupid accusations—I'm sure to make his point very clear. I thought I should keep it. It's proof that he tried to bribe me. I noticed, though, that it was written in a way that made his story sound true instead of just threatening me with it. If I use it against him, it won't give anything away, about wanting the discs, I mean—clever boy."

They spent the evening together, Roger joining them for drinks after dinner as they listened to a live band playing on the beach.

Shane walked the women to their condo, made a mock bow, and went to his own. He was just putting the key in the door when Diane came running down the hall. "Shane, come quick—you won't believe this." They rushed back to the other condo together. The door was open, and they went in. The place was torn apart, every drawer open, cushions were pulled off the couch, and mattresses had been pulled off the beds. Their suitcases were all open, and their clothes were strewn everywhere.

"We'd better go down and call the police," Ruby said. Shane moved closer to her and asked if anything was missing. "We haven't looked."

"Well, I'm not sure we shouldn't check. Just in case this has anything to do with our business here, we don't want to be explaining this to anyone." The women started slowly, picking at their things as if they had been contaminated, but then gradually began a real search. They started to pile things on their reassembled beds. Shane straightened up the living room and pushed in all the kitchen drawers. Half an hour later, no one was missing anything. All money and passports were in place, and any jewelry had been overlooked. They had nothing else of value.

"Just a minute," said Taylor as she went into the bathroom. Shortly, she returned to the living room, holding her toilet kit. "It's gone."

"What's gone?"

"The letter. I hid it in my toilet kit. It has a side pocket. I just wanted to put it somewhere safe. It was such a scary thing to read."

"Are you sure you put it there? Maybe you just meant to and then came downstairs before you did."

"No, I put it there. It wasn't something I was going to leave lying around."

"Okay," said Ruby, "let's sit down. We obviously aren't going to call the police. Why or who would take the letter? Kevin wouldn't need it back. If he didn't want anything in writing, then he could've just talked to you." Shane and Taylor sat back and took a deep breath.

Diane got up and started to walk around the room. "It has to be the same guy who's been after Patricia, someone we don't know and who has an interest in all of this. There's no other explanation."

"If he was trying to cover things up, he'd have taken something else. So he can't be too worried about us knowing what he's after."

CHAPTER 37

Together

Patricia was packing the last of her things. She was sorry to leave their little house but looking forward to feeling more secure, at least surrounded by people she knew. The added expense didn't seem that important anymore. So much had happened.

Taylor had come over earlier to explain about the recent break-in. The part about Kevin had been upsetting. It made her beginnings with Emma seem more sinister. Plus, she had so little family; it was sad to have him behave so poorly.

Taylor had been out to visit them a few times, and Patricia had enjoyed her company. It was nice to share concern for Emma with someone. Taylor maintained a distance that was comfortable and continued to respect Patricia's status as mother. Could it be possible that her worst nightmare could be so...livable? They had exchanged stories with as many details as they could remember but continued to avoid the question of Kevin. What *was* his part? They had silently agreed that that piece would have to come later.

Patricia glanced at her watch. Check-in time at the condos was 2:00 P.M., and she wanted to arrive then, to give Emma time to become acclimated. Being part of a group was a whole new experience for Patricia. So far, she had enjoyed the company...in small doses.

When they arrived at the condos, everyone was waiting for them around the pool. Emma immediately wanted to go for a swim. "Not right now, honey. We have to unpack and then take the golf cart back."

"That's all right; we can watch her if you like," offered Diane.

Patricia didn't know why she agreed to let Emma swim with them. As she unpacked, it all felt very squirmy or itchy or just too different. They usually did everything together. She was not used to relinquishing control. She wanted to abandon the drawers and rush down to the pool but thought that would look silly. How much was going to change? The prospect made her tired, so she lay on her bed, *just for a minute*.

Soon, someone was shaking her awake, "Mom, mom, we've been swimming this whole time. Taylor's been teaching me to jump off the side of the pool. Then we...then we put our heads under water and held our breath, and...and Shane, he would throw me up in the..."

"I can't do this," Patricia blurted out before she could stop herself. Fear had opened her mouth and formed the words. Emma looked confused, and Taylor, who was standing behind her, looked hurt.

"I'll let you talk to your mother now, Emma," and she was gone.

"What's the matter, mommy? I just wanted to tell you about what we'd been doing; it was so fun."

"I know, Emma; I'm sorry. I've just got a headache, and I think I'll sleep a little more. Do you want to go in your room and see where I put everything? Then, you can look around or read for a while. What do you think?"

"Okay, you sleep, mom, and I will take care of myself." Emma was feeling very old with all of her new grown-up friends.

"Don't leave the condo, okay?"

"Okay." Emma tiptoed out of the room and closed the door with an exaggerated effort to be quiet.

Patricia knew this wasn't going to be easy, but she hadn't expected such immediate encroachments. Somehow, she'd convinced herself that things would arrive in an orderly fashion, in single file, and she'd expected to have an appropriate reaction to each new experience.

She'd also refused to consider how important Taylor was now. She'd been too involved in her own side of the story. As much as she felt the need, this was not all about her. Patricia could see that Emma was stepping out, which she'd done in degrees through the years. Yet this time there were other people involved, people personally interested in Emma's life.

There was more: The truth was impossible to ignore. Taylor was trying harder than she was. Patricia's image of herself was being challenged.

Her self-sufficiency wanted to climb into bed and draw the curtains. Her practicality wanted to grab Emma and run deeper into Latin America. This serious and straightforward farm girl wanted to stomp her feet and scream and run in circles, tearing her hair out. *It isn't fair; it isn't fair.*

She knocked on the door. "Just a minute," she heard. Shortly after, a puffy-eyed Taylor was standing in front of her.

"Can I come in?" Taylor nodded and backed away to make room. "I've come to apologize; do you have time to talk?"

"I have lots of time." They sat opposite each other in the little living room, letting themselves sink into their chairs and avoiding each other's eyes.

"I have to be blunt if you don't mind."

"Please."

"I realized this afternoon that I haven't been trying very hard, and I'm sorry for that. I think I was hoping you would go away, but I know that isn't possible." Patricia paused as if her suggestion was something to consider. "I've been trying not to like you; you've represented the worst that could happen...for a long time."

"I can imagine." Taylor didn't want to talk; she just wanted to hear things.

"I've been a good mother to Emma. I've tried to give her everything I never had and more. Now, what I've been thinking I should say is that this isn't about us. It's only 'whatever is good for Emma.' But that isn't true; this *is* about us. In the short time we've had together, which I realize has been strained, it seems to me that we are somewhat alike. We've no choice now. If I took Emma and ran and she found out, she would never forgive me. And if you left, she would never forgive you for abandoning her. So, if we want to do what is good for Emma, we're stuck with each other. I don't mean to sound flip or rude. I just feel that we'll never get through this if we aren't as clear as possible."

Taylor was grateful for what was being said.

"I'm very grateful to you for respecting my position as mother. I'm sure it must be very hard for you." Patricia stopped and waited for Taylor's reply.

"I'm so glad you've come over. This is all so...odd," said Taylor. "There are just so many things to consider."

"That's it, isn't it? There's just so much to think about. We have to figure out her birth records, how to tell her, how we're all going to live…and where. There's so much to talk about, past stuff and future stuff. I think maybe it's time we worked on some of this before all my anxieties wrap me up for good."

Patricia looked up at Taylor. "I had a funny thought about this the other day, wondering if there was a guide for such a thing. Then it occurred to me that maybe we should get some professional help, somebody to keep us focused in the right direction. You'll have to be patient with me. I'm not used to a lot of people, and I certainly have no reference for behavior in this situation. I'm sure I'll mess up a lot, and I'm sorry if it hurts you."

Without planning it, Patricia simply ran out of words. Again, the women found themselves sitting quietly together. Taylor felt like it was her turn to say something but couldn't think of anything to say. Her mind was crowded with so many considerations that nothing was being processed. Patricia seemed to understand, and the silence continued.

"I know we can work all these things out," Taylor said after a few minutes. "But you know I'm worried about this thing with Kevin and your break-ins. It's hard to work on the future until we can figure out what's going on here. I mean, with all these robberies and people asking questions, I've this feeling there is more. Maybe I'm out of whack. As you said, we've no guide for all of this, but something else is up."

Taylor took a deep breath. "If we agree that we're in this together and at least try to work through the emotions we can't avoid and forgive each other and understand we're both trying, then I know we will be fine. As you say, we have no choice. Actually, if we're talking about the part of this that is just you and me, it can only get easier. I mean, finding each other and adjusting to the truth was tough enough. Right?" Taylor tilted her head and raised her shoulders in a gesture of inevitability, trying to give both of them permission. "My friends are great, and they're here to help." She sat back in her chair. They had done enough for one day.

Patricia got up to leave. They were both uncertain about a hug. It would have felt good, but they couldn't give in that far, yet.

CHAPTER 38

A Plan

July was getting hot on Isla Mujeres. Ruby had been on the island for three weeks now and had yet to miss her home or her husband. She was enjoying the ocean view as Taylor drove Jeannie's golf cart. Boo was riding in the backseat. He was sitting up, proudly displaying his status as a dog with an owner. He'd had a bath and was wearing a new collar.

Jeannie had sent Taylor to a lady on the island who took care of all the stray dogs. Ruby wanted to talk to her about Boo, to find out whether he had an owner and to see what she would need to do if she wanted to adopt him. She'd grown accustomed to having him next to her and now found herself looking for him if he wasn't.

They pulled off the road to admire the colors. On that side of the island, the road runs next to the shore, and the water stretches uninterrupted toward the sky. The water offered ten different shades of blue and green, depending on the ocean floor. The areas above sand were the lightest turquoise, and the shades of green varied over coral or sea grass or darkened with depth.

The east side of the island differs from the north. There are cliffs breaking the waves, with coarse, broken coral walls. There are also some beaches, but they are smaller and strewn with patches of rocks. This is the windward side, covered with fragments of shells and other sea-floor debris. They'd seen island women collecting things close to the water, and the shops were filled with an assortment of crafts made locally with these beach treasures. Mirrors, mobiles, boxes, and wall pieces were available everywhere. Jeannie had some examples in her store and told them that the ladies brought in different crafts according to the season. After hurricane season, there were more pieces of broken coral from the reefs that surround the island. With these they made mobiles and large wall hangings. Then, after the seas had been calmer for a few months, there were smaller shells, and the women would make boxes and mirrors.

They sat quietly and watched the water grow flatter until it finally rounded the globe and fell out of sight. "You know, Cuba is only one hundred miles from here," Ruby observed, "and there's no part of Mexico farther east than this."

As soon as they'd come to a stop, Boo jumped off his seat and ran directly into the surf. He dashed in and out of the water until he found some seaweed to roll in. "So much for his bath," Ruby said. They decided to walk south along the sand. Boo stayed just in front of them, darting from one scent to another.

"I've been thinking," Taylor started. "I'm going to talk to Kevin. We know what he wants, and when he gets it, he should leave us alone. Plus, there are questions we haven't asked, and he doesn't want us to ask." Ruby agreed: No one had discussed Kevin's part in the fire. Taylor continued, "You know, it was a long time ago, and I don't care anymore. It was probably an accident. Now, I just want to get on with my life."

"What about keeping Tennyson's work from him?"

"I've been thinking about that, too. We don't even know if we have all the research. All we know is that we got a package. After I talk to Kevin, I'm going to go to Boulder and have a look at that box, and then we can go from there."

"Do you want me to go with you?"

"No, but you do need to tell me where it is."

"I put it in a safe deposit box."

They ambled along the beach for a while, and then Taylor drove Ruby and Boo back to the condos. Afterward, she decided to walk along the town's main street, where colors and people oozed out of every doorway. Broomsticks propped between cinderblocks were strung with necklaces and bracelets. T-shirts and colorful blankets hung on every available wall. Pottery was stacked up in the most precarious ways, and people had to step around it to get into the stores. Every surface was painted with bright colors, and even if it had faded and chipped, the effect was appealing. The road ended at the town square, where the island is so narrow that, while sitting on the cement benches in the middle, Taylor could see the water on both sides.

She climbed the stairs at the edge of the square and sat on the sea wall to watch the ocean. It offered her relief by diminishing her life with its vast expanse. She'd been in a fish bowl, under observation as her world had been transformed. The pressure to perform and not reveal the ambiguous commotion in her head was consuming energy that she couldn't spare.

"Thinking about me, I hope."

"Pardon." Taylor turned around and saw Kevin for the first time in ten years. He hadn't changed, just seemed a little fuller everywhere. As Taylor looked up, the sun was behind him, and she had to shield her eyes. It was tempting to put both hands over her face and wait for him to go away, but not possible.

"We need to have a talk," he said.

"I know, but let's go some place where we can sit out of the sun and get something to drink." Taylor got up and started walking back to the main street. She wasn't about to be isolated with this lowlife. They settled in a small restaurant. This was a quiet time of the day, mid-afternoon and too hot to do anything. Inside, it was dark and cool, and overhead there was a ceiling fan earnestly trying to make a difference.

"You know what I…"

"Kevin, I don't even know where to start with you. Is it actually possible you have single-handedly ruined my life? Were you that resentful about Tennyson and me?" Taylor had thought this was going to be hard, but she felt very calm. She wanted to accuse him, and she wanted information. "Did you want him that badly?"

"You…you don't know anything about it—what did he tell you?"

"He told me enough, so don't mess with me. I know all about you, and you had already lost Tennyson by the time I came along. You know that's true. He'd gone way beyond any level that you could contribute to. So I didn't change him, and I didn't steal him. I'm not even going to ask you what happened at the cabin. I hope for your sake it was an accident. That's for you to live with. I just want my life. Patricia and I can work this out. We can deal with it, so just go away."

"Not a chance. I don't care about any of that old stuff. I just want that box you got from the university. That research is part mine, and I want it. How can you think it's okay to keep that information away from the rest of the world?"

"Don't you even try to pretend you care about anything other than getting rich or proving something to your daddy."

"You don't know me, and I don't care what you think of me. You always made it very clear you didn't want me around. Just give me the discs, and you'll never hear from me again. Otherwise, I'll have to stick to my story, and you and Patricia and Rebecca will be dragged through custody courts, and 'child abuser' will be your new name."

Taylor closed her eyes. She was getting too angry. "Tennyson didn't want you to have his research, and I could have you investigated for the fire."

"Investigate what? Everything is gone. There are no witnesses to anything, and my story explains it perfectly."

"How about the fact that you took my daughter?"

"Okay, let's go for it then. Let's see who suffers worse from bringing all this up. Go ahead."

Taylor was shocked by the challenge. "I need time to think about this," she said.

"No!" This came out of Kevin louder than he'd intended, but there was no one around to care. "You've had enough time; I want the research now."

"I'm going back to Boulder. I haven't even seen the box. I had it put away. I'm going to go home and get it, and I'll call you after that."

"I'll go back with you."

The thought of spending another minute with Kevin was repulsive. "You can go anywhere you want, but not with me. I'll call you; just give me a number, and then leave me alone."

CHAPTER 39

Boulder

Taylor had the number and a key to a safety deposit box in her purse. She was going to Ruby's house in Boulder, but first she was stopping at the bank to pick up this thing that had fragmented and demolished her life. She reached the bank before it closed and asked the taxi to wait.

When Taylor got to Ruby's, she sat on the back porch with a glass of wine. She sat there staring at the white box with Tennyson's name on it. So this was it. Just a box, but filled with something so potent it had first owned her husband and then, possibly, been the cause of his death. She watched it for a long time, giving it life. She reviewed its past, its power, and the place it held in her life. Its strength came from the flaws in the people involved: her husband's fears and indecision, Kevin's greed, and her lack of compassion. She deserved this. This was retribution for the patience she had run out of. She knew who Tennyson had been when she had married him. She'd thought she could bring him down to earth with love and devotion but had tired of the struggle. For Taylor, this box pulsated with accountability. It resurrected the guilt she had regulated over the years, only allowing it to seep in when she could not keep herself otherwise occupied. What if she'd been there that weekend? What if she hadn't run out of patience? What if she'd tried harder to understand Tennyson's struggles? What if she'd required less of him to be happy? These questions and a million more "what ifs" had added yet another ragged edge to the feelings she'd been struggling to come to terms with since the fire.

Then she came back to *It's just a box*. Right now, it belonged to her, and it was helpless without her. She knew she had to open it, and after a long while she did. There were two smaller boxes with dozens of discs. This, she expected. Each one was marked with a beginning and ending date. Taylor pulled them out and lined them up on the table in front of her. She knew which months had been critical in the discovery. Tennyson had been uncharacteristically animated during those months. It had been after that time that he had struggled.

She had to be sure that there were no more discs. The next morning, she walked across the same grassy area she had often covered with Tennyson. She'd avoided the university since his death, but this felt okay.

Oh, my god, she thought as she spotted George. He was sitting at a picnic table located on the same spot where he used to have his silent lunches with Tennyson.

"Do you remember me?" George turned in her direction. He looked exactly the same, maybe a few more lines and a bit heavier, but there he was.

"I wondered if I'd hear from you. I've already heard from the other fellow…but seeing you is a pleasure." Taylor sat on the bench across from him. "I'm guessing you got your package."

"I did. Thank you, George. I don't have many things of Tennyson's, so it was very kind of you."

"It was, you know. I didn't send out all that stuff, just to the ones I remembered—the guys who weren't too stuck up. But you know there wasn't nobody else like Tennyson." George looked a little uncomfortable. He wasn't used to saying nice things about anybody.

"George, is there any more?"

"More boxes?" Taylor nodded. "Nah, not where I was working. The big upstairs is adding onto the building, and I was told to clear out some storage rooms. They're all empty now."

"Could there be any more anywhere else?"

"Not in the storage rooms, but maybe somewhere in the offices or something. I wouldn't know about that." Never one for small talk, George started to gather the remnants of his sack lunch. Taylor got the hint.

"Thanks. I guess I'll check there. Good to see you, George."

"Yeah."

Taylor located the offices but found no further information. She decided that the final discs had to have been either in the cabin or in

198 |

Tennyson's head. So now what? She ran through the consequences of Kevin's challenge, trying to figure which of them would suffer more damage. On one hand, she was greatly relieved. She no longer had the responsibility of deciding what do with Tennyson's work. But now she needed to find a way to make it safe for her new family.

CHAPTER 40

Catch and Release

"Taylor just called." Ruby was sitting in Shane's condo. They were enjoying some coffee while he cooked breakfast.

"What did she find?" Shane asked.

"The last disc or discs are missing. Taylor thinks they either burned up in the fire or Tennyson had the last part of his research in his head, which, sadly, means the same thing." Ruby was sitting at the counter that divided the kitchen from the living room. "She's afraid Kevin won't believe her and that she'll never get rid of him."

"She must be a little relieved, don't you think?" asked Shane.

"Yeah, she said so. Now, at least, she doesn't have to decide what to do with it. She's flying back in the next day or two."

"Good. Maybe you can pay some attention to me, for a change."

"Why would I do that?"

"Because we're going fishing; I've chartered a boat. No one else is in need of a savior today, so you have to save me from fishing alone."

"Is it a big boat? I get seasick, you know."

"It's a big boat, and we have the whole thing to ourselves except for the captain and crew. I've made breakfast, and I have Dramamine."

After seeing Ruby and Shane off, Diane went to Jeannie's apartment. She and Jeannie were going to take José for lunch in a last-ditch effort to spot the man who had been so interested in Patricia.

"Where are we meeting him?" Jeannie yelled from the bathroom as she dressed.

"It's a little restaurant called Tres Amigos. Shane set it up."

"Great, I love that place, and I'm starved. They serve nice big portions, perfect for a growing girl like myself." Jeannie burst into the room like a leaping rainbow, adorned with bright birds and flowers from shoulders to the floor.

"Where do you get those wonderful things?" Diane asked.

"I actually make them—they're easy. It's just like sewing two tablecloths together. I'm trying to make up in color for what I lack in shape."

"Well, they're great.... Ready?" The two walked through town toward the restaurant. "You know, I just love it here, just the pace of things is so peaceful. I could use some time in a place like this."

"Well, it's not that hard to live here. You just have to decide that it's what you want. Isla has always fit me to a T. Here's the restaurant. Why don't you pick a table? I just need to talk to the owner for a minute." Diane found a table for four in the front by the street, so they could see passersby. She ordered them both bottled water and was starting to read the menu when she heard her name.

"Eating alone?" asked Kevin. Looking up, she wondered how she could've ever been happy to see him. He looked tired and pale and always caused trouble.

"I'm eating with a friend."

"Can I join you?"

"No!" Diane replied. He pulled out a chair and sat down.

"Is Taylor back yet?"

"No, she's still in Boulder, and we haven't heard from her." Diane was wishing Jeannie would get back. "You should leave her alone; she's had a rough enough time."

"I intend to, as soon as she gives me those discs. Then, she never has to see me again." José was walking toward the table, and Jeannie arrived at the same time. They all sat down and made introductions. Diane couldn't get Kevin to leave without making a scene, so he ordered lunch with the rest of them. Before their food came, Roger showed up, and they moved to a larger table to accommodate everyone. Luckily, Jeannie chatted away through the whole meal. No one else had much to say.

"I think we should get back to your store and start on the inventory, don't you?" Diane had jumped up, still chewing her last bite, and she hoped

Jeannie would take the hint. Diane couldn't take another minute next to Kevin.

"Oh, the inventory—right, I guess I've been trying to avoid it. José, *puedes ayudarnos?*" Jeannie wasn't about to leave José there. "Thanks for the lunch, Kevin." The three of them were down the street before the two men could say a word. Jeannie was grinning blissfully, and Diane was holding her hand over a huge smile. José was the only one who wasn't amused. He hadn't said a word during lunch. Jeannie thought it was the language barrier, but looking at him now, she knew there was something more. They walked back to her shop and up the stairs to her apartment. José hesitated at the door, but Jeannie practically dragged him inside. "*Què pasò*, José?"

"Roger *es el hombre.*"

"Roger? *El hombre que comio con nosotros hoy?*"

"*Si, ha habido mucho tiempo ahora, pero, creo que si. Nesacita regresar a mi restaurante, gracias, hasta luego.*" He was gone.

"Do you think he could be wrong?" asked Diane. "He didn't seem completely sure."

"I don't think José would've said anything if he wasn't sure. I mean, this is the first time he's identified anyone," Jeannie noted.

"Why would Roger care? I guess we really don't know that much about him. Let's ask Shane. He played golf with him the other day. He should know something about him."

Ruby was waiting to feel sick, but so far she felt fine. It was glorious to be out on the water. The sun was hot and bright, and the breeze stroked her with just enough cool air to make the ride soothing and comfortable. When they lost sight of land, she was struck by the vast expanse of the ocean and felt like a small speck sandwiched between the broad, turquoise-blue sky and the deep blue sea. She was surprised to find the boat clean and new and a crisp white. Inside, the cabin was a small kitchen with a dining booth. Then, down a few steps toward the bow, were a bathroom and two tiny bedrooms. The whole thing was comfortable, not at all what she'd expected. On the open deck in the rear of the boat were two swivel chairs bolted to the floor. They had all the hardware for fishing. Shane had caught one sailfish already. It'd taken him fifteen minutes to get it next to the boat, and then the captain had cut it loose. Shane told her that the next fish was hers, so they relaxed in their chairs and waited.

"I see one near the line," yelled the man steering the boat. He was on the top deck, where the view was better. The rods were attached to the back gunwale, ready to go if there was a strike, and then someone would bring the fish in. They both turned to the back of the boat and could see the fish, a blue-green streak in the waves, sliding back and forth two feet under the surface. Then there were two of them, two streaks of color moving at the same speed as the boat.

"Do we keep them if they're bigger?" asked Ruby.

"Nope, they're all catch and release, so you needn't worry." Shane was looking at her with an enormous grin. "It's your turn." Ruby had seen *Jaws*; she sat back in her chair and strapped herself in.

"He's on," the man yelled from the top of the boat. The captain unhooked the rod from the gunwale and placed the bottom of it in a metal cup between her legs. Ruby took it from him and steadied herself, then started to reel the fish in. She leaned forward as she cranked the handle to take up the slack in the line; then, she leaned back and pulled the fish toward the boat, just as she had seen Shane do. Back and forth, sometimes the fish put up resistance, and sometimes he helped her out. When it was about thirty feet from the boat, it burst out of a wave, shaking its head, trying to dislodge the hook. It took her ten minutes to get the fish next to the boat. It was a four-foot-long splendid rocket of shimmering color. She was glad to see it cut loose. As the hours passed, she became totally absorbed. Shane was a genius.

They arrived back at the condos, tired and refreshed, just in time to get the latest update from Diane. She was in the restaurant and waved them in. "You're just not going to believe this," she told them.

"Can we go up and wash the fish off, or do we have to hear this right away?"

"Okay, but I'm only giving you twenty minutes. I've been waiting to talk to you all afternoon." Diane had another margarita as she waited. She hadn't been able to make any sense out of José's discovery and was looking forward to asking Shane about Roger.

Twenty minutes later, she looked up and saw Ruby coming toward the restaurant; at the same moment, she felt a hand on her shoulder.

"Can I join you, or have you had enough of me for one day?"

"Um…yes, sorry. Yes, please sit." As Roger made himself comfortable, Diane stared at Ruby, hoping that her wide-eyed look would let her know something was askew. But Ruby only glanced at her as she sat down and said hello to Roger.

"We're pooped. Shane and I went fishing today, and being out on the water all day has just worn me out. Plus, I have to admit my arms are sore from reeling in a huge fish."

"You caught a fish?" asked Diane. She was desperate to tell Ruby about Roger. He looked different to her now, his pleasant face taking on a more sinister slant, his casual appearance seeming more planned. *Go away*, she thought.

"I actually caught two, but one was quite small, and I'm happy to say we let them all go. What an experience." Diane tried to give Shane the same wide-eyed look as he approached, but he was looking at Ruby. "You have to tell them about the boat, Shane," Ruby said.

"Oh, the boat was beautiful, big, totally equipped, and obviously well cared for. What a blast."

"Maybe we should all go one day. It's been a long time since I went fishing," Roger suggested.

"Where was that? Where you went fishing, I mean?" Diane asked.

"Just other vacations I've taken in Mexico."

"Did you say you were from New York?" Diane couldn't stand it—who was this guy?

"Yup, born and raised. Always thought I would get out, but I never did."

"What do you do there?"

"Research."

"I love research," Ruby said. "I write freelance, and that's the part I enjoy the most. It's incredible what you can find out." Ruby was trying to stop Diane before she had Roger fill out a personal information sheet.

"So, what kind of research do you do?" Diane persisted. She was now on her third margarita and leaning toward Roger with a scrutinizing look on her face.

"Depends what I'm hired for. I work freelance, too." The waiter arrived to take their orders, and the distraction gave Diane an opportunity to squeeze Ruby's leg under the table. Ruby didn't seem to notice.

"Where's your friend Taylor tonight?" Roger asked after the waiter left.

Ruby was about to answer when Diane just started to speak louder. "She just went on a sight-seeing excursion; none of us really felt like going, actually—that reminds me, I forgot to take my medicine today. I'll be right back."

Ruby was shocked as Diane hurried sloppily toward the condos, and then she smiled at the men. "She's having a bit of a rough time these days" was all she could think to say. After a few minutes had passed, Ruby excused herself to investigate. Something had to be going on. Diane wasn't in their condo, so she checked the ladies room. It was obvious to Ruby that Diane had been enjoying her margaritas. Empty-handed, she returned to the restaurant. Possibly Diane had gone on a short walk to clear her head and would return shortly.

CHAPTER 41

Reflections

Diane never did come back for dinner. After eating, Roger left quickly, so Ruby and Shane decided to take a walk on the beach. It was a luscious night. The stars were speckled upon the navy sky, and the plush sand felt velvety under their bare feet. The summer's heat had warmed the ocean so well that there was no temperature shock to it as it tumbled gently up the beach and over their toes. Ruby knew something was going on with Shane; she'd felt the difference for a week now. Maybe it'd been there longer, but she hadn't been paying enough attention to notice.

Now that Taylor would be spending time with Patricia and Emily, Ruby was feeling some space, enough to make room for her own life. *Ugh*, she thought, *I've moved through each moment and woken up every day, but I still don't know how I got here.*

"Does this happen to everyone?" she asked Shane, as if they were already having a conversation.

"What?"

"Well, with all that's going on, I've been thinking more about all the levels of my life. It feels as though we're all in a bit of a transition here, suspended, until we go home. Without my normal routines to pull me through the day, I've been pestered by repulsively profound reflections." She made a face. "They go all the way back, then forward and back again. I mean, get over it."

"Oh, come on; let it go. Tell me what's roaming around in that head of yours," Shane urged.

"Okay." Ruby was glad he had asked. "Well, along with the confusion of growing up, I remember there being a sense of who you are. Your family defines you, your school, your grades, sports, and hobbies, whatever. There goes Joan—her dad's the town doctor, and she gets all A's in school, plays basketball, has one best friend, and is kind of shy. You know what I mean?" Shane stayed quiet. "I mean, I was defined by my mother, at least to myself. What she was, I wasn't. Whatever she wanted, I didn't want. I was a daughter loved by my father. I was a pain in the ass to my brothers and considered radical by them all. I enjoyed writing, spent a lot of time by myself, but wasn't shy. I was well-liked, higher than average intelligence, and not interested in sports. There it is—me. Then, I marry. That's where things start to get cloudy. I mean, does my husband define me or, I should say, the life we've created? I'm not saying all my self-evaluations come from some outside source. I just mean that when we create a world for ourselves, we're the ones at the helm. Right? So if I've been the architect of my married life, then I hate the definition that comes with it. It's cold, distant, practical, and compromised—a woman who does too many things that no longer interest her. In this part of my life I don't have myself clearly pegged. Yuck. How did the first me turn into the second? I like the first me; she was bold and bright, and my family's reflection fit. How did I get here, and what've I done with my life? Ha, now there's an unusual question."

"That question may be a cliché, but it doesn't mean that asking it is a bad thing. At least you're looking. Finally, your distractions are diminishing." Shane moved closer and put his arm around Ruby. "So what *about* that husband?"

"Don't you flirt with me. I'm having a moment here."

"Yeah, but you're sharing it with me; therefore, I get to participate." He was looking down at Ruby with that clean-cut, boy-next-door smile. Ruby stood on her toes and gave him a kiss. She couldn't resist. It was on the lips but delivered as a genial gesture. He leaned into her and tried to prolong her touch, but she backed off.

"I just had to do that. You can't listen to me, hear all my foibles, and then smile at me like that. It's just too kind."

"Oh, great, I'm back to the kindly big brother again. Been there, done that."

"I know what you want. I know we could have something together, but I have this unavoidable urge to be honest with you. It's just so effortless. I don't want to mess with it. What if it doesn't work out between us? I'd have to talk to you about our relationship, and then you wouldn't smile at me like that." Ruby took a deep breath. "Who would listen to me objectively? What if you didn't like me? Then I'd never see that incredible smile again, not the way I saw it tonight."

"Do you always get to the end of things before they start? Can't we try this and see how it turns out?"

"Not now. I need you the way you are. There is…." Boo was growling. He was facing the palm trees near by. "Did you hear something?"

"Nope, maybe he's growling at me for getting too close. What are you going to do with that dog anyway? He's become your shadow."

"I know. I even look for him now when he isn't around." Boo growled again, and this time they both heard something. "It could be anything. Why don't we head back and see if Diane has appeared, so she can tell us why she was so strange."

"Okay, but I just have one question for you, and I mean it seriously. Ready?"

Ruby nodded.

"If you don't like the way you see yourself in your husband's eyes, maybe you should ask yourself something. Why are you still married to him?" There was no reply.

Diane was still not in the condo. No note, nothing. "Well, she's a grown woman. It's not like she has to ask permission to go out," Ruby proposed.

"Do you want me to go look for her?" Shane asked.

"No, I'm sure she's all right. I think I'll just go to bed. Thanks so much for listening to me. I'll see you in the morning." Ruby had Shane out the door before he could say a word. She needed sleep.

CHAPTER 42

Passports

Taylor arrived the next day. The first thing she wanted to do was to see Patricia and Emma. She had missed them both. Getting to know Patricia had become as important as getting to know her daughter, and she liked Patricia already.

The five of them spent the next day together as tourists, enjoying the space that the island offered. That morning Ruby had found a note on her door. It was from Diane, telling them that she'd run into an old friend and they'd gone to Tulum, a Mayan ruin on the mainland, for a few days. She apologized for the abrupt departure, explaining that this was a good bud and that she wanted to do some sightseeing while in Mexico. It seemed odd to Ruby and Taylor, but it reminded them once again that they really hadn't known her that long and she was capable of doing some strange things.

"I mean, she did go to Nicaragua to spy on you," Ruby remarked.

"I know, but she just seems so different from that person now," said Taylor.

Taylor had spent a few hours with Patricia discussing their future. It was time to go home, and they needed papers for Emma. Patricia had bluffed their way into the country with every paper she could find that had Emma's name on it, but they were worried that US and Canadian customs were going to need something more substantial.

Some of Patricia's fear had subsided as she had gotten to know Taylor. Relief was rising from her like a mist; slowly, one morning at a time. Her life had been so full with Emma, except for the fear. She'd done her best to tuck it away, and yet it had gnawed its way back into her life daily. The uncertainty of Emma's origins never waned in significance. Only when she noticed the anxiety fading did she realize the degree of struggle she'd embraced for too many years.

Yet, something new had arrived with the relief—guilt. She had not felt guilty about many things in her life. Emma was her pleasure, and though she had tried to convince herself that Kevin had told her the truth, she'd always known that there was a mother out there. Whether she was good or bad, she had lost what Patricia had gained. Now that mother had a face. She was everything Patricia had hoped she wouldn't be. She wanted her to have fangs, to smoke and drink in lowlife bars, to kick small dogs as she slimed along dirty streets. Now that mother was Taylor, and Patricia would have to live with that. The burden of Taylor's loss now replaced Patricia's fear, filling that space with a new struggle.

The following day was a Wednesday. It was hot now and uncomfortable to be anywhere but in the water or an air-conditioned room. Patricia stepped outside, and the heat felt thick and heavy, groping her with sticky hands. Then it would settle over her like a heavy coat. This was the hottest time of the day, so they were going to spend it at the beach. She and Emma liked to lie on the sand at the water's edge and let the waves wash over them.

"Hey, you guys," Taylor called as she walked across the beach toward them. Emma saw her and started to smooth the sand beside her.

"Taylor, you have to come in," Emma pleaded, "the waves land on you and then pull the sand out from under your tummy. It feels so weird."

"I'm going to come in later, okay? I have to make a few phone calls first. Can I borrow your mom for a minute?" Patricia was already standing, and Emma quickly lost interest in them as the next wave tugged at the sand beneath her belly.

"I have an idea. I'm going to call my father. He's a lawyer in New York, and maybe he could arrange the papers to get Emma home."

Patricia was shocked. It had never occurred to her that there might be grandparents or aunts and uncles. A mother was as far as she had allowed herself to go.

"Emma has a grandfather?"

"Not really. I mean, he is her grandfather, but he never wanted to be. I haven't seen him since the fire. He left my mother when she was pregnant. She told me he never wanted children. I've rarely considered him as anything in my life, but, you know, if he can help us…"

"Does he even know that Emma is alive?"

"No, isn't that funny? I haven't even thought to call him. Who knows what he'll say."

As the phone began to ring, Taylor started to get nervous. She never knew what to say to this man who was her father.

"Mr. Mendel's office."

"Hi…yeah…can I talk to Mr. Mendel?"

"Who may I say is calling?"

"I'm…Taylor…Taylor Barrett…I'm Mr. Mendel's daughter." There was a long silence on the line. "Hello," said Taylor, "are you there?"

"Yes, yes, I'll see if he's available." Again, a long pause.

"Hello, who is this?" He sounded very stern.

"It's me…Taylor." Just hearing his voice made Taylor feel small. There was another pause, and she considered hanging up but changed her mind. "You know, your daughter…ha ha…remember me?" She meant it as a joke, but it came out more like a plea.

"Taylor…how are you? Are you okay?"

"Yes, actually, I'm better than okay. I've found Rebecca." Taylor didn't know what she expected, but "cold" should have been at the top of the list; still, she wasn't prepared.

"How did you do that?"

"It's…it's a long story. But can you believe it? She's actually alive."

"It's amazing," he said without inflection. "Where are you?"

"Well, that's a long story, too, but I'm in Mexico, and I need your help."

"My help? Help with what?"

Why did this still hurt? He'd never been a father; in fact, he was a stranger, but this was even less than that. Once again, Taylor wanted to hang up, but she didn't. She needed his help. Somehow, he must owe her something.

"I need papers, papers for Rebecca…to get her back into the country. She doesn't have a birth certificate or anything. I don't want to have to explain all of this to anyone. Who knows what will happen? I just need to get her home. Can you help me?"

He said he would try, but the conversation left Taylor stunned, hurt, lonely, and angry with herself for being any of those things. What did she know about him anyway? Maybe he was an axe murderer. Her mother had barely mentioned him. She'd been honest and told her that he didn't want children. Then, she would say he'd been good to her because he had given her Taylor, her perfect daughter.

Taylor was tired. She just wanted a dark room or that numbing zone that had eased her through so many circumstances. She was hurt by her father, ached for her mother, and wanted her daughter. For the first time, she wanted Rebecca to know who she was; she wanted to be her mother. Something needed to fill this empty space.

CHAPTER 43

Small Spaces

The sound of drums was mixing into Ruby's dream. She was on the edge of being awake, aware that she was dreaming but enjoying it and staying on—yet, the drums didn't fit. They interrupted the soft space she was in. Soon, she crossed to wakefulness, and as her head cleared, she realized it was someone banging on the door.

"What, what?" she yelled as she wrapped a robe around her and headed for the door. "Who is it?"

"It's me. Ruby, you've got to let me in." Jeannie burst into the room with her usual flair. She was out of breath and agitated. "You have to come with me, Ruby. It's Diane."

"What's Diane? Talk to me."

"They found her. She's in the clinic next to the square."

"What are you talking about? She's in Tulum."

"Ruby, put on some clothes; we've got to go. I'll explain on the way." They were in the golf cart and en route in five minutes.

"Tell me what's going on."

"I don't know much. She's in the clinic, and she's unconscious. Some-one found her, and they brought her in. That's all I know. The morning guard at the clinic is a friend of mine, and since Diane is obviously not from here, he thought I might know something about her. The people there don't even know who she is."

They arrived at the clinic and rushed inside. It looked more like a run-down hotel, but Jeannie knew her way around, and soon they found Diane. Ruby was shocked. Some sort of battered Diane look-alike was lying in the bed. She had blood in her hair and crusted on her neck. Her face was an odd shade of gray, and her eyes were two deep, dark pools sinking into her skull. There was an IV running into her arm, and she was completely still.

Ruby had to sit down; she felt nauseated. Trying to put this together with the person she knew was difficult. There were so many questions. How do you walk away from the dinner table and end up like this? "Jeannie, I'd like to stay here if you don't mind. Could you go back and get Shane and Taylor?"

"No problem—we'll be right back."

What happened to you? She couldn't take her eyes off of Diane's face. This felt surreal, and Ruby found it hard to focus. Instead, she started to notice the peeling paint and broken tiles on the floor. The furniture looked like it had started out as secondhand and gone downhill from there. There was a window high in the wall with a crack arching over the lower corner. Piled on a table were some medical supplies, not neatly displayed, but more like they had been dumped out of a bag.

Diane was still wearing the clothes she'd had on at dinner. They were brown with blood and ripped in places or maybe cut to allow her to be examined. She was so still, unnaturally so.

Ruby heard talking in the hall. Then Shane and Taylor entered the room. They, too, were speechless. Jeannie came in behind them. "I'm going to see what I can find out. Do you all want to stay here?"

"I'll come with you," volunteered Shane. The door swung shut behind them and then open again as the nurse came in.

She checked the drip in Diane's IV bag and straightened her bed covers, all the time murmuring "*Pobrecita, pobrecita.*" She wore a white dress embroidered around the top with colorful flowers. This design was repeated on the hem just below her knees. Ruby had seen the maids at the condos wearing the same thing. The nurse was warm and attentive, and they numbly watched her tend to Diane. Her kind demeanor reassured Ruby, but this didn't feel like a hospital room, and it was obvious that her friend needed medical attention.

After a while Taylor suggested they get some air. "Come on, Ruby. Let's go outside and see what Shane and Jeannie have found out or talk to a doctor or something." Taylor gently lifted her out of the chair and led her into the hall, where Jeannie was waiting.

"All I've found out is that a lady came here early this morning to tell them where Diane was, so they sent the ambulance and brought her here. The nurse said the doctor is in with someone else but that we could talk to him soon after."

So they waited. No one spoke. There was no information to discuss. When the doctor arrived, Jeannie talked to him for a long time while the others watched, frustrated by the language barrier.

"Okay, this is it. She was found in a rented room. She was shut inside an armoire. She's suffered a bad blow to the head, loss of blood, severe dehydration, and he thinks she might have a broken arm, but they don't have an X-ray machine."

"Is she going to be okay?"

"He says he doesn't know. She's been unconscious since she got here. He says the worst of it is the blood loss and dehydration. He would like her to have a transfusion and X-rays, but she'll have to go to Cancún for that."

"How do we get her there?" Ruby asked.

"I asked him that. They have an emergency helicopter, but it's very expensive, and they won't come unless they know they're going to get paid."

"Okay, let's get that arranged," said Ruby, in need of a mission. "Taylor, do you want to go over there with her?" Taylor nodded. "Shane, you and I can stay here and try to find out what the hell happened."

Everything was arranged. A few phone calls from the bank guaranteed payment until they found out about Diane's health insurance. Clothes and toiletries were sent with the patient. They were told she would need to take sheets, toilet paper, soap, and other things that foreigners would normally expect the hospital to supply. Taylor accompanied the patient, and Ruby and Shane went with Jeannie. She'd found the woman who had come to the hospital. She was the maid and had been there to clean the room. No, she didn't know who had been staying there, but the manager would be back soon. They waited, working on different theories, starved for information. When the manager arrived, his records showed that the guest had moved out the day before. "Right here, yes, he paid in advance; here it is." He turned the book around so they could read the name: Kevin Levine.

CHAPTER 44

The Ocean

Taylor had known Kevin for a long time and thought he was many sad things—sad because she understood the dynamics of his family. Tennyson had tried to explain how his behavior was all about his overbearing, selfish, and abusive father. He didn't know whether Kevin had been beaten, but the verbal abuse was heartless and incessant. Kevin's mother rarely stepped in, fearing the fury would be turned on her. She had convinced herself that silence was the best defense. At that time Taylor couldn't understand a mother who wouldn't do anything to keep her child safe, but now she felt she had no right to judge anyone.

She was sitting in a chair in Diane's hospital room. Actually, it was more like a dorm. They'd been put in the maternity ward. Probably because Diane was still unconscious, the hospital didn't think the constant crying of babies would bother her. Well, it bothered Taylor. Since their arrival by helicopter two days earlier, she'd been alone by the bed. The hospital was clean, but the staff was inattentive. It seemed that most of the patients had their own imported caregiver. Figuring that these natives knew the situation better than she did, Taylor rarely left Diane's side.

But the idleness had not been a gift. She worried, and she wanted to be with Rebecca. There were so many years to make up. Taylor knew she couldn't replace those times, but their loss enhanced every moment they had together now. She wanted to be with Patricia, as well. It felt as though there was never enough time to talk about their past—and how they would plan for the future?

Both women felt they'd been given a reprieve. They enjoyed each other. As much as each tried to stay guarded, the affection came through.

It was obvious that in different circumstances they would have become friends.

That was where Taylor wanted to be now. Not in this chair, not in this room. Even if she managed to drift in other directions, the crying would bring her back. It was more than just an annoyance. It was an insult. She would have tended to her crying baby if she'd known she was alive. She wanted to be there. That was stolen from her, and now there was a chance to be with her daughter. But here she sat, stuck. She felt so stuck and then reprimanded herself for not wanting to be there for Diane.

Things went forever in circles. Unavoidably, as she started to know her daughter, as she saw parts of Tennyson in her gestures, the loss accompanied the joy. How could she have missed so much? How is that fair? This wasn't a usual occurrence; why did it happen to her? Taylor had other struggles, as well. She wanted to know everything. When Patricia talked, Taylor wanted to climb into her head and come out with the stories, somehow inserting herself into them. Hearing it all had stirred a need in her that had taken years to suppress. She was learning about the life she should have had, that she deserved, and she couldn't get enough of it. She wanted to be able to implant the memory where it belonged, not hear it from someone else. She suffered the loss of those years as she saw the joy Rebecca had brought to Patricia's life. She felt bruised and relieved at the same time by the array of emotions that were gathering while she listened to the stories of Rebecca's childhood.

If only Diane would wake up, Taylor would have something to do. She remembered after the fire when the numbness had started to subside; all she could think of had been Rebecca: Rebecca crying, Rebecca burning, Rebecca dragged off by animals. She knew she needed to block these images. They were torturing her. Everyone said, "Get busy; that always helps," but she hadn't had the energy to do anything.

This was different and yet the same. Now, she could and would do other things, and this time she was being forced to sit here, just sit here and think about it all, to think thoughts that she knew weren't good for her. Allowing her feelings to come around a few times was good, but this was brooding, and she was trapped.

The mystery of Kevin was something else that plagued her. Why would he hurt Diane? He was supposed to be waiting for her to come back. No one had told him that the last discs were missing. Diane didn't know, so what had happened? There were only frustrating questions. Shane had called Kevin's parents and posed as an old friend. He'd asked them whether Kevin was in Boulder and was told that he was still vacationing in Mexico. So where was he?

A nurse came into the ward to check on the new mothers. Finally, she came by Diane's bed, took her pulse, increased the drip in her IV, and took her temperature. Then she went back to the more interesting, awake patients. Taylor knew she should make conversation and ask questions; it just didn't happen. Luckily, Ruby was supposed to come over and spot her for a night. What a relief. She was concerned about Diane, trying to help, but she was spent; she'd had enough.

Relief did arrive. Ruby showed up about 4:00 that afternoon. Taylor wanted to talk to her but was overcome with the need for fresh air. They had a short chat, and then she was in a cab, on the ferry, and walking toward the condos as fast as she could. She was grateful for the exercise and anxious to see Rebecca and Patricia. Ruby had arranged for her to meet with Shane the next day; he could tell her what they'd been doing.

All was forgotten when Taylor knocked on Patricia's door and Emma opened it and squealed with glee. "Where've you been? We've missed you soooooooooooooo much. Mm said that Diane was sick, but you have to come see us, too. We've done all sorts of things on the beach and bought…"

"Whoa, up there; are you going to let Taylor come in or just keep talking to her in the hall?"

Emma was not the least bit deterred by her mother. She grabbed Taylor's hand and dragged her into the condo. It was just what Taylor needed. She flopped onto the couch and happily absorbed a barrage of Emma's stories. At the same time, Patricia watched her with concern, and Taylor felt at home. *Oh, my god, home,* she thought. She hadn't had this sense of family since she'd been in the cabin with Tennyson and Rebecca.

When Emma finally looked up in the middle of her beach story, she said, "The crabs were all right. Taylor, you don't need to cry. I'd be crying, too, if they hadn't made it back to the ocean."

"Emma, I think Taylor's tired. Do you want to put some crackers and cheese on a plate like we did yesterday? I'll set up some chairs on the porch." Emma was thrilled with the chance to show off her culinary expertise. Patricia signaled Taylor to follow her out the sliding glass doors. "Are you all right?"

"I am now."

Taylor slept in Emma's room that night. There were two single beds. She started out with Emma until she fell asleep and then moved to her own. She was filled with gratitude for having the opportunity to hold her daughter. Yet, there was that shadow. Why should she have to be grateful to anyone for the opportunity to fall asleep with her own child? As she faded off, she wondered how much resentment she was allowed to feel, where the line was that said, "That's enough"?

CHAPTER 45

Currents

Patricia was reading on a lounge chair by the pool while Shane and Taylor pushed a delighted Emma around on a floating mattress.

"This makes a pretty picture," said Ruby as she approached.

"What are you doing here?" asked Shane and Patricia in unison.

"Diane's sister, Mary, is here. She's at the hospital now. Diane still isn't conscious, and if she doesn't come out of it in the next few days, they're going to medevac her to a hospital in Miami. Personally, I don't know what they're waiting for."

"I'm so glad someone from her family is here," said Patricia.

Ruby sat on the end of Patricia's lounge. "I've some other news, as well. Some friend of Jeannie's who works in Cancún came to the hospital to show me an island newspaper. It had a picture of a body they found in the water near Contoy Island."

"She said she was going to ask around about it," offered Shane, who was now hanging on the side of the pool next to them.

"That's right. This paper had printed the picture of a man who'd drowned, because they didn't know who he was. I can't tell—it's so bloated—but I think it could be Kevin."

"You're joking." Taylor was out of the pool and drying off. "Do you have the picture?"

"Right here." She handed it over.

"My god, it could be." Taylor sat on the next lounge, staring at the newspaper. "I mean, it's really hard to be sure, but it does look a bit like him, and he's definitely not Mexican."

"The article says the man was drunk and definitely drowned."

"Why would Kevin have drowned off some island called Contoy?" asked Shane. "Where's that?"

"I asked the same question. Luckily, the guy spoke English. He told me Jeannie had asked him to check into things since she had to go to Mexico City for a few days. He was to ask the ferry workers and the local boat owners since it's hard to get off the island without being seen by somebody. I guess he was checking the papers, too, and found this article about a missing person. So I asked him the same question. 'Why does a body found near Contoy Island have anything to do with our guy?' He told me that whenever a person is missing here, inevitably someone says, 'Maybe they went to Contoy.' It all has to do with the ocean currents. If someone drowns close to this island, the body usually ends up near there."

"So where is this Contoy?" asked Shane.

"It's an island about twenty miles north of here. It's only five or six miles long, and he said that no one lives there except for a few biologists, maybe. It's a bird sanctuary. Anyway, it's right where the Caribbean Sea meets the Gulf of Mexico, and this causes some weird currents."

"Does he match Kevin's description?" Shane reached out for the picture. "I mean, it's hard to believe Kevin bashed Diane on the head, stuffed her in the closet, and then went out for a swim." He looked down. "Wow, it does look a bit like him."

"I'd better call his family. If it's him, they'll need to bring down some proof. Then again, maybe he's alive and home by now, and we can ask him some questions." Taylor started toward the office and then froze.

"What is it?" Ruby asked. There was no answer. Taylor had already turned and walked away. Ruby looked in the same direction Taylor had and then saw what had caused such an abrupt departure. There was a cab in the parking lot, and the man paying the driver was Robert Mendel.

"Oh, my god." She hadn't seen him since the fire, but he looked exactly the same. He was tall with thick dark hair and a face that looked like a handsome mask. Obviously, Taylor was in no hurry to see him. He was coming along the walkway toward the pool now, one small bag in hand. Ruby stepped toward him.

"Hello, Mr. Mendel. Do you remember me?"

He seemed surprised to hear his name but recovered immediately. "You're Ruby; you're the one who called me." It sounded like an accusation.

"That's right. We met after the fire. Are you looking for Taylor?" Ruby wanted to get him away from the pool, specifically from the people next to it. She took his arm and started to lead him toward the office. He was not easily moved. "I don't know if Taylor is here right now; why don't I go up and check?"

"I can check myself, thank you," he said as he pulled his arm out of Ruby's grasp.

"Does she know you're coming?"

"No."

"Then, come on, Mr. Mendel. Let me prepare her." He paused. "Please." They had reached the office.

"I will wait here."

What a scary guy, thought Ruby as she rushed upstairs. She let herself into the condo and found Taylor lying on her bed.

"I didn't know what to do. What's he doing here?"

"How did he even know you were here?" Ruby asked.

"I called him. I wanted him to get me papers so we could get Emma back to the States." Ruby noted that Taylor was not using the name Rebecca anymore. "I never asked for him to come, and I don't want to see him."

"Well, he's downstairs waiting for you. Boy, he's one cold guy." Ruby regretted the comment right away. "Look, I can go downstairs and tell him you're not here."

"No way, not after being up here for this long. He's a lawyer. Remember? Nothing gets by him." Taylor went over to the mirror and started brushing her hair. "Do me a favor and bring him up, but give me a few minutes to get dressed, and then we can see what he wants. Please don't point out Rebecca or Patricia to him."

Back to Rebecca, Ruby thought. "Okay, is ten minutes enough?"

"No time is enough, but I guess that'll do." Ruby left, and Taylor sat back down on the bed. What was he doing here? She didn't trust him, and she knew he didn't care. He couldn't possibly be here to see Rebecca. He didn't ask a thing about her on the phone. She got up and went into the bathroom and took half a Valium without any hesitation. She was determined to keep her cool.

"Hello, Robert," she said as she opened the door. "Come in. Ruby, you'll stay too, won't you?" Everything was coming out very formally, and

Taylor wondered how long it would take for the Valium to chill her out.

"Hello, Taylor." He strode into the condo like he had been there before. His presence filled every square inch of the room. Taylor had the feeling that she was going to have to squeeze past him to get to the couch. He sat stiffly in a chair and put his bag on the floor beside him. "I have brought you the papers for Rebecca. They are her original papers. A forgery wasn't necessary."

"Why did you bring them? You could've sent them."

"I thought I should come down and check on things—make sure everything is okay."

"What do you mean? I've found my daughter. Things are better than okay. Did you come to see her?" The question was too direct; she didn't want to hear the answer. "Can I see the papers?" she asked quickly. Her father always paused before he spoke, and she hoped the time for her first question had come and gone. He reached into his bag and brought out a large manila envelope and handed it over without a word. There it was: a birth certificate. It was incredible. Alive again, just like that. "Is this all I need?"

"To get across the border, that should do. Unless they look her up in the computer, but I can't imagine they will do that."

"And you will get rid of any record of her death?"

"I can't get rid of every mention of her death. Old newspapers and police reports are a matter of record. But I think I can get her out of the computer as far as a death certificate is concerned."

"Thank you, I really appreciate this. Would you like to see her?"

"I already did. I assume that was her by the pool."

"Yes, that was her." Gratitude had momentarily knocked down Taylor's guard, and she regretted it instantly.

"I have a reservation at the White Sands Hotel. I am going to stay for a few days and would like an opportunity to talk to you before I leave." Robert Mendel closed his bag and stood up as he talked. This meeting was over.

"You know where I am. I've a friend here who isn't well, so we'll be staying until she's better or leaves for treatment in the US. I'll contact you." Taylor opened the door for him, and he was gone.

"That was unbelievable," said Ruby. "He's like a robot. Has he ever shown any feelings at all?"

"I've never spent any time with him, so I wouldn't know. He helped after the fire, but all that's a little foggy now."

"What about your mother? Did she ever say anything?"

"My mother told me she loved him when she married him. She'd thought he might change if he had a home and someone who cared." Taylor started to smile. "Mom told me that she'd been more like him before I was born and that I saved her." Ruby was reminded of how little family Taylor actually had. There was a knock on the door. It was Patricia.

"Who was that?"

"That was Emma's grandfather."

"I thought that was it. I can see some resemblance. What's he doing here?"

"Let's sit on the porch. I need some air." Taylor could see how worried Patricia was, and she understood. The three of them sat around a table on the little deck that overlooked the pool. They watched Shane and Emma splashing each other.

"He's like a big kid," said Ruby as she watched Shane.

"Listen, Patricia, I can see that you're worried. You needn't be. He has absolutely no interest in Emma. He never did." Taylor went inside and came back with the manila envelope. "He brought us this." Patricia pulled the birth certificate out of the envelope.

"Is this real?"

"Yup." Taylor told her what her father had said. Patricia got very quiet, and then she gently placed the paper on the table. When she looked up, she was crying.

"I'm so sorry, Taylor. I should never have kept Emma. I knew that, but I needed her so badly; my life was so empty. I have excuses, the ones that helped me forget, but they don't mean anything. I'm so sorry." Patricia leaned forward with her face in her hands and cried. Taylor motioned Ruby to go. It was hard to witness this woman, this strong, kind, clear-headed woman, weep with such abandon.

Ruby went out to the beach and started to walk. Boo was beside her immediately. He was looking very handsome. He was with her now, and she wanted to take him home. "It's incredible, Boo. I watch these women suffer and then wonder what am I doing?" Boo sat next to her when she stopped to look at the ocean and listened to everything she had to say.

CHAPTER 46

Connections

Taylor couldn't sleep. What was he doing here? It just didn't make any sense. This man didn't want her. He hadn't wanted her mother once she was her mother, and he didn't want Rebecca.

Taylor was feeling stronger; she and Patricia were going to work this out. They were perfect together—they understood and forgave. That was all there was to it, and from that simple base things seemed so clear. They were becoming a family. When they both decided that this family with Emma didn't have to exclude either one of them, the conflict was over; no one had to choose.

This new future made old connections more expendable, as expendable as she'd been to him all these years. No more surprises: expect nothing, need nothing. How can he mess with that? She wanted to make this work but realized that knowing something and feeling something were not the same.

In the morning she was going to go to his hotel. She wanted to know why he was here. It had to be connected to her, of course, but she was sure it wasn't going to be to her advantage. That was the scariest part: What did he need? What could he possibly require from her or Rebecca?

Hours later, still determined, Taylor walked along the beach toward the White Sands Hotel. She wanted to decide when they met. Why should that be up to him? She got his room number from the front desk. He was in the old part of the hotel. When she got there, she sat by the pool for a moment to steady her nerves. This area looked like cabins in the jungle. There was a kidney-shaped cement pool with a stone patio around it. There were four two-story buildings with *palapa* roofs and wooden porches out front. Vines were growing up all the supports, and there was worn wooden furniture in front of each room. It all felt moist, tropical, and very different from the open-air beach where she was staying.

His room was on the second floor. Taylor hoped she would wake him up. She wanted to see how he looked when he was sleepy and rumpled. Somehow, he gave the impression that he always wore a suit and that sleeping was too vulnerable a thing for him to do.

He opened the door wearing khaki pants and a pressed shirt neatly tucked in at the waist. This was as close to formal island-wear as Taylor could have imagined.

"Good morning. I wasn't expecting you."

"Well, I'll need to see my friend this afternoon, so I thought it would be better if I saw you this morning. Is this a bad time?"

Robert turned and looked at the laptop on the bed and told her no, but the message was clear. He was used to deciding the time for things. "Why don't we go down to the restaurant and talk there." He reached for his keys, and they were on their way.

"Two coffees, please," he said as they sat at a table. The eating area was half inside and half outside.

"No, thank you; I'll have tea with a lemon." Taylor didn't want tea, she didn't even like tea, but she didn't want him ordering for her. He hadn't even asked what she wanted. How characteristic, she thought. He'd never asked what she wanted.

He was looking directly at her. "Taylor, what are you doing here? Do you want to tell me what is going on?"

"I don't understand? What are *you* doing here?"

"I came to bring you the papers and check on things."

"What things? You've never needed to know about me before."

"Well, these circumstances are a little unusual, wouldn't you say?"

"My circumstances are different, but yours aren't. You've never wanted my daughter or me around, so I still don't understand why you're here. You've shown absolutely no interest in us, so why did you come?"

"There are things you don't understand."

"Then explain them to me."

"What happened to your friend?"

Taylor was taken aback by the sudden change in subject. This was getting nowhere, and he was back to asking the questions.

"My friend had an accident."

"What kind of an accident?"

"We don't know. She hasn't woken up yet. Someone found her in a room downtown."

"Does this have anything to do with you?"

"You're making absolutely no sense. Why would you think that had anything to do with me, and why do you care about my friend?"

Taylor noticed a man approaching the table.

"Excuse me, are you Robert Mendel?"

"I am."

"There's a phone call for you. You can take it in the office."

Robert looked at his daughter. "I have been waiting for a call. Can you have dinner with me tonight?"

"I don't know if I'll be back early enough."

"I will leave a message at the office of your hotel. Please come if you can." Robert stood up and strode away. Again, that was it; she hadn't called the timing on anything. He'd told her nothing, and now he was deciding where they would meet next.

Taylor felt tired. She waved the waiter over and ordered a cup of coffee. When the waiter returned, she noticed Roger walking through the restaurant and waved him over.

"Hi, Roger. We haven't seen you for a few days. What've you been up to?"

"Hi, Taylor. May I join you? I've already eaten but didn't get enough coffee."

"Sure, have a seat." After he ordered his coffee, Taylor asked, "Aren't you here on vacation?"

"Well, it's more like a leave of absence. I'm just not ready to go back. I've been playing golf in Cancún, and I think I'm getting my swing back."

"Good for you. Everyone needs a break sometimes. My father's here; he's from New York, too. I wish he could chill out a bit." Roger looked at Taylor as if he had gone deaf and was trying to read her lips.

"What is it? Are you okay?"

He sat back in his chair and put one hand on his temple. "Sure, sorry, I've just had this headache all morning. Too much fun, I think." He did look a little pale. They sat quietly for a while and Taylor was struck, once again, by a feeling that she'd seen Roger before.

Taylor found Shane by the pool when she got back to the condos, and he motioned her over. Taylor told him about the meeting with her father.

"Why do you even bother with that guy?" he asked.

"You know, I'm just so nervous about why he's here. You've no idea; this man has never been the least bit interested in me or Rebecca, and now he's here. You just can't imagine how strange that is."

"Ruby told me about the meeting yesterday. He sounds like a real cold fish. I'm sorry you have to put up with this now, with so much else going on."

Taylor was warmed by Shane's concern; he was such a nice man. It had occurred to her that it was odd how he'd latched onto their lives, but who knows anything about anybody?

CHAPTER 47

Diane

Taylor stood on the ferry dock, watching needlefish dart around just beneath the ocean's surface. At first she'd thought they were ripples in the water, silver and fluid, but as she waited for the ferry, it became clear to her which ones were reflections and which were fish. It was fascinating how a school of them always faced in the same direction, and then some quiet influence suggested the time for change, and every fish would turn at that exact same moment. Occasionally, one would glide off on its own, and Taylor wondered whether that fish would join another group or spend some time alone.

The ferry arrived and gave up its island-bound passengers. Immediately, her line was motioned to fill the now-empty boat. There was a schedule. The unloading and reloading needed to be monitored. A man at the walkway had a clicker in his hand, and that was his job. If tourists had questions, they were going to have to find someone else.

Inside, the boat was cool, and the window seats were filling up fast. Taylor settled herself toward the rear and watched the last of the travelers come on board. She noticed that the seats on the sunny side filled up first, and as she felt the heat being amplified through the window, she considered it a poor choice. After the boat pulled away from the dock, she realized they would be heading in the opposite direction. As much as the tourists worshiped the sun, the islanders planned their movements to avoid it whenever possible.

The trip to Cancún took about twenty minutes because of the good weather. For Taylor it was a relief, a short period of time when all she had to do to accomplish her goal was to sit there. She'd been so annoyed by her father. Why would he ask whether Diane's situation had anything to do with her? She knew it probably did. But how did he know that? What could possibly have happened? When would Diane be able to tell them?

The Cancún side of the ferry was very busy, with luggage handlers and cab drivers all scrambling for business. As she walked toward the road, she had to work her way through the crowd. Everybody was selling something, anything to draw a tourist dollar. A short taxi ride had her at the hospital, and she climbed the stairs to Diane's room. Diane's sister, Mary, sat by the bed. They hadn't met, but the circumstance afforded them an easy connection.

"Hi, I'm Taylor. I came to Mexico with Diane."

"Oh, hi, I'm Mary; Diane's older sister. Ruby's told me about you. I hate to be rude, but did you bring the laundry?"

"No, not rude at all, and I've everything here with me. Do we need help, or can we change the sheets together?"

"She's awake, did you know?"

"No, I didn't. That's terrific. When did she wake up?"

"Just this morning. I didn't even notice at first. I'm not sure how much she's with us, but I think she'll roll from side to side if I ask her. Why don't we see what we can do?" Surprised by the news, Taylor focused on Diane. It was hard to tell how much she was registering, but it was so wonderful to see her eyes open. She weakly responded to commands as they changed her bedding and put a fresh nightgown on her. During their efforts Taylor noticed Diane looking directly at her, but that was all. There was a dullness in her stare. Mary told her that Diane already seemed more alert than she had that morning. Everything was feeling very positive, so they had delayed plans to take her home.

"Has she said anything about what happened?" Taylor asked.

"She hasn't said anything. I don't think she's all there yet. I know we all have questions, but I just want to let her come back to us gently."

There were loud voices in the hall. Everything was in Spanish but in angry tones. Then Jeannie Tull came charging around the corner toward their room. "Oh, my god, I can't believe it. She's opened her eyes, right?"

"Jeannie," Taylor rose to give her a hug, "this is Mary, Diane's sister."

"Grand to meet you. How is she?" Jeannie moved closer to the bed.

"What was all that noise?" Mary asked.

"Oh, just those dumb nurses, trying to tell me that two visitors is already one too many. What a crock! As if they care. Hey, Diane, are you with us now, darlin'?" There was no response; her eyes were on Jeannie, but they lacked enthusiasm. "What's up?" Jeannie turned her attention to Taylor.

"Why don't we go for a walk, and I'll tell you everything I know."

There was a small garden behind the hospital. Taylor led Jeannie to one of the benches, where they sat as she explained Diane's condition.

"Well, we really have to figure this out. Maybe it has something to do with Roger?" said Jeannie.

"What do you mean, something to do with Roger? What does he have to do with anything?"

"Wait a minute, you mean you don't know? I was sure she would've told you."

"Know what?"

"Well, that day Diane and I had lunch with José, bingo, we were joined by Kevin and Roger. José said that Roger was the guy. With Diane's situation and then leaving town right away, I never got a chance to talk about it, but I was sure Diane would have told you. I mean, there was so much going on and…"

"Roger? Was he sure?"

"He said he was pretty sure. It was the first time he had pointed to anybody."

"Oh, my god, that must've been why she was so excited to have Ruby and Shane come to dinner with her that night. She wanted to tell them, but Roger came to dinner as well, so she couldn't say anything. Then she disappeared. Ruby said she was acting weird at the table before she left."

"Yeah, that makes sense."

"Wow, I wonder who wrote that note? You know, the one on Ruby's door." Jeannie didn't know about it, so Taylor explained. They were both silent for a while.

"I saw Roger today. He looked a little pale," Taylor added.

"So, if Roger's the guy, who the hell is he, and what's he got to do with any of this?" Jeannie wondered out loud. Taylor thought about the questions her father had asked. Someone was giving him information. Why not Roger? He lived in New York, and he'd said he was in research. That could mean anything.

"Jeannie, do you plan to stay at the hospital for a while?"

"Yeah, I came here to spend some time with Diane, even though she doesn't seem to be into conversations right now."

"I just think someone should keep Mary company—maybe let her go out for a while. I'd really love to get back to Isla."

"That's fine with me. I could use some sitting time."

"Great. Will you say goodbye to Mary for me? Tell her some places to go if she would like some fresh air?"

Taylor was back on the island by mid-afternoon. There was a message from her father to meet him at one of the nicer restaurants in town at 7:00 P.M.

After changing her clothes, she joined Ruby by the pool. She wanted to be prepared—as if that were possible. But it was worth a try, and Ruby was her best sounding board. She filled her in on Diane's condition and what she'd learned from Jeannie. Boo sat between them, cementing his role as a permanent fixture.

"So, what would Roger be in all of this?"

"I don't know," answered Taylor, "but I wouldn't be surprised if he was connected to my father in some way. He's always looked a bit familiar. Maybe they're old friends, or maybe he was there after the fire. I've no idea.

"Tonight, I want to have some advantage when I meet my father for dinner." Taylor paused. "Ha, as if he couldn't mess me up in about one minute."

They worked on different possibilities and questions that Taylor should be prepared to ask or answer. Later, as she dressed, Taylor decided on half a Valium—no use in getting rattled, and it had helped with Emma.

She didn't show up until 7:20, in an effort to make him wonder whether she was coming. Of course, this backfired because ultimately she was worried he would leave. This upper-hand stuff wasn't easily achieved when it involved her father.

When she arrived, he was very polite. He stood as she approached the table and then asked her what she would like to drink. Already, this was an improvement. His work obviously required him to be observant and adaptable.

Taylor had taken extra time to make herself attractive. She knew she looked like her mother and wanted to remind him of her, of what he'd missed. She also knew this was all very silly, but she couldn't help herself. By the time her wine arrived, the Valium was relaxing her nicely. "Tell me, who's Roger?"

"Pardon me?"

"I want to know who Roger is. You obviously have some information from someone, and I deserve to know who you have spying on me." The waiter arrived and let him off the hook. They both gave some attention to the menu and ordered.

"I think you have things a bit askew."

Oh, how many other words could he have used? The English language is full of them. She thought of a thesaurus; there could've been so many alternatives. *"Askew": such a poor choice. So pompous. Like all their family life wasn't askew. Like everything wasn't askew.*

Taylor also wondered whether she should be mixing alcohol with the Valium, but it was too late. Her glass was half empty, far too quickly, and there was another one on the way. *Fuck it,* she thought, vaguely aware that she was moving away from her practical self.

"Askew, askew—you know what's askew? The fact that you're here; that's really askew. You're acting like it's a normal thing for you to show up. I'm thirty years old and have only seen you a few times in my entire life. That's askew. What are you doing here?"

Robert was taken aback. His daughter had always seemed so frail, and here she was pressing him in a direction he was not prepared for. He decided to change the flow of things, to ease the situation.

"I'm not sure what I'm doing here. You called, and I wanted to help."

This wasn't what Taylor had expected. It took the wind out of her angry sails. *No, no he did that on purpose. He's a trial lawyer; he manipulates for a living.* "I don't believe you. You've never wanted to help me at any other time except for the fire."

"That's exactly it. I helped you when you lost Emma, and now I want to help you when you have found her."

"You make her sound like a wallet. I only need the papers. I don't need any other help. Don't bother even trying to convince me that you have any interest in me or my daughter." Taylor was gaining momentum. "You know, mother never said a bad thing about you, just that you didn't want children. She actually told me once that she hadn't wanted children either, but when she got pregnant, that was all she wanted from then on. She always gave me enough love and support for two people. She easily filled any void that you created." Her father remained silent. "You've no idea what you missed."

"If you know about the agreement, then you must understand why I left." Taylor was surprised by such a practical answer to what she considered an emotional outburst. Why was she talking to this man?

"Why am I talking to you?" Her thoughts were making quick exits out of her mouth. "You haven't answered one of my questions."

"I told you I don't know."

"And I told you I don't believe you. How'd you get your information, and who's Roger?"

"I'm a lawyer. I know how to find things out."

"Again, you don't answer my questions. I don't know what I'm doing here." Taylor stood up. She was getting nowhere, and this was wearing her out.

"Okay, sit down. I will tell you some things." She remained standing. "Sit down, Taylor. We can talk. Please." It was an odd sensation hearing him say her name.

"I will stay, but don't mess with me. I've had enough. I'm not kidding; I really have. I don't need you." Taylor sat down, but she promised herself she would leave if he didn't stick to the bargain.

Dinner arrived, and they ate in silence. Taylor wasn't interested in her food but managed to eat some of it and remembered to chew before she swallowed. She was, however, enjoying her second glass of wine.

"I'm going to ask you again: How did you get your information, and who is Roger?"

"Okay, Roger works for me. I sent him down here to check things out. I didn't know if this child was yours or if it was some scam. You must admit the whole thing is a little unusual."

Taylor was surprised that she was right about Roger. Then, as the idea of it sank in, she felt contaminated. It all seemed so creepy, and it took a few minutes for her to regain her composure enough to continue the conversation. Annoyingly, her father allowed her the time.

"So, what does he have to do with Diane?"

"Nothing. He has worked for me for eight years, getting me information for my cases. He needed a vacation, and I needed to know what was going on, so he came to the island. I just wanted to know if everything was all right."

"That's disgusting. How dare you have me watched!"

"Wait a minute. I wasn't having you watched. He was merely getting a little information. Don't make this into something it isn't."

Taylor wasn't going to let him tell her what to think. She'd had enough. She stood up too fast, and all the blood rushed to her feet, and her head gave up.

CHAPTER 48

Roger

"Do you know how I got home last night?" Taylor asked as she sat in Patricia's condo, having coffee and trying to figure out how her evening had ended. Ruby had left before she woke, so she was hoping Patricia would know something about it.

"Well, it wasn't that late, and we got a call at the office from your father. He told us that you'd fainted, and he didn't know what to do with you."

"Ha, that's nothing new."

"Well, we all went into town and walked you home. You were really out of it."

"That's what a father can do to you."

"What happened?"

"It was so stupid. I was nervous, so I took a Valium. I'm not used to that kind of stuff, and then I had some wine. Part of me knew it was a bad idea, and that same part of me didn't care."

"Do you remember what you talked about?"

"Oh, I remember everything. The son-of-a-bitch sent Roger to spy on me." Taylor sat back and thought about that for a while. "But...you know the strangest thing...wait a minute...Roger was here before I called him...my god...I just realized that."

Just then Emma came charging into the room. She'd been packing for a day at the beach and was planning things carefully. "Mom, do you think I need an extra shirt? I'm wearing one, and I have my bathing suit, but you said to pack for a day, so do I need another shirt?"

"You're really thinking about this Emma. I'm proud of you. Okay, so if I were packing, I'd ask myself what I would need the extra shirt for. Then, if I could think of something that might make it necessary, I'd take it along. Shirts are small."

"Okay, so I could get splashed with my clothes on, or, I might get sick of this shirt, or, I might lend it to someone else. Okay, I'll put another shirt in my bag." Off she went—this was a lot of work, preparing for the beach.

"Patricia, you're such a good mom." The two women were silent and thought about this for a while. It was an odd situation. Then Taylor leaned forward again; she had to think about what her father had said. "This is too weird. Do you realize that my father sent Roger here before I called him to help us get the papers for Reb…Emma? What does that mean? Does he always have me followed? How did he even know I was in Mexico? This is really strange. Can you guys go ahead without me this morning? I need some time to think about this. Just give me a little while, and then I'll come and find you. Is that okay?"

"Of course, it's okay. I'm so sorry you have to deal with all this. You're making me grateful I've no one else to worry about other than you and Emma." Taylor was really touched at being included on Patricia's list of people she wanted to worry about. She was so grateful for Patricia and for the trust they were developing. They just seemed to know each other. *How incredible*.

She returned to her own condo. She wanted to think through things carefully. This was beginning to scare her. She wanted to organize her thoughts, so she decided to write a list of questions.

Number one…she drew a blank. *Okay, try this*, she told herself.

How did my father know where I was?

Why did he care?

What does he want to learn about me by sending someone to spy on me?

Why did Roger seem familiar?

Is this a real problem?

Are we safe?

The last question seemed odd. This was her father. He was a bad father, but she had never actually considered him dangerous. She was going to have to see him again. There were too many questions.

His hotel was a short ways down the beach, so Taylor walked along the water's edge to stay cool. What was she going to say about last night? *I don't have to tell him anything.* She found him sitting at the same table they'd sat at the morning before. *Was that only yesterday?*

"Good morning," she said as she approached the table. He looked up and didn't seem either surprised or happy to see her.

"How are you today? Feeling better?"

"I'm just fine." Taylor didn't want to discuss the night before. "Can I join you?"

"Please." He motioned toward a chair.

"I've some questions for you, and I really want some answers."

"I've already told you about Roger. What else do you need to know?"

"I want to know why you had him following me and how you knew where I was."

"You called me, remember?"

"Roger was here way before I called you about Rebecca's papers. So how'd you know I was here? Why was he following me?" Robert Mendel was surprised. He didn't know that Roger had introduced himself. It had not been part of the plan. His instructions were to watch, get information, and call if anything unusual was happening.

"Would you like some coffee or breakfast?" Robert needed time to think.

"No, I'm not here for coffee." Taylor was not interested in any extra time with her father. "Tell me, why was Roger following me? I've had enough of this."

"I do not like your tone. I have a right to watch out for my family."

"You have no rights." Taylor didn't like his answer and raised her voice to make that point very clear. "You've got something going on here, and I want to know what it is."

"Keep your voice down!"

"I will not, and don't tell me what to do. I want to know why he was following me." Her voice was getting louder, and Mr. Mendel was looking around. People were beginning to stare.

She was not going to let up on him, and she was pleased to see that this public commotion was upsetting him. "I want to know. It's time you gave me some answers."

"You are making a scene; now, lower your voice."

"If you don't tell me what I want to know, I'll just get louder. Answer me!" Taylor was relentless. "Answer me!"

"All right." He put up his hand like a stop sign. "All right, he was not following you; he was following Patricia." Robert's face went red instantly.

Taylor was stunned. She couldn't assimilate what he'd just told her. She looked down at her lap and tried to put the pieces together. The only reason he'd have to follow Patricia was if he knew she had Rebecca. So he must have known that at least by the first time they saw Roger. When was that? Something was welling up inside her, and she couldn't get her head to clear.

Following Patricia, following Patricia, following Patricia. She kept saying it over and over in her head. *What does it mean? How does he know Patricia?*

Taylor looked up at her father. He clearly had said something he regretted. She'd never seen him look vulnerable, but that was how he looked now. "You don't understand," he said.

It took a few attempts to start a sentence but something had to be said. "You're absolutely right. I don't understand. How did you know about Patricia?"

"I have always known about Patricia." Robert was tired. He just couldn't come up with a lie fast enough. After he said it, he felt relieved. Knowing this had always been complicated.

"What does that mean?" There were pictures in Taylor's head, pictures of her own pain. They were behind a screen, slightly out of focus, threatening, yet she felt the screen was shielding her, not hiding the pictures. It was the fog. Thank god for the fog.

Robert was talking. He was telling her things, important things. She could hear them if she wanted to.

"Don't talk any more." She was staring into her lap again, keeping her head as low as she could. This feeling was familiar. She wanted to fold herself. She liked the image of it. First, her head would go flat on her chest, and then her arms would fold in like you do with a sweater. Next, her legs would come straight up, giving way at the hips, and then the final fold at the knees. What a tidy bundle she would become. But she wasn't tidy. She was a miniature image of herself rattling around in her body.

And the pictures were there, trying to define themselves. *This is risky.* There were dangerous words coming out of her father's mouth.

No one could do that. Why would they? Nothing could be that evil. No one could do that.... No. She tried to think clearly, but the pictures were threatening her, those reminders of her pain. They weren't going to let her stay small. She was growing back into the body where her stomach was whirling, putting pressure on the back of her throat.

"You..." It was hard to make the words. She didn't want to hear the sound of them. "You...knew. You...knew Rebecca was alive?"

"You don't understand," he said again.

Oh, my god—he didn't deny it—he didn't deny it. Oh, my god. Taylor was crawling inside her skin; the fog was lifting. *No. No pictures. Please, no pictures.* Her throat was burning, and her stomach was upside down. She wanted to stand up but couldn't; that big, old, heavy body was weighing her down. Why couldn't she be small again? Her breath was getting shorter, and there was a crowded feeling in her lungs. *He knew.*

She'd lived the pictures. She didn't want to see them. There she was, curled up on the floor. Not dead but wishing she was dead. Then, she was in bed, the sheets pulled up over her head. She couldn't leave her apartment; dealing with the world was out of the question. There she was, curled into a ball, trying to focus on her breathing. There she was, in the dark. Food and nighttime were her worst enemies. If things could possibly be worse, it was always at night. Eating had become a battle with her throat. It felt impossible to keep it open enough. Peas were the biggest substance she could manage. Chewing was out of the question. This went on for months; she dropped thirty pounds. There she was, so strangely thin. Being that skinny made her feel weak and vulnerable, always cold.

It all went on and on. Time—everyone said it would take time. Time was her constant, unyielding enemy. Those hours in the dark, each moment felt to its fullest, like the magic children feel on Christmas morning, but in the opposite direction, or as strong as your first love, but heading down from the centerline of daily existence. There had been no culprit. She could only focus her pain on something as heartless as fire. The feel of it all was there in the pictures. *No more pictures, please.*

Her father started to speak again. He had to be stopped. There had been no culprit. That had saved her. No one to hate—until now.

Without conscious thought, she lunged at him. Her arms and fists out in front of her, she could hear herself screaming as she bashed her fists into his chest, his shoulders, his arms—it didn't matter—anywhere. She couldn't see. She knew what was happening but couldn't feel it. Then, there was something pulling at her, but she punched and punched until she was hitting air. As her eyes focused, she could see the horrified face of her father. Not her father: the offender. Taylor lunged back at him with all her strength. "You're the devil—you're the devil!" She punched forward with all her strength until an enormous pain brought some sense of time and space back to her.

Someone was sitting her in a chair. Everything was in her fist; it was screaming in pain, so she sat, overwrought, overburdened.

Robert was out of his chair. He asked the waiter who had tried to pull her off of him to get a doctor. Taylor had heard him saying she'd had a seizure and would need something to calm her down.

"Yes," she said, "that would be nice."

Then she felt the shot, and that was the last thing she remembered of that morning.

CHAPTER 49

Away

"Is she awake yet?" asked Ruby.

"Not the last time I checked," Patricia said as she closed the door.

"Do you know what happened?"

"All I know is her father brought her back this morning and we put her to bed. He said she'd had a seizure and the doctor had medicated her."

"What does that mean? She's never had a seizure as long as I've known her."

"How about the fact that every time she goes near that man she comes home completely out of it in some way?"

"Did you talk to her when he brought her back?"

"No, we practically had to carry her. She wasn't with us."

Taylor could hear them talking about her, but she couldn't join in. She wanted to get up but couldn't manage that either. She was hoping they would check on her soon and that would solve everything.

She must have faded off because the next thing she saw was Ruby standing over her with that wonderful "I-love-you," "are-you-all-right?" look. She wanted to tell Ruby everything but wished she could just plant the information in her head and not have to put the horrible truth into words.

"Oh, Ruby." The tears came with the words. She could feel the pain rising in her throat. Ruby lay on the bed beside her and wrapped her arms around her. That was all it took; sympathy cleared the path for her tears and heartache.

Then, Taylor was waking up again, and Ruby was still beside her. She felt more awake this time and wanted to get up, so the two women sat in the living room, and Taylor told her everything.

Ruby felt like it had happened to her. She was as demolished as Taylor, crying with her as she pictured the scene.

"I've got to leave," Taylor said. They'd been silent for a while. "I can't stay here. I have to start something good, some life I can live. I want to take Patricia and Emma to Boulder for now. Can we stay at your house, just until we have a plan?"

"Of course, you can. I'll call Mark right now."

"Okay, I need to talk to Patricia first." They sat together, offering each other a space to prepare.

It was evening now. The air was less oppressive but still nothing that could be called cool. Taylor knocked on Patricia's door and waited. It was opened by a pajama-clad Emma. Patricia appeared behind her and asked Emma to kiss Taylor good night. They both tucked Emma into bed and then returned to the living room. Then, Taylor told the incredible story again.

"I really want us to leave. We could go to Boulder, just until we figure things out. What do you think?"

"I can't believe this man has been watching me all these years. And how could he do that to you?"

"He never gave me a reason. I know he didn't want children, but I didn't know that meant he didn't want me to have children, too. It doesn't make any sense, and I don't care. I'll never see him again." Taylor was getting tired again. "Do you want to leave with me, Patricia?"

"Of course, I do. The only reason I was here was to hide from you, so it's time to go home. I need to get settled and get Emma back into school in the fall."

There was so much to say, and there were so many things to decide, but it was all going to have to wait until tomorrow. Taylor needed sleep.

Patricia joined Ruby and Taylor in their condo for coffee the next morning. "Emma is in our place looking at her books, so I can't stay too long, but it occurred to me that the document we have has her original name on it, so she'll have to cross the border with that. How are we going to explain that to her?"

"I guess we have two choices," said Taylor. "We tell her the truth now, or we tell her something that will work in the meantime. Something like…It's a mix-up because your passport got stolen, or something like that."

"I really want to tell her soon, but it would be nice to be home or settled a little. I'd rather not tell her and then rush off to someplace new."

"However you want to do it is fine with me. Just let me know before you tell her, or if it would be okay, I'd like to be there."

"Of course. How about if we make a game out of it for now? She can use the name on the birth certificate. That is, if they ask her at all. Then, when we get to Boulder, we can tell her the truth, explain why we lied. She's a very sensible girl, and I know she'll understand."

After Patricia left, Ruby and Taylor poured themselves more coffee. "I called Mark last night, but there was no answer, so I'll try him again today."

"Do you think he'll mind?"

"Not at all. He's probably out of town, and even if he's in Boulder, he's rarely home."

"How do you do that, Ruby? You two are more like roommates than husband and wife."

"It's true. I guess we'll change it when one of us needs out."

"Do you need out? I've seen you and Shane together, and there's definitely something there."

"Oh, I don't know. We do have a blast together. He would love to make it more, but it just feels too complicated right now."

"I hope you don't mean me, and if you do, you can relax. In a way, I've been set free. I'm moving on. I feel like I'm entering my next life. Everything in my past is shit, and I refuse to take anymore. I have everything I need to be happy. Patricia is a gift, and I know we can work this out. It feels like we're sisters."

Ruby felt excluded but happy to hear such a positive plan. It was time for them all to move on. Taylor's enthusiasm for a fresh start was contagious. *Funny how things work out. Maybe this trip wasn't all for Taylor.* The struggles they'd encountered on Isla Mujeres had imparted enough reality into Ruby's consciousness to make it impossible for her to go back to her old life.

Taylor, Patricia, and Emma left Mexico the next day. Ruby stayed on to help Diane and her sister and to do whatever was necessary to take Boo to Colorado. Besides, she wasn't ready to go home yet. She took turns staying at the hospital with Jeannie Tull, Shane, and Diane's sister, Mary, to keep an eye on things. Mary moved into Taylor's room, and when Diane could leave the hospital, she would stay there, too. She was up and walking around but not saying much, and she didn't appear to remember anything that had happened.

Three days after Taylor left, Ruby got a message to call home. She went down to the office to use the phone.

"Hi, Taylor; how's everything going?"

"It's so nice to be here. We had absolutely no trouble. They never asked Emma anything."

"How's my house? Still standing?"

"The house looks great, as always, but I've something strange to tell you."

"What, all my plants are dead, right? Mark didn't water them."

"Well, that's just it: Mark isn't here."

"Oh, he's never there; that's nothing different."

"No, I mean he's really not here. I didn't even notice at first. We were all staying in the guest room, and I never thought to look in your bedroom, but then I went in to borrow a jacket, and the closet was half-empty, so I started to look around, and all his things are gone, Ruby. Do you know anything about this?" There was silence on the Mexican end of the phone. "Ruby, are you there?"

"Yeah, I'm here and, no, I don't know what's going on." There was another long pause. "You know what? You make yourself at home there. I'll call Mark at work, and I'll call you again soon, okay?"

Ruby had always thought she would be the one to leave. She'd already decided that with Taylor gone and Diane getting out of the hospital in a few days she could no longer avoid her own future. This was ridiculous: She was actually hurt that Mark had left first. The feeling was more from the fact that they hadn't discussed it. She had thought of them as friends, companions, and assumed they'd pick the time together. They'd both known the truth for a long time, and the knowing had allowed a gap to widen between them. They liked each other, and it bothered Ruby to think him gone and to picture him packing his things alone in the house. She should've been there. She'd seen it many times. She would help him, and they would talk about their separate futures like old friends. Somehow, she'd convinced herself that the moving on would be the positive side of their marriage, that they'd given each other the gift of time to do it when it was right. *All in a row—all so tidy—I'm an idiot.* She felt miserable. She'd handled things shabbily. For the first time she felt unfaithful, not physically but from the heart. Friends or lovers, they'd wasted each other's time, and she'd let it happen. She'd allowed herself to miss a piece of her own life, and she had permitted Mark to do so as well. *Sorry, Mark.* Maybe they could still be friends. She would talk to him. At least this was definitely a more honest arrangement.

Then there was Shane. Shane was great. She'd been tempted many times to take things to the next level, and now she was glad she never had. It didn't seem right to jump into a new relationship before she'd come to terms with her marriage, but maybe she had. She'd taken no risks and offered no commitment. *Ugh, I'm pathetic.*

CHAPTER 50

Crossing

Big day: It was finally time to bring Diane home from the hospital. She was still abnormally quiet but physically recovering well and getting stronger every day. The doctors said she'd been suffering the effects of a chemical imbalance caused by the blow to her head and that she should recover completely. All she needed now was rest and time and possibly some therapy when she was ready. For now, Isla was perfect: quiet and sunny.

Ruby and Shane were hanging some balloons and cheering up the condo for her arrival. Jeannie and Mary had gone to Cancún to bring her back.

"Has she said anything about what happened yet?" Shane asked, slightly out of breath from blowing up a big red balloon.

"I don't think she remembers. She's been so quiet, and none of us has wanted to push it. Perhaps she doesn't want to remember." Ruby was also breathless from blowing up balloons, and her ears were ringing.

"I hope you aren't taking on too much, Ruby. Maybe Diane should've stayed in the hospital."

"Ugh, you saw the place. Nobody would want to stay there any longer than absolutely necessary. Besides, I've got you to help me, right?"

"I'm no nurse. I'm here solely as entertainment for the staff."

"I know what you're here for. I think you're hoping for a little entertainment yourself."

"I'd need more cooperation for that. Besides, you've seemed a little preoccupied lately. Looking for a new distraction, maybe?"

"You just think you're so clever, don't you? You haven't known me that long."

"I know you well enough, and you're avoiding the subject. Are you going to tell me what's up?"

"I don't have to tell you everything." Ruby was standing on a chair, hanging balloons from the curtain rod.

"You're right, but I wish you would." This struck Ruby as an abrupt step into the serious conversation. She dropped her arms and looked out the window.

"All right. Mark left me. When Taylor got to Boulder, he was gone, along with all his things."

Shane stopped what he was doing. "How do you feel about that?"

"You sound like a shrink."

"You probably need one. Or is it simpler than that?"

Ruby stepped down off the chair and faced Shane. "You know what I think, and that's what bothers me. I'm not that affected by the whole thing. I mean, yes, I'm sad. Mark's a good man, and we cared about each other, and he did the right thing. I'm actually a little ashamed of myself. I should've done something sooner." Shane held his tongue. "Now I need to adjust to being unmarried."

"I could adjust to that in a big hurry."

"I know. That's why I haven't told you. I don't want to rush into anything."

"You've got to be kidding. Rush into anything? We couldn't go any slower if we were in reverse."

"Hey, you're not the one with the commitment."

"Don't be ridiculous. You didn't have a commitment to Mark. Your only commitment was to not change anything."

Ruby knew this was true. She hadn't been able to think of anything else since she'd got the call.

"I guess the commitment you think is right," said Ruby, "is one to you?" Shane moved closer, put his arms around her, and held her head close to his chest.

"You're such an idiot. I'm not asking you to marry me, just to let us feel what we feel."

"You know that's not true. If we get involved, it wouldn't be some casual thing."

"First of all, we're involved already, and second, *you* need a push back into the real world."

"What's that supposed to mean?"

"Don't act like I'm telling you something you don't know. You're a volunteer, and you lived with a husband you didn't love. I mean, how chicken is that?" Ruby pushed him away and sat on the couch.

"Let's be honest," continued Shane. "If you volunteer, people are supposed to be grateful for whatever you have to offer—no stretch there. Plus, living with a person you aren't passionate about, no requirements there either—just boredom, I'd guess. Sounds pretty safe to me."

"If you want to have sex with me, this is hardly the way to go about it." Ruby was serious. This was pissing her off. She knew it was true; she'd already said the same things to herself.

"Sex is a big leap. I just want a kiss." Shane was trying to lighten things up. He knew she'd been struggling with something.

"I want to take a shower, and I don't want to talk to you anymore. Why don't you come back when Diane arrives? That way there'll be other people in the room, and we won't have to continue this conversation."

Shane shrugged and left the condo without another word. He wasn't wounded. He knew he was right, and she knew he was right. They'd always been honest with one other. It was one of the things he enjoyed the most.

Mary, Jeannie Tull, and Diane arrived just after one. Diane was tired but seemed pleased to be there. She still had a somewhat tranquilized demeanor that was disconcerting. They settled her in, and she loosened up a bit and then went to sleep. Shane had met them as they had entered the condo complex but had not come upstairs.

"Nothing yet," said Jeannie. "It's as if this mystery started at the hospital."

"What do you think we should do?" asked Mary. "I don't have to go home right away. In fact, I'm enjoying it here, other than worrying about Diane. The doctor said the best thing for her right now is rest and quiet. He wanted to see her a little stronger before she did any major traveling."

"Good advice," offered Jeannie. "There couldn't be a better place than Isla for that kind of recovery."

CHAPTER 51

Letters

Ruby was having breakfast when Nancy from the office approached her. "You seem to be quite popular," she said.

"Oh, good. I've always hoped so."

"I've got two letters for you. It was my day off yesterday, so I guess one has been here for a while. That Henry is such a moron. The other one was put through the slot this morning. It came in early today." Nancy dropped the two letters on the table and trotted officiously back to her office. "I hope it's all good news. Have a nice day."

Ruby picked up the envelopes. They both had her name on them but in different handwriting. She opened the first one and immediately scanned to the bottom to see whom it was from.

Dear Ruby,

I've already been here too long. I need to get back to work, and it's obvious to me that you need more time. I'd hoped you would give us a try, but as each obstacle was removed, you still hesitated to let us act on what we feel for each other.

I don't know what you're going to do or how long you'll be in Mexico, but I want you to be careful. There are still a lot of unanswered questions. If you have problems or think you're in danger, stick close to Jeannie—she knows the island.

You know how I feel. The rest is up to you. Be careful, and call me if you need me.

Love,
Shane

Ruby couldn't believe that Shane had left without saying goodbye. This was becoming a pattern in her life. She ran through their conversation the day before, looking for clues, but she already had the answer. How long could she expect him to hang around? She'd been fortunate to have him stay as long as he did. He was right about her. She'd kept everything at bay for so long—it had become a way of life.

Reaching for her coffee, she was reminded of the second letter. When she opened it, she was surprised to see it was from Robert Mendel. *My god, what could he have to say?*

Dear Ruby,

I am writing you because I know how much you mean to Taylor. I am sure you know what went on between the two of us and how she must be feeling about me now.

"No kidding," thought Ruby.

I am equally sure she told you I have been watching Patricia and Rebecca from the beginning. I am not used to explaining myself, but the explosive nature of Taylor's reaction has led me to appraise my behavior.

He writes as coldly as he acts. She laid the letter on the table and stared into space. The waiter approached her with a coffee pot, and she watched him pour her a fresh cup. When she was ready, she picked up the letter and continued to read.

I am a solitary man and have little experience in expressing my feelings or discussing my actions. Taylor has made me aware of the need to scrutinize my conduct. I need time for this and am contacting you with the hope that we may communicate in the future. You are my only link to Taylor. I am open to the idea that a family could be a good thing. I am sure that that sounds odd to you, but there is a great deal of history behind my choices.

I am aware that this is a lot to ask, but if you would consider staying in touch with me, it may offer some relief to Taylor as well. Please let me know.

Robert Mendel

P.S. Attached is a picture of Roger Bates. I asked him to go to Mexico to keep an eye on things, but apparently he has motives of his own, which I intend to look into. I am enclosing this picture in order that you may be aware of him as a potential problem.

P.P.S. He no longer works for me.

Ruby was actually feeling sorry for the man by the time she finished reading the letter for the second time. Imagine being that stiff, practically robotic, even when discussing personal matters! How pent-up and isolated he must be. The letter sounded like a business communication. Maybe it was?

She didn't need time to consider her response. She knew right away that she would listen to whatever he had to say, and she was grateful for the opportunity to screen what part of it reached Taylor. The part about Roger was another matter. It was impossible to know what his story was.

She wasn't sure, however, what her response was to Shane. She read his letter again and decided she was not going to be pushed into anything. Like Robert Mendel, she needed to scrutinize her own behavior before she started something new.

CHAPTER 52

Faces

"I 'm sorry, *señora*. We have not been able to find him anywhere on this island."

"Did you check the airlines to see if he left Cancún?" Ruby asked.

"*Por supuesto,* but there's no record of a Roger Bates on any flight leaving in the last week."

"Officer, do you realize how dangerous this man could be?"

"*Si, señora.* I checked with the hospital and was told how serious the injuries of your friend were. If the man is not on the island, then there is no more I can do."

"So that's it, then?" asked Ruby.

"*Si señora.* Unless this man shows up, or there's another incident."

Ruby stepped into the sun and instantly felt exhausted. The high temperatures were draining her, and her frustrations had the same quality of attempting a quick jog in knee-high water. She considered going to Jeannie's store but, after a moment on the hot sidewalk, changed her mind. Boo had waited for her outside the police station and trotted along beside her as she walked back to the condos and air conditioning.

This was the end of it, then. She had to assume Roger had left. No one had seen him, and no one could find him. Maybe he had gotten scared, or maybe he had found what he wanted, but there was nothing more she could do. She was going home. Roger was gone, and Diane was out of danger. She and her sister had decided to stay on. Diane needed more time to recuperate, and Ruby could see they were enjoying each other, maybe for the first time. They were going to take an apartment in town, near Jeannie's. It was cheaper and smaller and just perfect for the two of them.

That evening, Ruby booked a flight with Mexicana Airlines for herself and Boo; apparently, it was the most dog-friendly carrier. She'd already talked to the island dog-lady, who'd assured her that she had sent hundreds of dogs off the island and knew exactly what was needed. Earlier in the week Ruby had gone to her house to get a crate for the trip and had been greeted by fifteen or twenty dogs of all sizes and colors. The story was that the dog-lady took in any dog in need of help, and her love for them was obvious as they walked toward the stack of dog crates beside the house. She talked to every dog, calling each by name and petting any that came close to her.

The next day they were going to the local vet's office for a checkup and to get a health certificate. The last step was to arrange transport from the ferry dock in Cancún to the airport. Taxis wouldn't take dogs, so the dog-lady worked with a specific van company that was glad for the extra business, dogs or no dogs. Ruby was very grateful for the help. She was apprehensive enough about her return to Boulder; things there had changed in her absence.

Both Patricia and Taylor met her at the Denver airport. Ruby was the last one to come through the doors; it had taken extra time to claim Boo and get him through customs.

"That was so much easier than I thought it would be! Those guys really couldn't have cared less," Ruby said as they coaxed Boo into the back of the car and drove toward Boulder.

"I'm so glad you're home. Its strange being in your house without you," confessed Taylor.

"I'm really glad to be here. It was too hot in Mexico when I left. I've been a little nervous about this, though; having all Mark's things gone is going to be strange. It's going to be an adjustment to think of him as gone instead of away."

"Well, we've made you dinner. We thought it would be good for the dog to be in the yard with us all there on his first night." Patricia was driving Ruby's car and seemed to know her way around.

"Isn't it incredible, the thought of having Boo here? I hope he likes it. Funny, isn't it?—exit one husband—enter one dog. What does that say?"

They turned north toward Boulder. Ruby was thinking how good it was to see the mountains again. The air was so dry and cool. *Nice to be home.*

"You have to tell us everything that has happened since we left, and how Diane is. It sounds like she's doing better," Taylor said.

"Let's get home first," suggested Ruby.

They drove up to the house and parked in the street. Boo jumped out of the car with enthusiasm. He sniffed the air and then the ground and stayed very close to Ruby. Ruby smiled at her house. She loved this old, peculiar bunch of bricks. It had been an old folks' home once, so there was a sink in every bedroom and a drinking fountain behind the kitchen. It had two sets of stairs, five fireplaces, and a dirt cellar. There was a porch wrapped around the front and side of the building, and huge mature trees shaded all the right places. She left her bags by the front door and went into the kitchen with Boo at her side. Everything seemed the same. Maybe there wouldn't be any difference at all. They sat on the back patio and watched Boo check out the fenced yard. "So, how is Diane?"

"Oh, she's so much better. She's taking short walks every day and gaining strength quickly. Her thinking is getting clearer, too, but she's still very quiet."

"Was she relieved to remember what happened?"

"I think it frightened her. Up until then she didn't know someone had hurt her. We hadn't told her anything about what happened, even the little we knew. We just thought she would remember when she wanted to or was ready to, but it didn't work out that way."

"You read about people losing their memory, and then something brings it all back for them. What happened?" asked Taylor.

"Wait, I have to get Emma. She's next door with her newfound friend. They're such a nice family." Patricia left through the side gate. They could hear her footsteps on the stairs to their neighbor's porch.

Ruby turned to Taylor, "How's it going? I mean, with the three of you together?"

"It's really been great. Patricia and I are becoming good friends. We think alike."

"Have you told Emma yet?"

"No, it's an adjustment for her with the two of us around all the time, so we're waiting. Or maybe we're stalling, whatever; it just hasn't happened yet…it will."

"I'm sure you two will handle it just right. She's a lucky girl." Emma came running through the side gate.

"Hi, Ruby. Did you really bring Boo here?" Emma threw her arms around Ruby's neck and planted a big kiss on her cheek. Ruby loved it.

"I sure did. He's right over there, checking the place out."

"Wow, that's so cool. Can I play with him?"

"Sure, I bet he would love to see an old friend."

They ate dinner early, and then Ruby went upstairs to face the empty closet. She had prepared herself for gloom but only experienced acceptance. Perhaps other feelings would come with time, but for now she tentatively appreciated the extra space as she unpacked.

Ruby enjoyed sleeping in her own bed after so long and loved having Boo sleeping on the floor beside her. He was easily transitioning to indoor living. So far there were no messes in the house.

"You're such a good boy," she said when she woke up the next morning. She was rubbing his ears as he rested his head on the side of the bed. "What should we do today? I guess I've a little catching up to do." It was a fresh, clear morning. Ruby finished unpacking, chatting with Boo through it all. It was a treat to have someone to talk to in the mornings. The coffee pot would have to take second billing now.

In the kitchen there was a note from her roommates. They had gone to buy school clothes for Emma and would call before lunch. Ruby was relieved. She had a phone call to make, and it had to be private. It also needed to be done right away. It would be two hours later in New York.

"Mr. Mendel's office, can I help you?"

"Yes, I'd like to speak to Mr. Mendel."

"May I ask who is calling?"

"Tell Mr. Mendel that Ruby is calling and that it's personal."

"One moment, please." There was a short pause, and then Ruby was relieved to hear Robert Mendel's voice. It felt very different from the first time she'd called him.

"Hello, Ruby. I am glad that you have called."

"Hi. You asked me to get in touch with you."

"That's right. Where are you?"

"I'm back in Boulder. I arrived yesterday."

"Have you seen Taylor?"

"Yes, she's staying here at my house. I have some things I need to talk to you about. First, I wanted to let you know that I got your letter and that if you want to keep in touch that's fine…but you will have to trust me on what I tell Taylor."

"I understand."

"The other thing is I need your help. I need to tell you what happened after you left."

"I will help if I can; go ahead."

"Okay, I'm not sure when you actually left the island, but I received your letter the day after we brought Diane home from the hospital. Luckily, you included that picture of Roger, because I had it on the table in my condo. Diane saw the picture and picked it up and just stared at it for a while. She was getting agitated, so we sat her on the couch, and then she said she didn't feel well, so Mary took her to her room. The next day, Mary told me that Diane had remembered what happened. She'd had a terrible night, and early that morning the sisters talked, and it slowly came out. Do you have time for this right now? Should I keep going?"

"I have time, and I am very interested in what happened to your friend. Please go on."

"Okay, the night Diane left, she'd been very anxious to talk to Shane and me when we came back from fishing; but we went upstairs to clean up first. When we returned, Roger was at the table."

"I knew Roger had something to do with this."

"He sure does." Ruby had to restrain her anger. It was Mr. Mendel who'd sent Roger to Isla in the first place. *Not now.* "That night, we joined Diane and Roger for dinner. Diane acted so weird, and we had no idea what was going on. Then, before we finished dinner, Diane made some lame excuse and left the table and never came back. In fact, she didn't come back that night at all. The next morning, we got a note saying she'd gone to Tulum with a friend. It seemed odd, but we really hadn't known her that long. We had no reason to think there was any problem."

Well, she told Mary that she'd found out Roger was the guy who'd been spying on Patricia and Rebecca. She'd waited all afternoon to tell us but then couldn't because Roger had sat down at our table. Having Roger at the table, with us not knowing about him, was making her nuts, so she went for a walk on the beach. She said she was standing close to the water when Roger came up behind her and grabbed her arm. He asked her what she was going to tell us about him, and she said she knew he'd been spying on Patricia and wanted to know who he was. I guess he wouldn't let go of her and started to walk her along the beach. He told her that he would hurt her if she made a commotion."

"Wasn't her arm broken when they found her?"

"They X-rayed it in Cancún and found that it was just badly bruised. So he must've been really rough with her. Anyway, she said he was aggressive and frightening, so she went with him, but it really shocked her when he took her to Kevin's hotel room. I guess she'd been there before. Kevin was there, and they started to argue, because he was mad that Roger had brought Diane to his place. Diane said they knew each other, and Roger seemed to be the one in charge."

"How does Kevin know Roger?" Robert already knew how Roger knew Kevin; he had tracked him down after the fire.

"That's the really bizarre part. Kevin had met Roger a few times when he was at the university with Tennyson. It turns out that Roger is Tennyson's brother."

"What?" There was a long pause. "Are you sure?"

"I haven't seen any proof or ID, but I guess Kevin was pretty sure."

Robert put things together quickly. Roger had shown up right after he had returned to New York, right after the funerals of Tennyson and Rebecca. "That makes sense. The first time I ever saw him was in New York right after the fire. But what is this all about?"

"I think Roger has always wanted what Kevin wanted: the discs with Tennyson's research."

"I knew Tennyson was a scientist, but I never knew what he was working on."

"He was working on fuels, alternatives to fossil fuels. Taylor told me he'd come up with something incredible but then was daunted by the enormous ramifications of the discovery. He left the university, and they moved to the mountains to get away, so he could decide what to do. Taylor also told me that Kevin used to hound him for the material, saying he'd had some part in the discovery and should be part of its introduction into the world. They'd worked together at the beginning of the project, but it was Tennyson who finished it. Kevin's behavior was part of the reason Tennyson had second thoughts about what to do."

"I know this part. It was Kevin who led Roger to Patricia. I wanted to be sure that the fire had been an accident, so I hired someone to look into anyone who had been involved with Tennyson. It was easy to come up with Kevin. I didn't want anyone from my office to do the research, so I hired Roger. He had left his résumé with my secretary and…" There was a long pause. Ruby assumed that Robert was trying to remember the order of things, or perhaps it was just hard for him to talk about what he had done. She hoped it was the latter.

"He told me he was new in New York and was leaving résumés all over town, but in retrospect, he must have been targeting me. I hired him. He was a private investigator. I checked his credentials but obviously not well enough. Now I see the timing and the connection."

"Did you know anything about his past?"

"I knew he had been in the military."

"Well, he's a really creepy guy." Ruby was getting angry again. The thought of Robert sending someone he knew so little about after Rebecca was another reminder of his hideous behavior. She had to let it go. She wanted his help. "Okay, let me finish. The men argued for a long time. They both wanted the discs, and, according to what Diane remembered, they both thought they were entitled to them, Kevin because he had worked on them and Roger because he was Tennyson's brother. Then Roger told Kevin he wasn't going to need him anymore. Poor Diane must have been so terrified. Right there in front of her he said he was going to kill Diane in Kevin's room, and Kevin was going to be blamed for it. Mary said that at that point Diane had rushed toward the door, and that's all she remembers. We can't find any trace of Kevin since that night, so he must have either run away because he was afraid of being charged with Diane's murder—or Roger got rid of him."

"What makes you think Roger got rid of him?"

"Well, none of us could be sure, but there was a picture in the local newspaper of a man who'd drowned. We all saw it, and it could've been

Kevin. But he'd been in the water for a while, and none of us could be sure."

"My god! Do you know where Roger is now?"

"That's actually why I'm calling you. He's disappeared, too. I went to the police because they were investigating Diane's assault. After she remembered all of this, I took his picture to them. They couldn't find him, and there was no record of him flying out of Cancún. What scared me the most was that Taylor had recently left the island. What if he was following her to get the discs? This guy is dangerous. We've got to do something. What if he's already in Boulder?"

"Does Taylor know about this?"

"She knows that Diane remembered what happened to her and that Kevin and Roger were involved, but she doesn't have all the details, and she doesn't know that Roger is Tennyson's brother. I need help here. She could be in real danger. That's why I called you…you sounded like you might want to be involved in Taylor's life?"

Robert ignored the question. "I will call the police here. I work with them all the time. I will get them to contact the Boulder police, and I will call the sheriff in Nederland. He should remember the case and be familiar with the area we need to concentrate on."

Ruby was so relieved to hear his plan and mutual concern. She knew she was over her head. "What should I do?"

"You need to make Taylor aware of the situation and keep me informed of anything unusual going on. I am sure the police will be contacting you soon. They will be able to tell you what to do."

When Ruby hung up the phone, she felt relieved to have help and dread at the prospect of telling all this to Taylor.

CHAPTER 53

Old News

After the call from Ruby, Robert Mendel searched his records for any information he had on Roger Bates. He found surprisingly little and in hindsight couldn't believe he'd been so sloppy. He was mortified. He'd been duped and had put his daughter and granddaughter in danger.

Robert was tired. He hadn't slept well since his return. His steadfast perceptions were in question. He'd followed his program from the day he'd left his mother and sisters and stayed his path in a straight line. In actual fact, it had been easy. There had been no gray areas. He hadn't wasted an ounce of energy on doubt and was able to put all his drive into plowing forward—no pauses and never a stall. This steady pursuit had been his strength, his mantra during his climb, and for the first time he was suffering doubt. Was his behavior questionable? Wasn't his history enough justification?

During those early morning hours, when negative thoughts are magnified, he would crumble just a little. Mainly the outer edges, then fear would hold him together, just at the fringe of vulnerability. All this time, his consistent, forward motion had avoided retrospection, and distance had been his security. Now he was being drawn to connections he was used to avoiding. This was all unfamiliar territory and was accompanied by a plethora of remote possibilities. The magnitude of his errors could have crushed a weaker man, but Robert understood himself. He was uncomplicated and resolute. There had never been malicious intent. He'd spent enough time with criminals to know the difference. It was the stupidity that was hard to accept. He had to sift all of this and only let it settle when accompanied by comprehension. Being an organized thinker, he was able to consider this new perspective clearly.

He wondered how much a person had to change to move forward. He knew he was changing already. He hadn't planned it but couldn't halt the process either. He understood that he would have to help Taylor. He wanted to help her and, realizing this, questioned his motives. Was it guilt or need?

He knew he was an excellent lawyer. He'd put his father in jail over and over again. It felt good and had been enough to keep him satisfied. But he was lonely. There'd been nobody since his second marriage had ended. Relationships were distracting, but how does one divorce one's daughter? He'd tried, and for some reason she wouldn't go away—or, more precisely, he couldn't rid his heart of her.

Confusion was not something Robert was used to. There were so many unanswered questions. *Had watching Rebecca and Patricia been a connection? Had it been some kind of controlled, hands-off family for him?* It sounded ghoulish, and that was not the way Robert saw himself. His father had been sick, and his mother had let herself be corrupted. *Not me*, Robert thought, during those dark morning hours as he paced back and forth in his tidy, eighteenth-floor New York City apartment. He knew he could say "not me," but that didn't make it true.

First, he called the New York police. He'd worked with the captain often and had no trouble getting straight through to him. "This is Howard Becker."

"Howard, Robert Mendel here."

"Robert, how are you?"

"Fine, thanks, but I need your help with something. Got a minute?"

"Shoot—what's up?"

Robert told Howard the story. He didn't explain why he had kept the existence of his granddaughter from his daughter, and the captain didn't ask. Howard told him he would contact the Boulder police and see what he could find out about Roger Bates.

Next, Robert called Nederland, Colorado. "Sheriff Small, please."

"This is Sheriff Small. What can I do for you?"

"Sheriff, this is Robert Mendel. It was my daughter's cabin that burned down eight years ago."

"I remember, Mr. Mendel. It was a tough time."

"Well, there are some new developments in the case, and I may need your help."

"What case? The case is closed, but, you know, you're the second inquiry I've had about this in the last few months."

"I am aware of that. I am familiar with the woman who called you. Ruby Starkey, right?"

"Yeah, that sounds like it. What's going on?"

For the second time that day, Robert went through the story. This time he said he did his own investigation just to be sure and again did not explain why he had kept Rebecca's existence from Taylor. Again, he was not asked about it. Every time he repeated his story, no matter what he omitted or added, it made less sense to him. It was becoming more difficult to position himself in a positive role. He was reading himself out loud, and he was finding he wasn't the person he wanted to be.

"You know, I met that young fellow's brother. He came here after you and your daughter left. He wanted to see the site of the fire, so I took him up and showed him what was left of the cabin. Are you sure this Roger Bates is the same man?"

"I assume you have a fax?"

"Sure do."

"I will fax you his picture. I am coming to Colorado as soon as I can arrange it. Can you meet with me?"

"Sure, I work with the police in Boulder all the time. We can meet at the station there."

"Perfect. I will fax you the photo and then call you with my schedule."

"This is an amazing story, Mr. Mendel. I'll pull the files and wait for your call."

CHAPTER 54

Colorado

"Roger Bates is Tennyson's brother?" Taylor jumped up and started to walk around the room.

"That's what Diane heard Kevin and Roger talking about. I guess Kevin already knew him," said Ruby.

"I never met Tennyson's brother. He was in the army. Tennyson didn't like him and said they had nothing in common."

"Well, he sure doesn't act like Tennyson."

"Tennyson said he was a really unhappy guy and that he had always felt sorry for him. He told me they were never close. We just didn't talk about his family that much. I don't think it had been a warm home to grow up in. It was easier for Tennyson, though—there was always something brewing in that incredible mind of his. But Roger got into trouble, one thing after another. I've never heard the details except that his parents gave up on him pretty early on. Then, he just sort of disappeared, and no one looked for him."

"Well, we don't have a clue where this guy is now, either. We do know he wants those discs, and we do know he's capable of hurting people. Plus, we still aren't sure what happened to Kevin. If that body in the newspaper was Kevin, it must've had something to do with Roger. I think we need to be very watchful." Ruby hesitated for a moment. "The Boulder police have been told, and they want to talk to you. That old sheriff from Nederland is going to be there, too."

"You arranged all that?"

"Not just me...I had some help."

"So Patricia knows all this?"

"I've told Patricia everything, but she's not the one who called the police." Ruby reached for Taylor's arm. "Taylor…I called your father."

Taylor stared straight at Ruby. "My father is dead. I don't want to hear one word. Do you understand me? Not one more word about that." Taylor abruptly left the room.

They had been in Ruby's bedroom. Ruby lay back on her bed and thought about calling Shane. She was sure he would want to know she was back in the United States, and she needed someone to talk to. She wondered what it would mean to him if she called. Would he think that meant they were going to have a relationship? Ruby didn't think he wanted to go on being friends, unless, perhaps, if she told him that they would never be lovers, and she wasn't prepared to do that. *Oh, smart, Shane,* she thought resentfully, *either I take all of you, or I get none of you. Not fair.*

Ruby and Taylor had a meeting with the police at four o'clock that afternoon. Ruby called Robert to tell him they were going, but if he was already in town, she didn't think he should be there. She told him what Taylor had said but that she, Ruby, still really wanted his help. He said he was already in town and assured her he would stay out of sight.

After telling Patricia where they were going, Ruby and Taylor left for their appointment.

The police station was a cold, utilitarian brick building. Inside the front door was a glass partition. As they approached the glass, it slid to one side, and a policewoman asked what they were there for.

"We have an appointment at four o'clock with Sheriff Small."

"That's right; he just got here," said the policewoman as she looked at the papers on her desk. "Please hand me your purses and come through the side door." The two women proceeded through the door and a metal detector and were given back their purses. After passing through another door, they entered a large, noisy area full of cubicles. The outer walls were lined with offices, each with glass doors and walls. Sheriff Small approached them from an office on the right. He'd met both women before and appeared pleased to see them.

"Ms. Barrett, it's good to see you. It's been a long time. Ms. Starkey," he nodded, "nice to see you again."

"I wish it were under better circumstances, but it's nice to see you again too, sheriff. How's your father?" asked Ruby.

"He's fine, thank you. If you'll come with me, they've assigned an office for this case. We should be joined by detective Birmingham soon."

Everyone took a seat around a table in the center of the office. "Have you found anything out about Roger Bates?" asked Ruby.

"We've received a dossier from New York. He's got quite a history. Once they knew his real name, they were able to come up with a lot of information. Right now, Birmingham has the file, but I can give you the gist of it while we wait."

Taylor spoke up for the first time: "Sheriff, I've never met Tennyson's brother. My husband and his brother didn't get along. He was in the army at the time Tennyson and I were married."

"Well, he's a rough guy. He must be Tennyson's older brother, right?" Taylor nodded. "He has packed in quite a bit for his thirty-nine years. First, he wasn't in the army; he was in the Marines. After he put in his time, he spent eight years in South America. We made a few phone calls and found enough to know that when he left, staying there wasn't an option. When he came back to the US, he changed his name to Bates and became a private investigator. He's been charged with harassment a few times but never convicted. He presently has two ex-wives, one with a restraining order out on him. It seems he has a bad temper and can get violent with women as well as men. I've briefed Birmingham. If it's true he hurt your friend and that Kevin…," he checked his notes, "…Levine is still missing, then I think it's clear just how far he'll go to get what he wants."

"That's just it. He wants my husband's discs, and I don't have all of them. That's also what Kevin Levine wanted. It all started up again when the university sent me a box of Tennyson's work that they found in an old storage room. I opened it, and the final discs, the ones that are the most important, aren't there. I assume the final stages of Tennyson's work were either in his head or burned up in the fire. The date on the last disc is before…."

"Excuse me for being late." Gerry Birmingham entered the room. He was medium height and very sturdy, with short brown hair and dark brown eyes, and he looked like someone who could take care of things. Sheriff Small introduced him. "I've been going over the file on Roger Bates and the statement we received from New York, plus the sheriff's file on the fire. If I may say, this is an amazing case. Now, Ms. Barrett…"

"Please call me Taylor."

"Good, okay, Taylor—where are you staying at the moment? I understand you're not living with your husband. Is that right?"

"We're separated. I'm living with Ruby for now."

"Okay, it's clear to me that until this Bates shows up, we need to offer you some protection. For now, twenty-four hour surveillance is the plan."

"What does that mean?" asked Ruby.

"It means there will be an unmarked car outside your house at all times. They'll have a picture of Roger Bates, and you'll have a radiophone that will connect you to the officers on duty. The phone has a panic button, plus you can talk to whoever is in the car if necessary. You'll need to inform the officers if you're going anywhere, but we do recommend you keep your activities to a minimum."

"This sounds awful. How long will this go on?" asked Ruby.

"At least until we track this guy down. This is just a first step. He could show up back in New York, and they'll hold him there. We just have to wait and see."

"What'll you do if he shows up?" asked Ruby.

"We'll hold him for questioning. The details of the assault on Ms. Fentner are being sent from Mexico, so we'll start there. We've also been in touch with Kevin Levine's family, and he has not returned to Boulder. We would like to question him as well."

Ruby told the detective and the sheriff about the picture in the newspaper. The detective said he would look into it.

"I've got my father watching things in Nederland," said Sheriff Small, "so I'm going to stay in town for now and help with the surveillance. If you need anything, here's my card. It has my cell phone number on it, where I can be reached at any time."

"Thank you, Sheriff, that's very assuring," Taylor said.

"Can I add that I think it's incredible that you found your daughter? The thought of her dying in that fire has haunted me for years."

"It has been incredible. We're all still adjusting to it," said Taylor.

The sheriff walked Taylor and Ruby to the car and reiterated his offer of help, which Taylor appreciated. Sheriff Small seemed more personable than the officious detective.

CHAPTER 55

The Road to Nederland

It was 5:30 P.M. by the time they left the station, so they decided to pick up some takeout and then go straight home. Ruby bolted her front door after they entered the house. That was a first. She had never locked her house except before going to bed, figuring if someone wanted to get in, they would find a way. This was definitely different.

"Patricia!" Taylor called as they went down the hall to the kitchen.

"We're in here," Patricia answered, unenthusiastically.

"We thought you might be hungry, so we stopped and got some stir…" Taylor rounded the corner and stopped so suddenly that Ruby bumped into her. Sitting at the kitchen table were Roger and Emma. Patricia was standing at the sink. Ruby looked around Taylor.

Oh, my god. She thought when she saw Roger. *They aren't going to start the surveillance on the house until midnight.* She glanced at her watch. *That's five hours away.*

"Come on in, ladies; nice of you to bring us dinner." Emma was sitting next to him and started to get up. "You just stay there. They can bring the food to you."

When they entered the kitchen, Boo started to scratch on the backdoor. He was happy to see Ruby and wanted to come in. Ruby started toward the door. "Leave it," Roger snapped. "That dog's not coming in."

"What do you want?" Taylor could see now why Roger had looked familiar to her. Now that she knew who he was, the resemblance became more obvious. "We know who you are, Roger. What's this all about?"

"I wouldn't have known who you were. Tennyson never wrote me that he was getting married. What kind of a brother is that?"

"Don't be ridiculous. When did you ever write Tennyson?" Roger's smug demeanor had Taylor annoyed immediately. The situation wasn't clear yet, and based on what she knew, it wasn't going to be good. "He never knew where you were or what you were doing."

"That's true. But he wouldn't have cared."

"Of course he'd care. He was your brother."

"Oh, give me a break. What would you know?"

"He was my husband."

"Yeah, and you must be some sort of wacko. Who would marry a guy like that?"

"I've no idea what you're referring to. Tennyson was a wonderful, brilliant man."

"Brilliant, yes, but how about adding ego-maniacal asshole?"

"What has any of this to do with us?"

"That's easy; I want those discs."

"I knew you'd say that. I only have the beginning of his research. The university sent it to me. The discs that covered the last part of his work are gone. Maybe they were only in his head, or maybe they burned up in the fire."

"I thought you'd say that. It's bullshit. Tennyson always recorded everything. No way he wouldn't have had some record of his work."

"Maybe he did, but it must have burnt in the fire." Everyone else in the room was very quiet. They let Taylor do the talking.

"Not possible. Our friend Kevin looked everywhere for them."

"When are you talking about? Kevin never came to our house." Taylor was afraid to have the answer, but she had to ask.

"Haven't you figured that out yet? He searched the whole cabin after he killed Tennyson." Roger sat back, gloating over his prized piece of information.

Taylor felt lightheaded. It was hard to think about it. She knew he was telling the truth: Everything fit together. She didn't want him to see how shaken she was, but she had to sit down. Trying to appear casual, she moved toward the table and sat in one of the chairs. The closeness obviously bothered Roger. He slid his chair back from the table.

"Where's Kevin now?"

"He's gone."

"What does that mean?" asked Ruby. She knew why Taylor sat down and wanted to help her out.

"He's just gone." He looked back at Taylor. "You should be thrilled. He killed your husband."

"How do you know that?" asked Ruby.

"Because he told me. It's a miracle he never got caught." Roger turned to Taylor again. "I've watched your husband, my ridiculous brother, off and on, all my life. I knew with his smarts he would come up with something worth money, and I've been waiting for a piece of it. I deserve that much after growing up with the bastard. If he'd been normal instead of wonder-boy, I might have had a half-decent life."

"He never did anything to hurt you. He was never a mean man," said Taylor.

"He didn't have to do anything—just being so fucking smart and smug about it."

"He was never smug." Taylor couldn't take this scumbag tearing Tennyson apart, but she knew there was no point in arguing. She wanted information, and they needed time, so she needed to change her attitude. Roger, evidently, was happy to talk about it.

"Superior, smug, what's the difference? Do you know what it was like growing up with a brilliant brother? No amount of smarts was enough next to him. He was a star. I grew up thinking I was an idiot. I got out of there as soon as I could. But I paid. I deserve a piece of anything that weirdo came up with."

"He discovered something for the world, not for your greedy ambitions." Taylor knew as soon as she had said it that it was the wrong thing to say. She was trying to engage him, not annoy him.

Roger stood up and moved around the table, getting very close to Taylor. "You don't know shit. He never did anything to deserve being so smart. That was the biggest piss-off of all. He was born that way. He took over the day he was born." Taylor leaned back in her chair to put more distance between her face and his aggressive behavior. Roger sat back down, obviously trying to control his anger.

"Anyway, he's so stupid, he got himself murdered and almost killed his little girl here." Roger put his arm around Emma. Both Patricia and Ruby leaned toward the table, but Roger let her go and sat back in his chair, entwining his hands behind his head. "You're all so stupid. Your father actually paid me to find out what I wanted to know. What an idiot. He's been paying me for eight years to keep an eye on all of you. I was a little surprised that he didn't tell you that Rebecca was alive, but I didn't care. And Kevin," he turned to face Patricia, "was pathetic. It was so easy to find him; he drew a straight line right to you. Then he made a mistake: He went to Mexico without telling me he had new information."

"Where is Kevin?" asked Patricia.

"Never mind. He promised me he would let me know if anything came up. We both figured that the discs burned with the cabin, but we had a deal. Then he came up with that stupid story about Taylor being abusive. Luckily, I got the letter back before he could complicate things. I can't believe he thought he could mess with me. Not just because he was a wimp, but because I had so much on him. He told me everything when I first caught up with him. He'd just dropped off Rebecca, so that added kidnapping to murder and arson…. I'm pretty sure he'd get the chair for that. So he got what he deserved, anyway."

That was it. No one said a word. Roger realized he'd confessed. He sat forward in his chair, clearly indicating that the discussion was closed.

"I should've known who you were," Taylor said. She wanted to keep him talking until they could get some help. "You looked familiar to me the first time I saw you in Mexico. I can see some of Tennyson in you."

"There's no Tennyson in me. That was always the problem. But, then again, brainy boy is dead, and I'm still here. Just give me the research, and I'll leave you all in peace."

"Fine, I'll give you everything I have. It's in a box upstairs. You can have the whole thing."

"It's no good to me without those last discs. Where are the rest of them?"

"What do I have to do to convince you there are no…?" There was a knock on the front door, and everyone looked at Roger.

Roger stood up. "Are you expecting someone?"

"No."

"Good, then they'll go away."

The knocking continued, followed by a "Hello." Everyone was very quiet. Then it stopped.

"Why don't you get the box and let me have a look at it?"

"It's upstairs."

"Don't worry about the phone, it's busy, and don't be too long." Roger looked at Emma as he said that. The threat was clear.

Taylor went up the stairs quickly. She looked out the window over the front door. There was no one there. She came right back with the box. She had no intention of messing with Roger. As she re-entered the kitchen, there was a knock on the backdoor. It was a sliding glass door that entered the kitchen from the backyard. Taylor could see Sheriff Small looking right at her. She looked ahead without moving and talked to Roger.

"What do you want me to do? He's seen me."

"Hey, let him in, no problem." Taylor tried to smile as she walked toward the backdoor. She opened it and asked the sheriff to come in while trying desperately to communicate with her eyes. Whether he noticed anything or not, it didn't make any difference. She shut the door quickly behind him to block Boo.

The sheriff was calm. He told Roger that he remembered him and asked what was going on. Roger said it was no big deal, that he'd come over to pick up a package and then he'd be on his way. The sheriff asked whether he could help out in any way. He was trying to give the impression that he considered the whole scene to be normal.

"We have a slight problem," said Taylor. "I'm very happy to give Roger what he wants, but he seems to think I'm holding something back. You see, Roger is my late husband's brother, and he wants some of his research discs, but I don't have them all."

The sheriff looked at Roger, obviously trying to take in as much as he could as quickly as possible. "Roger and I have met. I took him up to the cabin after the fire." With his eyes still on Roger he continued. "What makes you think Taylor's lying?"

"I knew my brother; he recorded everything. He would have put it all on discs. But we can handle this. Why don't you stay out of it?"

The sheriff moved closer to Taylor and looked her straight in the eyes. "You know, this may well be the answer to something I've been wondering about for years."

"What are you talking about?" Roger was annoyed. The last thing he'd expected was for the sheriff to show up, and it was making him nervous. "What are you doing here anyway?"

"Just came to pay a visit. Taylor and I are old buds. She called to tell me the good news. I had to come over and see for myself."

"Do you stay close to the victims of all the crimes in your area?"

The sheriff moved next to Taylor and put an arm around her waist. "Nope, just had a big heart for this one." Taylor found the contact reassuring.

"So tell us, sheriff, what've you been wondering about all these years?" Roger asked sarcastically.

"Well, after the fire, we did some local research. There was no investigation, but we asked around a bit anyway. We found out that Tennyson had a safety deposit box in our bank. Those ladies at the bank are pretty chatty, and the head of the bank is a good friend of mine, so I asked him about it. He told me it was something he'd worked out with Tennyson. Tennyson wanted to rent a safety deposit box, but he wanted it just in his name. Then, he added a stipulation. If he died, the box was to be undisturbed for ten years. After that, only his wife could open it. I've always been dying to know what was inside that box."

"I don't know anything about a safety deposit box," said Taylor.

"You weren't supposed to. That was part of the deal."

"Is this bank still there?" asked Roger.

"Oh, yeah. Nothing much changes in Nederland."

"Well, what if I wanted to open it now?"

"You can't."

"What if I add a little persuasion?" Roger pulled a gun out of the pocket of his jacket and put it on the table. Emma tried to get up, but Roger put his hand on her shoulder.

"I don't think there's any need for that kind of thing around here," said Sheriff Small.

"How about if you and I and Rebecca…"

"No!" Taylor moved toward her daughter until Roger put his hand back on the gun. She stopped immediately, understanding the implication.

"As I was saying, how about you and I and Rebecca take a ride up to Nederland and see what's in that box?"

"The bank would be closed now."

"Come on, now, sheriff. Are you trying to tell me that you couldn't get your friend to open the bank?"

"I guess we could try. He lives just on the edge of town."

"Then we can pay him a visit and make a special request to open things up. Police business, you know."

Sheriff Small looked from Taylor to Ruby. "I suppose we can give him a call."

"I doubt that," said Roger. "We'll go right to his house, and if he isn't there, we can wait."

"We don't need to take Rebecca," said the sheriff. "Why don't we take her mother instead?" Emma looked a Patricia.

"No, Taylor is going to stay right here until we get back. She's just going to wait quietly, not use the phone or leave the house. Right, Taylor?"

"Mom?" Emma started to get up from the table, but Roger put his hand on her shoulder again. "I just want to talk to my mom. Let me go." Roger followed her gaze to Patricia.

"She doesn't know, does she?" Nobody said a word.

"I know lots of things. I want to talk to my mom." A malicious grin spread across Roger's face. He looked from Patricia to Taylor. "Why can't I talk to my mom?"

"You can. She's right there," Roger pointed to Taylor. Taylor gave Roger the most hateful look she could.

"There's no reason to do this," she said.

"You know, come to think of it, I'm Rebecca's uncle." Roger looked at Emma, "I'm your Uncle Roger."

"Mom?"

"Stop it! Do you hear me? You stop this!" Patricia strode toward her daughter, ignoring Roger's hand back on the gun. She raised Emma from her chair and wrapped her arms around her. "If you hurt any of us now, you won't get any of these things you want." Patricia pointed at the box. "Just go with the sheriff and take what you want and leave us alone."

"That's just what I'm going to do, but first Rebecca is coming with us. The rest of you are going to stay put until we get back. If I see one thing that looks suspicious, then Rebecca is going to go on a trip with her uncle."

Roger turned to the sheriff. "How long does it take to get to Nederland?" The sheriff looked at his watch.

"It's seven o'clock now. We'll just get the tail end of rush hour. I'd say about an hour."

"And then to the banker's house?"

"It's a small town; everything is right there."

Roger stood up and put his gun back in his pocket. He extended his other hand, palm up, signaling Patricia to hand over Emma. "It's time to go."

"Look, Roger, take me," Taylor said. "If the letter is addressed to me, then it will be easier with me there. She's just a little girl."

"Nope."

Patricia loosened her grip, and Emma moved reluctantly toward Roger. "Come on, Rebecca, you're just going to take a ride in the mountains with Uncle Roger."

"My name's not Rebecca!"

"We can talk about it in the car." Roger moved the gun in his pocket and scanned the people in the room. "I just want to remind you that I'll be very unhappy if I see any signs of interference. Just stay here and wait for us."

"We're not going to have any trouble." Sheriff Small looked at the two mothers. "It's an easy ride up there and back, and I'm sure the bank will cooperate under the circumstances." Ruby handed over the keys to her car. "We'll be back soon; don't worry." The sheriff put a protective arm around Emma as they walked toward the door.

CHAPTER 56

Waiting

Roger left a stunned silence behind him. Everything in the kitchen seemed like a normal evening, except for the absence of Emma. What remained had a surreal texture.

"We have to think…be very careful…I just don't…" Patricia lowered herself into a chair by the table, where her daughter had been moments before.

Taylor and Ruby joined her there and put their hands on Patricia's arm. "It'll be okay. The sheriff's with them, and Roger doesn't want to hurt anyone. He just wants those stupid discs, and then he'll leave us alone."

"What if that isn't what's in the safety deposit box?" Patricia asked.

"It has to be. There could be no other explanation. Tennyson would have done that for me. He must have assumed someone would come up with an alternative in ten years, and in the meantime I wouldn't inherit his struggle. So the discs have been there all this time." Taylor was touched by what her husband had done for her, and, for the first time in a long while, she suffered his loss again; but her reverie was short. "What we've got to decide is what to do now."

Ruby spoke for the first time: "I think we should call the police. They already know the circumstances, and if they stay out of sight, it won't increase the threat to Emma."

"No!" Patricia said. "He hurt Diane and practically confessed to killing Kevin. He might know somehow."

"I think Ruby's right," Taylor said, trying to sound calmer than she felt. "He wants those discs, and if they're in the box, then he won't have any reason to hurt anyone." She kept talking—she had to. "We don't have any proof he killed Kevin or about what happened to Diane. After the injuries she suffered, she may not be considered a reliable witness. Plus, it was Kevin's name on the hotel room. He can still walk away. But if he hurts someone now, he'd never get away with the discs. They would have to find him." Unsure, Taylor added, "Right?"

"That's right," Ruby said to Patricia. "He just wants any money he can get for the research. I mean, think about the possibilities. He doesn't want trouble, just money."

Patricia was listening, but nothing was going to alleviate her fears. "Oh, my god, I just can't stand the thought of Emma with him. I can't bear the thought of her being so frightened." Ruby leaned toward Patricia and put her arm around her. Patricia was trying to stay calm, but tears were rolling down her cheeks, and she looked like she was holding her breath.

Taylor wanted to say something to help but couldn't. She turned her back on the other two. She had to protect the tenuous hold she had on her own emotions. Along with her own fears, she was dealing with resentment again. As she watched Ruby comfort Patricia, the words "my daughter" started to repeat in her head. There was no time for this, she told herself, but she couldn't stop it. *Patricia was caring for her when I wasn't. It was easier to be on Patricia's side. I wanted to. Will it always be like this?* Then she felt a hand on her shoulder. Patricia turned her around and held her tight.

They both wept—for fear, for loss, for guilt, and for relief. They stayed like that for a long time. "Everything will be all right; there is no reason for him to hurt her," Patricia said. "Thank god for the sheriff."

"That's right. I vote we call the police," said Ruby. "They know how to deal with this kind of thing better than we do…I mean…I just don't know what else to do."

"I just can't stay here and do nothing." Patricia said this to Taylor, who reluctantly nodded her agreement.

"So, we're agreed. I should call the police?" Taylor and Patricia nodded. Ruby went to the phone. It had been off the hook since Roger had arrived, and she hoped it would work. He must have done something to it, however, because Ruby found it had the hollow sound of no connection. "He's done something to the phone. Now what?" They sat around the table, looking down, afraid to see the grief in each other's eyes, afraid of what it would do to their own limited control. "Wait! Mark had an unlisted line put in his basement office. We can try that."

They all hurried downstairs. Ruby opened the office door. She'd forgotten her present situation and felt an uncomfortable jolt at the sight of the empty office. The only thing in the room was the phone on the floor. *Please, don't have disconnected it yet.*

"Oh, thank god, it's working. I'll see if I can reach Detective Birmingham." Taylor went upstairs for her purse and returned with the detective's card. Ruby made the call.

"Detective Birmingham…how long will that be? Ruby Starkey…yes, he has the number…no wait…let me give you a different one." Ruby hung up and turned toward her friends. "They're going to find him and have him call us."

"Well, at least the police car is showing up at midnight, no matter what happens."

"No," said Taylor. "We can't let that happen. Roger will see it when he gets back."

"We'll ask the detective about it."

"Ruby, do you have any…" The ringing phone cut Patricia off. Taylor picked it up immediately.

"Hello. Oh, my god, I'm so glad it's you. He has Emma…Roger…he took her." There was a long pause as she listened. "The sheriff came over, and he and Emma and Roger are going up to Nederland. There's a safety deposit box that my husband left for me. We think it has the last part of his research in it." Taylor continued to explain the situation to Detective Birmingham and then listened for a long time before hanging up. "He wants to come here and talk to us. He can be here in less than ten minutes."

"How long has it been since they left?" asked Patricia. Ruby looked at her watch as they went back upstairs.

"Let's see. They left at seven-twenty, and it's seven forty-nine now, so they've been gone for half an hour. They'd still be on the road."

"It seems like hours. She didn't even get dinner or take a jacket." Patricia started to pace and wring her hands. "I can't stand this." It was easier when they had something to do. No one had said anything for a while, and time to think was not a good thing.

"If Roger gets the research, then he has no reason to hurt anyone and…"

"Did you see his face light up when he realized that Emma didn't know about Taylor? We should've told her. We should've told her sooner. He's going to tell her. It's so wrong that she should hear it from him."

"I've been thinking about that, and he probably will tell her. But it'll be okay," said Taylor. "It'll be confusing for her, but she isn't going to believe anything he says. Then, when this is all over, we can explain it to her properly."

"I should've insisted on going with them," Patricia said. Waiting was offering her nothing but time to panic. Ruby moved closer to touch her on the back.

"He wouldn't have taken you. He didn't want more people than he could control. He wants you and Taylor here, worrying and waiting and…" There was a knock on the front door. Ruby hurried to let the detective in. "Yes, yes, come in. We're all in the kitchen."

They sat down at the table and listened to what the detective thought should be done.

CHAPTER 57

Nederland

"Just keep driving, sheriff," Roger said. He was on the passenger side of the car. The sheriff was driving, and Emma was in the backseat. "Tell me, officer, why did you really come to the house?"

"I told you. I never could stand the thought of the baby in that fire. I just wanted to come and see her for myself."

"Did you hear that, Rebecca? The police thought you burned up in a fire."

"Why do you keep calling me Rebecca?"

"Because that's your name. That's the name Taylor and your dad gave you."

"My mom and dad were killed in a car accident. You don't know anything."

"Nope, Taylor is your mom, and your dad died in a fire, and she thought you did, too."

"That's not true. My mom would've told me. You're the liar."

"Not too fond of your Uncle Roger, eh? Well, it's true, and your daddy was my idiot-genius brother."

The sheriff hated the malicious pleasure Roger was getting from confusing Emma. "Rebecca, your mother didn't know. She was told the same story we were," Sheriff Small said.

"Quit calling me Rebecca. My name is Emma, and I'm not listening to either of you." Emma crossed her arms and slid herself into the rear corner of the car, putting as much space between her and the front seat as she could.

"How much farther?" asked Roger.

"Just a few more miles to the reservoir, then we drive down into Nederland."

"Okay, we'll drive straight to the banker's house. I want to get this done fast."

"Will do." They drove into the town, and a minute later they passed the sheriff's office and were through downtown Nederland in sixty seconds more. At the end of the main street they turned left. Sheriff Small stopped in front of the second house on the right. "This is it. What do we do now?"

"We're going to knock on the door and ask the banker to come with us, with all of his keys, of course."

"I don't want to go," Emma said. Roger was already getting out of the car. He walked around to the side that Emma had pressed herself into and opened the door.

"Come on, get out."

"But I don't..." The sheriff turned around from the driver seat and assured Emma that everything was going to be okay, but she needed to do what Roger asked.

Emma looked from one man to the other. Taylor seemed to like the sheriff, so she decided she would do what he said for now. There wasn't anyone else around. She slid off the seat onto the dirt road, and Roger closed the door behind her. The sheriff joined them, staying close, forever aware of the threat to Emma. He knew she would be Roger's first target if anything went wrong. The house was a two-story log cabin. There were two windows on the second floor and light around the front door. Looking straight at it with the soft pines on either side and on the hill behind, it bore an eerie resemblance to a smiling face.

They knocked and waited. They could hear footsteps coming toward them, and the door opened. A large man greeted the sheriff like they'd known each other for years. He invited them inside. The sheriff introduced Roger and Emma as a friend and his niece and explained they needed to get into the bank. They needed to open a safety deposit box.

"Can't this wait? The bank is closed." The banker peered over his shoulder at his family. "We were just sitting down to dinner." Roger had one hand in his pocket and the other on Emma's shoulder. He'd positioned her in front of his body, keeping the threat clear to the sheriff.

"You know, Jed, we really have to do this now. You know I wouldn't ask you if it wasn't extremely important." Jed hesitated. He looked back toward his family again and then sighed.

"It better be, Sheriff."

"I really appreciate it, Jed. I'll make it up to you sometime."

"Let me get my keys."

"You can ride with us," Roger said.

"I meant the keys to the bank. I don't care how we get there, young man." Jed was clearly annoyed. Roger sat in the backseat with Emma as they drove back into town. He'd pulled her aside as they walked toward the car and warned her not to say a word. She was too confused and scared to do anything. His menacing bearing was enough to ensure her cooperation.

The bank was in the middle of town, on the main street. The other businesses were closed down for the evening. This was a mountain town, and the area was deserted. They parked in front, and all four of them got out. The bank manager fumbled with the keys, seemingly nervous, but he managed to open the door; then, he went straight toward a keypad on the wall and punched in five numbers. The second door clicked, and he pushed it open. The bank was dark and empty.

"I won't be able to open the safety deposit box without the owner's key."

"I think you have the key, Jed. This is the box opened by Tennyson Garland. Remember? That's the man who died in the fire eight years ago."

"Yes, I remember him."

"You told me you had the key in a letter to his wife."

"That's right. Where's his wife?"

"She's in Boulder, but this is his brother."

"Sheriff, I'm trying to cooperate with you, but I can't open that letter if it's addressed to his wife. It's just not possible."

"Just get the letter, and let's get this done fast." Roger could see that this approach was getting nowhere. He also knew that the longer this went on, the more chances there were for problems.

"Now, you wait a minute, young…" The sheriff put his hand on the banker's arm and told him that he'd better do what the man said. Jed turned to Roger for more information. Roger moved out from behind Emma, just enough to draw attention to his hand around something in his pocket. The message was clear.

"The letter's in the safe in my office—this way." He led them into his office and turned the lights on. Kneeling in front of the safe, he opened it and then riffled through the contents before coming out with an envelope addressed to Taylor Garland. "You'll have to open this," he said to the sheriff, holding it toward him.

"Give it to him," the sheriff gestured at Roger. Roger took his hand off Emma's shoulder and reached for the envelope. It was sealed, so he started to take his right hand out of his pocket to open it. As soon as his right hand became visible, the sheriff shoved Emma to the floor. At the same instant the banker hit Roger in the chest with his shoulder, knocking him off balance. Roger hit the wall with the banker still pressed against him. He was struggling to free his right arm so he could reach the gun in his pocket. He managed to work his arm out from under the banker's weight, but the flimsy fabric of his jacket made it hard to find the opening to his pocket.

After the sheriff was sure Emma was out of the way, he grabbed at Roger's coat, caught the collar, and yanked as hard as he could. The force jerked the coat off Roger's shoulder, and the sheriff put all of his weight into pinning Roger's arm back against the wall. The pocket with the gun was hanging almost to the floor. "Get the gun," yelled the sheriff. "It's in his pocket."

Two officers appeared at the door to the office. One of them snatched the loose side of the jacket and removed the gun. Then the sheriff and the banker stood Roger up and away from the wall. The second officer pulled Roger's jacket all the way off and handcuffed him.

"Get him out of here," said the sheriff. They were all breathless from their struggle, and Roger said nothing as they led him away.

The capture was over quickly, and as the officers escorted Roger from the room, the sheriff looked for Emma. She had braced herself behind a chair and curled into a ball as small as her little body would allow. Her head was lowered on her knees, but she looked up as the sheriff touched her hair.

"Emma, it's over now. You're a very brave girl."

CHAPTER 58

Emma

I don't remember being frightened that day. I can remember other instances of fear in those young years, but not the day I was taken to Nederland. Mother and Taylor took me back there a few weeks later, and we visited the cabin site where my life changed one night during a snow-storm. Who knows what my life would have been like if my father and I hadn't had a visitor that night? I can't even say that things began there. I could go back to the day my father was conceived from some perfect mix of whatever creates a genius: a man who would create something worth killing for. Then, as well, we would have to go back to find the moment Kevin became a man who could kill: a slower process, in which he finally sustained enough wounds to generate that level of hate, enough unidentified pain and frustration that could funnel into one desperate act.

It's all part of my history now—the circumstances that caused me to end up so far from where I began. Other than the death of my father and the sorrow my mother endured, I'm grateful. I love my life the way it is. I love my history. Not all of it, but the sum of it.

I am still Emma, but once again I am also Rebecca. Emma needed Rebecca in the beginning, and then she needed her again to have her whole story, her history, and her life.

As we stood in front of the fireplace, I felt the presence of my father for the first time. Taylor told me that he had laid some of the rocks himself, ones he had collected from the property. They were obscured now by the summer's growth—it had the feel of something ancient, a ruin of something monumental.

It had been monumental. My father's research had influenced the lives of every person who knew it existed. He knew it would. Creating it had been much easier for him than having created it. He had understood science better than he understood people. Yet he knew enough to be wary.

Roger went to prison. It takes a special kind of person to live in someone else's shadow. I expect that if my father were alive he would have acknowledged Roger's suffering. From what my mother told me, my father lived in his head, and it was difficult to engage him. It must have been very lonely for Roger, and then the accumulation of his later years magnified the bitterness and resentment to the destructive level that endangered us all.

Now my father is there for me. Taylor has suggested he was probably a better father in his absence than he would have been had I shared my childhood with him. She tried to explain how difficult it had been. That she had loved him dearly but was often lonely in his presence. She said he lived in his head and that she felt as though she only existed to him for short pieces of time during their life together.

As I grew, I realized I did get so much from him. I studied until I knew enough to work with him, using his research as a place to begin. He inspired me, and his research became mine, and now I feel him with me every day.

There never were any final discs. There wasn't even a safety deposit box. The sheriff had made the whole thing up. His goal had been to draw Roger out of the house, where he would be more vulnerable. The sheriff had been working with my grandfather. They had followed Ruby and Taylor home from the police station that day. When no one had answered the door, they knew something was wrong. The sheriff had a cell phone in his pocket with an open line to my grandfather, who was in the car outside. He had heard everything that had been said in the house and called ahead to Nederland to set the whole thing up. He'd placed one of the sheriff's deputies in the house, posing as the bank manager. All they'd needed was a moment when they could safely get me away from Roger. Poor Roger; after all those years of experience, it only took one moment of greedy excitement for him to slip his hand off the gun—just one small move, and the sheriff had the opportunity he'd been waiting for.

Taylor had been relieved that there were no final discs. She dreaded inheriting the struggle that had tormented my father. But I became inspired—the answers had been found once.

We stayed in Boulder for two months after they arrested Roger. I was told the story of why I had been born in Colorado but grew up in Ontario. I think I was lucky. I have two incredible mothers. The three of us moved to the family farm and worked out a loving way to live under unique circumstances. Patricia ran the farm, and Taylor set up a pottery studio in the barn. We did everything together, and, as they both came to trust one another completely, they worked out our lives without fear. Sometimes we all fought and stomped and pouted, but we always came back to trust and love. Actually, I don't think it was that difficult for the two of them. They are very much alike and agreed on most things. It was usually me who caused the trouble.

Then, eventually, there were two men in my family. It took some time, but Taylor slowly began to forgive my grandfather. He wrote her letters. They started arriving a few weeks after we settled in Ontario. He told her about his family, about his history, and about his fears. At first, Taylor wouldn't open them, but when they kept coming, she gave in. She still has them all. She said it was like reading a journey and told me that after the anger subsided, the letters enlightened her. Robert had let fear run his life, and, when his worst fear caught up with him, it turned out to be also what delivered him. Patricia read the letters as well, saying she'd suffered the same thing—she had been confronted by her worst fears, and they had liberated her.

While I was growing up, they both constantly reminded me that fear is never your friend; it robs you of clarity. That was what my grandfather's letters were all about. From his rough beginnings, Robert had a well-honed sense of control, but he was controlling the wrong things. Fear had done that to him, fear of being sucked into some sort of low-life existence and then stuck there without options. Fear of carrying some polluted genetics had traumatized his judgments.

Taylor's mother had said Taylor was her greatest gift, that she'd saved her from the part of herself that was like my grandfather. Well, in the most roundabout way, Taylor was also the gift that brought clarity to the father who had rejected her. Then, one generation removed, my rebirth had been her rebirth.

We visit Isla Mujeres often. Diane ended up staying there with Jeannie Tull. They opened a bed and breakfast, which they close every time we come to town. Jeannie says they'd opened it to bring in new listeners for her stories, but Diane simply loved running the place from the very beginning. They started very small and now have a warm and colorful eight-room hotel.

Shane and Ruby would often join us there, and one year we were all there for Christmas. Other years we would go to Boulder, or Shane and Ruby would come to the farm. Shane finally got Ruby to marry him. He used to make a joke of it. He'd say he got Ruby pregnant so she'd have to marry him. Ruby would roll her eyes and say, "As if." They have two daughters now, as strong and bright as their mother and as sweet and generous as their father. Shane was always running some business involving sports equipment, and Ruby went back to writing. She had written four wonderful books before this one. She has asked me to finish *No Urn for the Ashes* for her, saying that it's my story and I deserve the last word.

ABOUT THE AUTHOR

Alison Sawyer Current is a writer, a potter, and the operator of the unofficial humane society of Isla Mujeres, Mexico. In 2005 she received The Doris Day Animal Kindred Spirit Award, and in 2007 she was invited to Mexico City for the first Forum on Small Animal Overpopulation in Mexico. She and her husband Jeff divide their time between Colorado, Canada, and Mexico. They have five grown children.

Give the Gift of

No Urn for the Ashes

to Your Friends and Colleagues

CHECK YOUR LEADING BOOKSTORE OR ORDER HERE

❑ **YES**, I want _____ copies of *No Urn for the Ashes* at $16.99 each, plus $4.95 shipping per book (Colorado residents please add $.49 sales tax per book). Canadian orders must be accompanied by a postal money order in U.S. funds. Allow 15 days for delivery.

My check or money order for $_____ is enclosed.

Please charge my: ❑ Visa ❑ MasterCard
❑ Discover ❑ American Express

Name _____

Organization _____

Address _____

City/State/Zip _____

Phone_____ Email _____

Card # _____

Exp. Date_____ Signature _____

Please make your check payable and return to:

Bayfire Press
1750 30th Street, #197
Boulder, CO 80301

Call your credit card order to: 303-718-6395

www.bayfirepress.com